MW01233987

MIGUEL'S BAY

A NOVEL

PEGGY DONOHO

&

RON PROUTY

Miguel's Bay

Publishing

2018

Miguel's Bay©
Publishing
2018
P.O. Box 14044
Bradenton, FL 34280

Dedicated
to my mother,
Marian "Tookie" Anderson
for keeping us rooted in our family and
connecting us to our past.

Thank you,
Larry "Bub" Anderson
(my daddy), for all the bare-footed,
ride-in-the-back-of-the-truck
Saturday morning fishing
trips that sparked in me
my love of Florida,
water, and fish.

Acknowledgements

Ronnie and I would like to acknowledge some special people who inspired, supported, and helped during the development of this book.

Marian Anderson started the family research years ago, and Cindy McPheeters helped organize her files and pictures, so they were easily accessible.

The Lee family, the Bailey family, and the Poirrier family, grandchildren of Edmund Miguel Lee, have supplied valuable information for this book and supported family projects.

Cathy Slusser wrote a trilogy about my great-great-great Aunt Madam Joe (Julia) Atzeroth, her daughter Eliza, and her daughter-in-law Caroline, who were an important part of Frederica's story.

Ollie Fogarty spent ten years writing a book about pioneer families which included the Guerreros, the Lees, and the Fogartys.

Cindy Russell, Krysten Miner, Pam Gibson, and Phaedra Carter directed us to historical documents and valuable information.

Josep Gornes, Marc Pallicer Benejam, Nieta Cardona and Gordon Byron were our Menorcan contacts. They helped us with research when we traveled to Menorca.

Bob Pitt, Bill Burger, and Jeff Moates shared their years of research with us.

Joy Harshman allowed me to examine the old church records from the 1800's of the Manatee Methodist Church of Bradenton.

Daughters of Ollie Fogarty, Mickey Lee, her sister Jean Smith, and granddaughter, Anita Colonia spent a few days with us and shared stories from the Fogarty side of the family.

Lynn Prouty shared creative ideas along the course of our writing.

Dona Lee assisted with the formatting process to prepare the book for printing.

Mary Audrey Hornsby took us on a tour, pointing out old Terra Ceia landmarks and told us stories of the original pioneer families and their descendants.

Paul Iasevoli was our Beta Reader and helped with the foreign languages.

Peggy's son, Landon Donoho traveled to Menorca with us. He navigated and translated the trip via iPhone and helped us find our way in a foreign land.

Finally, thank you to everyone who assisted us whose name is not listed here, making it possible to bring Miguel and Frederica's story to life.

***

The spelling of many proper names in the book have evolved or completely changed over time. Here are the names as they appear in historical records and used in the novel, followed by how they are spelled or known today.

Place Names

Braidentown, Bradentown	Bradenton
Sarazota	Sarasota
Teo Rocia, Terra Rocia, Terrasilla	Terra Ceia
Manitee	Manatee
Ft. Brooke	Tampa
Peas River, Peas Creek	Peace River
Miguel's Bay, McGill Bay	Miguel Bay

Personal Names

Gerrero, Guerro, Garedo, Gerro, Ganero	Guerrero
Madam Joe Atzeroth, Aunt Julia	Julia Atzeroth
Migel, Michael, McGill	Miguel
Fredericke, Frederika	Frederica
Cramer	Kramer
Robbie, Captain Rob, Rob	Robert Fogarty
Eddie, Ed, E.M.	Edmund Lee

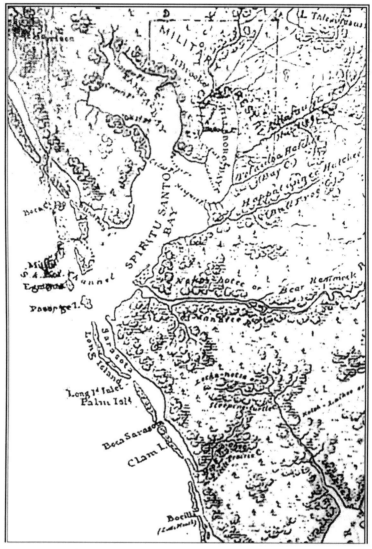

Map of the Peninsula of Florida, compiled by Capt. McClellan &
Lt. Humphreys, USTE, 1845, NA

An 1845 map of Tampa Bay as Miguel would have known it when
he arrived from Menorca via New Orleans sometime between
1840 and 1848

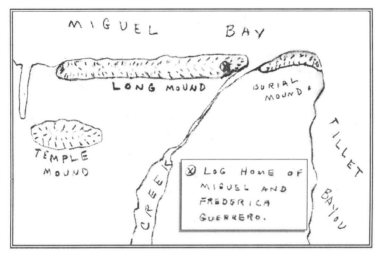

A section of a hand-drawn map found in Ollie Fogarty's files showing the location of the Guerrero Cabin on Terra Ceia Island near Boots Point.

Map of Terra Ceia by Clinton F. Smith/Ollie Fogarty

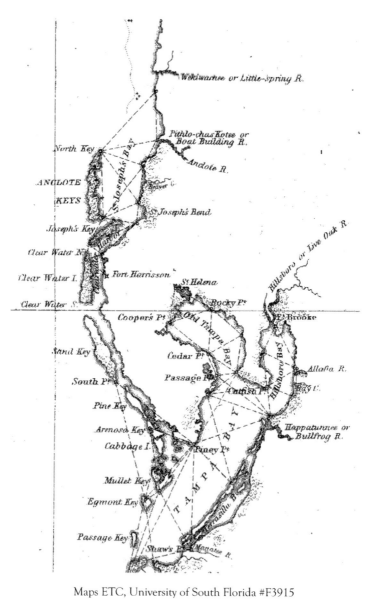

Maps ETC, University of South Florida #F3915

Tampa Bay: A General Reconnaissance of the
West Coast of Florida, 1851

Table of Contents

The Hurricane of 1848

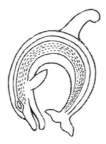

The bow of the sloop *Cazadora* rose, plunged, and shot high arcs of spray onto the deck. Fisherman Miguel Guerrero felt the hull shudder beneath his feet as the boat slapped down into the smooth valley between the white-capped leaden-grey waves.

A brisk wind whipped at his blond hair and tore at his blood-stained shirt. He tasted salt water on his lips, and his blue-grey eyes were stinging from the relentless spray. Miguel looked younger than his thirty-one years—in better shape than most of the younger men. His fair skin had become ruddy and worn from years spent outside in all types of weather. First, he had sailed in the bright sunshine of his home island of Menorca, and then as a crewman on a commercial schooner making runs from New Orleans to Pensacola, Ft. Brooke, and Key West. On a visit to the Port of Tampa one spring day, he met Philippi Bermudez, who urged him to sign on at Perico Pompon's fishing rancho.

The tropical paradise Miguel found at Tampa Bay captivated him as did the opportunity to claim free land. So, for five years, he learned the Florida fishing business and saved money, so he could one day strike out on his own.

It was Sunday, the twenty-fourth of September. The date triggered a memory in Miguel from his Catholic upbringing. He remembered today was the Feast of Our Lady of Ransom, the principal Patroness of Barcelona. On this day, faithful Catholics celebrated the founding of the Mercedarian religious order.

As he surveyed the mangrove coast, he looked for the pass that opened between the barrier islands into Tampa Bay. He recalled the stories about the heroic Mercedarian friar-knights who had guarded the *Spanish coast* against the Moors. They had taken a special vow to ransom and possibly lose their own lives in exchange for a captive who was in danger of losing his faith under Muslim rule.

When he was a child growing up on Menorca, Miguel had been taught that laying down one's life to save another person was the greatest act of love. He recalled how the thought of it scared him. He wondered, would God require that of him someday? If so, would he have the strength and the courage to make that precious sacrifice?

Pedro Felis, at the helm, called out, "Keep a sharp lookout. We must be close to the pass!" He was older than Miguel, and he'd fished these waters for over twenty years. He was the owner and captain of the *Cazadora*. The rest of the crew consisted of Miguel's friend Philippi Bermudez and Pedro's teenage sons, Nassau and Rofeno. They were slowly working their way down Florida's west coast on a return voyage to Perico's fishing rancho located on an island on the south side of Tampa Bay, not far from the mouth of the Manatee River.

Miguel spotted the break in the barrier islands for which he had been searching. "Bunce's Pass!" he shouted above the sound of wind beating the sails. They were stopping for the night at the rancho of Máximo Hernandez, an old friend of Pedro's, to refill their water barrels and salt down their catch. Bunce's Pass was a short cut located above Tampa Bay's main channel. It led to the peninsula inside of the Bay and the rancho called Punta Piñal.

The crew arrived and set anchor just before dark. Hernandez's men greeted them and helped them offload their water casks and load of fish. As he worked, Miguel noticed something peculiar about the evening sky. Toward the south-southwest, far out in the Gulf of Mexico, towering thunderheads were piling up. The sky had a strange glow as if it were reflecting the flames of a massive, distant inferno. For a moment, Miguel felt uneasy, but his uneasiness faded as he lost himself in the work once again.

The crew of the *Cazadora* enjoyed barbecued venison compliments of their host. This was followed by rum, tall-tales, and singing that went on well into the night. Worn out from a full day, the crew retired to a palm-thatched hut. They would clean and salt down their catch in the morning.

The sound of the wind rustling the palm branches of his hut awakened Miguel. From outside came the sound of excited voices and footsteps running. He leaped from his hammock and hurried out to see a camp bustling with activity. Indian women were salvaging what fish they could from the drying racks and packed them into barrels with salt. The men loaded wagons preparing for a move further inland. Others were moving their fishing boats away from the rancho to a safer location behind the barrier islands.

When he ran down to the beach, he found Máximo and Pedro surveying the thin, wispy clouds that circled counterclockwise above them. Towering thunderheads were boiling up in the sky far out in the southern Gulf. Beneath them, the sky was as black and deadly as a shark's eye.

"It's an equinoctial," Máximo told Pedro. "It could be right on top of us by tonight. I think you should stay here with us until it blows over. But if you insist on going, you must leave now and not wait."

Pedro walked briskly to the hut where the rest of the crew slept. Before he reached the door he yelled, "Up. Hurry!" There was concern in his voice, and the crew was quick to respond.

Pedro gathered his men and explained the gravity of the situation. He took a vote, and the crew decided they would try to make a run for home to save their catch. A great deal of money was at stake, and these men depended on the profits from their catch to feed their families. Within minutes his crew was reloading their fish and water barrels, and soon they were headed home.

The water of Tampa Bay kicked up a chop, and Pedro knew he needed to cross it before it got too rough. He would have to hug the coastline where the water would be less turbulent.

The crew's concern mounted as flocks of seabirds flew inland. Miguel had experienced an equinoctial here two years ago, but it had come from the east. That one pushed the water out of the river and bays and into the Gulf. This time the storm was coming from the southwest bearing north-northeast. Miguel felt in his gut that the winds would be much stronger than the previous storm he'd experienced. The cruel equinoctial winds would push the sea into the bays and rivers. Villages, homes, and farmland would be flooded and saturated with saltwater.

As the skies grew overcast and sultry, a steady wind hammered the *Cazadora's* sails. "It's going to be a bad one!" Pedro called out to Philippi, who was busy trimming sail.

Pedro heard the canvas ripping and ordered Nassau to drop the mainsail to keep it from tearing apart—they would have to tack the rest of the way in with the jib. It became increasingly difficult to hold the boat on a steady course toward the harbor.

Pedro fought with the rudder to keep the boat on course. "The wind is picking up very fast. I don't think we'll make it all the way to the rancho."

"Puerto crítico!" Philippi shouted.

"Sí, we'll ride it out there!" Pedro shouted back.

Miguel didn't understand what they meant. "What harbor?"

"Right over there, through that pass up ahead." Philippi pointed to the coastline ahead of them. "At the head of that little bay there's high ground where we can ride out the storm."

Miguel wiped his eyes from the sea spray and strained to see an inlet, but he could only make out an impenetrable wall of mangroves silhouetted against a sky that grew darker by the minute. The clouds were angry spirits furiously racing overhead.

The spray and rain parted for a moment, and Miguel thought he could make out an inlet. "There! I see a pass." He pointed to a spot to the starboard of the mast.

Pedro ordered the sails furled and centerboard raised for shallow waters. The crew would pull with oars until they reached safety. As the *Cazadora* entered the narrow pass, Miguel saw it was a small bay enclosed on its north, south, and west by a ring of green mangroves. The waters were relatively calm—they looked as if they belonged to an inland lake. Mullet jumped all around the boat. Miguel immediately fell in love with the place in spite of the impending storm.

The *Cazadora* glided through the channel toward a large mangrove-covered shoal in the center of the bay. Pedro would attempt to secure the boat in a little bayou between the mangrove trees, so they could be protected during the worst of the storm. Philippi stood on the bow sounding the depth of the bay. It was very shallow and, as they approached the bayou, the hull scraped over oyster shells. Finally, the little craft wedged in and held fast.

"Drop the centerboard and pound it in. Secure the lines!" Pedro ordered.

The four crewmen dropped over the side into waist-deep water. They each took a line and chain to tie to the mangrove trees on either side of the boat. That would hold the *Cazadora* fast while allowing her to rise with the incoming tide.

Pedro began filling the skiff with supplies. "Rofeno, load up all the food we have left along with the water cask. Then bring what digging tools you can find below. Don't forget the ax and the tarp. Philippi, you and Miguel strip the sails.

We're going ashore. It won't be safe here for long." Pedro bellowed above the howling wind.

It was late in the afternoon when the men climbed aboard the skiff and left the *Cazadora* to her fate. They headed east for the high ground at the head of the bay.

The wind became stronger, and it was raining in torrents. Miguel's arms burned as they rowed against the wind, so he was relieved when they reached the beach. He looked longingly at the shell ridge with the large mound on its far end and thought about how good it would be to stay on dry land for a while.

The bedraggled sailors dragged the skiff into a little creek, tied it securely to the mangroves, and unloaded their supplies.

Pedro had experienced devastating equinoctials in Cuba, so he knew that the real danger would come from the sea. "We need to get to high ground fast—we have to be above the water surge. Once there, we must dig a shelter so we can keep out of the wind."

"How about over there?" Rofeno motioned to a high mound on the north point by the bay.

"No, it's too close to the water. I know a better one. It's just a ways south of here, and it's not so close to the shoreline," Philippi said.

The rain had abated, but the men knew this was a temporary reprieve. There were only a few hours of daylight remaining to dig a shelter. The men gathered the supplies and headed down the trail to the mound. Miguel and Philippi shouldered the heavy water cask. "You seem to know this place well," Miguel said.

"Yes, I fished and camped here years ago with Perico. He told me there was once an old rancho here that belonged to a man named de Rosie." Philippi's words came out in huffs and puffs as he struggled to speak while carrying the heavy cask. "Before that it was an Indian village—native people who made these mounds lived there."

By the time Miguel and Perico hauled the heavy water cask up the side of the mound, Pedro and the others had already selected a spot to dig a pit. Their shelter would be located just over the summit on the southern side of the mound.

While Pedro, Rofeno, and Nassau dug, Philippi and Miguel chopped down a small oak. Digging into the oyster shell mound was slow, difficult work. The wind was howling and ripping branches from trees, and the rain felt like bee stings on their exposed skin. Night fell, and the men felt they were running out of time. They worked frantically to build their shelter.

Pedro's design was simple—he had used it to survive a bad storm in the mountains of Cuba. The hole was four feet deep, and large enough for five men to sit close together inside. A covered entrance in its center sloped down the side of the mound so water would drain away from the shelter. The logs Miguel and Philippi cut were placed across the top of the hole and entranceway. This layer was followed by a tarp, that was covered up by a thick layer of oyster shells.

The wind ripped palm fronds and cracked the limbs of oaks growing on top of the mound. Pedro stood on the roof and jumped up and down to make sure it would hold. "This will have to do!" he yelled.

As morning broke, the sky remained dark and oppressive. Miguel looked to the west and saw that the bay was no longer calm. Barely 200 yards away, waves were rolling in and crashing over the shell ridge where they had landed yesterday. The surge was coming.

They topped off their water jugs from the cask then buried it in a pit with their other provisions and equipment. Each man took his water jug, some salt pork and hard bread, then crawled into the shelter to ride out the storm.

Miguel found the damp, dark shelter to be incredibly unnerving. He and Philippi were sitting on the left side of the doorway. Nassau, Rofeno, and Pedro were crammed into the space on the right. A makeshift door of palm fronds and moss was stuffed inside the entrance tunnel to help keep out the wind and rain. Miguel felt like he sat in his grave waiting for the end to come.

Outside the shelter, lightning erupted all around, and rain came down in torrents. An overwhelming fear the likes of which he had never experienced washed over him. He felt utterly helpless and out of control, at the mercy of nature's forces.

Whenever lightning flashed, he could see Nassau sitting just on the other side of the entrance—he was crying with his head between his knees. Beside him Rofeno prayed the rosary in a low voice as each of the small beads slipped between his fingers.

Pedro handed a bottle to Philippi. "Here, this will help pass the time." As Philippi reached for it, there was an explosion outside that momentarily lit up their dark hole, and he dropped the bottle.

"Well, there goes some good rum!" Pedro snapped. There was a deafening *crack*, and something large fell onto the roof. A small section of the side of the pit next to Miguel caved in, and shells and dirt dumped into his lap. The roof held fast, but rivulets of water were now seeping into the pit and puddling around them.

"Ay, Diós mío!" Rofeno hid his face between his knees again and continued saying his prayers more fervently than before.

With every flash of lightning, Miguel would peer through the small, open space between the roof and wall. He picked out a particular tree at the base of the mound and watched horrified as the water level climbed higher and higher up the trunk as the hours passed.

The wind increased in intensity and the sound reminded Miguel of a locomotive. Suddenly the palm frond hatch Pedro had used to block the entrance was sucked out of the passage and into the darkness. Rain blew in from the tunnel and soaked them all. They feared the pressure would lift the roof and expose them to the storm, so they took turns sitting with their backs up against the entrance to block as much wind as possible.

Philippi handed Miguel his jacket. "Here, stick this into that hole by your head so it doesn't suck your brains out." Philippi laughed.

Miguel reflected that Philippi always tried to make light of every bad situation. *Perhaps that's how he copes with stress*, he thought.

As Miguel stuffed the jacket into the gap, lightning flashed, and he could see his tree and the surrounding mangroves and palmettos nearly covered by water. He closed up the space and decided he wouldn't tell the others. He sat in silence and wondered if the entire mound would soon be engulfed by the sea.

Sometime later, Philippi shook Miguel awake. "What? What's wrong?" Miguel couldn't believe he had dozed off in the midst of the roaring storm.

"The wind has stopped," Philippi said. "Come on, we're going outside."

Miguel crawled out behind the others and joined them on top of the mound. They were soaked to the bone and covered in crushed oyster shells and sand.

The sound of the waves seemed very close. Pedro stared up at the sky framed by the great limbs of the mighty oaks standing on top of the mound. He pointed out to a clear patch of blue sky above his head. "We're in the eye of the storm." A towering wall of clouds circled around the oasis of blue. "We only have a short time before it starts up again."

Working as fast as they could, the men bailed water out of the hole and repaired the collapsed roof. They finished just as the rain started again, and suddenly the back side of the storm pressed in upon them.

Lightning and thunder erupted from the sky. The surface of the flood waters encircling their mound reflected blinding electrical bolts. Miguel estimated that the water was less than ten feet below them.

He knew that the mangrove swamp, the woods surrounding the mound, and the trail they had hiked up yesterday must be completely submerged by floodwaters.

"Get back inside now!" Pedro screamed as the wind regained its intensity. He knew the other side of the eye wall would bring another wave of devastation and a huge tidal surge.

The interior of the shelter was clear of debris, and the frantic bailing had removed most of the water. Miguel hoped they could keep the water out of the pit. Again, they stuffed the doorway with palmetto and moss thatch, but this time they secured it with rope. Perhaps this time the seal would hold.

A violent gust of wind suddenly battered against the outside of the hatch. It howled like a hungry demon being eluded by its prey. The roof logs shuddered and rose upward, as soil and shells poured into the hole again.

"That didn't last long," Philippi shouted. The men watched as rivulets of water began to carve snake-like canyons into the sandy walls of the shelter.

They could hear the crash of the surf against the mound below and wondered how much higher the water would rise. Rofeno still muttered his prayers.

"If we can make it through the next couple of hours, we should be all right," Pedro said. "The winds will start to weaken, and the water will recede."

Only the occasional flicker of lightning lit the shelter with light strong enough to barely illuminate the men as they cowered in their perilous perch atop the besieged mound.

They were soaking wet and shivering. "The rum would've been nice right about now." Pedro laughed, as he poked Philippi in the ribs.

While they were chastising Philippi about the rum, something dropped down from between the roof logs and came to rest on Nassau's shoulder. He grabbed at it, thinking it was Rofeno poking him, only to discover that a large snake had descended from the roof and sought shelter on his shoulder. "Ay, Dios mío!" he cried, and in his terror, he stood up. Shells and dirt fell in on everyone's heads as they tried to back away from Nassau and the snake.

A close lightning strike boomed outside, and Miguel could see the snake's triangular head and shimmering, black skin in the pale light. The wide-open mouth glowed white in the dim light, and Miguel imagined he could see a drop of venom on the tip of its needle-like fangs. "Cottonmouth!" he yelled as he grabbed the snake by the throat and pulled it to the floor.

Philippi drew his sheath knife and decapitated the snake before it could bite. "We'll save this, it's a good-sized one—it'll make a good meal," Philippi told the others. Miguel thought that Philippi had been living with the Indians far too long.

Miguel's eyes grew heavy—he was entirely worn out from the day, and his need for rest overcame his discomfort from being soaked to the skin and terrified by the storm. He shut his eyes and let the droning of the wind lull him to sleep.

When he woke up, the sun streamed through the spaces between the logs. There was no sound of wind, and the rain had stopped. He and Pedro's sons were the only crew members who remained in the shelter—the boys were still sound asleep.

He pushed out through the doorway and into the sunshine. His legs cramped from the hours spent sitting in awkward positions, but he was relieved to see the sun again. The storm had moved out across the state and far toward the northeast. They had survived.

Miguel walked to the top of the mound where Pedro and Philippi sat around a small fire trying to dry out. Philippi was skinning his snake, and Pedro was smoking his clay pipe.

Pedro pointed toward the bay. "You ever see anything like that?" he asked Miguel.

Miguel looked around and was shocked by the devastation he saw. The small bay they had sailed into yesterday on the *Cazadora* merged with Tampa Bay. The mangrove shoals in its center and the islands around the perimeter had all vanished. Now, only the tops of the trees appeared above the surface of the water. Shattered trees and debris floated on the surface. He guessed there must have been a tidal surge of up to fifteen feet, or perhaps more. This was a scene that would be forever etched in his memory.

Pedro joined him and stared out at the bay. "The *Cazadora* was a good boat," Pedro said. "She will be missed but thank God we have our lives. I worry about Máximo. His place must surely have been destroyed. I hope they made it to safety."

"There won't be anything left of our rancho either. It was sitting so close to the Gulf with only that thin barrier island to protect it," Miguel said.

Pedro nodded as he began to comprehend how devastating the aftermath of this storm would be for the fishing community. All of the huts, flakes, boats, nets, and gear would be gone. They would have to start again from scratch. There were still six months of the season remaining and, right now, the entire industry was completely ruined.

Pedro's eyes were downcast. "This might mean the end of Perico's enterprise at Tampa Bay." He met Miguel's eyes. "I don't know what I'm going to do," he murmured.

Miguel realized at that moment they would all be starting over from scratch. He thought of the gold coins he had hidden under a gumbo limbo tree on the back side of Perico

Island's long mound. He hoped to God that the tree survived the storm, so he could find his stash again.

Philippi handed a stick with a piece of snake meat on it to Miguel. "Eat up, my friend. It tastes just like chicken." he said with a grin.

"No thank you brother. I wouldn't want to rob you of such a delicacy." Miguel smirked.

He felt awful for his friends. Ten years ago, the Army had deported Pedro's Seminole wife, and Philippi had lost two wives and his five children. Now he had probably lost his boat and all of his fishing gear, but Miguel understood that he was a survivor and would start over. Miguel also knew he would have to make a new start for himself as well. It was time to break away on his own.

The floodwaters had begun to recede, and the land of Terrasilla was reemerging. It was a resurrection, and Miguel took this as a sign that it was time for him to resurrect *his* life and career. It was time for him to carve out his place in the world and forge his own path.

As evening fell, the sky turned magnificent shades of violet and purple. It was the most beautiful sky Miguel had ever seen. He felt a storm-surge of exhilaration rise within him. This was a validation of life, *his* life. This place had saved him. He recalled the scene he'd fallen in love with yesterday—a secluded paradise, teeming with fish and rich with beauty. What better place could he find to start his rancho than this beautiful bay? What better place could there be to settle down and start a family?

Off Anna Maria Island, 1854

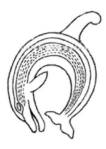

Miguel threw his blanket aside and got up from his hammock. He walked over and stood by the mast; it was a dark silhouette against the starry sky. He was anchored off the north end of Anna Maria Island. He had awakened abruptly and found himself drenched with sweat—his heart still drummed from a recurring dream. Lately, the image of a woman's face rising up from deep black waters had been haunting his dreams.

He shuddered in the chill night air and wiped sweat from his face with his sleeve. There would be no more sleeping tonight. He found his water jug, pulled the cork, and took a long drink as he stared sleepily at the reflection of the waning moon—it was shimmering like a bride's veil on the face of the dark water.

Despite the deathly pallor of the woman's face, he had known her immediately. Her name was Teresa Gavas-Font of Genova, Mallorca. She had been his first wife.

20

She looked so beautiful that summer night in 1840 as they stood by the railing of a steamer departing from a dock in Barcelona. Her olive skin glowed in the afternoon sun, and a strand of her black hair fell from its bonds and streamed in the warm, Mediterranean breeze like a pennant. Her ice-blue eyes glazed over with tears as she waved goodbye to her loved ones. Miguel understood that her heart was breaking at the possibility of never seeing her family again.

***

He met Teresa at the home of her father Francisco Gavas when she was only sixteen. Francisco owned the merchant vessel upon which Miguel served as navigator before the Carlista War began.

They set June sixteenth as their wedding date, but when the day finally arrived, Miguel had not yet returned from sea. Teresa's father agreed to stand in for him at the Church of Santa Maria.

All of Spain had become a place of economic distress and hardship following seven years of civil war, so the young couple decided there was no future for them near the Iberian Peninsula. They chose to do as many others had done—seek a new life in America. They sailed first to Barcelona on the Spanish mainland, where they lived for a time with Teresa's uncle until Miguel could secure a crew position on a schooner bound for New Orleans.

Miguel and Teresa drifted in their own thoughts as they watched the coast of Spain vanish behind them. It was as if the door to their past had been shut and bolted, and they had been cut off from everything they knew and loved. Miguel remembered how Teresa had read his thoughts and tried to reassure him that they were sailing toward a better life.

They watched the receding glow of an orange sunset behind the Serra de Collserola mountain range on the western horizon. The first star of the evening appeared. "Make a wish!" Teresa said.

"My wish is to have my own land in America". Then he corrected himself and said, "I meant *our* own place!"

"No, you're not supposed to tell me. Now it won't come true." Teresa slapped his shoulder and smiled.

Miguel pulled her close and kissed the top of her head. He was exhilarated at the thought of the new life which lay just over the horizon.

He took Teresa down to their quarters and descended a narrow ladder to the 'tween-deck. She was immediately overcome by the foul, damp air, and she pulled her shawl across her face, all the while straining to see her new accommodations in near-total darkness. She worried that the only ventilation and light was what filtered through the small open hatch.

On either side of the deck sat two tiers of bunks from fore to aft, each berthing three to five persons. Everything else was shared—there was a long table in the center aisle and a toilet was located on each side of the deck. Miguel sighed as he realized they would be sharing the toilet with at least thirty-five other travelers.

Meal rations provided were uncooked, so Miguel and Teresa had to cook for themselves. On the first night they shared a meal of salt pork, rice, and beans which Teresa couldn't digest and lost immediately. "Not to worry," Miguel said. "Seasickness is very common for passengers during their first few days at sea."

He helped Teresa into their upper birth and spread out their blankets on the straw-filled mattress. They talked about their new home in New Orleans, Miguel's prospects of finding work on a ship's crew, and the names of their future children. Soon Teresa was lulled to sleep by the motion of the ship. When eight bells struck, Miguel went topside to work the night watch with the other seamen.

Teresa thought she was getting used to life at sea after two weeks of sailing, but the vomiting started again. The spasms emptied her stomach until she had dry heaves soon followed by painful diarrhea.

The sickness had affected several of the passengers, and the toilets were always occupied. It became impossible for Teresa to reach them anyway, because she soon was too weak to walk. The air below decks was foul with the stench of vomit and human waste. Still two weeks from their destination, the sounds of human misery were becoming unbearable.

One by one, other sick passengers began to die. The ship's doctor declared the scourge to be cholera. Miguel was frantic when he noticed Teresa's heart beat very fast. She became delusional and had severe muscle cramps. There was little he could do for her but try to keep her clean and dry. He dripped water between her parched, cracked lips while praying fervently.

Teresa was burning with fever and the lower decks were unbearably hot as the ship moved closer to the Americas. Miguel decided he must take her up on deck where she could get some fresh air and cool down. He found a place on the foredeck where she could bed down and see the ocean. Her sunken eyes seemed to brighten while she gazed across the blue, watery expanse that lay ahead. Miguel held her close while singing softly in her ear as sun vanished in the west.

Suddenly, Teresa's mouth began moving like she was trying to speak, but Miguel couldn't understand her. He rested his head lightly against her chest and heard that her heartbeat was slow and faint. He fell asleep as he had every night since they were married, with his hand holding hers.

He awoke with a start from a strange dream where he lay beside a cold marble statue. He reached over to touch

Teresa. She was deathly cold and her skin hard. Her dark eyes were wide open and lifeless. Miguel felt like something inside of him had died with her—he was utterly empty.

He held his wife close for what seemed like hours, until the ship's doctor came for her body. Seventeen passengers, mostly women and children, had died on the voyage. Their bodies were carried up from the lower decks and sewn into canvas bags, then laid side by side next to the ship's rail on the upper deck. An old priest performed last rites over the dead as their families stood by in a drizzling rain, then each bag was dropped overboard as the names of the dead were spoken aloud.

Miguel heard nothing that was said. He was numb and could feel nothing until the sailors lifted the canvas bag containing Teresa's corpse onto the plank. One man called her name, and her body slid over the rail into the foamy sea.

Miguel watched the place where her body sank into the cold Atlantic until he lost sight of it. He wanted to drop over the side and join her in the dark abyss. He was overcome with grief at the loss of his wife and the erasure of their joyous life together.

***

A sudden spray of warm sea water aroused him from his sleep. Miguel believed that his feelings of guilt must have conjured up memories of his young wife out of the dark sea of his subconscious mind.

The dream was the same every time. Teresa's beautiful, pale face floating below the surface of the water—her hair splayed out and drifting with the current. His wife's lips moved but made no sound. He would always awaken with a start and feel overcome with sadness.

He knew he had to let her go, even though she would always have a place in his heart. He pulled a gold chain from around his neck with a St. Christopher's medal and gold ring suspended on it. He slid the ring off the chain and tossed it overboard. His chest heaved as he watched it disappear into the deep. He finally had a sense of closure.

The Atzeroth Store

When Frederica awoke she glanced around the small room, but it took a few minutes for her eyes to adjust to the light. They arrived on Terrasilla Island to the Atzeroth farm so late the night before she was unable to, "get her bearings," as Uncle Joe would say. Now she was wide awake and alert, but she felt completely drained of energy.

Because of Frederica's excitement about finally seeing her Aunt Julia again after so many years, the trip from New Orleans had seemed exceptionally long and arduous. She slept motionless in the small bed that first night, but still felt like she was rocking along with the waves on the schooner. She hoped it would only last a day or two. Frederica was ready to have her land legs back, and to stay on solid ground for a while. Little did she know that in Florida, the water was the highway. She would be on boats a lot—like it or not.

The smell of tobacco burning in Uncle Joe's carved German pipe wafted through the door. The soothing, familiar scent reminded her of home. Joe poked his head through the door and startled her. He let out his booming laugh when she jumped.

"Good morning sweet girl. I hope you are rested and ready to start your newest adventure?" Uncle Joe brought in a tray of biscuits, bacon, eggs, and a steaming hot cup of coffee. It smelled so delicious, and the coffee was so hot and strong it made her heart race. The eggs had a different flavor than she was used to, and the amber-colored jelly was a bit tart, but it was all delicious. She had never tasted seagull eggs or guava jelly—two things that would soon become a staple.

Joe smiled. "You eat your aunt's good cooking and wash up. Your carriage will be waiting to take our Bavarian princess to the river property shortly. Your new home is ready to welcome you." Frederica realized Uncle Joe had been anxious for her to rise so that they could start the day. It would be a long ride to reach the Atzeroth store on the north side of Manatee River.

She pulled the last set of clean clothes out of her bag and hurried to get dressed—she didn't want to hold her uncle up for another second. Her hair was in tangles, but it would have to wait for a good cleaning until she got to the river. She wondered if a hot bath would even be an option in this new wilderness.

Her two brothers were already up and dressed. Down by the water, they took in the new scenery. When Frederica walked out of the cabin and onto the porch, she felt like she'd stepped onto a different planet. The trees, flowers, grass, water, sky, the birds—nothing looked familiar. Everything was wonderfully beautiful and new.

Joe's loud whistle drew the boys' attention, and they ran toward the wagon. Frederica pulled herself up into the passenger seat and her uncle handed her a shotgun. As she looked down at the weapon, she realized her life was about to transform into an entirely unanticipated and novel adventure.

Aunt Julia, Eliza, and Mary had departed earlier so they could open the store, and Frederica was anxious to see what the place was like. The Atzeroths were so generous to pay her passage to Florida and offer her a place to live and work. It would be rewarding and fun to be with her cousins, Eliza and Mary, after growing up with only brothers. Her brothers had done nothing but complain since they arrived in New Orleans. The list was long—it was too hot here, there were too many bugs, there was no familiar hardwood for the crafting of furniture, and the land was too flat and wet. The complaints went on and on, and Frederica began to wonder if they would ever stop.

She was convinced the road to the store was merely a cattle trail—it was so rough and bumpy. At one point, Uncle Joe grabbed the shotgun, cocked it, and shot into the bushes, scaring her to death. They heard the loud crash of an animal in the brush, and Frederica screamed, "What was that?"

Joe set the rifle down and gave Frederica a wink, "There is no need for you to worry about that now."

The wagon continued on and about an hour into the trip, they had to ford a shallow river. All of the passengers climbed down in order to lighten the load, and all hands were needed to push the wagon through the mud. After the effort, Frederica was left hot and dirty—her shoes soaking wet.

Once they'd forded the river, they rounded a corner and a herd of wild cattle crossed the path to get to water. It seemed strange to Frederica to see cattle roaming freely through the brush instead of grazing in grassy fenced-in pastures. Uncle Joe explained to her they were descended from the cattle brought over by Spanish explorers hundreds of years earlier.

The wagon had no choice but to wait until the last animal went by. The sun beat down on them, and a cloud of flies surrounded the cattle as they passed the travelers. The stench of the beasts along with the oppressive heat made Frederica sick to her stomach.

Her younger brother jumped out of the wagon and walked into a palmetto thicket to relieve himself. He was out of sight within seconds but, a minute later, he came running back with his pants still unfastened. He saw his first Florida rattlesnake, and it made him scream like a little girl. Uncle Joe laughed so hard tears ran down his cheeks.

Frederica was hungry and thirsty, but she vowed not to speak a word of complaint. She wouldn't show discomfort or weakness in front of these men. She closed her eyes against the bright sun for a few moments. She suddenly felt a cool breeze on her face that prompted her to open her eyes. The sun had disappeared behind a cloud. It was a single dark cloud. It opened up and dropped what felt like buckets of rain on them in just a few short minutes.

When the rain shower ended, Frederica squeezed the water out of her hair. The shower had been surprisingly refreshing, but now she was drenched to the skin. "Uncle Joe, are we almost there?" she asked. He reached over and squeezed her hand. "It's right up ahead!"

Frederica peered into the distance. She was excited to see Aunt Julia's beautiful store. She had pictured it in her mind for so long—it would be whitewashed and bright with blue shutters and a big porch, she thought. Eliza might have painted German folk art around a beautifully carved, wooden door. There would be roses and wildflowers growing in front, welcoming patrons with beauty and a sweet fragrance. There would be a stone walkway, perfectly straight, leading up from the river to a bench where travelers could sit and rest. The big tree in front would have homemade bird feeders hanging from it, and it would attract tropical birds for the children to watch as their mothers shopped. The smell of baked goods would lure the local fishermen and workers in for a snack.

Frederica held her hand up to her forehead to shield the sun from her eyes. There it was, the Atzeroth store—the beginning of her American dream. The structure was a large box, and the walls were built of grey, weathered pine. The windows were small, and no curtains could be seen on the inside. The porch was made of straight, plain planks, the banister to the stairs was made of a sanded tree limb. The ground around the store was a mixture of sand, weeds, and unsightly sticker plants which Frederica had never seen. Strange, thin-trunked palm trees grew in bunches around the store. Horses were tied up to tree stumps and branches. Boats were anchored by the shore, and Frederica wondered why there was no dock.

Frederica smelled some kind of meaty stew cooking—a huge black pot hung over an open fire. She thought that this must just be a stop on the way to the Atzeroth store. But when Aunt Julia emerged from the front door waving and smiling, Frederica realized this was indeed their destination.

Frederica turned her back to the river and faced the small, homespun store. Aunt Julia came running toward her—she was smiling that big grin of hers, and she motioned for everyone to come inside. Frederica put on a happy face and tried to muster up some excitement about what she saw.

As she entered the front door of the store, she was surprised at how many people were actually inside. The Atzeroth store must have been a meeting place for everyone who lived in this tropical wilderness. Frederica immediately noticed several languages were being spoken. There were women and children, old men, and even a couple of girls who may have been around her age. The whole world seemed to be represented in this little store—a small Indian family, light-skinned people, black people, olive-skinned people, and two red-headed boys.

Julia took a pencil and struck a small glass cup to capture everyone's attention. Then it dawned on Frederica that she and her brothers *were* the reason for the announcement. These people had traveled miles to welcome them to the area. She choked back tears as she realized all of these folks had given up a precious workday so that she and her brothers would feel welcome.

An old man with only two teeth in his head and a beat up straw hat yelled out, "What do you want Madam Joe?" A soft chuckle spread through the crowd. He called her Madam Joe because he couldn't remember the name Julia, nor pronounce the name Atzeroth. But he could remember Joe's name, so that would have to do. "Madam Joe" became Julia's nickname until the day she died.

Julia introduced her niece and two nephews saying their names slowly as she pointed to each one. She knew that many of those gathered could not understand what she said, but language does not always keep people from communicating. The joy and love on her face was contagious, and soon the music and dancing began, as wonderful food was brought out for all to share.

After an evening of eating, dancing, and countless awkward conversations in multiple languages, the party began to wind down. Folks said their goodbyes and headed to their homes. Some planned to sleep in their wagons or on the porch of the store before striking out for home the next morning.

Julia found Frederica in the crowd and pulled her through the back door. She shared the plans and dreams she had for the house, the store, and the property. Julia spoke with confidence, hope, and joy. She had already embraced the potential of this place and had grown to love it.

The first project would be a dock. She envisioned schooners, sailboats, skiffs, row boats, and eventually huge steamers bringing in people with goods to sell and trade. She talked about a church and a school. There were plans for a vegetable farm, fruit orchards, and barns for animals. *This woman is a dreamer,* Frederica thought, *and she has the determination to make it all happen.*

What Julia told her overwhelmed Frederica—these tasks seemed daunting if not impossible to complete in a single lifetime. How could one woman, one family, build an entire town?

Julia took Frederica by the shoulders and looked at her with her big, blue eyes. "My dear, your future can be anything you want it to be. Look at this land, this water, these people. We are the first to write this story. We left a country of famine, economic strife, poverty, and hopelessness. We have been given the gift of a new beginning."

Eliza called for her mother, and Julia turned to go inside.

Frederica sat on the steps of the front porch and put her face in her hands as she thought about everything she had seen and heard that day. A little boy played in the sand a few yards away. He wore a worn-out pair of pants with suspenders that were too long. He was barefooted, and on his head sat a little red hat.

The boy walked to the fence and stared at a beautiful, pink hibiscus flower that was as big as his face. He struggled to pull the flower free, but it wouldn't budge. He reached in his pocket, pulled out a small knife, and cut the blossom from its stem, then smiled with pride at his achievement.

The boy turned and looked at Frederica. As he walked toward her he shuffled and stared at the ground as he approached. When he was directly in front of her, he lifted his head and held out the flower. Frederica was so taken by his kindness that she reached out and hugged him. He smiled shyly and ran away. It wasn't long before she saw him leave with his father and two little sisters, but there was no sign of a mother in the wagon.

Frederica watched the little boy's wagon fade into the distance and wondered what had happened to his mother. This was a beautiful but dangerous territory. Men died trying to build their houses, and strange illnesses brewed in the jungle. Young women died in childbirth, and the sea claimed bodies each week. Not many people lived long enough to see their hair turn white.

Frederica's two brothers came through the door and sat down on either side of her. They seemed excited about something. This was the happiest she had seen them since they had left Bavaria. The boys explained that they had met a German tradesman who was visiting from a place called Indiana. He described it as a beautiful state with four clearly defined seasons, fertile farmland, forests of sturdy hardwoods, and a large community of Germans. Their towns were already furnished with schools, churches, and doctors.

The man himself owned a profitable furniture business and had been looking for young men to be his apprentices. He offered the Kramer boys jobs in one of his shops. His plan was to return to the Atzeroth store in six months, and they could return with him to Indiana should they choose to accept the offer.

"Why don't you come with us, sister?" they pleaded. "Look at this place, there is nothing here for you. You will work for Aunt Julia and be lonely without friends. You are cut off from civilization here. It will take years to grow a township, and did you see any young men your age anywhere today?"

The decision her brothers asked her to make shocked Frederica. It had been hard enough to emigrate from Bavaria. How could she live without her brothers? They had all come here hoping that their parents would eventually join and reunite the Kramer family.

By now the sun had set, and bugs buzzed around her hair. Frederica was suddenly very tired and hungry. She just wanted to eat and go to bed—she would have to make her decision tomorrow.

***

With so much to be done, the days passed by quickly. Frederica was a fast learner, and she soon was ready to run the store for Aunt Julia. The customers who came in were drawn to her friendliness and kindness in spite of the language barrier. She tried hard to remember everyone's names in order to make them feel welcome and appreciated.

There was no other place in the world like this little store on the north side of the Manatee River. It amused Frederica to think about the stores in Bavaria, particularly the shops in the larger cities. She remembered going into fancy places that sold fine jewelry and china, and she recalled the clothing stores and art galleries. Her father's own furniture shop that seemed modest to her family would be extravagant here. She thought of the fine bakeries, markets, and shops that sold musical instruments. No stores like those could be found on the banks of the Manatee.

But the Atzeroth's shop was so much more than a store. It was the lifeblood of this area—it was the meeting place, the source of information, the doctor's office, the trading post, and the post office. On Sundays, it was the church, and on weekday mornings the front porch served as the school.

True to her word, Aunt Julia had begun her long list of improvements to the store, and the local men had accomplished an incredible feat of engineering when they built the dock within two weeks. One workman had almost drowned but was saved by a young girl who saw him hit his head and fall in the water.

Young boys fished from the dock and brought in large fish on their bacon-baited homemade poles. The dock also made it much more convenient to moor boats and bring in catches of fish and produce. Wagons could load and unload cargo, and boxes and crates could be stacked. The end of the dock made an excellent lookout point to view the mouth of the Manatee River.

Whenever the little boy with the red hat, who Frederica later learned was named Henry, came around he loved being the watchman for the store. He would call out in a loud voice when he saw any boat enter the river from the bay. Colored flags could be flown to inform residents along the river if danger was near.

The end of the dock was Frederica's personal sanctuary. At the close of the day, she would sit and let the sound of the water wash away her stress. Never had she seen such brilliant sunsets, and there was not one star hidden from view on cloudless nights. In six short months, she would have to leave with her brothers to go north, or would she? It would be a difficult decision to make. Aunt Julia, Uncle Joe, Eliza, and Mary hoped her decision would be to stay with them. Frederica had no idea what her answer would be, but she prayed every day for a sign.

Every time she walked into the store, a hundred smells flooded her nose—fresh flowers and vegetables, Seminole blankets, wood carvings, bottles of herbs and medicinal oils made from local plants, paper, fabric, tools, baked items, staples like flour, sugar, and tobacco seeds and cuttings. Aunt Julia would buy anything the local people wanted to sell. Soon Uncle Joe would start making runs to Ft. Brooke and all the way up to New Orleans to procure goods. The Spanish fishermen continually brought in treasures from the sea and items they'd traded for in other ports. It was a living, changing collection that was never the same from day to day.

Frederica had learned so much about the world from working at the store. It was never boring, and every day was unique. After being there for only a few weeks, she knew it would be difficult to leave, and she knew that she might never return. But Indiana might hold an exciting future for her as well. She longed for a sign that would help her make her decision.

One bright, clear day, Frederica rode Eliza's horse down the road running alongside the river to a beautiful spot she had recently found around the river's bend. It was a sandy, white, little beach with a great view, and many beautiful white birds congregated there. The air felt heavy, and Frederica suspected that a little squall might be coming up. She had learned that they typically came late in the day during the summer. As she gazed out toward the bay, the clouds began their swift march toward the shore.

She knew she should rush back to the store, but instead she decided to pull herself under some palmetto fronds to wait out the storm. As the winds blew cooler, the water turned grey and churned. The river amazed her—it was always moving and finding new paths and patterns. The water could change color from one hour to the next. The sky was also that way—it was never the same color as the day before, and no sunset was ever repeated. The clouds always created new pictures in the sky every day.

As a gentle rain fell, Frederica closed her eyes and tried to imagine what her life might look like if she stayed here. Would she find a good man to love, and would he love her as well? Would her home be blessed with happy children? Would Florida be a peaceful and productive place to live?

She opened her eyes, stood up, and brushed the sand off her skirt. There had been no blaring trumpets from the sky, no regal voice from the heavens, and no writing in the sand. She climbed onto her horse and headed back to the store.

She still didn't know what to do. The horse trotted slowly back down the path alongside the river. The wind blew through the trees, and it sounded like an eerie song from a supernatural throat. The words came back to her, "always moving, never standing still, always finding a new path." Maybe the river itself had been her sign. Living here would always be an adventure full of the unexpected, but it would also be grounded in the rhythm of the changing tides, the setting of the sun, and the rising of the moon.

As Frederica tied the horse's tether to a tree, Aunt Julia rounded the corner of the house. She put her arm around Frederica's shoulders and walked her down to the dock. "My dear, before you make the decision to go with your brothers, I want to show you something." They reached the end of the dock, and Julia turned her toward the horizon. There was a perfect double rainbow in the sky. Julia whispered, "In all of my born days, I have never seen one of these.

If the rainbow is a covenant, a promise, then you my dear, have been given a double portion," her aunt said.

Frederica's decision was made—she would stay in Florida.

Dolphins

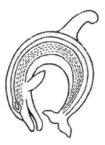

Miguel felt most alone at night. He was anchored in a dark, little estuary somewhere between Havana and his Tampa Bay rancho. His eyelids grew heavy as he sipped Cuban rum, and he watched an eruption of distant lightning on the horizon. The air smelled of rain and seaweed collecting among the mangrove roots growing along the shore. The sound of gentle waves slapping rhythmically along the side of his fishing smack lulled the tired fisherman to sleep.

As his body slept, his mind wandered the shadowy corridors of the deep nighttime, and his dreams focused into one clear vision. *He drifted slowly at first then slid faster and faster into a dark tunnel, and all that was recognizable and familiar was obscured from his eyes. The enveloping darkness seemed to smother him, and he thought that he must surely die at any moment. Suddenly a flicker of light appeared like an ember glowing in the heart of a campfire. It grew larger as he moved toward it, and his sleeping mind told him that the ember was beckoning to him.*

The silhouette of a woman appeared in the light, but her face was a blur. Her long, dark hair blew freely in the wind, and her arms outstretched toward Miguel. She urged him forward. Radiant light warmed his face as he approached her, and hope and unspeakable joy rose in his breast. Almost near enough to touch her now, he could hear the fabric of her dress whipping in the wind...

He awoke to find the morning sun baking his face and the sound of wind tearing at the jib sail. It interrupted his vision, and the realization that it was all a dream frustrated him beyond measure. The memory of the dark-haired woman haunted him for hours as he worked his nets in the heat of the Florida sun. Was she someone from his past that he had forgotten? He smiled nervously as he realized that perhaps she was someone who had yet to enter his life.

***

Months later, Miguel slackened the jib and allowed the warm morning breeze to fill it. The winds blew out of the northwest, as he turned the bow of his yawl *Margarita* into the mouth of Tampa Bay. He adjusted the mainsail to keep the boat headed eastward through Passage Key Inlet and set his course for the mouth of the Manatee River. The bow rose and fell with the churning current of the inlet and sprayed salt water on his weathered face, which was reddened from a week at sea.

Miguel smiled as a school of seven or eight dolphins encircled his boat. The closest one swam on the port side of the yawl, and Miguel could swear it looked up at him, hoping that he would throw it a fish.

Miguel loved the company of dolphins. On his home island of Menorca, there was an ancient legend that the appearance of dolphins was a sign of good fortune. As a child, his father had recited stories of dolphins that rescued sailors at sea. "If your ship is accompanied by dolphins, you are sure to find calm seas and safe harbor," the old man had told him.

As a young man, Miguel enjoyed the story about the Greek god Poseidon, who sent dolphin messengers to bring him a nymph whom he loved. Poseidon later married the nymph, and as a reward, he set the dolphin in the night sky as a constellation.

Miguel laughed as he remembered his shipmates' course jokes about what awaited them at their port of call after seeing a school of dolphins. Having been raised in the teachings of the Church, he didn't believe these ancient omens, yet sometimes he wondered if the Creator, who had placed signs in the heavens for navigation, might also use nature to guide man.

A sudden gust of wind snapped the mainsail taut, and Miguel jolted back to his task. The dolphin guides were now well ahead of him and leading the yawl into the mouth of the Manatee. He slackened the mizzen and allowed it to fill. This would turn him into the center of the channel and thus avoid the sandbars.

On his starboard was Shaw's Point—named after his friend William Shaw. Shaw was a hard-working homesteader who had staked his claim to the land in 1843. Miguel once worked on Shaw's sixty-ton schooner, *Mary Washington*, as it transported government provisions from New Orleans to Pensacola, Tampa Bay, and Key West. After Miguel established his own rancho, Shaw bought fish from him and shipped them to Key West. Miguel shook his head when he thought about the huge loss of income all the fishermen had suffered when Shaw panicked and returned to Key West after hearing about a Seminole uprising.

Shaw's vacant house of tabby brick stood near the shore. Miguel's fisherman friends, Perico Pompon and Philippi Bermudez told him it had been used by Spanish fishermen decades before Shaw arrived.

Perico and Philippi had helped Miguel set up his rancho on Terrasilla in 1848. Six years earlier, they had directed Josiah Gates six miles upriver to a fresh mineral spring, where he established his home site that would eventually become known as Manatee.

***

Miguel thought about how much times had changed since he left New Orleans and arrived at Perico's rancho. The Armed Occupation Act of 1842 had opened the Florida wilderness to settlement, and Gates was soon joined by a diverse group of armed claimants: northerners, southerners, merchants, sea captains, farmers, planters, cowboys, and fishermen. It was called Manatee after the sea cow that lived there in abundance.

The settlement, on the edge of the wilderness, was the only white development south of Tampa. The new settlers clustered tightly together for defense, and their staked claims looked like a patchwork quilt laid out among the choice riverbank hammocks on both sides of the river. Manatee Village now had a wharf, a blacksmith's shop, and two stores. Further upriver, three sugarcane plantations were in full production.

Miguel dropped the mainsail. Just ahead of him on his port side, the pilings of a wharf emerged from the grey mist hovering over the river. The dock belonged to Joseph and Julia Atzeroth—immigrants from Bavaria, and their store was the closest place for him to purchase supplies.

A woman stood on the dock against a peach-colored sky. The morning breeze whipped her dark brown hair around her face as she watched him approach. Suddenly, the sun broke through the purple clouds in the east, and her shape was outlined in fiery light for a moment. She waved at him and then ran back to the store. The leather soles of her shoes gently slapped the dock as she raced into the building and disappeared.

Miguel knew in that moment he had found the woman he saw in his dream.

Frederica's Diary

August 13, 1855

It's not that I don't enjoy keeping cousin Mary during the day. She is sweet, and I adore her, and I am so grateful to have been given my passage from Bavaria to come live with this family. It's just that all she ever wants to do is read books and bake! She definitely has Aunt Julia's love of sweets, but I would rather have a delicious mango or juicy orange while walking through Uncle Joe's grove.

It seems to be such a waste of time to spend two hours baking a cake, when you could be riding one of the horses alongside the Indian mounds or looking for beautiful shells and brightly colored tropical flowers to brighten up the rooms of the house! Why not bake after the sun goes down?

It is torture for me to sit in this house all day! I look through the window and watch the bright sun dancing on the water and I feel like a prisoner. When I have my own

47

children, the land will be their playground, and I will be outdoors with them!

When I have a home, it will be plain and simple; I don't want to spend all of my time cleaning and keeping house! We will eat out of the garden and the ocean, and we won't waste hours in the kitchen making fancy dishes!

August 30, 1855

Today I begged Mary to go for a walk down by the river, but she insisted on starting a new piece of needlework. I tried to convince her that fresh air is good for the body, and that sun on the skin can fight illnesses, but she just looked at me with a grimace and said, "Bugs. I hate bugs."

I sat and watched her for hours and yearned to be with Uncle Joe at the Terrasilla farm. He was planting with his hired hand, Henry. I love the smell of freshly-turned dirt, and Henry plows perfectly straight lines. Each area looks like a geometric piece of art when he finishes!

By the time Aunt Julia and Uncle Joe came home it was dark, and I'm not allowed to go out alone. I just wanted to dash out of the door, take off my shoes, and run to the river to see the sunset at the end of the dock! I have to find a way out of this stifling boredom.

September 8, 1855

Today at breakfast, Aunt Julia asked me if I wanted to go work with her at the store while Uncle Joe was on a trip. I said yes of course!

The girls have started school with one of the neighbors, and I have finally been set free from the house. I am ready to get out into this new world! I'm so anxious to meet some of the other young women here, but I think that some of them may talk behind my back about the fact that I'm not married yet. Many of them my age already have three children or more. I've heard the words, "old maid" whispered more than once as I've walked past a group of gossiping women. Mary has told me what these words mean.

I am trying very hard to learn English. Eliza works with me constantly but is hard to learn so many new things at once at my age. I try to use only English words around the dinner table. Uncle Joe told me last night that I said, "Please pass the snake." They laugh at me as though I am the entertainment for the evening, but it is a kind laughter, and I don't mind it too much. I will also probably make a fool of myself many times at the store!

Aunt Julia is very protective of me. She keeps me away from any of the young men who come around, and she constantly tells me to wait and marry a well-educated man with a nice house and a respectable profession. I doubt that the Lord Jesus himself would be approved for courtship by Julia. The truth is that I have not met anyone yet that has caught my eye. The pioneer men are rough and crude, but new people arrive every day. Maybe my 25th year will bring a husband tailor-made for me. I just try to remember that God knows what is best for me. I do hope that whoever God chooses has a beautiful sailboat and bathes regularly.

October 4, 1855

I really enjoy working at Julia's store and meeting the interesting people that come through the door! It's the only dock and store on the north shore of the river, so the local families come in to meet with their neighbors and socialize in addition to buying supplies. The building is almost always buzzing with conversation, and it smells of rich coffee, sawdust, and the sea. Traders and merchants bring in new merchandise from different places every week, and they love to trade with Madam Joe. Seminole Indians and the Spanish rancho fishermen have also found us. They are so different and fascinating to me, and we can learn a lot from them since they were here first.

Now every day is so different, and I'm very happy that I'm no longer trapped and brooding indoors. Aunt Julia and I are a good team, and she tells me that I work harder than most of the men she knows! I feel strong and fit, and I sleep so well at night. My homesickness is passing, and I welcome each new day that God gives me.

October 12, 1855

Today Aunt Julia left me in charge of the store for several hours. I love running the store alone, and I made many sales! I'm no longer nervous when left alone, and I know enough of the area's languages to trade and exchange pleasantries.

This afternoon a Spanish fisherman came in to buy supplies and food. I recognized his accent immediately, but he didn't look and act like the other rancho fishermen. He seemed very mature and polite, and he left me with the impression that he is probably educated and well-traveled. He may be a little older, but when he smiled I could see that he is handsome in a rugged sort of way.

He seemed a little self-conscious at first, and he spoke his Spanish so fast that I couldn't pick out any words that I knew. I realized that he was asking for something, so I encouraged him to repeat himself. Instead of speaking again, he began to strut around like a chicken, and he actually started clucking! Then he mimicked a chicken producing an egg! I laughed until my sides hurt and tears were rolling down my cheeks.

He bought two fresh chickens that had been plucked and cleaned earlier, a dozen eggs, and some flour, sugar, and salt. As he handed me his money, he grasped my hand and said, "Miguel." I replied, "Frederica." He walked to the door, turned, and gave me a big, toothy grin. I could not help but smile in return. His light-hearted spirit was contagious.

October 20, 1855

The Spanish fisherman, Miguel, has become a frequent customer. I have to admit that my heart beats a little faster when I see him come through the door. He comes in a small sailboat, and Uncle Joe told me that he has a fish camp on the west side of Terrasilla. I try not to ask too many questions about him, but I want to know more!

Miguel and I use sign language to communicate, and we always end up laughing at our mistakes. Every time he comes in, he points to items and yells out the Spanish word. I reply with the Bavarian word, and then he usually shakes his head. Sometimes another customer will yell out the English word. There are just too many languages to learn in this place! Despite the language barrier, he always finds what he needs, but he only buys a few items at a time. I wonder if he's spreading out his shopping so that he can see me more often? Should I even dare to think about that?

Miguel may be a bit older than I am, yet he has a youthful, attractive spirit. He has beautiful eyes. They are light in color, and they are ever-changing like the waters of the Manatee. His hair is thick and tied back with a bit of string, and it has been lightened by the sun. His skin doesn't appear to be rough like the other fishermen, instead it looks smooth and tanned. Maybe he trades for the oils that the Indian women use to prevent the sun from lining their faces? I'll have to ask him, but I'll have to figure out how to say it in Spanish!

October 30, 1855

Today Miguel came in with two fellow rancho fishermen. One of the men spoke English, and after so many weeks of half-communicating with Miguel, it was nice that his friend Manuel could interpret in simple English words. He even knows a little German!

Through his friend, Miguel asked me if I ever left the store, or if I slept in the vegetable bin at night! I laughed and said, "Of course I can leave the store, but only when my Aunt approves of my reason to go out."

He then asked if I had ever been on a sailboat with an expert navigator from Menorca, Spain. I suddenly felt self-conscious and nervous. I am quite sure I blushed at his invitation. About that time, a scowling Aunt Julia appeared and whisked me away to load potatoes in the back of the store, all the while cutting her eyes angrily at Miguel.

I saw the three men leaving, and I wished I could have said a proper goodbye to them. I have always felt that good manners are very important for a lady. When I heard the bell on the front door jingle, I crept from the back of the store and peered through the window. Miguel, who was walking alongside his friend, turned around and waved a piece of paper in the air. He then placed it in a crack in the wooden store sign, smiled his beautiful smile, and walked down to his waiting boat.

When I felt sure that there were no spying aunts around, I rushed out to the sign to collect the note. It was a well-written and thoughtful invitation for an afternoon date. He obviously had Manuel write it, but he signed his own name and made a small drawing of a dolphin beside it. I noticed that the salutation had also been written in his own hand. I've stored the note away in my keepsake box, just in case Miguel is to have a special place in my life.

Nov. 4, 1855

Today was our date, and it was wonderful! Miguel invited me to go out on his boat for the afternoon. I feel a little guilty about being dishonest with Aunt Julia, but I know that she would never let me go if I asked her! I told her that I wanted to stay home to do my laundry and write letters back to Bavaria. She told me to keep the

54

door barred because they would be taking the girls to visit neighbors, and they would not be home until dark. I cannot imagine her anger if she finds out what I really did, but it was worth it!

The clock chimed ten in the morning, and I walked to the dock on the Manatee River. I waited impatiently and hoped that no one would see me waiting for Miguel. I looked to the west, and right away I saw the silhouette of a small sailboat in the bright morning sun. I grabbed the basket of food that I had packed and then waved at the boat.

Miguel skillfully pulled the boat right up to the dock and reached out his hand to me. I was surprised at how tenderly he helped me into the boat. The wind caught the sails and we were off on a great adventure. Today was absolutely perfect, but I'll have to write more about it later. I hear the family arriving!

Nov. 14, 1855

Tonight, Miguel picked me up at the dock again as the sun was setting. Aunt Julia, Uncle Joseph, and the girls were at a church meeting.

As we glided through the clear, cool water, Miguel suddenly jumped to his feet and took off his shirt. He threw down the anchor, grabbed a knife, and jumped into the water. It all happened so fast that I didn't know what to do! Then I saw the reason that Miguel had jumped overboard.

A beautiful dolphin lay lifeless in the water, and Miguel was struggling to cut away the net that had entangled the poor creature. Without a thought, I jumped in to help him. Together we freed the frightened dolphin and then laughed as she swam away from us and leapt into the air.

The water was not rough, but after we freed her, we pulled ourselves back into the boat, exhausted. The excitement and stress of the situation had made us both very tired! The happy dolphin circled the boat until we arrived back at the dock. It was almost as if she realized that we had saved her life. I will never forget the patience and compassion Miguel showed as he worked to save that dolphin. That was the night I fell in love with him.

Eden

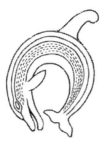

Miguel walked out the door of Julia Atzeroth's store and into the bright sunlight. His heart felt as hollow as the sound his footsteps made as he walked down the long dock to his boat. He paused and looked back at the covered porch. He had hoped to catch another glimpse of Frederica, instead he noticed a handsome, young man in his Sunday clothes. The young man held a bouquet and sat by the old barrel where the old-timers played checkers. He gave Miguel a curt smile then stood up and strutted confidently through the door of the shop. The bell jingled brightly, but to Miguel, it sounded like the door of a tomb slamming shut. He had seen this man before, and there were others. These men were visiting Madam Joe's store for the same reason he was—to be waited on by Frederica.

As he untied and pushed off from the dock, Miguel spotted a couple of young boys fishing with their cane poles. They smiled and whispered to each other, then quickly looked away when they saw Miguel had noticed them. Miguel didn't catch their words, but he imagined what they said, *the old fisherman's been courting again.* He felt ridiculous. *What must Frederica think of me making multiple visits a week, like today, coming in to buy one tomato!*

It was customary for him to come to the store only once or twice a month, but these days he often pretended he had forgotten some item like coffee or lamp oil. "I'm a fool," he mumbled to himself.

What did Frederica think when the door jingled and he walked into the shop? He was a sun-weathered older man who smelled of fish, sweat and salt water. He knew she must be at least ten years younger. *Did she think him a desperate fool?* She was always very kind and cordial, although they couldn't communicate. Yet, he felt there was something magical between them. Miguel wondered if this was all in his head. He thought about how silly he must look as he used sign language to act out his requests. He had made her laugh, but was she laughing with him, or at him?

Miguel didn't see himself as a man lacking confidence, especially after all he had endured in life, but when it came to Frederica, things were different. Her eyes stripped his soul bare, so much so that he felt there was no hidden dark corner within him she couldn't see. It made him feel vulnerable, childish. It was ridiculous that a man his age should feel so insecure and unworthy. He grieved the loss of a woman he had not yet won. This realization made him feel even more ridiculous.

With a shadow on his heart, Miguel turned his boat into the warm wind and sailed out of the mouth of the Manatee River, past Terrasilla Bay, then north along the mangrove coast. He headed home to the little bay where he'd established his fishing camp eight years before.

Miguel's Bay, as folks started to call it, had two semi-hidden entrances. His friend and fellow fisherman, Philippi Bermudez, had shown the entrances to Miguel when they worked at Perico's rancho. This was a place used by boat captains in the old days. It was called *el pantano crítico*, a critical bayou, and it was used in dire circumstances such as hiding from fierce storms or enemy pursuits.

The schooner's bow turned toward the coast and threaded the narrow southern inlet into Miguel's Bay. Dark summer thunderheads towered majestically in the distance and deepened the dark-green hues of the mangroves. Fingers of lightning lit up the jungle hammock of Miguel's Island and gave it a primordial atmosphere.

After passing the twin keys in the center of the bay, Miguel could see home. The chalky-white shell ridge along the beach in front of him contrasted sharply with the deep-violet sky. On the northern end of the ridge rose a large shell mound where his palm-thatched fisherman's hut sat twenty feet above the black mangrove jungle.

Miguel had anchored off the beach when a vivid memory of his mother struck him. She was reading the story of the

"Garden of Eden"—the scene where man walks with God. Miguel had felt that same closeness to the Divine, when as a child, he walked among the olive trees on Menorca, but life has a way of complicating a childlike faith.

He had been driven here by his despair after the loss of his wife. This remote place halfway around the world was Miguel's *el pantano crítico*—his place of refuge. It was indeed, his Eden, where he hoped he could find inner peace. Perhaps, with luck, he could even find God again. This island was abundant with fish, wildlife, and warm sunshine. But would Frederica love this island as much as he did?

Frederica's Secret

It had been three weeks since Miguel met Frederica at the dock and took her out on his boat. She learned from one of Miguel's fishing mates that he was gone on an extended fishing trip down the coast, where he would trade with the Indians and catch many fish. Frederica was surprised at how much she had thought about Miguel lately. She wondered if Aunt Julia would notice her daydreaming and be suspicious that a man had captured her thoughts.

The memory of freeing the dolphin from the net played over and over in her mind. She recalled every minute of that beautiful day—how it felt, the color of the sky, and the briny smell of the water. Most of all, she remembered how it had felt to hold Miguel's hand when he helped her in and out of the boat. He had been a perfect gentleman to her, but she had been a bit startled at how comfortable he was about taking off his shirt and jumping in the water. He seemed to be perfectly at home in the sea. He showed it respect, and there was no sign of fear in him.

Frederica wondered if Miguel was thinking about her. She also pondered how many other women he might have taken out on his boat. She supposed he could have a girlfriend in every fishing village he visited, but her instincts told her that this was not true. Perhaps one of the other men would be kind enough to tell her more about him.

The bell on the store's door jingled and jolted her from her thoughts. She hurried out of the back room to greet the guest who had just entered. It was Miguel. He stood in the doorway with the sun at his back, and it made his hair appear to glow. He stepped inside and let his eyes adjust for a moment before his gaze fell on Frederica. A smile broke out on his face and he called out to her with his deep voice and thick accent, "Frederica!" She suddenly had trouble making eye contact with him. Without warning, he grabbed her in a quick hug. This was not an unusual move for Miguel, but Frederica's Bavarian roots made her feel a bit awkward. She was, after all, hugging a man she didn't know very well.

She would later reflect, that in that brief connection she learned a lot about him—he was open and honest, his confidence was contagious, and his positive spirit lifted the hearts of everyone around him. She was also very impressed that he smelled so good in spite of working outdoors.

She was glad that Aunt Julia had gone to gather the girls from school. Her aunt would have quickly ushered Miguel out the door after seeing his brazen greeting. In Julia's mind, such a greeting should be reserved for married couples.

Miguel looked around, and his expression portrayed that he was glad he and Frederica were the only two people in the store. He pulled a package from under his shirt and proudly handed it to her. It was wrapped in coarse, brown paper. She looked up into his eyes and hesitated for a moment. She wondered if she should take this next step with him. When she pulled the paper away, she revealed a beautifully woven blanket. Frederica knew by the colors and design that a Seminole woman had created it, and there was no telling what Miguel had traded to acquire such a treasure.

As she fluffed the blanket to see the whole design, emotion caught in Frederica's throat. The beautiful scene was of a dolphin swimming in shallow water with the setting sun in the background. The colors in the weave were the same colors as the sunset they had shared on their first boat ride together. Was this a coincidence, or had he been so thoughtful that he requested the weaver to make this blanket in commemoration of their special evening together?

As Frederica pondered this question, Aunt Julia's wagon came up the road. She hurriedly stashed the blanket under the counter, and Miguel secretly slipped a note into her hand. With a nod and a wink, he retreated through the back door. She put the note in the pocket of her apron—she would have to wait until later to read it.

The rituals of preparing dinner dragged on slowly that night, and the meal itself seemed to take years to complete. Frederica couldn't wait to read the note. "I think I will turn in early tonight," she told the family. "It was a very busy day at the store." She kissed Julia and Joe on the cheek and climbed the stairs to her small loft bedroom.

The note was written on very delicate paper, and she feared it would tear. Slowly, carefully, Frederica unfolded the paper. She sat in a chair by the window, so she had plenty of light. The note was written in German, and the penmanship was excellent. It read, "I would like to request a picnic with you on Saturday afternoon. Please meet me at the bend of the river on the small beach at one o'clock."

She fell back onto her bed and held the note to her chest. How many days was it until Saturday, and where in the world did Miguel find someone to write this note? Frederica was impressed at the extra effort that he must have made to have the note written, and that he had come so far to hand deliver it. He sure found the back door in a hurry when Aunt Julia showed up! She quietly giggled while thinking about it.

Five days passed in agonizingly slow fashion, but Saturday finally came. Frederica put her hair up because it was so warm outside, and she put a few orchid blooms in her hair clip to create a subtle perfume. She knew that Julia and Joe would strongly object to a second date with Miguel, so she kept it to herself. It was her day off from the store, and the

Atzeroths had gone to Terrasilla for the day. As long as Frederica was back by sundown, and she was careful not to be spotted, her aunt and uncle would never know about her secret date.

Her mother's cloth handkerchief rested snugly in her sleeve, and every time she patted the sweat from her face, she felt that her mother was with her. She wished so many times she could tell her mother about meeting Miguel. She would explain how he had touched her heart in such a short time, and her mother would love the story about the dolphin.

Miguel was right where he said he would be—punctual as usual. Frederica marveled that the fishermen could navigate their schedules without clocks or calendars—they always knew what time it was by simply looking at the sky. She handed Miguel the picnic basket of food and waited for him to help her gracefully board the boat. When the sails filled, Frederica was surprised that they were not taking the same route as last time. Instead of staying close to the shore in shallow waters, they were headed straight out into the vast ocean.

Frederica didn't expect this, and she clung to the side of the boat until her knuckles were white. She refused to make eye contact with Miguel. He pulled on the sails and began to sing. They continued to sail away from land. One of Frederica's worst fears was that someone might discover her secret fear of swimming. She murmured a quiet prayer, "Oh

Lord, please don't make me reveal this weakness to him today."

They anchored in beautiful, deep-blue water and ate the packed lunch. Miguel nodded and smiled as he ate, letting Frederica know how much he enjoyed her food. He pointed out animals to her—giant birds, a group of manta rays, millions of tiny fish being chased by a larger school of fish. He gestured at a point on shore that might have been a special fishing hole for him, or perhaps a favorite spot to rest, but Frederica could not decipher the description that he gave in Spanish.

After lunch the wind subsided, and the stillness made the heat feel quite intense. Just like last time, Miguel took off his shirt, without hesitation or modesty, and made a perfect dive off of the bow of the boat into the deep water. She thought that surely, he must be part fish. Wouldn't it be funny to call him *Mullet Miguel* after the abundant local fish? She smiled at the thought and for a moment forgot about her nervousness. Then the unthinkable happened. Miguel popped up from the water and motioned for her to join him. Frederica wanted to disappear. She had no idea what to do.

Her awful secret was about to be exposed. Frederica had never learned to swim. She felt like a little girl again, she was so scared, and she wished that she had never come on this picnic.

Their last trip had been in waist-deep water, but this time Miguel had executed a perfectly vertical dive from the tallest part of the boat, so the water must be very deep. He treaded water and looked at her expectantly. Without warning, tears rushed down her cheeks, and she felt totally exposed and embarrassed. She mimicked a swimming motion and shook her head, "No. I can't!"

Miguel's countenance changed to concern, and he climbed back into the boat. He pulled up the anchor and headed back to shore. His back was to Frederica, and she imagined him being very upset with her for wasting his afternoon—he probably thought it so stupid that she did not know how to swim. How could a woman her age not know how to swim? She mentally prepared herself for a very long and awkward trip home.

Miguel adjusted the sails and brought the boat to a stop several yards from shore on a secluded sandbar. The anchor splashed into the water once again. This time Miguel lowered himself into the shallow water and motioned for her to join him. It dawned on her that he was offering to teach her how to swim. Once again, the fear rose in her chest, and she struggled to breathe. She looked into his kind eyes as he walked toward her with outstretched arms.

Frederica removed her dress, but she was still covered with enough underclothes to be somewhat modest. She waited a few more moments and tried to find the courage to go to Miguel. She reached out and closed her eyes as he lowered her into the warm water. As the water covered her up to her waist, she remembered all of the nightmares about drowning she had as a little girl.

Miguel held her in the water for what seemed like a long time. He let her get used to the movement of the water, and little by little, she relaxed. He gently laid her back in the water and taught her to float. He supported her with strong arms, and she could feel the water holding her up. For two hours, Miguel lovingly and patiently worked with Frederica, and by the end of their time in the water, she swam several yards with no help from him.

It was such a relief for her to put away a fear that had crippled her for so long. Now she could enjoy the serenity that the ocean offered, and she wouldn't be tormented by fear and nightmares.

By the time the couple reached the shore, the wind and sun had dried them both. It was time to sneak back in before anyone noticed her absence, but Frederica took a moment to embrace Miguel and give him a quick kiss. She hoped he could feel her appreciation for the gift he had given her. He had taught her to swim, but he also proved that she could trust him with her life.

A Talk with Frederica

Several days had passed since her swimming lesson, so when Frederica saw Miguel on the North River dock, she greeted him enthusiastically. She wanted to spend the afternoon with him, but she had promised Aunt Julia she would run the store for the rest of the day.

When she was with Miguel the minutes flew by. She had fallen completely in love with him. Neither one of them had expressed their feelings for one another yet, but she knew how she felt about him. How strange that such an unlikely pair would find each other in this new land.

She ran from the dock back to the store, knowing that Aunt Julia would be waiting to relieve her of her duties. That woman always had a plan, and she never slowed down. Frederica burst through the door gasping for breath, and her cheeks flushed a bright crimson. Aunt Julia met her with hands on her hips and a solemn face. "Eliza!" she called. "You and Mary mind the counter for a few minutes while Frederica and I go outside for a chat."

Frederica walked through the back door with her aunt and wondered what Julia had to say. They sat on a wooden bench in awkward silence. Her aunt seemed to be searching for the right words to express some awful news. Frederica braced herself.

Aunt Julia's face softened, and she made a conscious effort to make her voice quiet and even. "My dear niece, you know that you are like a daughter to me. There is a special place in my heart for you." Her voice cracked as she spoke, and it was as if she were holding back some particularly strong emotions. "I can tell by your demeanor that you have fallen in love with the old fisherman, Miguel. I can see that he treats you with respect and thoughtfulness, but there are a few things I would like you to consider."

Frederica was surprised that her aunt had read her so easily. Bavarian women were usually careful to hide such matters from others, and they rarely talked about affairs of the heart.

Julia continued, "Miguel is also smitten with you, and I expect that he may offer you a proposal soon. I want to tell you of my concerns, and then you must make a decision on your own."

Julia paused for a moment while she organized her thoughts. "This man is different from you in so many ways. He was raised in a different part of the world, and he speaks another language. He is also Catholic and looks old enough to be your father. As if these things weren't enough to make a marriage difficult, I would like you to think about this," she leaned in as if afraid of being overheard, "You are still young. It is your first time to feel love and attraction for a man, so you are wide-eyed with expectations of love and romance. Miguel, on the other hand, has probably been in love before. We don't know what secrets his past might reveal to us. He may have had a beautiful and delicate wife in his past, or perhaps he was wed to a fiery Spanish woman who became hateful and overbearing. Maybe this prompted Miguel to escape to the other side of the world, yes?"

Frederica interrupted, "Aunt Julia, I know these things are possible, but—"

Julia cut her off, "If he has experienced and lost true love with a young wife, you will always live with her ghost. He will always compare you to her. He may whisper her name and not yours as he dreams. You may not measure up to her in his heart of hearts. You will be able to sense this in him and will suffer deep sadness as long as you are married. If he had a wretched first wife, you might do or say something that reminds Miguel of her. She may have wounded his confidence or made him feel weak as a man. Frustrated by a distant memory, he could take it out on you, though you would not deserve it."

As Julia continued, Frederica's eyes welled up with tears. "We know that the Spanish fishermen were here long before we arrived in Terrasilla. Many of them took Seminole wives and had children. It's possible that Miguel had a family with a Seminole woman, and she may return to find him when the conflict is over." Frederica felt as if the wind had been knocked out of her. She stared off into the distance, numbed by her aunt's words. Aunt Julia reached over and rubbed her hand gently. "You have an important decision to make, my dear. My desire is that you guard your heart as you would a precious and perfect jewel. Do not give it away in haste."

Frederica looked up at her aunt. "No one respects you more than I do, and I am so grateful that you brought me here to share your home. I love this wild, exciting land and I am learning from you, the strongest woman that I know, how to survive here."

She stopped talking and took a deep breath before continuing, "I am twenty-five years old, much older than most of the unmarried women here. Don't you think I should have found a man to marry me by now? I have been patient, and I've begged God to send the right man for me. I need someone who can tolerate my ambition and need for adventure. Yes, I am ready to become a wife and mother, but I want a husband who will love me for my strength and determination, and who will see me as a valuable partner in life. I am not interested in being treated as a woman who needs to be molded like a piece of clay into what my husband desires me to be. I am who I am, and I don't want to change. I'm not sure I *could* change to please a man."

The passion in Frederica's voice surprised Julia. She allowed a slight grin to dance across her face. This girl sounded very much like herself at a younger age. For the first time, she was looking into the face of a grown woman. Had Miguel given her this new confidence? Julia wondered how in the world they could communicate without speaking a common language.

"But Frederica," Julia said urgently, "What about Miguel's past? What do you know about him? There are so many rumors about him, and have you thought about what being the wife of a fisherman will be like? He will leave often to sail dangerous seas, and he may be drawn into military causes because of his skill on the water. You might soon find yourself widowed if you marry such a man."

Frederica reached over and held Julia's hand. "What about love? Doesn't it come at the most unexpected times, to the most unexpected people, in the most unexpected places?"

***

Julia remembered the day Joseph, a man despised by her uncle, had proposed to her. He asked her to move across the world with him, to cross a vast ocean, even though he knew she had never been on a boat. She looked out of the window and recalled the months of back-breaking toil while clearing land for their home and farm. She thought of the letter that she had written to the Kramer family, it begged them to risk their lives to come to this land of opportunity and adventure. How dare she try to hold Frederica back in any way? Julia's heart understood what Frederica was telling her, and she knew that if Miguel had suffered a broken heart in his mysterious past, Frederica was the one to mend it. She understood that Frederica had what it took to be a real pioneer wife—she and Miguel would make an excellent team.

With that thought, Julia accepted that Miguel and Frederica loved one another. In a time and place where so many people had to marry for safety, convenience, or obligation—how special it would be for them to be able to marry for love.

Visiting Miguel's Rancho

While riding home from church in the back of the wagon, Frederica could hardly keep her eyes open. The visiting pastor's message had been long and tedious. He had to cover a lot of scripture since he only came around once every six weeks after all, but today she felt like he had covered the whole Bible!

She lay back on the hay as the wagon bumped along the rough country road. The sun felt good on her face, Eliza and Mary were asleep beside her. Frederica couldn't wait to get back to Aunt Julia's house so she could go down to the swimming hole and practice her strokes while no one was there.

Frederica began to feel as if she belonged on this island. For a long time, it seemed as though she was just drifting with the tide, but now her life was starting to take direction. She felt like a young sailor might feel when he finally takes control of the rudder. For the first time in her life, Frederica felt that she was her own person.

Her thoughts turned to Miguel, as they so often did these days. His fishing trips seemed so long to her. Why couldn't he have been a farmer or a tradesman? The call of the sea seemed to mesmerize him. Even on the days when he didn't have to fish, he chose to be on the water.

Frederica knew that Miguel loved her, but she wondered if she would ever be his true love, or if the ocean would always hold that special place in his heart. She smiled as she imagined their wedding—it needn't be a large gathering, but she surely hoped it would take place soon. Aunt Julia was still not happy with the idea of her niece marrying a fisherman, but she knew that Miguel would eventually win her over.

The wagon pulled up to the house and the jerk of the sudden stop woke up the sleeping girls. Aunt Julia gave orders before she had even stepped down from the wagon.

"Eliza and Mary, go inside the house and fix yourselves lunch. Then finish your schoolwork and weed the garden. Joe and Frederica have somewhere to go with me." Frederica was surprised that plans had been made for her. "Where are we going?" she asked impatiently, "I really wanted to practice my swimming."

Frederica followed her aunt and uncle down to the dock. Joseph jumped into the small boat and called to his niece, "Your aunt and I want you to go on a short trip in the boat with us. I have some supplies to take to Miguel's rancho."

Frederica hesitated. "But uncle, he's not there to receive them."

"We will drop them off anyway, my dear," Joe said. "Go change out of your church dress and into some cooler clothes."

***

Aunt Julia had packed a lunch for the three of them to eat on the trip, and Frederica reflected that food tastes better when eaten on a boat. The seagulls swarmed overhead and called anxiously for the travelers to drop something delicious into the water for them. Frederica threw a crust of bread overboard and giggled at the white-winged chaos that ensued. Her grin disappeared when Julia snapped, "We feed people, not birds."

Frederica had not yet been to the rancho where Miguel worked and lived. He probably didn't want her to come during the busy days when boats and men filled the cove, because he knew that she might be self-conscious around the men. It would not have been proper for him to bring her there alone on the weekend, of course. She was actually very curious to find out more about Miguel's world, but she hoped he would not be bothered that she visited without an invitation from him. Maybe Uncle Joe wouldn't even tell him that she had joined her aunt and uncle on the errand.

They carefully maneuvered into the shallow waters of the cove, where Indian burial mounds lined the shore. It was so unusual to see the long shell mounds in Florida. In the distance, behind the mounds, the thatched roofs of the huts peeked up. Her heart raced. She was arriving unannounced and uninvited. She was relieved to see that no one was there. Frederica was entering Miguel's world, and she was quite nervous about it.

Hammocks hung from the trees and fire pits were dug into the ground next to the small huts. There were racks where fishermen hung their nets to dry and crude pine tables where the fish were cleaned, salted, and put into barrels. Clothes were hung to dry from ropes stretched between trees, and in the center of the clearing, sat a large barrel to serve as a cistern for collecting rainwater.

Uncle Joe carried the boxes of supplies toward the largest hut. Frederica guessed this must be Miguel's home.

Aunt Julia walked up next to Frederica, took her by the elbow, and led her to the door of the hut. "Niece, you are about to see where the man you love lives." The tone of her voice was grim. "This is where you will live, should you marry him."

Uncle Joseph untied the seaman's knot that held the rough-hewn door closed. As it creaked open they walked inside, and their eyes slowly adjusted to the dark room. Frederica's eyes widened with surprise at what she saw. Julia and Joe waited for their niece's reaction.

The hut was only one room. There was a very modest, homemade cot covered with an old Seminole blanket pushed up against a wall. Lying on top of the blanket was a small pillow stuffed with moss. In a corner stood an unfinished square table with one wooden stool. On the table sat a kerosene lamp, that looked to be the only source of light in the whole place. In the back of the hut, a piece of an old sail had been repurposed as a windowpane to cover a small window. It was hot and stuffy inside the hut, and the space smelled of dried seaweed and dirt. Miguel's wooden trunk had been pushed underneath the cot. Frederica imagined it contained cherished reminders of the fisherman's past. His neatly folded clothes rested on a mat of pine needles. A bucket, ladle, two plates, and one cup sat on a shelf. Secured to the wall with a bit of twine—it appeared to be made from an oddly-shaped piece of driftwood.

Frederica took all of this in and let out a heavy sigh. She pulled back the canvas curtain to reveal a single outhouse in the thicket behind the dwelling. She saw no paths cut into the dense and dangerous looking woods, and she could only imagine what the bugs would be like when they swarmed out of the mangroves at dusk. Could Indians be lurking in the woods behind the rancho? Perhaps they were watching her even now and plotting to kidnap her when she emerged from the hut.

Maybe a panther had silently stalked into the deserted settlement. It could hide itself in a tree and leap onto them with no warning whatsoever? A chill ran up Frederica's spine, and she shivered in spite of the heat.

She was standing in Miguel's home—the home she would share with him if she became his wife. What if he never felt the need to build a log cabin for her? Could she birth and raise a child here? Could she survive alone for long periods of time while Miguel harvested a living from the sea? Would she ever be safe here?

Frederica went silent on the trip home. She had a great deal to think about.

In the Nick of Time

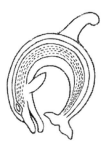

Christmas had long since passed and the days were getting longer. The mornings and evenings were cool and clear. The sun warmed in the afternoons, and the breezes were mild.

Miguel and the other fishermen had worked the waters hard since October. The mullet were running strong, and they worked six days a week salting and drying as many barrels of fish as possible. The men hoped the profits from the sales of the barrels would carry them through the long hot days of summer.

Every seventh day, the mullet rested, but the fisherman received no such reprieve on the Sabbath. For them, the morning of the seventh day was set aside to mend and dry the nets, then empty and clean the boats. The gardens around the rancho also needed tending, so free time for the men was limited to Sunday afternoons. Some men drew a hot bath, shaved, and washed their clothes. Others gathered with like-minded shore folk to worship God, and there were some who hit the rum and slept all day. Those in charge of rations for the boats gathered food and supplies for the next trip.

Miguel woke up before the gulls started calling out their early morning song. As he left his hut to feed his horse and dog, he thought about how happy he was to have a full day on shore. The men would handle the necessary chores, so he could complete his special errand. He was full of nervous energy and excitement to see his Frederica today. It would be a perfect day to surprise her—the sky was brightening into a sapphire blue, and the slight onshore breeze cooled his face. He imagined how the proposal would go—*He would profess his love. She would say, "Yes," and fall into his welcoming arms while weeping tears of joy.*

He scrubbed himself with a fresh bar of lye soap, shaved his sun-weathered face and trimmed his mustache, hoping he would appear a bit younger to Frederica. He also trimmed his bushy Menorcan eyebrows and ran coconut oil through his wavy hair in a futile attempt to tame it. He brushed his teeth with salt and lemon juice and put on clean clothes.

He didn't stop to eat breakfast since he knew Madam Joe would have delicious German pastries to sell today, and no one made coffee like she did. He grabbed his hat and a burlap sack for the supplies he needed to buy in town that afternoon. After being penned up for a few days, his horse, Bella, was well-rested, saddled, and ready for a long ride. She pawed at the ground when she saw Miguel open the rusted gate of the pen—she would not be happy until they were flying down the shell path at a full gallop.

A short time later, Miguel pulled on the reins to slow Bella down and jumped off to gather some fragrant lilies growing by the creek. She was content to snack on clover and take a quick drink. He was careful not to get mud on his clean shirt and shoes. Once again, he imagined Frederica smiling as he handed her the flowers. "Let's go Bella." He laughed. "It's an important day for us!"

When he rode into sight of the Atzeroth's homestead, a small crowd of folks milled about in the front yard. He reined Bella in and strained his eyes to see if he could discern some details about the situation. They slowed down to a walk, and as he drew closer, a very disturbing scene came into clear view. He dismounted and pulled Bella over to the side of the path, so they would not be seen. His heart pounded in his chest as he watched.

Heavy steamer trunks were packed and lined up on the dusty front porch steps. It was obvious someone in the household was prepared for a long trip. Full bags of food were being carefully carried to a wagon already fully loaded with furniture, a large clock, and trunks. Someone moving away from Terrasilla.

Joe and two young men walked out onto the porch. Miguel's heart skipped a beat and then stopped momentarily as he recognized Frederica's two brothers. Were they leaving

Terrasilla? They were dressed for travel. Miguel hid behind a huge cedar tree as the scene unfolded. He thought they were here to stay to help Joe on the farm. Frederica had come to help her Aunt Julia with the house and the store. Surely, they had not changed their minds!

When Frederica walked out of the front door, time stood still, and Miguel felt as though the breath had been knocked out of him. She was wearing her best clothes, and the crimson ribbon on her black silk hat meant she had dressed for an important day. She was openly weeping. The people who had gathered, hugged Frederica and her brothers. Julia desperately clung to the boys as though her heart was breaking with their unexpected departure.

***

Miguel pondered why the Kramers were leaving. Had they not been captivated by the lush beauty of the island? Or maybe they were not cut out for the stifling climate and hardships of the Florida wilderness.

He stared longingly at Frederica as Joe attempted to comfort her. He turned his head before he saw her get in the wagon. He did not want that scene to be etched in his mind. He could not afford to have this image torment him for the rest of his life. Weak-kneed, Miguel leaned against Bella's warm flank—his eyes brimmed with tears. Frederica was leaving and she had not even taken the time to tell him.

He felt like an old fool. How silly for him to think a beauty like her would find him attractive. In a dark and insecure corner of his mind, a whisper told him she had found another man, a younger man, and she was leaving to join him.

The flowers dropped from his shaking hand. He mounted Bella and swiftly rode away before anyone from the homestead noticed him standing in the distance. The joy he had come to know since meeting Frederica was gone. He felt empty. His heart ached, and he had a lump in his throat that would not go away. "Never again," he murmured. Never again would he allow himself to fall in love. A piece of his heart was leaving Terrasilla Island on that wagon, and it would never be whole again.

***

After goodbyes were said, the collection of friends and families went their separate ways. Frederica stood in the middle of the shell road, watching as the wagon drove away until it was a small speck on the horizon. She knew she would see her brothers again, but that reunion would probably not come for several years. This was a painful test for her, and far worse than leaving Bavaria. She could no longer lean on her brothers. Everything had happened so fast. The boys decided to move to Indiana and had given her only two days to decide if she would stay in Florida or join them. She had chosen to stay.

Aunt Julia and Uncle Joe had not pressured her into staying, but she knew they really needed her. They had been gracious enough to get her to Terrasilla, and in doing so they had given her a chance at a new life in a beautiful place. The small island had captured her heart in a very short time. How strange life could be—it was as unpredictable as the weather in this new land. Maybe this unpredictability is what attracted so many risk-takers to Florida.

The island was attractive to brave, adventurous men who would not settle for the mundane lives of their fathers and grandfathers. The women were strong, industrious, independent, and fearless. The children growing up here were wild and free by the sea, where the days were long and warm. It was this freedom that made it easier to endure the hardships of this life.

How could she have ever considered leaving this place? The day she met Miguel, her life was transformed. She saw the world in brilliant colors rather than the muted pallet it had been before Miguel. Every day was filled with expectation and joy. She had found her life's purpose in him, and she knew they could achieve their dreams together.

She would love and respect him as the captain of their ship. He would trust and depend on her as his first mate. They would navigate the calm or stormy waters of life as a team. She had never felt completely safe and comfortable with a man until she met Miguel. He was humble and kind, but he was also strong and fearless. He felt so familiar to her, but she knew it would take her a lifetime to explore the depths of his character. She daydreamed of marrying Miguel and living on Terrasilla Island, of having a large healthy family, putting their mark on this new territory.

She had prepared for the challenge of marriage by learning as much as she could from Aunt Julia and the other women. If he didn't propose to her soon, she may just have to ask him herself. She went inside and changed from her church clothes into her work dress. Since it was Sunday, she would work in her flower garden, and then hopefully, Miguel would show up and take her on an adventure. She loved the anticipation in this new chapter of her life.

***

The ride home for Miguel was a tear-streaked blur. He felt like his heart had been ripped from his chest. How cruel life could be. He had found love, but suddenly it was torn from his grasp without explanation or apology.

He imagined Frederica boarding a schooner at Ft. Brooke. Maybe she and her brothers were returning to their homeland? Maybe they had found a better opportunity somewhere else in America? Perhaps she had written him a letter and left it with Joe. How could she leave without seeing him one final time? It was hard to imagine Frederica being so heartless. Maybe he had misinterpreted her kindness for love—it was entirely possible he had expected too much from her because of his infatuation. Once again, an insecure voice in his head whispered to him, "Keep to the sea, you old fool! Do what you know best. Follow the trade winds, and the salt water will soothe you." Miguel knew the voice was right. The only way to deal with this pain was to get back out on the water.

That afternoon he told his fellow fishermen he would be leaving the following morning on an extended fishing trip. He needed to put space between himself and Terrasilla for a while—he needed to lose himself in his work. Manuel pulled Miguel aside after his announcement. "What is happening with you my friend?" he whispered. "You had a ring in your pocket? Did she turn you down? Why are you leaving so soon?"

Miguel lowered his head. She is gone Manuel, without a word said to me." Miguel's voice cracked. I am a broken man. I ask that you never speak of her or mention her name again."

Manuel grabbed his friend in a strong hug. Miguel tried to resist, but Manuel's wiry arms held him tight. "You will survive this storm, brother. The sea will heal you, and you will have a new start. I will stay here and manage the rancho so you can sail without worry."

The next morning a dense fog covered Miguel's Bay. It was eerie and quiet. Word of Miguel's loss had spread through the camp in hushed whispers, and no one dared speak of it aloud. The boats were floating specters on the water, and their rhythmic, creaking voices called to the men. Quietly, they set sail and disappeared into the mist of the bay. They would not be back for at least two weeks. Manuel felt as though he was mourning a death in the family. Life would never be the same for Miguel in Terrasilla. Frederica's memory would haunt him forever, and for the first time, he wondered if he would ever return.

***

Frederica got up early after a miserable and sleepless night. The sadness of her brothers' departure lay heavy on her heart. As the hours of darkness crept by, she played the scene of the wagon pulling away over and over in her head. Finally, the sun came up and there was no reason to stay in bed. Perhaps the promise of a new day would lift her spirits. She did not question her decision to stay—it was right. It was the only choice that would satisfy her personal happiness and give her dreams a chance to come true.

Frederica thought it odd that Miguel had not come for a visit yesterday, *maybe there was a problem with the boats? Maybe he was too tired from the trip home and needed another day to rest.* She was sorry he didn't get a chance to see her brothers off. He would be surprised they decided to move to Indiana so quickly, but he would be happy they left her behind!

***

Two days passed with no word from Miguel, Frederica kept herself busy with chores. She would be leaving with Julia for the store on the river the next day. If he did not appear by this afternoon, she would borrow Eliza's horse and ride over to the rancho to check on him. She made food to take in case he was sick.

After lunch, Frederica told Aunt Julia where she was headed and set off for the western part of the island. Her mind wandered as she rode. *Maybe she had not remembered his schedule correctly and he would return from a trip today.* She remembered his fishing log indicated that he should definitely be on the island now.

As she neared the point, she noticed that the fishing yawls were gone. *Had they returned from a trip and then left again?* She tied up her horse and looked around. The camp was very quiet without the fishermen there. Frederica was used to it bustling with activity. The wife of one of Miguel's crew was in the camp's grove picking fruit with her two small children. Frederica smiled and waved to them. She had learned a little Spanish from Miguel, but her simple knowledge of the language made it difficult to carry on a conversation

"Hola!" Frederica said to the young woman. The woman smiled. "Hola Señorita!" She told Frederica her name was Margarita, and one of her children offered her an orange from his bag. She accepted the fruit with a "muchas gracias," and put it in her dress pocket for the ride home.

"Margarita, ¿Dónde está Miguel?" The woman shook her head "No" and pointed toward the bay. Frederica understood that Miguel must have left on another fishing trip. "Por cuánto tiempo?" Frederica asked. The woman held up two fingers. Two weeks! He had left for a two-week trip without telling her?

Anger and disappointment rose within her. *How dare he disappear without even leaving a note?* She dug her heels into the sides of the horse and left at a full gallop. She imagined Miguel sailing through calm waters, the wind in his sails, laughing and singing with the other men without a care in the world. The words of Aunt Julia echoed through her mind. She had warned Frederica about men who dedicated their lives to the sea, "They have wandering hearts and wandering eyes, my dear. Their boats can take them away in a moment's notice, and they can disappear over the horizon and never return."

Frederica's imagination spun out of control. Maybe Aunt Julia was right. Maybe he was like the other men who came to America to escape trouble and responsibility, quenching their burning desires in ports and towns along the way. Hot tears burned her eyes and cheeks. *Had she given her heart to a man, only for him to break it?* She wanted to be filled with hope that this was all a misunderstanding, but the burden of reality now rested heavily on her shoulders. Miguel was gone. He may have run off to another woman in another port, or perhaps he simply had grown tired of her, but the result was the same—he was gone. She felt like a naive schoolgirl. How could she have let her emotions rule her so? She had been raised to be a strong, intelligent woman, and now she found herself alone and heartbroken.

The sun hung low and heavy on the horizon when she returned to the house. Frederica wiped her face with a kerchief and held her head high. She would not show her weakness to her aunt. She would dust her skirt off and move on with her life. She would seal off her heart so that she would never feel this awful pain again.

Frederica stayed at the river store and refused to come back to Terrasilla despite her aunt's pleas. Aunt Julia suspected that her soul had moved into a very dark spiritual place. She would not let anyone touch or console her. Julia had never seen her like that before. It was as though the light in her soul had been dimmed to its lowest point before going completely out. Frederica moved silently through her days, numb to all around her. She could not eat more than a few mouthfuls of food at a time, and she went to bed early every night without speaking to anyone.

*****

One bright morning, Frederica came down to join the family for breakfast, the first time since the day she had gone in search of Miguel. She told them she had made an important decision during the night. She spoke to her family in a low, tight voice, "I wish to tell you something and ask that you do not respond. I will not change my mind." The room went silent, and there was a long pause before Frederica spoke again.

Her eyes met her Aunt Julia's, but she looked away before her emotions could interfere with the news she wished to share. She stared out the window toward the sea, "I sent a letter to my brothers in Indiana to inform them that I will join them next week. The spring storms begin soon, so I must leave immediately. My decision to part with my brothers was poorly thought out. I leave in four days. This is best for all of us."

Julia gasped and covered her mouth. Eliza started to cry. Mary ran to her room. Joe rushed over and rested his hands on Frederica's tense shoulders. "You will always have a home with us, sweet girl," his voice wavered as he spoke. "I hope that you know that."

She reached up and covered Joe's hand with her own. "I know that Uncle Joe."

The following days were tinged with dread as Frederica rushed through the preparations for her journey. The morning Frederica left was stormy and grey, but the captain of the small schooner decided they could outrun the weather. Hopefully, they could make it to Fort Brooke before the clouds broke. Frederica walked solemnly down the dock like a man walking toward the gallows. She did not waiver, and she never looked back. She moved to the bow of the boat that faced the mouth of the river. As the wind filled the sails, Frederica and her broken dreams were whisked away. She never wanted to return again.

***

A day later, Manuel Amon sauntered through the front door of the Atzeroth store on one of his regular visits. He brought the usual basket of fresh mullet to Madam Joe and a pouch of fragrant Cuban tobacco to Mr. Joe.

Hearing the bell, Julia rushed out to greet her customer. When her eyes met Manuel's, she stopped in her tracks. Here was the best friend of Miguel Guerrero, the scoundrel who had just broken her precious niece's heart. Madam Joe's face turned red with rage and disappointment. Miguel had put a dark blot on Frederica's soul and was driving her away.

Manuel returned the icy stare. He didn't offer his typical friendly smile or hug. He stared back at Madam Joe with anger for what Frederica had done to his longtime friend Miguel. He dropped the basket of fish on the counter and threw the tobacco onto Joe's chair. "I need sugar, flour and coffee, old woman."

Madam Joe raised her crooked finger and pointed at him. "You and your old fishing friend are not welcome in my store from this day forward, that is, if he ever comes back!"

Manuel was taken aback. "Of course, he will come back to his island! He was here first, and a young, fickle woman turning her back on him and running away will not keep him from enjoying a long, successful life here!"

"Miguel disappeared into the waves without a word to Frederica!" Madam Joe continued her rant, "She has not slept or eaten in days and will never be the same again! I suppose Miguel will move on to another woman while Frederica tries to put the shattered pieces of her life back together." Sweat beaded on her forehead, and her Bavaria accent became thicker as her speech grew in volume and intensity.

Manuel moved in closer. "Miguel Guerrero came here on Sunday to ask your precious Frederica to marry him. As he got close to your house, he saw Frederica and her brothers preparing to leave. She did not even have the courage to leave him a letter of explanation," he said under his breath. "She is a deceptive and heartless girl!"

Madam Joe was stunned for a few seconds as she tried to process what Manuel had said. She replied in a low, breathless voice, "Dear God, Manuel, something terrible has happened here. Sit down and share a cup of coffee with me. We have an enormous problem to fix."

As they talked, Manuel's demeanor shifted from simmering rage to understanding. He was overcome with sadness at the tragic turn of events that had brought about such a grave misunderstanding between two people so much in love. Now their lives were on opposite paths, never to cross again.

Manuel hoped that there was still time to try to right this wrong, but he was afraid it might be too late. He left the store in a state of near panic and ran to his boat. He found Joe on the dock skipping stones across the placid water. Manuel grabbed his arm and pulled him toward the boat.

Joe snapped, "Manuel have you lost your mind? Where are we going in such a rush?"

"Just get in and hoist the sail." Manuel responded as he clambered aboard the boat. "We have to find Miguel and we don't have much time! I'll explain it to you once we are on our way to Fort Brooke."

The dark, ominous clouds continued to gather in the sky. The waves became choppy and were topped with caps of foam as they tossed the small boat around like a toy. The men found it difficult to hold the sails true. Rain fell in heavy torrents. Manuel was nervous about heading into the unprotected waters outside of the bay. Joe had not even had time to bring a hat or coat, and exhaustion set in. "Manuel, this looks bad. I don't think it's wise to carry on."

Manuel wiped the spray from his eyes. Fifteen feet beyond the bow, the sea faded into a deadly shifting tapestry of water and wind. The boat was taking on a lot of water from the relentless downpour. Manuel knew he would have to call off this trip. They headed toward a stand of mangroves and struggled to anchor the heaving boat. Once ashore, they found an abandoned fishing hut and decided to weather the storm there. The two men sat quietly as the storm raged around them. Both felt hopeless and helpless, and they grieved that Miguel would never know the truth about Frederica in time to stop her.

***

Miguel and his crew docked the *Margarita* and dropped off the first part of an order of salted fish at the Ft. Brooke wharf. The men had hoped to spend some time in town, but they heard talk about a nasty storm coming up from the south. It would take several hours to get back to Terrasilla, so they cut the trip short and headed home to safe harbor. Miguel planned to return with the rest of the barrels of fish after the storm passed.

The sails unfurled and caught the wind with an audible snap, and the boat was hurled across the whitecaps toward home. The rain had not started yet, but the men could see the flicker of rapid lightning beyond the horizon. These storms could come out of nowhere. This storm reminded him of the storm that raged in his soul—both were unexpected, and he was not prepared for either of them. Miguel felt sick, exhausted and hopeless.

He leaned against the side of the boat and closed his eyes, knowing that as the storm intensified, there would be no rest for any man on board. A sinister voice in his mind urged him to slip into the black water, unnoticed. He would find a watery grave with no rescue in these violent seas. His tormented soul would find peace. It would be an easy exit—there was no family to leave behind and no one to miss him. The men he fished with would divide up his few earthly possessions and take over his rancho. Their lives would go on. They would continue to refer to *Miguel's Bay* and remember he was one of the first settlers of Terrasilla. Some might tell stories about him to their children, or they might just want to forget the disease, storms and hardships they had gone through to tame the wilderness. Memories of Miguel would surely fade with time, and the next generation would not know who Miguel Guerrero was. Miguel's Bay, Miguel's Island, Miguel Loop Road and Miguel's Pass would eventually be called something else and dropped from the maps.

His family in Menorca would never know how he lived and died in America. His brothers and sisters would only remember him as the handsome young sailor who set out for America to chase a dream of freedom and prosperity. More than anything, he wanted to establish land ownership and pass it down to sons and grandsons, but at his age, his prospects were limited. He had tried to live his life with dignity and honor. He respected his fellow men and showed them kindness in an effort to make his God proud, but he despaired that he had no family to continue his legacy.

He looked over the side of the boat as rain dimpled the surface of the sea. He was so cold. The stars were held captive behind the massive clouds. They were covered in darkness and the wind was picking up. The boat hugged the shoreline in an attempt to find familiar waters. One lantern lit their way. At the bow, Miguel suddenly felt a familiar sense of obligation stir in his chest. It was his responsibility to get his men to safety. They had families, they had futures, full of hope and opportunity. He stood up and took charge of his boat again, barking orders and using his intuition and experience to steer them to safe harbor.

Miguel was in his element amidst the crashing thunder and freezing spray. Just when he felt the boat could take no more punishment, the wind subsided, and a soft rain began to fall. The men found themselves gliding into the protected waters of Miguel's Bay. They were home.

The men quickly unloaded the empty barrels and headed for shelter. Miguel hoped they could rest, in spite of the rain. He would wake up at sunrise to take the last of the loaded barrels back to Fort Brooke to complete the order and meet his deadline. After that, he was unsure of the course he would follow. The storm continued to howl all night, but in the wee hours of the morning it finally passed. By sunrise, the sea was tranquil again, and the golden rays of the Florida sun had burned the clouds away.

Miguel still had no appetite, but he knew he must eat to keep his strength up for at least one more trip. He boiled some coffee and cooked a few gull eggs he found on the beach. He grilled a fish over a small fire and ate an orange. After a quick change of clothes, he left for the fort.

He was alone, but focused on making it through another day. Miguel had made this trip many times. He set the sail and laid down in the warm morning sun. The boat skimmed through the glass-like water. The birds had returned, and it was strange to think that this peaceful sea had violently raged around him the night before.

Fort Brooke was already teeming with activity when he sailed into the harbor. Hundreds of people passed through on any given day. Faces from all over the world came to America through the busy port of New Orleans, stopping in Fort Brooke for rest and supplies as they headed to the southern Florida ports.

Miguel found an empty slip and secured the boat with two tight anchor bend knots. He paid a dock boy to unload the barrels and then deliver them to a woman who owned the food market on Dock Street. He could have turned around and gone back to Terrasilla immediately, but he decided to stretch his legs and find a hot meal.

Miguel's old hat had been battered into a tattered mess by the wind and rain, so he thought he might shop for a new one while in port. He walked along the narrow streets and breathed deep the smells of civilization. He watched as boats dropped off passengers who were eager to set foot on land once again. Watching families reunite and children rejoice in those reunions was especially enjoyable to him.

He rounded the corner and started toward Elsie's Food Market. He hoped she had enough cash to pay him so that he didn't have to hang around another day. The welcoming smell of fresh bread, coffee, and streusel met him as the old door creaked open. He was suddenly very hungry.

Elsie stood behind the counter. She was a large woman who always smelled of cinnamon. He had never seen her without white patches of flour on her clothes and in her hair. Her skin was wrinkled, but she had a youthful spirit. When she saw Miguel, she held out her arms for a hug. As she squeezed him, she muttered something he didn't understand—no doubt it was something about how she needed to fatten him up.

Elsie motioned for Miguel to walk over to a small closet with a blue door she called her office. With a skilled push and pull, she dislodged a floorboard and pulled out a leather pouch full money that was hidden there. Being a good Lutheran, she rounded up the amount as she paid him. Elsie's traditional catch phrase caused Miguel to smile, "Grass-e-ass Senor Migilly!"

Miguel folded the money and tucked it into his shirt pocket. It was another job well done and another commitment kept. For a few moments he forgot the pain in his heart, but he suddenly felt very alone, despite the fact that he was standing in one of the busiest ports on the Gulf Coast. He walked over to look at some hats on a rack. The low roar of so many conversations happening at once made him want to leave and go outside. Without any warning the background noise faded, and one conversation stood out from the rest.

Miguel turned around and looked through the sea of customers toward the counter where Elsie stood. She was laughing and speaking in her native tongue while gesturing wildly with her hands. He recognized the Bavarian accent immediately. Miguel felt drawn to listen to the conversation, and even though he had not yet seen the other woman Elsie was speaking to, he knew her voice immediately.

He walked up behind the young woman. "Frederica Kramer," he whispered.

The world paused for a moment, and she turned around in slow motion. She looked up into Miguel's face, her face full of shock and disbelief. Neither of them knew what to do or say. It took a moment for both of them to believe the moment was real.

The tremendous pain they had experienced started to melt away as they stared at one another. Miguel pulled Frederica to him and held her tightly. He whispered her name over and over as he held her. He managed to choke out a few English words, "Brothers, gone. You gone!"

Frederica recognized the words "brothers" and "gone," and she instantly understood what had happened. Miguel must have learned her brothers were leaving the area and assumed that she had gone with them. Worse yet, he thought she had done so without giving him a proper goodbye. He surely must have thought the worst of her, but where had *he* been? "No Miguel, I stay here. You gone!" She took his hand and led him outside, so they could speak in private.

As Frederica talked, Miguel began to piece the story together. He recognized a few key words and understood the tone of her voice. She had not left with her brothers, and she never knew he had attempted to visit her on the day of her brothers' departure. If he had not come to the house and left so suddenly, this misunderstanding would have never have occurred. She showed Miguel her ticket and told him she had come to Ft. Brooke, so she could book passage to meet her brothers. Knowing she would not be with Miguel, she said a final farewell to her family and to Terrasilla.

It was truly a miracle to find one another again. A chain of misunderstandings had torn them apart, and a series of seemingly random events brought them back together. That evening was a sweet time for the reunited couple. They were able to retrieve Frederica's belongings minutes before the ship to New Orleans set sail. Elsie gave them a big basket of home-cooked food and some leftover cake she had catered for a wedding. They ate under the stars at a small table behind the store.

The warm sea breeze whispered across the water as Miguel and Frederica made their way back to Miguel's boat. Their hands were clasped tightly, and Frederica could not stop talking. Miguel smiled and nodded, content to listen to the lilting tones of her voice.

The light of the full moon guided them back to the small boat, and Miguel motioned for Frederica to sit down on the starboard bench. He pulled out a small wooden chest that had been secured in the bow of the boat. When he opened it, moonlight glinted on a tiny, linen sack closed with a drawstring. Miguel had placed Frederica's ring in this bag on the day he saw the Kramers leaving town. After they left, his intent was to wait until the next full moon, sail out to deep waters, and drop the ring into the depths—another love lost.

Miguel held the bag to his heart. He closed his eyes and offered a sincere prayer of gratitude as he walked back to sit beside Frederica. "Open your hand," he said shaking, and placed the tiny bag in her palm. Her radiant smile was all the answer that he needed.

That night they slept on the deck of his boat under the stars. They had found each other, against against all odds, and they vowed that only death would ever separate them.

The Guerrero Wedding, 1856

On Saturday, the fifteenth of March in the year of 1856, Frederica was awakened by a cool breeze coming through her bedroom window, and the sun peeked over the horizon like a curious child. She rushed to look outside and see what the day's weather would bring.

It was the day she had hoped for—clear blue skies, a warm spring sun, and not a cloud in the sky. The river was calm and the light of the rising sun twinkled across its perfect blue-green surface. She felt a wave of happiness and excitement wash over her. She couldn't believe this day had finally arrived—her wedding day!

Frederica had heard talk that many women were filled with last minute thoughts of doubt or dread on their wedding day. She had none of these. Miguel was her man. He wasn't the perfect man she had dreamed of as a young girl, not even the man she had dreamed of a year ago. Miguel was certainly not the man Aunt Julia dreamed of for her, but in the last several months she had learned to love him more deeply than she could ever have imagined. No matter where they were or what they were doing, being with Miguel always felt right. When they were apart, Frederica didn't feel complete. She wanted her days to begin and end with him.

She and Miguel had a multitude of differences. The most glaring was their age difference, with the language barrier coming in a close second. There was, of course, the cultural difference, for they came from two very different homelands. Miguel was dark-skinned. Frederica was fair. He was quiet but friendly, and a little mysterious at times. She loved to talk, had boundless energy, seemed always happy, and was an open book to those around her. In spite of all the differences, she thought they seemed to complement one another and would continue to grow closer for many years to come.

On this day, the couple would make their bond official in the eyes of the law, the Church, their family and friends. Reverend Lee and his wife, Electa, would arrive by ten o'clock to perform the wedding ceremony, bringing the marriage certificate with them. Frederica was unaware that Mary had been secretly practicing with Miguel to sign his full name when the time came.

Aunt Julia had originally disapproved of their plans to marry, and she wasn't the only one. After they heard the announcement, some of the women who knew the family couldn't understand why a young lady with Frederica's upbringing would choose the life of a fisherman's wife. Why wouldn't she want an educated young man from Ft. Brooke, or Manatee? Then she would be assured of having a nice home in town, and life would be simple and secure. Why would such a beautiful young woman choose a man of the sea who was so rough around the edges?

Despite these murmurings, Frederica knew that her heart wanted Miguel. She whispered a little prayer of thanks to God for finally sending a man to her in her twenty-sixth year. She dreamed of a future in a paradise filled with love and beautiful children. She knew they would be happy in spite of the hardships and dangers.

Well, there's no turning back now, she thought as she saw Miguel pulling up to the front of the house in his wagon. She wondered why he had traveled by wagon and not by boat. Maybe they wouldn't be going straight home to the rancho? *Could he have planned a honeymoon for them?* She felt a thrill of excitement as she thought about getting away from their normal lives and going on a trip together.

She smiled when she saw Miguel wearing a suit, and she knew how uncomfortable he must be. The coat had to be hot, and it was a little big on him—*probably loaned to him by a friend.* He wore a silk puff tie instead of his red bandana, and it was strange to see him without his fishing hat. The starched white shirt made his skin look especially tanned. Getting all fancied up was the first act of love and sacrifice as a new husband for Frederica on this special day. Aunt Julia would certainly be impressed by his effort, and the other women would have to admit he was a handsome groom.

The wagon had been cleaned and decorated with vines covered with white blooms. He must have used fishing twine to secure them to the sides. She imagined bees following behind the wagon as he drove through the palmetto thickets and smiled.

As Miguel walked toward the house, he glanced up at Frederica's window and caught her staring down at him. He blew her a kiss. Frederica, not wanting to be seen by her groom before the wedding, quickly stepped away from the glass.

Frederica heard Joe's joyful greeting as he rushed out to meet Miguel, and she imagined there was vigorous hand shaking and even some shoulder-punching happening. She could hear them talking and could imagine the wide smiles on their faces. She wished she could make out their words.

Frederica heard people arriving, moving slowly up the shell path. Soon, boats would be tying up to the dock. She felt very nervous thinking about the attention she and Miguel would get from all of these people today. Aunt Julia loved to plan a party, and this one would surely last all day. She cringed at the thought of being the center of attention for so long.

Eliza and Mary burst through the door and jumped on Frederica's bed. "You better start getting dressed! Are you going to get married in your nightclothes?" The girls giggled at the thought of her facing her nuptials in such a state. Frederica glanced at herself in the mirror as she washed and dried her face and realized this would be the last time she would see herself as an unmarried woman.

Downstairs, Aunt Julia ordered Uncle Joe around like a drill sergeant. "Move those chairs! Bring in the flowers! Get that dog out of here!" Other women bustled about to bring out baskets of food while others decorated the tables.

Meanwhile, Miguel sat in a rocking chair on the back porch. His goal was to stay out of the way, not sweat too much, and not mess up his suit. Thinking about these simple things took the edge off the anxiety he was feeling. The men stood around him, smoked their pipes, and told funny stories about their wives. Miguel knew they were trying to make him nervous about getting married, but he just smiled and shook his head at each new joke. He knew Frederica would not be like other women—he had found someone perfect and unique.

Three men from Manatee brought a violin, a guitar, and a harmonica. It seemed like an odd combination, but it resulted in beautiful, harmonious music. As the guests trickled in and seated themselves, Miguel's fishing buddies slipped in and stood against the back wall. They were self-conscious because of their work clothes, but Reverend Lee pulled them up to the front, so Miguel would know they were there to support him.

The house filled up quickly, and the children were directed to sit on the floor under the window, so they could see the ceremony. The doors were opened to let in the breeze, and the smell of wild roses filled the room.

Aunt Julia took a deep breath and started up the stairs to fetch the bride. Reverend Lee and Miguel stood in front of the fireplace and faced the seated crowd. Miguel blushed as everyone stared at him. It seemed like an hour passed while he waited for Frederica to be ushered into the room on Joe's arm.

The trio began playing, and the small crowd stood and turned to see the smiling bride. Frederica glided down the stairs and stopped briefly at the back of the room. She was overcome by the scene—there were so many faces she had grown to love since coming to Terrasilla, and the log house had been transformed into a beautiful wedding chapel. She squeezed her uncle's arm, a subtle message to let him know it was time to walk down the aisle. She glanced up at him for a moment, but she quickly looked away so the two of them wouldn't get emotional.

Looking down the aisle, she noticed rose petals lining the rough pine floors. She saw her Miguel waiting at the front of the room. Never in her life had she felt such optimism and promise. He was so happy that he seemed to glow, and he couldn't stop smiling.

As the crowd respectfully stood for the entrance of the bride, Miguel nervously trotted halfway down the aisle to meet her, removing Frederica's arm from Joe's arm. He escorted her to where Reverend Lee waited, to the amusement of the crowd.

Julia whispered to Eliza, "That man has waited a long time to receive this gift."

The reverend read scripture verses about marriage and selflessness and took the opportunity to slip in a short sermon about the abundance of the Lord's mercy. When it came time for the vows, Frederica spoke first. Her voice was clear and unwavering as she held Miguel's hands and looked into his eyes. When Miguel said his vows, his voice softened and cracked, and tears rolled down his cheeks. A tiny girl left her seat, came to the front, and offered him her pink handkerchief. In that sweet moment, many eyes went moist.

The bride and groom turned to face their friends and family for the first time as a married couple. Reverend Lee's voice boomed out, "I present to you, Mr. and Mrs. Guerrero! Miguel, my friend, you may kiss your bride!" Miguel gave Frederica a long, passionate kiss that lasted just a little longer than conservative custom dictated. Upon finishing the kiss, he looked up and waved to Aunt Julia. Everyone understood this was a good-natured taunt directed toward his new aunt. He had married her niece in spite of Julia's objections, and

Miguel was rightfully celebrating his victory. Julia tried to look angry, but after a moment she broke into a big smile. Everyone cheered, and the children clapped energetically as the newlyweds walked down the aisle.

The small crowd walked outside and around to the back of the house where Julia's flower garden flourished, and her fruit trees blossomed. The tables were filled with savory meats, fresh fruits, vegetables, cheeses, and loaves of crusty bread. The wedding cake waited for the newlyweds on the outdoor kitchen table.

Friends and family celebrated the new marriage and enjoyed a feast fit for royalty. The bride and groom took the time to walk to each table and greet the people who had come to celebrate. They were a mix of fishermen, farmers, landowners, and tradesmen. Some had formal educations, while others were students of the land and sea. The guests were as diverse as the two newlyweds they celebrated—a true picture of the new America.

A few hours of fellowship passed quickly, and Miguel and Frederica slipped back inside to change clothes and gather their belongings. Frederica had already moved most of her possessions to the rancho the day before, so she didn't have much to pack. They hurried out to the wagon to escape a string of long farewells. There was a hand-painted sign nailed to the back of the wagon that read, "Just married," and the strings of oyster shells trailing from the back of the cart clacked as they rode away from the party.

The setting sun lit the canvas of the sky with a palette of brilliant colors. The peaceful water reflected the sunset like a beautiful oil painting. Frederica leaned closer to Miguel and held his hand. Their adventure was beginning.

Love Language

Back from their short honeymoon, Frederica was adjusting to her new life as Mrs. Guerrero. On this particular morning she was returning from a trip to the spring for fresh water when she saw the door to the hut stood wide open.

Miguel's old fishing hat and muddy shoes lay on the little porch. A bait net had been spread across her rocking chair to dry. The drying seaweed gave off a putrid scent that wrinkled her nose.

She walked through the front door and noticed fish guts beginning their fragrant journey to decay on the small table. Miguel had been cleaning fish inside the hut again. A stray cat jumped up on a chair and was doing its best to clean the table of the fish scraps and it left muddy footprints everywhere it walked.

Miguel's shotgun lay on the ground beside his chair, along with rags and the foul-smelling brushes he used to clean the firearm. A plate of crumbs and orange peels covered with sugar ants teetered on the arm of the chair.

She discovered her dirty, naked husband napping on the clean linen sheets that Aunt Julia had given them as a wedding gift. Miguel's dog, wet and covered with mangrove slime, slept next to him. A large, tattered old pelican had let itself in and was perched on Frederica's hand-carved hope chest. Mosquitoes buzzed around her head.

Suddenly the bird flew from its perch, grabbed a piece of bread off of the teetering plate, and flew out the door. The puff of air from the pelican's wings caused the plate to fall and break.

Frederica crept quietly and stood over Miguel. Then, at the top of her lungs, she yelled, "*Aufstehe, du alten Fischer!*" Get up you old fisherman.

Miguel catapulted out of bed, his hair wild and his eyes wide. He looked around the room as if a cannon had gone off next to his head. "*Mujer, tratas de darme un ataque al corazón?*" Woman are you trying to give me a heart attack?

"*Reinige dieses chaos, oder ich dich skalpeire wie ein Indianer in der Nacht wehrand du schläfst!*" Clean up this mess or I will scalp you like an Indian in the night as you sleep.

"*Quién cogió el pescado para comprar la madera para construir esta casa?*" Who caught the fish that paid for this house?

115

Frederica grabbed a broom and a cleaning rag and threw them at Miguel.

The broom landed next to Miguel, but he caught the rag in mid-air and put it on his head like an old woman's bonnet. He took the broom and began to sweep as though he was dancing. He sang a Spanish love song in a loud falsetto voice and over enunciated all of the words. He waved to Frederica and winked as he swept.

She was taken aback by the scene. She had been so angry, but the sight of him imitating an old woman was comical and completely out of character for a grizzled fisherman like Miguel. He stayed in character as he continued to clean and sing—still as naked as the day he was born.

She tried to stifle her rising amusement, but it was no use. She laughed uncontrollably, so hard so she could not catch her breath. Miguel pretended to realize that he was naked and quickly covered himself with the rag. He screamed in a high-pitched voice and ran out of the house, which made Frederica laugh even harder.

On the way past the door, Miguel stubbed his toe on a chair leg. He held his toe with both hands and jumped around on one foot. He ran outside as if he could escape from the pain if he ran into the bay.

Frederica, exhausted from laughing so long and hard, fell into the rocking chair. As she calmed herself down and wiped her eyes, Miguel appeared at the front door. He was carrying a handful of flowers, a stringer of mullet, and a basket of beautiful, ripe mangoes. Her anger melted away and her eyes lit up. Her husband had learned that a spoken apology is not always the path to redemption. Miguel had discovered a great deal about his wife in a relatively short time. At this point, the fact that she spoke another language made no difference—he had become fluent in her love language.

The Shell Path

It was springtime in Terrasilla. Frederica marked each completed day on her calendar so that she could keep track of the months. The seasons seamlessly ran together here, and she felt obligated to mark each passing day, so they didn't get away from her.

At Julia's store the previous day, a neighbor woman had asked Frederica if she missed the cool autumns and frigid winters of her childhood. Without hesitation Frederica said, "Absolutely not! I love being able to open the front door and windows in the morning. In Bavaria, winter often lasts well into May, and I remember wearing heavy layers of clothing to go outside for a short time. This place is paradise in comparison."

Frederica remembered that she had never slept well in Bavaria. She often awoke twisted up in her nightgown and smothered by heavy, musty-smelling quilts. Her body would warm up in the night, but her face was always cold, and the smoky hearth-fires made her sneeze a lot.

The darkness of winter in Bavaria was perhaps the worst thing of all. Windows stayed covered with heavy draperies to keep the howling wind out of the house. The days were short, and even when the sun was out it seemed dim.

People became sad or downright mean during the wintertime in Bavaria. Men grew long hair and beards and would come home drunk and smelling of beer at the end of the day. Folks only bathed every two weeks or so because it was so cold, and this meant that the sour smell of body odor permeated the air wherever Frederica went.

The ghostly memory of that long-ago odor made her think about how grateful she was to have a husband like Miguel. He liked to be clean-shaven, and every day he would swim in the river on his way home from fishing. He always smelled like freshwater and sun to her.

Miguel was getting up in years, but the physical work that he did kept him lean. He could outwork most of the young men in Terrasilla, and he didn't complain like they did. Friends and neighbors often sought his assistance when faced with a difficult task because they knew that Miguel could be counted on to work hard and work well.

Frederica hoped that his job and his love of fish and vegetables would keep him healthy so that they could grow very old together. She could imagine him as a grandfather with many grandchildren around him—that would make him so happy.

The fact that flowers grew year-round in Florida was a blessing to Frederica. She learned how to take cuttings from bushes and put them in jars of water until they grew new roots, then she would transfer them to the rich Terrasilla soil. Sometimes she forgot where the cuttings came from, so the first blooms were always a fresh surprise.

Frederica truly loved Terrasilla, even though it was very hard to carve a life from the wilderness. There was something special about being one of the first settlers in a new state, and she took great pride in the success of her home and family. If given the choice to leave for a new place, she would turn it down without hesitation.

For a moment she tried to imagine the future of Terrasilla and the state of Florida. Once the land was tamed, she knew that many people would be drawn to it. She wondered if her great-great-granddaughters would still live nearby. Would they love Florida as passionately as she did? Would they have her strength and her faith to endure the many hardships of life? Would they look like her?

She hoped the stories of her family would be passed down to her descendants. She wished she had time to write down all of the wonderful secrets this place had taught her. She would write about how she and Miguel had loved one another despite their many differences, and how that love produced beautiful children and loyal friends.

She would want them to know how hard she struggled to blaze this beautiful path for them to follow. After lunch she would take her father's knife and carve her name into the gumbo limbo tree on the mound.

Perhaps years later a granddaughter would come along and find the name Frederica Kramer Guerrero carved into the tree. Maybe the girl would be curious about Frederica's life and want to learn more about her.

Bella

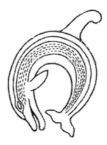

Terrasilla Island, March 1856

Miguel rested a boot on the split-rail fence. With his elbows hanging over the top rail, he smiled proudly as his wife slow-trotted Bella, his grey cracker pony. Frederica rode the mare across the field to the edge of the hammock and turned back toward him.

Miguel thought he was going to give his wife a basic riding lesson today, but Frederica snatched the reins from his hands, mounted up, and rode off confidently.

He could hear her joyous laughter in the distance as she dug her heels into Bella's flanks. Suddenly, the horse flared and burst into a full gallop. Frederica held the reins tight in both hands. She was riding bareback with only a bridle—her bare legs astride the mare's ribs—her skirt tails and mahogany hair blowing behind her like the horse's dark mane.

Miguel thought Frederica rode Bella beautifully. Bent forward with her hands up, his wife nearly touched the horse's ears as she urged her mount to run faster. She gracefully jumped Bella over a creek bed, and as she came close to Miguel, she slowed to a canter and stopped in front of him. She looked down at her husband, raised a dark eyebrow, and smiled. "See there, I *can* ride as well as any man!"

Miguel was impressed and wondered if he really knew this woman at all. What kind of life had she lived in Bavaria before she had come here?

He reached up and stroked Bella's nose. She had come so far since the first day he saw her. What a good, gentle horse she had become for him to trust with his new bride.

***

He smiled and thought, *I wonder if Frederica had known Bella when I first got her back in 1850, would she have still wanted to ride her?* Miguel remembered a spring morning and how one seemingly ordinary choice led to something exciting and completely unexpected.

It was six years ago that Miguel had agreed to help his neighbors John Craig, John Addison, and Henry Peterson hunt their cattle for branding. Wilderness living necessitated the cooperation of neighbors in order to survive. At any time, a cracker might need to ask a favor of his neighbors, so doing right by them was the smart thing to do. Miguel helped his neighbors without hesitation, no matter how it might set him back. When his neighbors called on that day, he decided the fish would have to wait until tomorrow.

Miguel was horseless, but he borrowed one of Addison's mounts for the duration of the job. It was a week-long trip hunting the free-ranging herd out into the scrub country northeast of Terrasilla Island. They could possibly end up as far out as the Little Manatee River.

This would be his first roundup since settling the island two years ago. Cowboy life was a big change for Miguel. He would go from sleeping in the bow of his boat on the open water to camping in the pine scrub, spending hours in the saddle, and living off of beans, jerky, and parched corn—instead of his usual rice and mullet.

The second day out, the men found a herd of cattle grazing on a floodplain along the lower part of the Little Manatee River. The cowboys spread out and encircled the group to contain them. There were several new calves with their mothers, and they needed to be identified and branded with their owners' marks.

Miguel was chasing a young cow that was trying to break free when something caught his eye through the trees. An animal thrashed about in the river. At first, he thought a gator had grabbed a calf, but then he saw it was a little mare struggling wildly. She was stuck on a sandbar in the middle of the river, and the frantic animal had sunk all the way up to her belly in the wet sand.

Miguel shouted to Peterson, who was the rider closest to him, that he was headed to the riverbank. The horse screamed when she saw Miguel and struggled harder to free herself, but she sank even further into the sand.

The horse was now up to her shoulders in the muck. Miguel dismounted, tied his mount to a tree, and cautiously entered the shallow water. He hushed the horse and avoided looking her directly in the eye.

Peterson arrived on the bank, tied one end of a rope to his saddle horn, and tossed the other end to Miguel. Miguel waded out and stopped on the solid river bottom next to the sandbar. The horse snorted, eyes wide with fear and ears pinned back, but she had exhausted herself and could no longer struggle. He slowly reached out his hand and stroked her neck while speaking softly to her.

Peterson shouted to Miguel and made a circular motion with his hands under his arms and around his chest.

Miguel waved back, took the end of the rope, and pushed it carefully through the mud and under the horse's left leg, and then back up behind her right leg. When he threw the rope over the animal's back, the horse snorted at him, but she made no attempt to buck or bite.

Having secured the slip knot, Miguel signaled to Peterson that all was well. Peterson began backing his horse to take the slack out of the line. Once Miguel backed away to a safe distance, Peterson slowly began to pull.

The horse felt the tug and found a hidden reserve of strength. She kicked with her front legs and broke through to the surface of the sandbar, but her rear legs were still sunk in the mud up to her rump.

Miguel went back to his borrowed horse and grabbed a rope—he needed to make a halter so that he could control the animal once she was pulled free. He had already decided that he was going to keep this horse. He whispered to the exhausted animal while he secured the halter around her head, then he attached the lead rope to the loop under her jaw.

Miguel returned to his borrowed horse, mounted up, and signaled to Peterson to pull. The action was over in an instant as the horse made one great leap out of the hole. She fell to her knees in the shallow river water for a few moments, stood up again, and shook herself off violently.

The horse erupted with renewed strength and all hell broke loose. She screamed with fear and anger as she pulled against the ropes. She rose suddenly on her rear legs and flashed her front hooves at Peterson's horse.

Miguel realized they were dealing with a wild horse that had never been broken. He urged his horse backwards, took the slack out of the line, and pulled the wild horse back down and away from Peterson. The enraged mare charged Miguel and Peterson pulled his line taut. This dance continued until the horse wore herself out and reluctantly allowed herself to be led back to camp.

That evening after supper, while the others sat around the campfire drinking coffee, Miguel walked cautiously over to the wild horse. He stopped when he saw that the animal was wide-eyed and nervous.

The young mare was three or four years old. In spite of the sand on her coat, Miguel could tell she was a real beauty. Her charcoal mane and tail contrasted starkly with her light-grey color. Her hindquarters and legs were dark-grey and dappled with white spots. The marks reminded Miguel of a starry sky.

"Bella, that will be your name, for you could be a Menorcan beauty!" Miguel said. He approached slowly from the side, once again careful not to look her in the eyes. Bella snorted and pinned her ears back. Miguel got the message—she felt pressured—so he stopped.

He spoke softly to her, stepped forward again, and stroked her neck. She took a deep breath and her ears came back up, which told Miguel she had relaxed. He backed away from her. Bella studied him for a moment, then moved toward him and touched him with her nose. It was a good sign, and a big step for their first day together.

Miguel patted Bella's nose, before he turned in for the night. He rolled up in his blanket, listened to the crackling of the campfire, and watched the sparks fly up into a starry sky. A couple of the men spoke quietly by the fire, and although Miguel couldn't understand them, he heard his name mentioned. He was sure they were wondering what a fisherman was going to do with a wild horse. He smiled to himself and thought, *they know nothing of Menorca. If they only knew how important the horse is to our people and our ancient traditions!*

Miguel looked at Bella in the glow of the campfire. She was tied up near the other horses. His eyes grew blurry. He was exhausted from the rescue, and he knew that he had a lot of hard work ahead of him. As he drifted toward sleep, he thought about Menorca and "Jaleo," the annual festival that honored the purebred, jet-black Menorcan horses. He remembered what it had felt like to be a child and ride his grandfather's beautiful horses.

***

Miguel snapped back to the present as Frederica dismounted Bella and hugged him tightly for a long moment. She smiled at him coyly and glanced over her shoulder toward home.

Miguel mounted Bella and reached down to pull Frederica up behind him. He made a clucking sound that directed Bella to head home. The sun was beginning to fall behind the mangrove jungle that sat between them and the bay. Miguel found his mood changing as the blue sky shifted to orange and violet. He knew something that Frederica did not know. Joseph had received news from the village. A Seminole war party had attacked and burned Senator Snell, William Whitaker, and Joseph Woodruff's homes on Sarasota Bay a few days ago. The people on the south side of the Manatee River were abandoning their homes and seeking refuge at the stockade and on river boats.

Joseph told him that any day now the militia would be called up. This meant that Miguel would have to ride Bella off to war. He would be gone for at least six months, and there was a good chance Miguel could be gone for much longer than that. He touched the arm that was wrapped tightly around his waist. How could he tell his wife the honeymoon was over—that she would have to go back to live at Aunt Julia's store?

Bella suddenly snorted. *I know Bella*, Miguel thought, *Frederica will probably feel the same way.*

Good News, Bad News

Frederica sat up in bed and slowly lowered herself back down into the pillows. The smell of frying eggs from the kitchen made her queasy. She knew if she got up too quickly, she would throw up. In a few minutes her husband would appear at the bedroom door. He was so anxious to please his new wife and would bring her thick-sliced bacon and fried eggs on a plate along with fresh-squeezed orange juice, biscuits, and orange-blossom honey. Only a week ago she would have welcomed breakfast in bed, but things had suddenly changed.

Frederica completed a quick calculation in her head, added it to the morning nausea, and formulated the likely conclusion their family would expand this year. In a perfect world, Frederica would have chosen to have more time to adjust to marriage before children came, but this was truly a blessing, especially since Miguel was older than the typical husband for a woman Frederica's age. She rested her hands on her stomach and her imagination painted the picture of their perfect future. The child would be a strong baby boy, healthy and bright. He would help his father with the fishing business and his mama in the garden. Or perhaps it would be a sweet little girl who would love to go out on the boat with her papa to look for sand dollars on a sandbar. If it was a boy, they would surely name him Michael, the English version of Miguel. With a strong name like Michael, he would have no problems fitting in and being accepted in this new country. Frederica and Miguel still felt like foreigners at times since they didn't speak English very well.

She decided not to tell Miguel about the pregnancy, at least not for now. So many women lost their babies due to the hard conditions and disease in this wilderness. It would be terrible to raise her husband's hopes, only to have them dashed by a miscarriage. She thanked God for this fresh miracle, and she begged protection for her child. A safe pregnancy and easy delivery would be the focus of every ounce of her willpower for the next nine months.

Miguel balanced a tray and a half-spilled glass of orange juice as he rushed across the threshold. He was in a joyous mood already, and it was all that Frederica could do to keep her new secret to herself. She was much better at keeping sad secrets than she was at keeping happy ones.

Miguel look at her as if she glowed in the early morning light, but Frederica knew her skin was probably pallid from the bout of nausea. *If he thinks I'm beautiful in this state,* she thought, *he is indeed my soul mate.*

Miguel sat on the bed. "What did I ever do to deserve such a beautiful wife?" He set the tray of the delicious breakfast he had prepared in front of his wife.

Frederica needed an excuse to get him out of the room before she was violently ill again, so she asked if he would fetch some cold water from the rain barrel. "I'm so thirsty," she said. Miguel didn't hesitate to scurry from the room and head out to the rain cistern. "Thank you my dear!" she called after him. As soon as he disappeared with the bucket, she ran to the window and sent the eggs flying.

As she stood at the window, the news of the previous day came rushing back, and her joy at the pregnancy was suddenly tempered by a bitter dose of reality. There had been a Seminole attack across the river. The alarms had been sounded, and the call had gone out for the militia to gather at Manatee Village. Miguel would have to leave, and his departure would come very soon.

***

The Seminoles had worked beside the settlers, traded with them, became friends with them, and taught them valuable knowledge about the land. Now, tragically, they were bitter enemies. The conflict seemed so unfair to Frederica, and she could sympathize with the plight of the Seminoles. The white men had arrived in droves and told the Seminoles they would have to give up their land, their waterways, and their very way of life. The sacred lands of their ancestors

132

were forfeited, and they were forced to move to the southern swamplands or to the unfamiliar western territories. The Seminole nation had reached their breaking point, and now they were willing to fight and lay down their lives for the right to live freely on their native lands.

Mrs. Wyatt, who lived on the Braden ranch, was a friend of the Seminole chief Billy Bowlegs—the white man's name for him. One night, the chief sat at the Wyatt's kitchen table to share dinner with the family, and Mrs. Wyatt asked Billy if he would kill her if war broke out. He responded, "Yes ma'am, but I would kill you in a kind way." Frederica supposed that this meant that Billy would not torture Mrs. Wyatt. And why shouldn't Billy fight, thought Frederica? Wouldn't Mr. Wyatt fight for his home and family if strangers told them to leave? Wouldn't Mr. Wyatt fight a friend who threatened his family?

She pondered the evils of war—it demanded that friend kill friend and brother kill brother, and sometimes it even drove men to kill innocent women and children. It made it necessary that women defend their homesteads while men fought and died. Many of the farms and homes the white men built during years of back-breaking toil would be destroyed in the blink of an eye. The sacred lands of the Seminole would be desecrated. No man, white or native, would be spared the horrors of war.

***

When Miguel came back into the bedroom, his look had changed. He lingered in the doorway and watched Frederica's moments of reflection, and he knew the thoughts that troubled her, for they were the same thoughts that plagued him. The reality of a long, bloody battle was inevitable. He put down the water bucket, smiled at his wife, and began to gather his travel gear.

He was somber and swift as he packed. He knew the militia would be deployed immediately to confront the Seminoles and that this confrontation would be extremely dangerous and destructive. He had come to America hoping to find peace and opportunity, but now he prepared for war. He was leaving his new wife behind, and he didn't know if he would ever return. If he did survive, would he find his house burned to the ground and his wife murdered and scalped?

When Joe Atzeroth arrived, they would have to decide how to ensure the women's survival. Would they cross the river to stay in the stockade with the other women and children from the village of Manatee? Would they stay in Terrasilla to protect their homesteads? The Indian raids did not come to Terrasilla as often as other settlements in the region, but that didn't guarantee that the women would be safe. What about Julia's store, would it be destroyed?

Miguel's head swam with worry and doubt, but one fact gave him comfort—Julia and Frederica were strong European women. They would listen to his suggestions, but ultimately, they would do what they thought best for everyone. They were stubborn and resourceful, and Miguel felt they could defend themselves against most enemies. *Woe be to the man who crosses our women*, thought Miguel. He smiled wryly as he oiled his rifle and packed his bag.

Billy Bowlegs' War

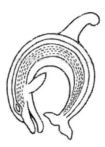

Manatee Village

On a cool Saturday morning in early April of 1856, an alarm was raised after Dr. Braden's plantation was attacked and several of his slaves carried off. Men from all around the Manatee and Sarasota districts were converging on the village to muster into Captain John Addison's Company of Florida Mounted Militia.

A schooner from the north side of the river offloaded men and horses at the Manatee wharf. Frederica and Julia followed Joseph and Miguel somberly as they led their horses down the dock. The clacking of hooves on the weathered boards was the only sound to be heard.

Miguel pulled Frederica close, held her tight, and whispered a Spanish phrase she had heard often and knew well—"Te amo," he said softly, his voice breaking. Joseph gave Julia some final instructions and a hug. Then he and Miguel mounted up to join the other enlistees at Branch Fort.

Fear had been hanging in the air like dense fog since early March. A band of Seminoles burned the homes of William Whitaker, Joseph Woodruff, and Col. Hamlin Snell to the ground near Sarasota Bay. The colonel had wisely decided to remove his family to Branch's stockade, but his caretaker, Owen Cunningham, stayed behind and was burned alive during the attack. Whitaker told the townsfolk, "The flames were so hot, fueled by the pitch in the pine logs, that Cunningham's body was entirely consumed, except for the large leg bones and the thick muscle of his heart."

As the soldiers signed the muster roll, townspeople huddled together to listen to reports of the most recent attack. The victim was Dr. Braden, and his homestead was only three miles from the village. The Indians were seen prowling around on the porch, but Dr. Braden thought it was a neighbor playing a prank until he shouted, "Who's out there?" At that point the marauders opened fire through dining room windows where the family was hosting a dinner. Braden and the guests were able to return a brisk fire with Robert Gamble's new repeating rifle, and the attackers quickly retreated.

The raiding party was unsuccessful in setting the house on fire, but they carried off seven slaves, several mules, and some food and blankets from the sugar mill before they fled south along the Braden River.

John Addison, with seven men from Manatee, set out early the next morning and rendezvoused with Captain Leroy Lesley's company. On the morning of the second day of marching, they caught up with the Seminole war band at Joshua Creek near the Peace River. Their attack was swift and virtually unopposed. The fierce sub-chief Oscen Tustenuggee and another warrior made their escape, but three Indians were killed—Addison and his men scalped two of them. One scalp was put on display in front of Clark's store.

Anxious settlers from the outlying regions poured into the village looking for refuge at Braden's tabby mansion or at Branch's stockade. Miguel pondered how stifling it would be behind those pine log walls. Despite the oppressive heat, he wished Frederica had been willing to stay there. Julia would have none of it and insisted on remaining at the store because Joseph believed there was no real threat to the north side of the Manatee.

The command was given to mount up, and the horse company formed up by columns of two. The men rode south under the outstretched limbs of ancient live oaks that lined the main road that meandered south and out of town. Miguel turned in his saddle and saw Frederica running behind him, tears streaming down her face. She caught up and handed him a lock of her hair. Miguel tucked the braid of hair into the breast pocket of his coat and set his jaw. He knew that it was going to be a long six months.

At the head of the Braden River, First Lieutenant John Addison's volunteers took the trail that led to Wyatt's place, then rode northeast to Addison's homestead at the ford of the upper Manatee.

The men had ridden during the heat of the day through miles of slash pine and palmetto scrub, until they arrived at the fort in the middle of the afternoon tired and saddle-sore. Like Dr. Branch's fort in Manatee Village, Fort "Rough n' Ready" was a square stockade post consisting of an eighteen-foot pine-log palisade fence with interior catwalks that enclosed the home and outbuildings. It was located on the Tampa Road near the south side of the ford of the Upper Manatee. For the next six months, this would be home to the Manatee Mounted Volunteers.

The company unsaddled and watered their horses and spent the remainder of the afternoon putting up tents and shelters. These were made with canvas and thatched palm leaves to protect them from the spring rains. Campfires were made, and men huddled around in small groups, taking turns cooking their rations and speculating about the war.

Sergeant David Townsend barked out the names of the men assigned to guard duty. Miguel and Joseph Woodruff were posted on the catwalk on the northwest corner wall. The two men needed longer-ranged weapons than their shotguns, so they each collected a '42 musket from the arsenal. Miguel strapped on his cartridge box, belt, and cap pouch. He slung his haversack over his shoulder and followed Joseph up the ladder to the catwalk.

Miguel's musket leaned against the wall beside him, cocked and ready. He was confident with Woodruff beside him. He knew his grizzled partner—a veteran of the first two Seminole Wars as well as the Mexican War—had done this, many times before.

Joseph fumbled around in his haversack for his pipe, placed it in his mouth, and lit it. Miguel knew Joseph Woodruff well. They had met at Hamlin Snell's commercial fishing operation on Sarasota Bay several years ago. They were close to the same age and had become good friends. Joseph had picked up some Spanish working at the rancho, so they could communicate by using basic vocabulary. He was often helpful as an interpreter for Miguel.

Suddenly Miguel heard a strange chirping sound far off in the woods.

He looked at Joseph. He had heard it as well. Miguel stared intently into the dense jungle across the river. It was quickly getting dark, and soon it would be impossible to see anyone hidden in the dense vegetation. Out of the corner of his eye, he caught a glint of light on the other side of the river. Maybe his eyes were playing tricks on him. He stared intently at the place where he thought he had seen the light. Then, just when he began to doubt himself, he saw the reflection again.

His heart pounded within his chest. There in the darkness stood a man in a dark hunting shirt. He wore a turban stuffed with feathers, and he was navigating his way slowly between the trees. Around his neck hung a silver disc, that reflected the same glint Miguel had just seen. The chirping was a subtle signal from this man to his followers. The leader moved into the jungle and was lost from Miguel's sight.

"Seminole." Miguel whispered. He jabbed Joseph in the ribs and pointed to the spot where he had last seen the leader. As they watched, one dark shape after another passed through the clearing and melted into the dark woods. Miguel could feel his pulse throbbing in his neck. There was no question that this was a war party. Miguel couldn't tell how many men there were, but they were definitely headed downriver.

As light rain fell, it was impossible for the two guards to see anything.

Joseph looked down into the fort and saw that Lieutenant Addison was standing on the porch of his house, his pipe puffing out tobacco smoke like a tiny locomotive. He shouted down to the lieutenant, "Sir, Seminoles across the river, movin' west." Addison stepped off the porch and walked across the yard. Rain spotted his brown frock coat and dripped off the brim of his black, slouch hat.

John Addison was an old soldier from North Carolina who had fought with the North Carolina militia during the War of 1812. He had also participated in the two preceding Indian Wars with the Mounted Florida Militia. "How many you reckon, Woodruff?" he called back.

"It's too dark to tell, sir. Maybe a dozen?" Joseph called out.

The lieutenant turned to his adjutant, "Light the perimeter fires and keep the men at the walls. Tomorrow we'll send out a patrol." Addison doubted that there would be an attack, because he was almost sure where the Seminoles were heading. Asa Goddard sat nearby, and his eyes briefly met Addison's. There was no more sign of the Seminoles during the night, but their celebratory whoops could be heard echoing up the river valley from the west. Addison and Goddard knew where they came from—Asa's place was only a couple of miles downriver.

Dawn chased away the grey of morning as the militia patrol drove their horses across the ford and up the muddy north bank of the Manatee. Lieutenant Addison left half of his militia to man the fort and led a twenty-man scouting party to determine the size of the raiding party. He needed to find their trail before mounting a full-scale pursuit. The line of horsemen headed northwest. They rode single file through the pine scrub along a narrow, sandy trail that curled around clumps of saw palmettos like a rattler hunting its prey.

Asa Goddard rode at the head of the column with the lieutenant. They knew these trails like the backs of their hands. The men were neighbors and had hunted these pine

142

woods together, but today was a much more serious kind of expedition.

Miguel rode in the center of the column. There was no sound except the squeak of saddle leather and the occasional snort of a horse. The men riding with him were men of all ages, backgrounds, and walks of life. None of them were professional soldiers, though he did know a few, like John Addison and Joseph Woodruff had spent much of their adult lives fighting Indians.

The men included a state senator, judge, sea captain, blacksmith, and shopkeeper, but most were farmers trying to make a living in the south Florida frontier. They had come from all over the country, and really, from all over the world. There were Southerners, New Englanders, and recent immigrants from Europe like himself. The volunteers were as different as the clothing each wore and the arms and equipment they carried, yet they were unified in purpose. They all wanted to create new lives for themselves and their families, and they would protect their dreams with their lives.

Before they reached Goddard Creek, the unmistakable smell of burning pine pitch in the damp morning air confirmed that Goddard's place had been burned. As they rounded a bend in the trail, they could see black smoke rising above the trees. When Miguel rode into the clearing, he could see that the cabin had been burned to the ground—the blackened bricks of the chimney stood as a stark reminder that this smoldering wreckage had been a home.

Addison and his scout walked around the property, looked at footprints, and tried to estimate how many Indians had been there. Sergeant Townsend was sent out with Addison's sons to scour the surrounding woods for tracks and determine which direction the war party had gone. Asa dismounted and walked up to what had been his front door. The roof had fallen in, and tongues of orange flame still licked at the pine beams and cedar shingles.

Miguel felt a heaviness in his heart as Asa stood alone in the embers. Goddard picked up an ash-covered doll that belonged to his daughter and gently brushed the soot from its face. Miguel knew how he would feel had this been his home—he would despair at seeing all the work, family heirlooms, and happy memories of the place reduced to ash. Reverend Edmund Lee, the preacher of the Manatee Settlement, put his hand on Asa's shoulder and tried to console him.

Miguel and Joseph led their horses to the creek bank where Lieutenant Addison and John Craig were refreshing their mounts. Both had been neighbors of Miguel's at Terrasilla Bay until last year when they moved to the Upper Manatee River.

"She's turned out to be a fine horse, Miguel." Addison said. He reached out, stroked Bella's neck, and remembered the day that Miguel captured her while helping him on his cattle drive. Addison turned to Joseph. "Woodruff, ask Guerrero something for me. Ask him why he is the only fisherman from these parts to enlist in this company."

Woodruff relayed the lieutenant's question.

Miguel thought for a moment, shrugged his shoulders, and answered, "*Florida es mi hogar.*" Joseph interpreted, "Sir, he says, 'Florida is his home.'"

Addison countered, "You were married only three weeks ago! The other fishermen obviously want no part in this war, so why would you?"

"*Sois mis vecinos.*" Miguel replied, and smiled back at Addison.

"What did he say?" Addison asked Woodruff.

"You're my neighbors," Woodruff translated.

The lieutenant listened intently to the scouting report. "Sir, the tracks continue west," Sergeant Townsend said. Miguel had followed Addison, and now he looked around and saw the worried expressions on the faces of his North River neighbors. Only a handful of settlers lived on the north side of the river, and there were no troops there except for Addison's men. The women and children had taken refuge at Gamble Plantation, but their farms were left unprotected.

Lieutenant Addison understood the North River men's fears, and he was concerned his volunteers might desert him in order to tend to their own interests. "We've sent word to Captain Lesley. He'll send some men and rendezvous with us at the fort, then we'll run them down," he assured the men.

"May be too late to save my place by then!" Henry Peterson barked back.

Addison knelt by the creek bank, scooped up some water, and splashed his face. His look was etched with lines of deep concern. He stood up and studied his men. "Sergeant Townsend, take your scouts and follow their tracks. Take Atzeroth, the Petersons, and Michael Guerrero with you. See where they're headed, then send word back to me." He hoped desperately his words would console his men.

Miguel looked up at Joseph. "Michael?" he asked, wondering if the lieutenant had slipped up.

"Your American name! He considers you one of us now," Joseph explained.

The name caught on quickly among the rest of the men, and Miguel liked the sound of it. It made him feel like he had finally been accepted by his Manatee neighbors. It made him feel like an American.

Addison mounted up and sloshed across Goddard Creek, leading his main force back to the fort while the scouting party continued west downriver.

Sergeant Townsend rode at the head of the ten-man patrol following tracks imprinted in the dew-covered grass and sandy soil. His Indian pony had been captured from one of the Seminoles who attacked Dr. Braden's plantation the previous week. The North River men followed behind him with shotguns at the ready. Miguel rode as a flanker, so he was off the trail in the palmetto scrub on lookout for an ambush. The morning sun warmed his back as it rose behind him in the clear morning sky. The rhythmic strides of his horse along with the solitude lured his thoughts into a place where he didn't want them to go.

Miguel thought about Frederica, Julia, and her daughters alone at the store. The images of the smoldering ruins of Asa's cabin haunted him. The war party was on this side of the river now, and they could be headed toward his home. He wished now he had made Frederica stay at Branch Fort.

Midday approached, and the sun climbed high in the blue April sky. A red-tailed hawk perched at the top of a dead pine tree and watched as the scouting party passed below him. They rode mile after mile and wove through pine and oak scrub, always wondering if an ambush waited behind the next turn in the trail. The stress unnerved Miguel, and his thoughts continued to fixate on the safety of his family.

Just then, Joel Addison and his horse crashed through the bushes lining the creek bank and sloshed through the shallow water. "I can't find any signs on that side. I think they walked upstream to hide their tracks. Might be headin' north," he said, and pointed up the winding, narrow creek.

Sergeant Townsend's brow tensed, and his face turned red. He spat on the ground. "Might? Well, I'll be a son-of-a—" he started to belt out, but he saw that Reverend Lee stood nearby and stopped himself. Townsend looked around at his men and said, "We need to get back! Mount up!"

Dark clouds moved in from the east and brought with them a cool gust of wind and the scent of rain. Miguel pushed his wide-brimmed hat down tighter on his head. Every mile they rode toward the fort took him farther away from home. Miguel wondered if anything would remain of his fish camp and livestock when he got back.

The scouting party arrived back at the fort late in the afternoon just as the rain began. The gate creaked on its hinges and swung wide open, and the horsemen entered the inner courtyard. Miguel was safely behind the log palisade again and could get a good night's sleep.

***

Just before dawn, a sentry yelled out, "Who goes there?" and roused everyone in the fort.

Miguel peered through a space in the wall. The silhouettes of horsemen stood on the other side of the morning fog-cloaked river. They looked like ghost riders. On the parapet above him, rifles clicked to full cock. "It's Lesley's men!" someone shouted, and a loud "Huzzah!" rose up from inside the garrison.

The gate opened, and two dozen riders followed a tall, lanky man wearing a black, frock coat and knee-high riding boots into the fort. A rain-soaked, slouch hat drooped over his face, but Joseph recognized the leader by his tuft of red chin whiskers. "That's Captain Lesley," Joseph pointed out to Miguel. "He's the fighting preacher. That man can preach a snake out of its hole!"

Lieutenant Addison had sent twenty men under Senator Hamlin Snell to support Captain Lesley's company in their pursuit of the raiders. Miguel's name was called, as was Joe Atzeroth's and the other North River men. Before the sun rose above the treetops, the men had eaten, saddled their mounts, and stowed seven days of rations in their saddlebags. By mid-morning, they were once again at Gamble Creek searching for tracks.

Miguel reached for the lock of Frederica's hair he kept in his vest pocket. He remembered how she liked to wear it bound up on the top of her head. The strands would break free and whip in the ocean breeze like black pennants as they sailed on his boat across the bay. He pulled it out so the sun could catch the auburn highlights, then he pressed it to his cheek.

He felt its softness and thought he could still smell her perfume. He tucked it away again and looked up at the mid-afternoon sun. It was an unusually warm day. He pulled off his hat and poured water from his canteen over his head to cool himself.

They found a skinned rabbit, evidence of a hasty meal, and tracks heading north toward the Little Manatee. Several minutes later, the scouts returned with the disheartening news that the raiders had made it to the ford and the footprints were once again lost in the river.

The sun sank into grey clouds in the west. The order was given to dismount, water the horses, and make camp. The hunt would have to resume at daybreak. The horses were concealed in a nearby hardwood hummock, and the men bedded down just over the rim of a sink pond.

The first rays of golden dawn peeked through the oak leaves, found a place between the edge of Miguel's blanket and the brim of his hat, and awakened him. He saw Sergeant Rawls as he moved quietly down the edge of the pond and woke the slumbering men. A dense fog hung over the fields between the hummocks, and it reminded Miguel of the sight that greeted him every morning as he looked across his little bay. He rolled up his blanket, slung it over his shoulder, and joined the others as they fetched the horses. They would eat in the saddle again.

There were no signs of Indians until they reached Little Bullfrog Creek, where a scout found hoof prints in the mud. The war party had tried to conceal their trail with branches and leaves, but they missed some clear tracks. The patrol followed the trail as it meandered north to Bullfrog Creek and then to the Alafia.

It was dusk by the time they crossed at Alderman's Ford and arrived at the Wordehoff store and post office located on the crossroads of the north-south trail running between Tampa and Manatee. The buildings were at the juncture of the military road that ran east from Fort Brooke to Fort Meade. The store was the only such business between the two settlements. It served the surrounding area and was also used as a base camp for the local militia.

Miguel joined Captain Lesley and a group of men inside the store. Suddenly a man burst through the door, wide-eyed with fear, "Indians!" he yelled, "They got him!"

Captain Lesley seemed to recognize the man. It was a local farmer, John Vickers, "Slow down, what are you saying, John? Got who?"

"They got Carney!" Vickers yelled frantically. John Carney was one of Lesley's men. He had taken his family up to Fort Brooke along with the others when they heard about the attacks at Manatee. Lesley had reluctantly let him stay behind so he could tend to his summer planting and join them later.

151

Vickers went on, "He was worried about Indians, stayed with me at my place last night. He couldn't sleep. Had a bad feelin'. He paced the floor most of the night. This mornin' he went right back to his fields. Said he had to get the rest of his plantin' done. I told him not to, but he wouldn't listen. I should've gone along! When I heard the gunshots, I rode out to his place. His horse and plow were just standin' right there in the middle of the field, but I saw no sign of him. I searched the field and found this." Vickers held up a blood-soaked handkerchief and a fawn-colored hat pierced with a bullet hole. "Oh Lord, forgive me, I should've gone with him and taken my gun." Grief choked off Vickers words.

"Then you'd be dead too." Captain Lesley said. The blood on the handkerchief made the captain assume the worst, although there was the possibility that Carney might have been captured. "At sunup you'll lead us to the spot, John." He looked around the store at his men. "We'll find them, by God, and justice will be done!" he said through clenched, yellowed teeth. Flames from the fireplace danced in his steel blue eyes.

The captain stormed out of the store. Miguel understood this had become personal for him. Until now, they had suffered loss of property, but now a settler had lost his life. The captain lost one of his own men, and the offenders would pay. This was a turning point, and the men all felt it.

The crackling of the campfire lulled Miguel into a deep sleep. In the dead of night, he had a disturbing dream about

Frederica. *Night descended on their Terrasilla Island home. He saw Frederica working outside their hut. She was unaware of the black, slithering shapes coming up out of the creek toward her.* Her screams awakened Miguel, and he found himself soaked in a cold sweat.

Excitement hung in the air like morning mist as the troop set out down the road. The sun was not up when they arrived at Carney's place, so Captain Lesley sent his men out with torches to search the fields. Snell's detachment and the men from Tampa were sent farther out to guard against an attack. Miguel rode perimeter along the edge of the field and watched the scene of horsemen slowly searching up and down the rows of Carney's fields by torchlight.

The search went on until the sun rose above the pine forest to the east and bathed the fields in a pale, amber light. Miguel could now make out the Carney homestead in the distance. Midway between here and there was a plow stuck in the furrow where Carney had left it. Lesley and his men thundered across the field toward them, their horses kicked up the freshly plowed turf, and they stopped where Colonel Snell searched the edge of the woods.

Miguel was a short distance away and could hear the officers confer. "There's no sign of Carney's body, but we did find tracks heading south toward the Alafia." Lesley told Snell. "I figure they may have an eighteen-hour head start, so I'm not wasting any more time here," he said. Snell nodded in agreement. He knew Lesley was concerned they may have

153

taken Carney alive. "We'll finish up here, Captain. You go on now, we'll catch up to you."

"I found him! He's over here!" One of the Tampa men yelled.

Miguel turned Bella and galloped across the fields to the spot where the four Tampa men were patrolling. They had found John Carney. He lay on his back and stared wide-eyed into a cloudless sky. Miguel counted five bullet holes in the chest of his blood-soaked shirt. Due to the distance that the body was from the plow where Vinson had found the bloody handkerchief, Miguel surmised that Indians must have wounded him there then chased him across the fields for several hundred yards. Carney must have turned to fire on his attackers and then was cut down by a hail of lead.

As Colonel Snell and the others converged on the scene, Miguel noted their sober looks and the eerie silence of the moment. The breathing of the horses was the only sound. The men stared down at the body. Reverend Lee dismounted, knelt over Carney, and gently closed his eyelids. He whispered a prayer over the man that only those who stood close by could hear. Two of the Tampa men agreed to stay and bury the body, so Snell's men could join the pursuit. The others mounted up and thundered across the fields in the wake of Captain Lesley's troop.

They crossed the Alafia at Alderman's Ford and caught up with Lesley at the headwaters of the Little Manatee. Here the trackers found two clear sets of tracks. They indicated that three or four warriors had crossed the river and headed toward the coast, possibly to the North River settlement. The larger group of Seminoles had followed the trail to Gamble Creek at the ford of the Manatee.

"They know we're right behind them, so they've split up." Lesley told Snell.

Captain Lesley had a decision to make. The sun was already high, and there were only six hours of daylight left. He knew there was no way to catch the band before dark. He decided he would take his main force and ride all night to intercept the Indians before they crossed the Manatee. He called on the six North River men under Corporal Rawls to track the smaller group of Seminoles and check their own property.

Miguel was relieved they were finally heading for home. The dream of Frederica had greatly disturbed him. Captain Lesley said they were tracking four warriors to the coast, but they were several hours ahead of pursuit. He didn't believe in omens and such, but the dream had caused him great anxiety that the four warriors could already be at Terrasilla or even the Atzeroth store by now.

The war party's trail was easy to follow in the flattened sawgrass, but it soon faded into the shadows as the day waned. They concealed themselves and their horses in a hammock until morning.

Miguel placed Bella's feed bag over her head and gently stroked her neck. "Are you as tired of this as I am, girl?" he whispered. "Tomorrow you'll be going home to see your friend Frederica."

Night of Terror

Frederica's mother had trained her early on to hide her emotions. It was a subtle and unspoken training, and Frederica often wondered if this was a Bavarian characteristic or simply her mother's nature. The only time she ever heard her mother cry was through a closed and locked door.

The women who had settled the Manatee area proved to Frederica that quiet suffering was not exclusively Bavarian. Her neighbors didn't talk about their suffering or heartbreak. Frederica supposed that they showed strength in their silence—perhaps they feared that once the floodgates opened, they might not easily be closed.

Miguel had left Frederica at the Azteroth river house with Julia, Eliza and Mary weeks ago, when he set out to fight in the Seminole Indian conflict. He, Uncle Joe, and many other young men were part of the militia. This was the first time Miguel had taken up arms, and she prayed that it would be the last

Frederica had missed her period, was unusually tired, and often nauseated throughout the day. Aunt Julia pampered her and made sure that she ate well and got plenty of sleep. She grimaced when she first suspected that Frederica might be pregnant, for a first pregnancy couldn't have come at a worse time. Both mother and aunt were nervous and worried at first, but they soon remembered that babies are a blessing from God, regardless of the time or the circumstances.

Seemingly by divine providence, Terrasilla had been virtually untouched by the Seminole path of destruction. Fort Brooke and many ranches east of Manatee were hit hard. A renegade band of young Seminole warriors from the Peas River area had gained a fearsome reputation and were being tracked by the militia. The citizens of Manatee all fervently prayed that they would continue to pass through the war unnoticed and unmolested.

The days passed slowly as they seem to do during times of strife. Julia wanted to check on Henry and needed to pick up produce and supplies from her farm on Terrasilla. The four women set sail after lunch. Upon arrival they immediately began to gather up fruit and vegetables to take back to the store the following day.

Once the boat was loaded, Frederica longed to check on the condition of her own home but knew that Julia would never allow it. Not knowing how long she'd be away, she wanted to get some of her books and sewing supplies, so she could start making clothes for the baby. She also had run out of writing paper and ink. Besides, she was craving the oranges and mangoes that grew in her backyard.

Frederica knew Miguel had hidden her horse and small wagon in case of an emergency. He and his friends had moved the boats to the mangroves on a secluded part of the island. They camouflaged the nets and drying racks with palm fronds and moss, so they would not be visible from the water. The cows were let loose in the woods with whispered prayers that they would not wander too far from home.

She knew she could get back home, grab her things, and be back in an hour. Aunt Julia went to bed early, so there would be about an hour of daylight left for her to make the journey. If she could get back safely before nightfall, her aunt would never have to worry.

After supper, Eliza and Mary cleaned up the dishes and went upstairs. Julia always read to her daughters before bed, and after the reading they would sing the same Lutheran hymns together and pray. The nightly ritual never failed to settle Eliza and Mary down, calming their fears. Frederica could hear the quiet voices fading, she knew they had fallen asleep.

She crept out of the house, avoiding squeaky floorboards as she went. When she reached the edge of the Atzeroth property, she quietly walked the horse and wagon over the pine trails, so the thick carpet of needles would muffle the sound of the wagon wheels. Frederica relaxed as she drew closer to home, and when the narrow shell road appeared before her, she knew she had arrived. She couldn't wait to be in her thatched-roof home and see all of the pleasant reminders of her married life, despite the fact that her time there would be fleeting.

The clearing was quiet and peaceful as the sun began to set in an explosion of light over the water. She loved this small piece of heaven on earth, and she was anxious for the war to be over, so she could resume her life with Miguel.

She quickly gathered the items she needed, mindful of the setting sun and her need to return to her sleeping aunt. Once everything was in the wagon, she grabbed a burlap bag for the ripe fruit. Her mouth watered in anticipation of the juicy mangoes. So much fruit hung heavy on the trees, and she wished she had the time and space to collect more than just one bag.

Frederica dropped the last mango into the sack and set out for the wagon. As she rounded the corner of the fishing shack, she heard the horse nickering and snorting. "She must have seen a snake." Frederica said to herself, as she watched the mare stomping at the ground.

A feeling that she was being watched crept over her. As she hurried to the wagon, her shoes slapped loudly on the ground, and her dress flew out behind her in the evening, onshore breeze.

She was stopped in her tracks when a strong arm wrapped around her waist. She dropped the bag of fruit. Terror paralyzed her as she struggled to breathe in the grips of her attacker.

How could she have taken such a stupid risk? What had made her think that she was invincible and immune to danger?

When her captor spun her around, Frederica could see four young Seminole braves walking toward her. They were wild with anger and their faces were painted for war. Her fear reached new heights as she looked into their eyes. She had never seen such hate.

One of them laughed as he played with Frederica's hair. She imagined that it would be a fine scalp to show his friends. He would brag on his victory as he displayed other souvenirs collected from the rancho.

The man who first grabbed her passed Frederica off to one of his companions, who examined her carefully. The others inspected the horse and wagon. They led her to a fencepost and bound her hands and feet with leather strips. She sobbed as she imagined what the next hour held for her and the baby she carried.

The Indians built a small fire and sat around it. They ate the fruit she'd gathered and talked in quiet voices. Occasionally, one of them would look over at Frederica and smile. He enjoyed tormenting her with anticipation of what they may be planning.

One of them brought items out of the huts so they could choose what they wanted to take. Frederica knew once they had their plunder, scalped and killed her, their final act would be to burn the rancho to the ground.

The conversation grew louder, and she heard a tone of consensus in the words the men spoke. They turned their gaze to Frederica. A fresh wave of terror welled up inside her and she knew her death was minutes away. She begged God to save her and her unborn child.

Suddenly an ear-piercing shot rang out from the woods and one of the young braves fell to the ground. Frederica was frantically untied from the post and dragged toward the wagon. She let out a scream and fought the man with all her strength but her bound hands kept her from striking him.

Another loud crack came from the tree line, and a second man clutched his bleeding arm and stumbled into the mangroves.

Again, a firing pin struck brass, and a bullet found the target. The man holding Frederica convulsed, and she could see a perfectly round hole in the center of his forehead. She rolled out from under the collapsing man and looked up into the face of the last young warrior. He froze when the gunfire started, and in the flickering light of the fire he looked like a frightened little boy. The last shot fired jolted him from his confusion. He turned and ran into the water, disappearing into the night.

The air seemed utterly silent in the absence of gunfire—no birds sang their usual night songs. Completely exhausted after the terrifying ordeal, Frederica leaned against the wagon trying to catch her breath.

She turned her head toward the sound of a cracking branch. Aunt Julia emerged from the woods, her face red with rage. She held Uncle Joe's new repeating rifle that he left with her. Eliza and Mary appeared from behind their mother and ran crying to Frederica.

When the girls tried to help her up, they realized she was bound, so they began loosening the leather straps. They quickly looked for any injuries that she might have sustained.

For a time, the four huddled together by the fire and tried to gather enough strength to return home. They were alive but exhausted. Frederica and Julia agreed that another band of Seminoles could return at any moment. They needed to get home quickly.

Frederica motioned toward the bodies by the wagon. "What do we do with them? We can't just leave him here."

"Our only concern right now is to get off this island." Julia whispered. "There might be more of them out there, and they might come back to finish the job."

In later years, Frederica wouldn't remember much about the dark journey back to the Atzeroth home that awful night. She felt an angel had surely directed her aunt to come downstairs to check on her. When Julia discovered her niece and wagon were missing, she surmised Frederica's most likely destination was the rancho.

Julia had heard men's voices before she turned the final bend of the shell road, so she and her two daughters crept through the woods until they saw the frightening scene unfolding. Frederica could only imagine the steely will that enabled Julia to raise the rifle, put a man in her sights, and pull the trigger.

Frederica had wanted to tell Julia that everything was all right, that she had done what she had to do, that she had taken two lives in order to save hers. But Julia was unusually quiet, and Frederica understood her aunt needed time and silence to process what had happened.

Eliza held Frederica's hand so tightly that it almost hurt, and Mary kept her arm around her shoulder. Frederica cried that night as she rubbed her stomach to assure her baby that he was safe now—that everything would be all right, and she would always protect him.

Frederica and her aunt never spoke to one another, or anyone else, about the events of that night. Frederica knew she owed her aunt her life, but Julia's stern eyes silenced her any time she tried to speak words of gratitude. Frederica grew to accept that her aunt would never speak of her heroic act, and she suspected that Julia struggled with the guilt of what she'd done. But occasionally, during a quiet moment together over a chore or dinner, a look would pass between the two women, and they sensed the bond of love and respect that had come together on that night of terror.

Miguel Arrives Home

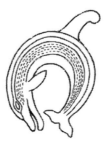

Miguel spent a sleepless night watching the horses, listening to the chorus of tree frogs, and worrying. He couldn't explain it, but he knew something wasn't right, and he was filled with worry. At the first glow of dawn on the eastern horizon, he woke everyone up. The men boiled coffee and ate their rations while they waited for the sun to burn off enough morning haze for them to find the Indians' tracks.

When Miguel recognized the jungle of towering palm trees growing near the coast he knew he was close to home. Just as he feared, the tracks led directly to the Terrasilla River.

When they reached the bank and saw that warriors had crossed over to his island, he feared his home had been raided and destroyed. In a panic, Miguel dug his heels into Bella's sides, so she bolted through the shallow water and galloped down the trail leading home. Corporal Rawls and the others followed closely behind, shotguns up and at the ready.

As the patrol thundered along the shoreline of Terrasilla Bay, Joe Atzeroth was relieved to find his home was still standing just as he had left it.

Miguel, who was several yards ahead of the others, was the first to arrive at his property. At first, he was relieved to see his huts were still standing, but his heart jumped into his throat when he saw two bodies lying in the yard. He drew his shotgun from his saddle roll, reigned in Bella, and jumped to the ground. He kneeled by the bodies and quickly surveyed the surrounding area for signs of others. One had been shot in the chest, the other in the head. Their blood had already soaked into the ground. The bodies were rigid, which told Miguel they had been dead for several hours. He looked at their young, painted faces for a moment.

So, these are the men we've been chasing all this time—two of the men who killed John Carney.

He walked up the shell ridge toward his hut just as the others arrived. The door hung wide open and household items were scattered everywhere. Miguel's mind raced as he tried to process what had happened. Then he saw Frederica's white dress on the floor. It was ripped from the neckline to the waist. His blood ran cold with fear. Had Frederica returned home? He ran back outside and followed the creek that fed into the estuary where they had hidden her little boat. It was still there. So was the horse and wagon.

Miguel couldn't help but think the worst. *Frederica had been raped and taken hostage. She might even be dead.* He frantically searched the mangroves for her body. The other men joined the search. Christian Peterson called out that he found shell casings laying on the ground at the edge of the woods.

"These are .44 caliber, like my Colt repeating rifle uses," Joe Atzeroth said, and a suspicion began to form in his mind. *Julia was here!*

"She's not here, Miguel. Maybe she's with Julia at the store," Joe said to reassure himself as well as Miguel that the four women were safe. This hope was diminished by the fact that they had tracked at least four Indians and two were still at large.

The men mounted up and rode back to thoroughly check Joe's farm before heading to the Peterson homestead on the south side of Terrasilla Bay. They were relieved that their homes had been untouched, and they continued on to the Atzeroth store at the Manatee River. The ride to the river took less than an hour, but for Miguel it felt like forever. Julia and her daughters were in the garden when the horsemen thundered down the river road. Julia shielded her eyes from the bright mid-morning sun, but she couldn't make out who the riders were, so she sent her daughters into the store to keep them safe.

From a distance, Miguel recognized Julia, Eliza, and Mary, but there was no sign of his wife. Any hope he had that she was safe here at the store began to waver, but just as they rode into the yard, the door flew open and a young woman appeared. She leveled a shotgun at the horsemen.

"Frederica!" Miguel yelled out, unable to contain the joy and relief he felt.

"*Miguel, bist du, wirklich?*" she cried out. She hardly recognized her husband—dirty and unshaven after a week on the trail. She lowered the shotgun, handed it to Julia, and ran to him. Miguel jumped from Bella and ran to Frederica. He swept her up into his arms and held her close. He was relieved that she appeared to be unharmed.

The reunion was short lived by necessity, for there were still two renegades at large in the region, and the families seeking refuge at Gamble's plantation had to be warned. While the horses were watered and fed, Julia and Eliza prepared breakfast for the men. When the food was ready, Julia instructed everyone, in no uncertain terms, that they eat their breakfast outside.

She informed Frederica that she and Miguel would enjoy their meal in the cabin, alone, together.

***

The next morning, Miguel and the rest of the squad were up before sunrise, back in the saddle, and bound for Fort Rough n' Ready. They made a stop at Gamble's plantation and found the families holed up behind its thick tabby walls, safe and sound. There had been no sign of the war party during the night, so they returned to Addison's Fort.

The area quieted down over the following weeks as regular U.S. Army troops arrived on the river to protect the Manatee settlers. When his first enlistment expired in October, Miguel re-enlisted along with most of the men of Addison's company into Captain John Parker's Florida Mounted Militia.

Parker's company was sent to do garrison duty at Fort Green, which always seemed to be undersupplied. While cooped up behind the pine log stockade, the Manatee militiamen fought boredom, hunger, and disease rather than Indians. Miguel counted off the days until his enlistment expired by carving notches in the log by his bunk. He was so relieved the day he was mustered out in December.

Miguel and Joseph packed their belongings, mounted up, and set off on the long ride home from Fort Meade. Miguel couldn't wait to surprise Frederica and get back on the water again.

Fish for Dinner

Frederica lay in bed, staring at the ceiling. She could tell the sun was about to come up because birds had started to chirp. She had not slept at all. She feared that this day would be just like yesterday and the day before last. A multitude of identical days stretched out behind her, and none of them included Miguel.

Her husband had been gone so long, and he had sent no word about his health or location. The men had departed the area in haste as they chased a band of Seminole Indians southward. Since then, there had been no news and she couldn't help worrying.

She got up and gazed into the small silver-backed mirror above her dresser. She was wearing the same dress she had worn for the last three days. The night before she had been too tired to change into her nightgown, and strange dreams had plagued her. Worry and fear kept sleep away, and her hair looked like the seaweed rotting in Miguel's nets. *A brush*

will just become hopelessly entangled and pull it out by the roots,
she thought.

Frederica walked out to the cooking area in a sleepy haze
and made coffee. As the pleasing smell of coffee rose to her
nose, she saw Aunt Julia walking up the path toward the
hut. Horrified that her aunt might see her in such a state of
dishevelment, she ran to the basin and hurriedly washed her
face.

Aunt Julia marched right into the yard and poured herself a
cup of coffee like she owned the place. She took one look at
Frederica and said, "Child, what has happened to you? You
look awful, and this house looks like it has been ransacked
by Indians!"

"Aunt Julia, I am just so..." and then the tears unexpectedly
began to stream down her face.

As Frederica wept, her aunt finished her sentence, "...so
worn out with worry, and you look like death warmed over.
Go get a clean dress and a bar of soap. Take the boat over to
the river and bathe and wash that hair before I cut it off
myself!"

Frederica obeyed gladly. She kissed her aunt on the cheek
and walked briskly toward the dock. As she hurried along,
Aunt Julia called after her, "Throw the net and bring us
some fish for dinner!"

Frederica was relieved to know that Aunt Julia would be there all day and would cook for her. Her aunt was like the cavalry that arrived at the last minute to save the day.

Julia grabbed a bucket and went outside to see what was ripe and ready to pick. Frederica had neglected her garden and the fruit trees for several days, so there was plenty to gather. Julia used her slingshot to the detriment of a few squirrels that had dared to encroach upon the mango and orange trees. She was a good shot and three squirrels hit the ground. After a few seconds, each squirrel got up and scampered away.

While her aunt worked at the house, Frederica swam in the refreshing river. She rubbed a bar of soap in her hair, rinsed it, and then slowly combed the tangles out of it. She felt like she was coming back to life.

As she lay in the sun on the deck of the boat, she realized just how tired and threadbare her soul had become as she struggled to survive without Miguel. Julia had spared her a mundane day of work. Frederica drifted off into a peaceful nap.

The sound of mullet slapping the water woke her from her slumber. She grabbed the net just in time, threw a perfect circle, and pulled up six fat fish. She couldn't wait to get them home. Now that she had rested, she felt she could eat two of the fish by herself. The bath and the rest brought back her appetite, and she began to feel like herself again.

Frederica smiled and remembered the day Miguel had given her the small net. He was boyishly excited as he taught her how to cast the unwieldy thing. She was skeptical at first as to whether she'd be able to use the net. He had worked on the specially designed net for weeks. Frederica practiced diligently. She was surprised to discover that she was actually quite talented with the net, and soon she was able to throw better than some of Miguel's men. They teased Miguel that he should take fishing lessons from his wife.

Frederica had been gone for a few hours, so she prepared to head home. She didn't want to wear Aunt Julia out. Besides, she was getting hungry and looked forward to chatting with her.

She let her hair dry in the wind as the boat cut through the water. Frederica felt free and peaceful, and she wished her husband was there to experience the moment. She didn't know if she could ever live a landlocked life again. Now she understood the call of the sea, and why her husband always had to say "yes" to its call.

When Frederica walked up the path her aunt was busy washing dishes out back. There was a full bucket of vegetables on the porch and fresh fruit in a large wicker basket. Fresh flowers had been cut for the dinner table. She could smell something delicious cooking in the back, on the woodstove.

Frederica dropped the heavy basket of fish onto the table.

"How many did you get?" Aunt Julia asked.

Frederica raised her chin up high. "Six big ones!"

A smile lit up Aunt Julia's face. "Great! We will need all of them for dinner tonight because a couple more folks will be joining us."

"Really? Who else will be having dinner with us?" Frederica asked nervously.

Aunt Julia pointed toward the path. Miguel and Uncle Joe arrived, as if on cue. Frederica let out a happy scream and ran to greet them.

As Miguel and Frederica embraced she took his hand and guided it to rest on her belly. Immediately, he noticed the change in her size and it dawned on him that she was carrying his child.

He pulled back and looked into Frederica's eyes. His face beamed with joy and excitement and he laughed out loud for the first time in a long while. There could not have been a better homecoming for him than to receive the news that he would be a father for the first time.

A morning that had started so poorly turned into one of Frederica's favorite days. It had become apparent to her that there would be precious few times in her life when her family would be together, so she tried to memorize every detail of every one of her loved ones' faces around the dinner table. She kept this memory tucked away, for she knew that life was sometimes hard, and her pleasant memories might one day be needed to sustain her during dark times.

Michael is Born

Frederica was quiet as she rode next to her Uncle Joe in his wagon. She dreaded every bump in the road—each jolt added to the pain she was already in.

"I am so sorry my dear! I know this is such a rough ride for you. We had no idea this little baby of yours would decide to come so early!" Uncle Joe put his arm around Frederica's shoulder. She reached up to touch his hand, grateful that she had family nearby to help her with this new adventure.

Her life had moved so slowly before she came to America. Her days had all been the same—she saw the same people, the seasons changed on time, and she could predict exactly what would happen each and every day— life was predictable. Then the invitation from Aunt Julia arrived, and everything changed.

Just as another contraction started, the old mule pulling the wagon jolted to the side of the road to avoid a snake. Frederica let out a moan "It hurts so bad, Uncle Joe!"

Uncle Joe winced with sympathy. He didn't have the heart to tell her that it would get worse much worse.

A cold wind blew in from the bay as they approached the house. Frederica hoped she had remembered to bring her blue shawl and stockings. She had gathered up her things so quickly. *If I can just get inside and lie down*, she thought, *surely that will ease the pain.*

Aunt Julia and the girls met Frederica and Joe at the gate. Eliza and Mary grabbed her things, while Aunt Julia eased Frederica out of the wagon. When Frederica's eyes met Julia's, she broke into tears. "Now don't you start girlie," Julia said. "Women have been having babies since God made himself a man and a woman, and I have helped deliver enough babies to fill this yard. Frederica, this is a joyous day, and by tomorrow, you'll agree."

Frederica was starving from the ride over, but Aunt Julia would only allow her to drink some warm broth. She put pillows under Frederica's lower back to help ease the pressure and pain.

Uncle Joe galloped off on his horse to fetch Dr. Branch from across the river. As he rode he mumbled, "Why do babies always pick the coldest nights to be born?"

The house fell quiet, and Frederica dozed off. Aunt Julia snored quietly in the corner rocking chair. The creak of the front door woke them. Joe rushed in, wet from the cold rain, and he struggled to push the door closed against the howling wind.

Julia could tell by the look on his face Joe was about to give them bad news. "I found Dr. Branch—he was at the Smith house. Fannie has been in labor for eight hours, and hopefully she will have her baby soon."

"Well, that's not so bad," said Julia. "Frederica can surely hold out until then."

"That's not all." Joe grimaced. "After the Smith baby is born, he has been summoned to the Felt's house. But he told me that he will get here as soon as he can."

Frederica grew very still and serious. After a moment, she spoke. "But it feels like my baby is coming soon. What if there's trouble that we can't handle?" She fell back on the pillows and closed her eyes. "And why does Miguel have to be off fishing? What if I don't know what to do. I have never even seen a birth." An intense contraction interrupted Frederica, and she let out a tortured scream.

"Joseph." Julia called. "Bring me your whiskey and a big spoon and don't you dare drink even a sip! It's going to be a long night, and I need you to be alert."

Eliza and Mary heard the scream from upstairs and ran down to peek into the bedroom. Julia shooed them back to their rooms.

179

"Maybe Frederica saw a palmetto bug in the corner," Mary wondered aloud to her sister as they left the room. She couldn't imagine another reason why someone would scream like that.

Joe returned from his hidden nook with a brown bottle in his hand. Julia snatched it away from him and gave a spoonful of whiskey to Frederica. The girl ignored the spoon, choosing instead to snatch the bottle from her aunt and took two long swigs before Julia could wrestle it away from her. Joe snickered, but the scathing look from his wife silenced him. The warm whiskey in her belly allowed Frederica to relax enough to doze again, and her thoughts wandered.

The events of the last year ran through her mind like a book magically turning its own pages. *The arrival in Terrasilla, the Atzeroth store and dock, fishing boats and warm water, the farm, the people, the Indians, the bugs, the heat, the fish...lots of fish, new trees and flowers, powerful storms, the wild land, the animals she had never seen before, so many birds...and, of course, Miguel Guerrero.*

As her thoughts focused on her husband, it became real that she was having the baby without him. She wanted so badly for Miguel to be here to share this miracle with her. She also wanted him to see the pain and suffering that she was going through to bring their child into the world. Another intense contraction swept over her, and Julia leapt to her feet to inspect Frederica's progress.

"This child is not going to wait on Dr. Branch! Dr. Julia and Nurse Joe will have to guide this little one into your arms. Joe, bring towels and clean water now!"

The urge to push returned, but Frederica held it back. "I really want to wait to see if Miguel comes home from his trip in time. I want him to be here."

Julia wiped Frederica's forehead with a damp cloth. "The baby is in charge, and neither of us can make it wait. It looks like maybe three more pushes and this will all be over. This is the hardest part, but you are a strong girl, Frederica. You have got to push this baby out now!" No sooner than the words had left Julia's lips, the door crashed open and in rushed Miguel.

Julia turned to him. "You! Go wait in the other room—this is woman's work."

Miguel ran to Frederica's side and grabbed her hand. "I am the Papa. We are going to welcome this child together."

The excitement and relief of having Miguel by her side gave Frederica a burst of new energy and strength. One giant push later, she delivered a handsome, healthy baby boy. His robust cries drew the girls and Uncle Joe back into the room. The nervous tension was broken, and they shared hugs and excited words of congratulations.

Julia had the baby wrapped up within moments, and she put

him in the arms of his exhausted new mother. Julia was relieved that the baby was large and healthy. Childbirth took the lives of so many young women in the wilderness, and many babies were still-born or died soon after being delivered. She felt like angels were surely standing in the four corners of the room and watching over all of them.

When Julia finished tending to Frederica, she stood to get a basin of water to wash the newborn. She had been so intent on her task that she hadn't noticed what was happening in the room. She saw Miguel holding his new son like a precious treasure. He was gently washing the baby with warm water, and the child's eyes were fully open staring up at his father. The baby was peaceful and still. He seemed completely comfortable in his father's arms.

"Hello my son," Miguel whispered. "Hello Michael." He wrapped him in a clean blanket and kissed him on the head over and over again. "I am the happiest old fisherman on the ocean. Frederica, my love, you are the bravest person I know."

Frederica was overcome with emotion as she watched Miguel hold his new son. The scene was forever etched in her memory, and Julia and Joe saw a new side of Miguel that night. Something brittle and painful had broken in Miguel as he watched the birth of his son. The Atzeroths were not sure what it was. Perhaps it was a painful memory, or maybe it was a childhood injustice, but watching the birth of his son had erased it from Miguel's psyche as surely as the tide erased fresh footprints in the sand.

Julia's eyes briefly met Miguel's. For the first time she caught a glimpse of the man that Frederica saw every day. She had no doubt that he would be a great father.

Eliza and Mary delivered a cup of hot tea and cookies to Frederica, and they giggled as they watched Miguel grin and coo at the baby.

There came a frantic knock at the door. Dr. Branch bustled into the room. "Well, did I miss it? Does this mean you won't name the baby after me?" They all laughed. The night had begun with pain and fear, but it had ended with the gift of a healthy child. This was truly a blessing everyone shared.

Into the Big Cypress

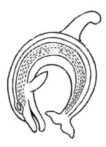

In June, Miguel reenlisted again for six months in Captain James F.P. Johnston's Company. After weeks of long fruitless patrols looking for signs of Indians in the Myakka shrub, he found himself wishing for some excitement. The abundance of game encountered on their patrols in southern Manatee County indicated that the Indians were no longer crossing Peas Creek, but rather seemed to have moved farther south into the Big Cypress Swamp. The immediate threat to the Manatee settlement had abated, and the militiamen were allowed to return home.

As the year 1857 came to a close, the call for volunteers was posted once again at the Atzeroth store. Colonel Gustavus Loomis was in need of militiamen to pursue the Seminoles who had sought refuge in the Big Cypress Swamp. Miguel was conflicted, he felt he had done his part, but as a citizen and member of the militia, he felt obligated to sign up once again. He reluctantly took the old shotgun down from above the fireplace and packed his gear.

He jumped on Bella and trotted down the shell path. His heart broke as he turned in the saddle and waved goodbye to Frederica standing on the porch with Michael in her arms. The rancho vanished into the mangroves as Miguel set off for Fort Meade, situated on Peas Creek in eastern Manatee County. When Miguel arrived, he would enlist in Captain Leroy Lesley's company of mounted volunteers.

***

On Christmas Day, Captain Lesley's company set off from Fort Meade for Camp Rogers, on the edge of the Big Cypress Swamp. The Camp had once been a village governed by Chief Billy Bowlegs.

When the company arrived, Miguel unsaddled Bella and put her out to graze in a field called Bowlegs Garden. Once he was sure his horse was content, Miguel found a bonfire and joined the group of soldiers who were standing around it. He was pleased to find two familiar faces from Manatee—his old friend Philippi and his Seminole wife Polly, who had once been wed to a famous Seminole chief named Chi-ee.

Philippi and Miguel reminisced about the old days when Miguel had first come to Tampa Bay from New Orleans. They had met on the job at Perico's rancho, and Philippi taught Miguel the lay of the land and the best Florida fishing techniques. Everyone laughed when Philippi told the story of the roasted rattlesnake breakfast that he prepared after the great hurricane.

Miguel was relieved when he learned that Philippi and Polly had been hired by the army to guide the company into the Big Cypress. He knew that without experienced guides, their chances of capturing the Seminoles were slim.

The following day they mounted up and set off under the gilded rays of the morning sun, but each man knew that they would soon find themselves immersed in the deep shadows of the Big Cypress Swamp. As they rode along, Polly rattled everyone's nerves by telling them strange, unwholesome Seminole legends. Miguel was particularly unnerved by the tales of the gruesome Stikini. These evil witches were rumored to look like normal Seminoles during the day, but at night they would vomit up their souls and become undead creatures that fed on human hearts. The rational part of Miguel's mind knew these were just bogeymen created to frighten children away from the dangerous swamp, but the pitch-black shadows and gnarled tree trunks of the Big Cypress made his imagination run wild.

The guides led the company down a barely visible trail to a large Indian village. The settlement was completely deserted, but there were signs that the residents had fled just moments before their arrival. A large cook pot simmered over a fire, an overturned bucket lay in the middle of a puddle of water next to the well, and Miguel felt eyes watching the company from the shadows.

Captain Lesley ordered one of the men to set torches to the palm-thatched roofs before they moved deeper into the swamp. Miguel watched the thick black smoke as it curled up into the cloudless, winter sky. A red-tailed hawk circled around the smoky column, and Miguel grew increasingly unsettled as he thought about the Seminole ancestral spirits that Polly had so vividly described. Once again, he felt the sensation of unfamiliar eyes crawling over him, but he was certain the eyes belonged to men, not ghosts.

The long column of horsemen continued along the trail and into a thick hammock. Miguel rode behind Philippi at the front of the column. His old friend halted as he came across some fresh tracks and Captain Lesley trotted up beside him to see what he had found.

Miguel noticed Polly shifting nervously in her saddle and craning her neck as she peered into the shadowy woods. "This not good!" she whispered.

Bella snorted and pranced about, then bolted in front of Philippi and the captain. Miguel didn't know what had spooked his mount, so he frantically pulled back on her reins in an effort to control her, but she was unresponsive. She reared up on her hindquarters and thrashed her front hooves at the saw palmettos sprouting from the edge of the trail. A gunshot rang out, and Bella screamed in pain.

Suddenly, shrill war whoops sounded in the woods. Hidden Indians opened fire on the company from their camouflaged positions. Scores of shots were fired, one soldier was struck and killed, and several others injured. The remaining militiamen thrashed through the woods in frantic pursuit of the ambush party.

A deadly pattern began to emerge as the Seminoles would stop and fire from a distance of three to four hundred yards and, after the volley was complete, they would turn and run. The horses continued to bog down in the saturated soil, and when they did, the Seminoles stopped to fire again. Using this strategy, the Indians repeatedly evaded capture.

Bella knelt in the road and Miguel jumped off of her as she rolled onto her side. Miguel could hear the volleys of rifle fire going off in the woods, but he could not leave Bella in her moment of need. He and Philippi looked for the entry wound on the underside of her body. Miguel expected the worst when he saw the bright red blood under her thick leather saddle strap and he prepared himself for the loss of his loyal friend. Philippi found a bullet hole in the strap and he lifted it up to examine the wound underneath.

A laugh burst forth from Philippi when he pulled a round shot from under the strap. Bella shifted, strained, grunted, and to Miguel's utter amazement, stood up.

"Bella is a very lucky horse, amigo!" Philippi said. "The shooter must have spilled some of the powder when he loaded, and the bullet had enough velocity to penetrate the strap, but not enough to pierce her hide. It stings, but she will be fine."

Captain Lesley walked over and patted Bella on her rump. "This wild horse of yours just saved my life Guerrero! A warrior hidden that close to the path had one objective, to kill the enemy commander. I saw a wild horse stomp a gator once, but I never reckoned I'd be saved by one."

Most of the men regrouped on the trail after their mad dash through the swamp, and Lesley's eyes widened when he saw two soaked and dirty militiamen carrying a wounded Seminole warrior.

"Polly," he said. "I have a job for you. Convince this Indian to tell us where his camp is located. Be sure to tell him how uncomfortable he will be if he remains quiet."

Polly nodded and followed the soldiers a short distance down the path.

The wounded Seminole saw the light of reason, and he soon informed Captain Lesley that Sam Jones, Assinwah, and other chiefs were encamped nearby with approximately thirty-five warriors.

Lesley led the company deeper into the swamp and found the island camp, but there were no Indians. They discovered a twenty-five-acre field of potatoes and beans, and a nearby hammock held nearly 100 bushels of corn and twelve bushels of rice. The captain ordered the men to take or destroy everything. "If we can't find them, we will starve them," he said.

Miguel and Philippi searched one of the Chickee huts and found a young girl rolled up in a blanket hidden beneath a table. Philippi climbed up the ladder to the second floor of the hut and found the child's mother, who had been left behind because she was sick. He questioned the woman and learned that she was the wife of Assinwah himself.

Miguel's saw fear in the child's eyes and thought about the horror she must have felt as she watched strangers descend upon her village, burn their crops, and ransack their homes.

When Miguel arrived in Florida, the Seminole land extended all the way to the head of Peas Creek, which lay 100 miles to the north in eastern Hillsborough County. He remembered the Indian families he worked with at Philippi's rancho. They worked together and lived in peace. Now they were forced into a mosquito-infested swamp, but still the greedy tyrants in Washington were not satisfied. *War destroys everyone's lives*, he thought. *After all of these years, why can't people learn to get along?*

Assinwah's wife pleaded, if they would take the child to Fort Myers, she would willingly bring the children and old people out of their hiding places in the hammock to surrender. The company watched as a wretched line of emaciated and dirty Seminoles filed out of their hiding places. Some were crying, but most wore blank looks on their faces as if they couldn't stand any more horror.

Captain Lesley chose to end the pursuit of the warriors and return to Fort Myers. Miguel suspected that the sight of the elderly and the children hiding in the hammock had taken the fighting spirit out of him. The child sat in the saddle in front of Miguel, and he held her tightly with one arm as they made their way back to civilization. He learned that her name was Hachi, which meant "river," and as they rode along, her little hand grasped his tightly. She looked up at him, and her jet-black eyes filled with tears. Eventually she leaned her head back against Miguel's chest and fell asleep.

The company passed through the gates of Fort Myers, and Miguel was forced to hand Hachi down to a soldier who took her to the stockade. Miguel's heart broke, but he had no other choice. She had to be placed with the other prisoners. He wanted to take the girl home with him so that he and Frederica could give her a happy life.

Taking in an orphan is one of the greatest sacrifices a person can make for another human being and Miguel was willing to make it. He knew his government would never allow it.

In March of 1858, the Seminole leaders surrendered. The discovery of the Indian sanctuary in the Big Cypress Swamp left the Seminoles no choice. On May fourth, most of the warriors of Billy Bowlegs, Assinwah, and Sam Jones, plus eighty-five women and children, departed Fort Myers aboard the *Grey Cloud*. They traveled to Egmont Key and then were sent into exile in the west. The war was declared over on May eighth.

Miguel mustered out of service from Fort Brooke on May seventeenth. He and Bella began the long journey home. He was thankful to finally hang up the rusty shotgun and concentrate on being a good husband and father. He desperately hoped he was done with war for good.

Wooden Box

Frederica woke up excited and ready to start the day. Miguel had gotten up ahead of her, made breakfast, packed up two-year old Michael, and sailed off for a day of fun and fishing. With her men out of the house, today would finally be the day she could complete a project that had been nagging at her for weeks.

She barely slept the night before as she rehearsed every move she would need to make so that the work progressed efficiently. Over the last several weeks she had sketched out the plan and collected the supplies she would need. With her hair tied back in a ponytail and an old apron tied around her waist, Frederica rushed through the cabin, ignoring the multitude of chores that called out to her.

Her first stop was her bedroom. There she fumbled around under the bed until she pulled out a small wooden box. It was polished smooth and beautifully crafted, with the name *Kramer and Sons* neatly carved into its lid. The scent of the polished wood opened a floodgate of memories for

Frederica. Her finger traced the name *Kramer,* and tears welled up in her eyes.

Her father was a third-generation Bavarian craftsman who made some of the finest furniture in his village. His skills earned him an excellent reputation, which in turn allowed him to comfortably support his family. When Frederica was a little girl, perhaps three or four, her father made a little stool for her to sit on in his shop. His ability to turn rough, ugly planks of wood into beautiful tables and chairs mesmerized her for hours. Her father would let his sons assist, but he would say to Frederica, "I cannot let you help me with this rough work. A woman needs to keep her hands protected, so that one day she can sew beautiful clothes and cook for her family."

When Frederica grew older, she would run into the furniture shop as soon as she got home from school. Once there, she would pester her father for work. She had learned the trade from hours of watching and listening, young Frederica argued that a few small jobs wouldn't harm her hands. Eventually her constant begging wore her father down, and he gave her some of his smaller jobs. Much to her dismay, however, she was always sent home in time to help her mother with dinner.

Her brothers taunted her. "Go home woman," they'd say. "It's time to make our dinner and mend our shirts." Frederica smiled as she remembered her older brother would forever have a permanent scar on his forehead from the block of wood she threw at him. *I'm a lot more patient now*, she mused.

As a young woman, Frederica discovered one of the truths everyone discovers when they become an adult—the world is always changing. She saw sweeping changes in her village and country. Factories were moving in and taking up the farmland and newly invented machines made mass production possible, taking jobs away from the common people. As a result, tradesmen and craftsmen found it difficult to support their families.

Economic and social changes went hand in hand, and political unrest was not far behind. Enticed by the promise of free land and religious freedom, many Europeans packed their bags and set out for the United States. One night at dinner, Frederica's father said, "If you own your own land, you will always have a home. If you are free to worship, you will always be strengthened by God."

Frederica's Aunt Julia and Uncle Joseph Atzeroth agreed with this sentiment, and so they were the first of Frederica's family to accept the challenge of the long voyage west.

The voyage to America was perilous and took many lives, and once they arrived, the brave travelers were required to build a life from next to nothing. The Atzeroths were clearly the best suited family members for this trailblazer role. Frederica once commented to her father, "I hope Aunt Julia is ready for America." He immediately replied, "I hope America is ready for Julia Atzeroth!"

As Frederica grew older, life continued to change. Her father's furniture business began to fail. Her brothers were hired by a lumber mill, but they both hated their jobs. Her mother took in laundry to make ends meet because money was scarce for the Kramers.

When Frederica left school, she had two choices—she could marry a man of means, or she could work at the local textile mill. Sometimes Frederica watched the women of the mill as they walked home from their shifts. They looked so sad and tired, almost as if they never saw the light of day, and their hands were swollen and gnarled from the grueling work.

One night at dinner, Mr. Kramer told the family one of his friends had recently lost his wife in childbirth. Because he had three young children, he needed to remarry as soon as possible. After he told the story, he looked at Frederica and paused. There was a long, awkward silence, and Frederica didn't need to ask her father why he had brought up the subject.

The following day a letter arrived, and its timing convinced Frederica that the message was heaven-sent. The Atzeroths had safely arrived in America, and after many months they settled on an island called Terrasilla. The island was located in the Florida Territory, and it sounded like paradise to Frederica. Aunt Julia wrote of their new home in great detail. She described the beautiful land, the water teeming with fish, the rich and fertile soil, and the wonderful climate. What Frederica found most intriguing was Aunt Julia's idea that anyone could start a new life in the Florida Territory.

The frigid month of January was the right time of year to entice the Kramer children to leave Bavaria. They all dreamed of tropical lands of year-round warm weather and calm waters.

Aunt Julia had lost two young sons to Scarlet Fever before leaving Bavaria. Her daughter, Eliza was three years old when they left. The Kramers heard that Julia's sister, Monica and her husband Franz Nicholas had later traveled there to live with them. They had a small girl named Mary. Monica died in childbirth along with the baby and Franz later died of an illness. Julia and Joe took in little Mary to raise as their own daughter.

The Atzeroths owned a farm on Terrasilla Island and built a cabin and successful store on a beautiful river named the Manatee. Their life sounded perfect, and Frederica was eager to follow her aunt and uncle to this new land of opportunity.

It took Frederica's brothers no time at all to decide to leave. In the blink of an eye they completed their immigration papers and booked passage on the next ship to the Americas. She wanted to escape her life too—she wanted a new life of adventure and excitement. If she stayed in Bavaria, she would have to marry a much older man and care for his children. Frederica didn't want to be just a character in someone else's life—she wanted to be the author of her own story. Trapped in her dismal life, she had never felt such despair.

The next day, Frederica arrived at breakfast with Julia's letter in hand. Her mother started to cry, for she knew the request that was coming. Frederica took a deep breath and wiped a tear from her eye. "As much as I love you and appreciate the life you have made for me here, I am asking you to let me go. Let me spread my wings and make a new start in a new world with my brothers, Aunt Julia, and Uncle Joseph."

Sadly, but with love, Frederica's parents gave their blessing for the young Kramers to accept the invitation to move to America.

So, here she was, finally living in their newly-built log cabin instead of in a palm-thatched hut, on a wild, tropical island, married with a son and another baby on the way. She and Miguel were creating a wonderful life for their growing family.

Frederica was heartbroken when her brothers decided to move to Indiana rather than stay in Terrasilla. The memory of that day still upset her if she allowed her mind to dwell on it. Hours after her brothers' wagon had pulled away, she found a box on the kitchen table. *Oh no*, she thought. *They have left something important and will miss it.* She wondered how she might send it to them by a courier. Until she read the attached note:

> *This is for our dear sister. Remember your brothers always and know that we will think of you often. We will continue to carry on the proud trade of our family. And now that we are separated, we will admit to you that your skills indeed outshone ours. Though we are separated by distance, our bond will never be diminished.*

The ticking clock brought her back to the present. Frederica picked it up and ran out to the back porch. She pulled back the old canvas sail to reveal the long, wide table she had built over the past week. Uncle Joe had brought her the wood and loaned her his tools to use, but she proudly declined his labor by telling him, "I'm still a Kramer, and I will do this on my own!"

The table was made of local pine, not the mahogany or oak of her childhood. It was simple, beautiful, and uniquely Floridian. The legs of the table were chunky and strong, unlike the mill-turned legs of a fine table. The top was thick and heavy, the grain full of interesting swirls and turns. This was the table of a wilderness family. She would polish it with lemon oil and beeswax to protect it from water damage, and many hearty meals would be served on it. If Miguel had to use it as a work table, any nicks or scratches would only add to its charm. Children would be schooled at this table, baby baskets would sit on top of it as she cooked and cleaned, and if the home was ever threatened, it could be turned on its side to protect the family to barricade the door. Frederica's only hard and fast rule for the table would be, "Absolutely no fish are ever to be cleaned on my table!"

She looked forward to serving the many guests and friends who would visit them and sit down for food and fellowship around this simple piece of furniture. It would be a family heirloom that would be passed down for generations, and it would surely stand the test of time if her descendants took care of it. She prayed that fire would never destroy it or their home, and that it would be a symbol of the love and life of Frederica and Miguel long after they were gone.

Frederica giggled as she realized she was talking to a table as if it were alive, "You are just like me, strong and sturdy, ready to take on any challenges this life may throw at you. You will not be pampered like the tables of the rich or be adorned with beautiful linens and china dishes, but you will serve us well. We are beautiful in our own right, are we not? We are certainly both unique. I wish my father could see you." She imagined her father walking into the cabin—he would rub his large hands down the grain of the wood. When he found it free of imperfections, he would try to rock it to see if it wobbled. He would smile up at Frederica and say, "Now *this* is a Kramer table."

She took the carving tools out of the small wooden box her brothers had left her and began her work. She let her mind drift back to her family's old woodshop, and she could hear her father humming his favorite tune as he worked. She tasted her mother's gingerbread cookies she had so often snacked on. She felt as though her brothers would burst through the door at any moment in the midst of arguing or roughhousing.

Frederica's fingers worked fast. They remembered how to make every cut as if the plan was in her very blood. Carving had been passed down to her and ingrained in her soul. She worked tirelessly for hours, without a break to eat until the sun started to set. Time flew by, and the buried memories of her family continued to surface, each one a beautiful and fleeting gift brought forth by the familiar act of carving. She mused that carving and living are truly linked, for they are both acts of destruction and creation. The carver destroys wood as he creates art, and each person destroys time as he creates his life.

She brushed the sawdust from the table then washed it with warm water. When she wiped it with a clean cloth, the new design appeared. Frederica saw that it was beautiful.

A Bavarian carver might have created a snow-covered mountain with tall fir trees and alpine meadows. Frederica's design was made up of large tropical leaves, flowers, and water birds. She had carved the image of a net in one corner. It was realistic enough to look like it actually draped over one end of the table. On the bottom right corner there were two playful dolphins, and carefully hidden in the design she had added the initials M.G. and F.K. framed by a heart.

Frederica stood back and admired her masterpiece. The table still needed a day in the sun to dry and she would bring it into the house and apply the protective oils. It was so gratifying to finish a project when so much of her work was of the never-ending variety.

Looking down at her tired, sawdust-covered hands, Frederica realized how hungry she was. *First a swim, then a meal,* she thought. She headed toward the tranquil waters of Miguel's Bay. The weather was often hot in her paradise home, but the closeness of the water and the constant sea breezes were more than enough to cool her.

As she floated in the gentle waves, she looked at her growing belly and wondered if the new baby would be a girl or a boy. Since the name Michael was the English version of the name Miguel, she wanted this next baby to be named after her.

One night, she had dreamed so vividly that it would be another boy. Maybe they could name him Frederick? She hoped to have a little brother for Michael to play with, an instant friend for life. She was suddenly anxious to tell Miguel her idea for the perfect name.

Frederica's Busy Life

Outside the cabin, a seagull screeched as if it had been caught by a gator. The noise woke up the new baby Frederick, who cried with great gusto. Frederica had gotten him to go to sleep after two hours of incessant crying, but now he was up again and, this time, he was hungry. The sun was coming up, and she knew that Michael would also wake up soon. She was still in her clothes from the day before—she had been too tired to change into her nightgown.

The cow in the backyard let out a baritone bellow to let the world know she needed to be milked. The noise from the uncomfortable cow made the dog bark, which woke Michael before the sun had fulfilled its daily duty. Frederica reached over to shake Miguel in the hope that he would get Michael his breakfast while she fed the baby.

This day and all of its trials would be solely up to her. She scooped up Frederick and placed him in the crook of her arm so that he could nurse. Then she walked outside, grabbed a bucket off of a hook, and using her foot, pushed the stool underneath Rosie the cow. She moved Fredrick from her right to her left side, and then she began to give Rosie some relief.

Michael appeared on the porch calling, "Mutter!" at the top of his lungs. Frederick was milk-drunk and sound asleep. He felt heavy on her left arm, but not as heavy as the pail of milk that she carried with her right hand. She put Frederick back in his cradle and said a silent prayer that he would make up for last night's sleep by dozing most of the day. Frederica would have loved to curl up in her bed with the covers over her head to muffle the noises of the day—exhausted as she was.

What little patience Michael had initially displayed was gone. He clung to Frederica's skirt and pulled on her, all the while chanting, "Behfast, behfast." She dodged her son and made her way to the chicken house to gather eggs but was interrupted by a familiar whistle. Miguel had taken in two young apprentices, Juan and Enrique, and their boat was entering the bay. They always seemed to fetch the dried nets right at breakfast time. Frederica sighed and grabbed another cup of flour to make a few extra biscuits for the men. She knew they would be looking for her guava jelly, and she didn't want to disappoint them. She put the coffee on and grabbed several oranges to squeeze for juice.

Within minutes they were sitting around her little pinewood table. As they ate, she gazed out the window and thought about how she needed to weed the garden and bring in some vegetables to Aunt Julia's store. Thoughts of weeding the garden turned to thoughts of the boys, who were indeed growing like weeds. They both needed new pants, so that was one more chore to add to her ever-growing list.

The supper dishes, which had been left in the water from the night before, attracted ants, and Michael was trying to kill them with his little fingers. That reminded her that the dishes and the clothes needed washing, but she was out of soap. The men would be taking the dry nets and leaving the wet ones on the porch. They would need to be washed and dried before tomorrow. The men also left a basket of fish they'd speared that morning. Frederica would need to clean and salt them before they spoiled.

Footsteps crunching up the shell path made Frederica look up. Mrs. Peterson approached carrying two large glass jars. Frederica vaguely remembered promising to help her fetch some wild honey for her baking, and lo and behold, here she came. Frederick was awake and hungry again. It was only seven-thirty, according to Uncle Joe's old Bavarian cuckoo clock that hung by the door, and the day was already in busy.

Frederica looked into the faces of Michael, Enrique, Juan, and Mrs. Peterson. She could hear Frederick stirring in his crib. She imagined Aunt Julia impatiently waiting for her vegetables. She could smell the dirty dishes in the basin. The garden, the nets, the laundry, the baby, the fish, the honey, the cabin, the animals, everyone needed something—

everyone needed her! All of her responsibilities swirled around and around in her head, and even the smallest noises seemed to intensify and echo in her brain. She put her head in her hands, sat down on the stoop, and allowed tears to come. Her strength was gone, and she couldn't move.

Michael was the only one in the cabin who noticed Frederica's collapse. The adults in the cabin continued to chat and point and laugh. They used multiple languages to communicate, and they found the process amusing. Michael walked over, put his hand under Frederica's chin, and tilted it up so he could see her face.

She looked into his bright-blue eyes. They were more beautiful than the water around the island, and his lashes were long and full. His hands were sticky with jelly, but Frederica didn't mind. He touched her hair and kissed her cheek, then he put his little arms around her neck and hugged her tight. "I love you Mutter. Don't cry." She breathed in the smell of this little boy who was as precious to her as pure sunshine.

A breeze came through the window and filled the room with a refreshing coolness. Frederica felt a burst of energy, she supposed that it might be the effect of the coffee. But deep down she knew it came from her son. The world came back into focus. "I love you too, Michael," she whispered. "Let's go get your brother. We have a busy day ahead. We need to make Papa proud of how well we take care of things while he's gone. Frederica stood up, and armored by the love of her son, she approached the day with new-found hope and vigor.

War Comes to Tampa Bay, July 1861

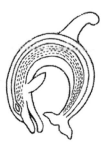

Miguel thought the day had all the makings of a joyous Fourth of July as he sailed his yawl across the calm waters of Miguel's Bay, through the mangrove-lined cut, and out into Terrasilla Bay. Frederica sat on the starboard side with Frederick snuggled in her lap—he rubbed sleep from his eyes. Michael sat beside his Papa in the stern—his little hands resting on the rudder post in an effort to help his father steer the boat.

Frederica's face beamed with excitement. Today would be an extra special holiday—they were having a double wedding at the Atzeroth's home. Frederica's cousin, Eliza, would marry Michael Dickens, and cousin, Mary, would wed William O'Neil. They were also celebrating the United States' eighty-fifth year of independence.

As Miguel sailed out of Terrasilla Bay, black smoke rose into the sky. It came from the twin stacks of a large, black steamship anchored in the main channel off Egmont Key.

208

The sails of several smaller vessels swarmed around the ship. It was a familiar scene he remembered from the Carlista War in Spain.

The War Between the States had arrived at their very doorstep in the form of a Union gunboat and her tenders threatening to pursue any vessel that might sail in or out of Tampa Bay.

Frederica had her back to the river, so she hadn't seen it yet. Miguel didn't want to scare her or ruin the day, so he vowed to keep the grim news to himself until after the wedding. The ramifications of a blockade preoccupied his thoughts as the double-wedding rushed by in a blur. The next thing he knew, Judge Glazier pronounced each of the two couples "man and wife."

While Frederica and the women were busy with the new brides, Miguel excused himself and walked down to the dock where he found his friend Manuel Amon talking with ship owners, Archibald McNeil, John Curry, and Captain Samuel Bishop. Miguel reported what he saw to the men—Manuel interpreted for him.

"Well, I suppose it was just a matter of time," McNeil said. "This is going to make life interesting, Sam!" McNeil was the owner of the sloop, *Mary Nevis*, that carried mail and passengers between the Manatee River and Tampa. Sam Bishop was her captain.

"They are trying to starve the South by sealing off every means of supply. Gentlemen, times are quickly going to become very difficult. This will cut off all means of trade into Manatee—medicine, fabric, manufactured goods, weapons, and currency. The only food we'll have is what we can produce ourselves," McNeil grumbled.

"We must continue our runs to Havana and Nassau, but we'll have to use the shallow inter-coastal waterways, and that will necessitate small, shallow draft vessels sailing in the dead of night." Curry said.

McNeil nodded, "They caught the *Salvo* running up from Key West with a load of cattle last month. They gave Captain McKay a warning and threatened to seize his boat the next time they caught him. They also threatened to send him to the Dry Tortugas."

The threat of war had seemed distant and unreal. It was an event reserved for the front page of the *Florida Peninsular*. Rumors of battles were brought to the wharf by folks arriving from Key West, and they spread like wildfire to everyone in the region. With the arrival of a Union warship off Egmont Key, the war was now a local danger to the people of Manatee.

The men of the wedding party were summoned by their ladies to join them for refreshments. As they walked, Manuel translated for Miguel. They were in need of boats, and Miguel's yawl had come up during the discussion. He

210

considered the financial consequences he faced if his boat was seized by the Yankee Navy. He shivered as he pondered the hardships that Frederica would endure if he was imprisoned on the Tortugas.

Frederica passed steins of Julia's homemade cane beer to each of the men, kissed Miguel on the cheek, then hurried off to help Eliza and Mary change out of their wedding dresses to prepare to leave on their honeymoons.

McNeil and the others continued the conversation by the refreshment table under the shade of a giant oak. "We need boats here as well—coast watchers of sorts. Men in small sloops and yawls will watch the blockade, supply the militia, and make the supply trips to Fort Brooke."

Manuel stared at Miguel. Miguel weighed the risks and dreaded the heavy burden, but he knew he must offer his help.

"*Mi barco está a tu servicio,*" Miguel said.

"My boat is at your service," Manuel interpreted.

McNeil laughed, " Excellent! We have the beginnings of our coast guard."

Eliza's groom, Michael Dickens, overheard and joined the conversation. "Soon, they'll be calling for volunteers from Manatee for the infantry, and I intend on joining at the first opportunity." He pulled a flask from his vest pocket and offered it to the others. "Gentlemen, please join me in a toast. To the South!" Dickens bellowed.

"To the South!" the others replied, as they lifted their drinks in unison.

The commotion under the oak tree caught everyone's attention. Julia shot a displeased look at the men. Judge Glazier went over to calm the raucous group. "Gentlemen, we all applaud your patriotism, but this is not the time. I'm afraid you are upsetting the ladies. They don't want to think about their men going off to war, especially on a joyful occasion like this. Mr. Dickens, I do believe Mrs. Dickens is looking for you."

He laughed. "I'm sure she is, and I bet she can't wait to get on with the evening."

Frederica noticed that Miguel was unusually quiet on the trip home. She wanted him to tell her what disturbed him. It was apparent that she noticed his fatigue, and he tried to lift his spirits out of the dark depths of fear and concern over the looming war. The day started out hopeful and happy, and he was determined it would end the same. He vowed he would make every day special for his family, until God or country dictated differently.

A Day Off of Palma Sola Bay, August 1861

It had only been daylight for a couple of hours and the crew of the *Margarita* had already stripped to the waist—every man's skin glistening with sweat. The yawl's sails billowed as she left Sarasota Pass and entered the open water of Tampa Bay. Rodrigo hauled in a line that had taken a hit, and José cut up strips of mullet for bait. Manuel stood by the forward mast looking like a pirate from days gone by—his head wrapped in a red bandana. His eyes scanned the horizon for enemy ships.

Miguel sat at the helm in the yawl's stern, setting a course for the Manatee River. Now that it was daylight, it would only be safe to fish close to shore. He knew the blockade ships were keeping a keen eye out for sails. They were like osprey on the hunt for unsuspecting fish. Captain Duvall of the 20th Florida Militia had encouraged them to fish just outside the mouth of the river. He hoped to draw Yankee schooners within range of the loaded cannon at Shaw's Point.

"¡Ay, *Dios mío*! It's going to be as hot as Hades, today!" Manuel said, as he wiped the sweat from his face with his bandana.

The men worked most of the night trolling the oyster beds and shallows in Sarasota Bay, but they only caught a few red snappers. The rest were junk fish and had to be thrown back. Each of the lines were rigged with two leaders and hooks baited with strips of mullet. They trailed at different lengths to keep them from tangling.

"¡*Caramba*! Another catfish!" Rodrigo said. He released the struggling fish off the hook and tossed it back into the bay.

Off the north shore of Palma Sola, they approached the spot called Seven Pines. Miguel watched small, grey and white birds swoop down to the surface of the water, diving and looping up with bits of fish in their black bills. It was a sure sign of predator fish feeding in the area.

"I'm glad *someone* is catching something!" Manuel joked, and he threw his line over the stern.

Miguel turned toward the coast as the birds squawked and scattered when the yawl got closer to them. Manuel was in the bow, keeping an eye on the depth of the water. Then he saw them, a school of large fish darting about in the sea grass chasing hundreds of small shiners.

"Mackerel!" he called out.

Miguel turned to watch the lines that floated in the wake of the boat. He held a line loosely between his thumb and forefinger and waited for a nibble. He felt a vibration followed by a sharp tug on the starboard line.

"Got one!" Miguel shouted. The center and port lines also dipped, and Manuel quickly made his way back to the stern to haul them onboard. Manuel pulled the fish up to the gunwale and Miguel gaffed them, hauling them into the boat, careful to avoid their razor-sharp teeth.

Miguel circled for another run, and the course took them just outside the mouth of the Manatee around Shaw's Point. They were within range of the bronze cannon of the Manatee militia stationed on the top of the Indian mound. The morning sun reflected off the tip of its bronze barrel, and he could hear the flag snapping above it in the morning breeze. He concentrated to see a person in a black derby on top of the mound scanning the bay with a transit on a tripod. Another man in military uniform, probably Captain Duvall, stood beside him. Duvall appeared to be waving his arms trying to attract their attention.

Miguel quickly turned and looked toward Egmont Key. He thought the Captain might be warning him of an approaching Yankee vessel, but didn't see any sails. Miguel looked at the pitiful catch in the fish hold, then looked at Manuel.

Manuel sighed. He knew his friend well enough to read his thoughts. The fishing would have to wait. He threw a mackerel in the bottom of the boat and watched it thrash on top of the few snappers they caught during the night. The birds had returned. They repeated their circling and diving, reminding the two men of the big mackerel they might have caught if they could stay. They both needed money the fish would bring, but the times re-set their priorities.

Miguel waved at the officer and looked at his friend, "*Lo siento amigo.*" They trimmed the sail and pointed the boat back toward Shaw's Point.

The yawl moved toward the beach until the hull scraped oyster shells. Manuel tossed the anchor and Miguel jumped overboard into knee-deep water to wade ashore. He could see the captain striding down to the beach. Two of his men followed with their muskets and military accoutrements. Miguel recognized his friend, Asa Bishop. The other was the man in the black derby he had seen watching from the top of the mound.

"*Hola,* Miguel," the captain said, and he stretched out a hand to help him out of the water. Once they were under the shade of the mangroves, he continued, "I apologize for interrupting your fishing." He paused, and Manuel interpreted his apology into Spanish.

"*Buenos días, Capitán*, how can I help?" Miguel asked.

"There's a load ready to be picked up at the salt works," the captain explained. "These men will take you there and load the salt. Bring it back here, and the *Mary Nevis* will take it to Tampa tomorrow."

Miguel detected resentment in Manuel's voice as he interpreted the captain's request.

"*No hay problema.* The fishing not so good today," Miguel told the captain. He turned to Manuel and said, "Tell him his men may have these few fish we caught and Rodrigo will stay here to help clean and salt them."

"*Ayyyyy.*" Manuel whispered under his breath. He shot Miguel a disgusted look and then interpreted for the captain, who thanked Miguel and climbed back up the mound.

Asa climbed aboard, followed by the soldier wearing the derby. He was Levi Heaton from New Orleans. Following Asa's directions, Miguel pointed the *Margarita* towards Sarasota Pass and entered Palma Sola Bay.

Asa placed a hand on Miguel's shoulder, "I'm sorry, friend. We would've taken my boat, but she is being fitted with a new mast."

"No, it is good. Don't worry," Miguel reassured him.

Miguel was calm on the outside, but inside he was nervous about sailing in broad daylight. The tide was low enough to worry about oyster beds, scraping over sharp shells from time to time.

Asa pointed to a ribbon of smoke rising above the eastern shoreline. "The salt work is over there, up a little creek," he told Manuel.

Miguel guided the *Margarita* through an opening in the mangroves, entering a hidden cove surrounded by towering palms and hardwoods. He could see the salt works situated on a little bluff at the far end. The smell of burning pine drifting from the furnace filled the air. Two men emerged from the smoke to greet them. Miguel recognized Archibald McNeil immediately. The man following him was Major William Iredell Turner, commander of a company of mounted volunteers. Beside him was the stern-faced Judge Josiah Gates—Miguel couldn't remember a time when he'd seen him smile.

"Hola, Miguel!" McNeil called out. "I knew we could count on you and your crew. Gentlemen, the service you are rendering today might not seem important, but salt is vital

218

to winning this war. We need it to preserve meat, cure leather and make shoes. Hell, it even sets the dyes in our uniforms. Let me show you around."

The machinery consisted of a small steam engine, a large steam pump used to extract seawater from the cove, an old single-tube boiler, and several cast iron sugar kettles to evaporate the seawater. McNeil, who managed Gamble's sugar plantation, had supplied two kettles to use for the boiler pans along with some slaves for labor.

Major Turner interjected, "And once we're completely up and running, we aim to supply a hundred bushels a day at $30 a bushel!"

McNeil nodded in agreement but sheepishly added, "Today, we seem to be a few bags short on the order due to a pump failure. Please ask Captain Duvall to extend my sincerest apologies to General Taylor. Tell him we'll have the rest of his sacks delivered this week."

"I will be sure to pass that along," Asa assured McNeil. He signed the delivery receipt and handed it back. He saluted Major Turner and joined the others as they loaded up the bags of salt.

When they pushed the yawl away from the dock, Miguel looked back at the salt work. He wondered what he would see and was impressed by its simplicity. He eased the *Margarita* through the narrow channel and back out into

Palma Sola Bay. It was midday and the tide was rising, making grounding in the bay less likely. They sailed into a headwind and Miguel navigated the final starboard tack out of the bay. The men relaxed and ate a lunch of hard bread, salt beef, and cheese. Levi walked to the bow of the boat to hand Manuel the water jug when he saw the hunter.

"Schooner ahead!" Levi screamed. The jug slipped from his fingers and shattered on the deck. He was stunned by the fear that coursed through his body.

The bow of a schooner was seen crossing the mouth of Palma Sola Bay about 1,000 yards ahead. Manuel pulled out his pocket-spyglass. "Yankee gunboat!" he called back to the men.

The chatter of the men and the sounds of the sea faded as Miguel focused on the schooner that loomed larger and larger as it came closer.

"*Miguel. Miguel!*" Manuel yelled frantically at him from the bow. "They're heaving to!" The schooner had spotted the *Margarita* and positioned themselves at the mouth of the bay to block the smaller craft's escape.

Miguel turned back to look at the schooner. It was holding its position in Sarasota Pass, but a second sloop-rigged vessel appeared out of nowhere and was following them. Running out of time, he would have to turn northward, beach the boat, and escape over land. He remembered Perico Island

220

and what his friend taught him about sailors using *critical harbors* in desperate situations.

Perico had always feared an attack on his rancho, especially since Captain Bunce's place had been destroyed. As a safeguard, he kept a small fleet of shallow draft boats behind his island in a little bayou. He called it his back door to Palma Sola Bay, serving as *his* critical harbor.

Miguel could barely make out the entrance to Perico's Bayou. It ran from the north side of Palma Sola Bay to Tampa Bay. It was very shallow, hopefully too shallow for the Yankee sloop to follow. Miguel prayed his own yawl would make it through. He feared the enemy schooner would be waiting for them when they emerged from the bayou.

Miguel sheeted in the foresail tight, loosened the mizzen, and quickly turned the yawl about and headed her downwind. The foresail billowed, and the *Margarita* lurched forward. They accelerated away from the sloop and toward the northeast.

Miguel heard a whooshing sound, and a split-second later a geyser of water erupted just beyond their bow. A loud boom followed, resonating across the bay. The Yankee sloop had fired its deck gun as a warning to the *Margarita's* crew to stand down and prepare to be boarded.

"We go through Perico's Bayou!" Miguel called out.

Asa couldn't believe his ears. "No! The bayou is too shallow! We'll never make it!"

"This boat has a very shallow draft and the flood tide is coming in. We've done it before!" Manuel answered.

"Maybe so, but loaded down with salt?" Asa asked. "I sure hope you're right!"

As the *Margarita* passed behind a mangrove shoal, the trees shielded them from view. Miguel knew that once the sloop moved past the mangroves, the Yankee sailors would spot them as they headed into the bayou. His boat and crew would be a clear target, but this time there would be no warning shot. There would be no time to beach and get the crew off his boat.

Manuel crouched over the edge of the bow and kept a close eye on the depth. He guided Miguel into deeper parts of the narrow channel, but suddenly the *Margarita* struck sand and stopped dead.

"We're stuck!" Manuel called out. "Quickly. Everyone out. Get her off the bar!"

Miguel looked back over his shoulder and expected to see the sloop training her deck gun on them, but there was no sign of the Union vessel. She must have grounded when she tried to make the turn around the mangrove shoal. They would be safe for the moment, but the rising tide would eventually float the sloop off of the bar.

The men dropped over the side and into the waist-deep water. This lightened the load and they began to push from the stern. The *Margarita* wouldn't budge. Just as they were beginning to consider dumping bags of salt, the *Margarita* began to slide off the bar with a scraping rasp. Walking the yawl through the bayou was a slow process. Finally, the water rose back to chest-deep levels and the men were able to jump aboard.

Miguel whispered a prayer as they emerged from the mouth of the bayou. There was no sign of the Yankee boats, but smoke rising from a ship at anchor in the southwest channel off Anna Maria Island caught his eye. It was the war steamer. No doubt the captain of the vessel could see his sails. Miguel was at least four miles away and out of the range of her powerful guns. The weary crew relaxed as they realized the steamer posed no threat to them.

The *Margarita* made it safely to the cove at Shaw's Point, delivering her precious cargo. Miguel and his crew had dinner with the Bishop family as they waited for nightfall. They could make the crossing to Terrasilla under the protection of darkness.

It was after midnight before Miguel opened the door of his cabin. He walked over to the fireplace to warm himself. He stood there for a long moment and watched the faces of his sleeping family lit by the warmth of the fire. He thought about the events of the day and how it could have turned out so differently. What if the *Margarita* had taken on a full load of salt? What if the Yankee sloop hadn't grounded? What would tomorrow have been like for his family if he hadn't come home?

A log settled in the fireplace and sent up a flurry of sparks. The noise awakened Frederick, who saw his father looking down at him. He could see Miguel's eyes moist with tears.

"Papa?" Frederick whispered.

"Yes, Frederick. Go back to sleep, son. I'm home, and we are all safe."

The Raid on Egmont Key,
August 1861

The pale light of a crescent moon shimmered on the surface of the Manatee River as the *Margarita* slipped into Tampa Bay. Miguel looked intently toward the fixed beam of the Egmont lighthouse as it pierced the inky blackness of night. He strained to see any blockade vessels they may be lurking in wait—clues might be a flicker of light from a deck lantern, the outline of a mast, or the glow of a careless man's cigar. He was sure that enemy ships were out there, their lookouts ever vigilant.

The bow pointed north toward the far side of Tampa Bay. Manuel Amon and Rofeno Fallis lowered the mainsail and used only the jib and mizzen, lessening the chance of the *Margarita* reflecting the moonlight and attracting unwanted attention. To the north, Miguel could see the dim glow of a bonfire on Pinellas Point, made by Abel Miranda's men to help the boat company navigate at night.

Miguel served with the boat company Miranda proposed to raise for General Taylor, so he wasn't surprised when Captain Duvall found him at the Atzeroth's dock, loading supplies onto the *Margarita*. The captain gave Miguel his orders and Manuel interpreted them.

Michael Gerrero

Sir,

Please fit out your yawl for sea, recruiting a crew as you deem necessary. Your responsibility is to cruise between the Manatee River and Point Pinellas, reporting to the officer in command of the Coast Guard. The State of Florida is amply able to pay you for your services. For the hire of your yawl, crew, and self, you will be paid sixty dollars a month, a fair amount, deemed as sufficient. You will also carry news and men when required. You must not change members of your crew without notifying me directly.

Joseph M. Taylor
Brigadier General
Florida Militia
Brooksville, August 22, 1861
Order of Brig Genl Taylor

The blockade had seriously hindered fishing, so the wages would be a tremendous help to Miguel. He was proud to do his part to protect his community, yet he worried about risking his boat and source of income. The lives of his crew, as well as his own life, would be in serious danger.

Sailing ahead of them now was William Curry's schooner the *Eliza Fisk*. Curry had also received orders regarding the use of his boat, which was under the command of Captain Frederick Tresca.

Manuel kept a vigilant watch from the bow of the *Margarita*. In order to locate the coastline, he had to squint to see where the land mass appeared darker than the starry sky. The boats anchored a long way from Pinellas Point to avoid grounding on the oyster beds—they awaited further instructions. Moments after the *Margarita's* anchor splashed into the deep waters, an unexpected voice called out from the darkness. It broke the silence of the night and resonated across the bay. "Identify yourselves!"

"*Eliza Fisk* and the *Margarita*," Captain Tresca shouted back.

The synchronized splash of oars broke the surface of the water as they came near. Manuel unshielded his lantern to illuminate the bay, revealing a fourteen-oar longboat carrying an armed crew. A small brass cannon was mounted on its bow.

"Follow us!" the gruff voice commanded.

The Manatee boats silently followed the longboat up the coast and into the entrance of Big Bayou. Once inside the

227

inlet, Miguel spotted a bonfire on the north shore—its glow illuminated the leaves of overhanging oak trees and reflected off the water. He could make out the shapes of two small schooners at anchor in the bayou.

Rofeno tossed the bowline to a large man who was waiting for them on the dock. He secured the line, then offered a hand to the crew as they scrambled out of the boat.

"Welcome to Big Bayou, friends!" the man said. He was built like a bull and had a full, black beard with piercing, black eyes. It was his voice they had heard back at the point.

"John. John Lowe," the man said as he helped Miguel out of the boat. "The lieutenant is over by the fire. He's expecting you."

When Abel Miranda saw Miguel, he jumped up, embraced him in a strong hug, and kissed him on both cheeks. "Aha! Welcome to the Coast Guard, my old friend!" He turned and saw Captain Tresca and the crew of the *Eliza Fiske* coming up the dock. "Greetings, gentlemen! Please come with me and enjoy some clams."

After the lieutenant saw they had eaten their fill, he invited Miguel, Captain Tresca, and their crews into the parlor of his home to sign his muster roll. He asked Miguel and Captain Tresca to remain behind after the others had returned to the fire.

He poured them a drink from a crystal decanter then spread a navigational chart across his desk. He placed a stubby finger on Egmont Key and his friendly expression turned grave. For a moment, Miguel didn't recognize his old friend.

"The mission at hand is to cripple the blockaders by any means possible. George Rickards, the lighthouse keeper and a good southern man, is feigning allegiance to the Union for as long as he can in order to obtain information. Rickards reports that the Yankees have not yet occupied the island. The general is concerned they will soon make Egmont Key a base of operations for the East Gulf blockading squadron. The light must be put out of operation. The Fresnel lens must be brought to Tampa for safekeeping." Miranda said.

Captain Tresca looked at Miranda for a moment with a blank expression, then asked, "Sir, begging your pardon, but what about the blockade boats?"

"Captain, I'm glad you've brought that up," Miranda said, pouring himself a glass of whiskey. His dark eyes focused on the men as he downed the shot. "They will be off chasing sails. *Your* sails, gentlemen."

Miguel suddenly realized the danger in the mission he had accepted and became increasingly anxious as the lieutenant returned to the chart to explain his plan.

***

The following afternoon, Miranda's fleet of four vessels set sail for Mullet Key. They used a thunderstorm for cover, harnessing its cool winds. The squall continued as they dropped anchor north of the key in Bunce's Pass. For a short time they were hidden from the view of the blockade boats.

From the *Margarita*, Miguel watched two men in a small boat drop from Miranda's schooner. They rowed across the bayou and disappeared among the mangroves. The pair beached their boat, hiked across the narrow key, and set up watch for enemy boats. A signal would be sent when all of the blockade boats were anchored in the main channel.

As the sun dipped below the horizon, the signal finally came from Mullet Key. A small, blue light glowed in the jungle of black mangroves across the bayou. It signaled that all of the blockade boats were now present and at anchor for the night. Miranda's boat signaled to the *Margarita* and the *Eliza Fisk* that the mission would proceed. Manuel signaled back that they had received and understood.

Miguel spent a sleepless night thinking about the mission. An hour before sunrise, the crew hoisted the jib and mizzen sails and followed the *Eliza Fisk* across Tampa Bay. They headed toward the eastern horizon where Venus was suspended in a blue-violet sky. Miranda and John Bethell's schooners waited expectantly behind him to see if the Yankees took the bait.

They sailed into a brisk northeast wind. When they arrived at the coast of Piney Point, they turned south to run to Sarasota Pass. Soon the sun would be up, and they would be in full view of the blockade boats. Miguel bellowed, "Raise the mainsail!" The sails snapped taut, and the *Margarita* lunged forward at full speed.

The *Eliza Fisk* neared Terrasilla at sunrise. Miguel's Bay reflected the golden light. Manuel trimmed the sail as he looked over his shoulder toward Egmont Key. He could see the black shadows of the three blockade ships at anchor. He barely noticed a faint signal light on the steamer—It appeared to be blinking in code. He yelled, "I think we've been spotted! The sea monsters are awake!"

In a matter of moments, the chase was on. Miguel watched uneasily as the Yankee sloops crossed the bay toward him. He had an advantage with the wind at his stern while his pursuers had to tack across the bay in a crosswind. Every tack closed the distance, and Miguel knew that it wouldn't be long before they were in range of the enemy guns. The war steamer belched black smoke, running full steam as it made its way through the southwest channel. It would head south down the coast of Anna Maria Island while the smaller boats chased the blockade runners through Sarasota Pass.

Miguel knew that Lieutenant Miranda would make his move through Bunce's Pass and out into the Gulf, then he would sail to the north end of Egmont to land and retrieve the lighthouse lens.

The *Eliza Fisk* was under full sail and well inside the mouth of Sarasota Pass. She ran well ahead of Miguel, and he began to feel vulnerable and exposed. He felt like a young dolphin lagging behind its mother while trying to escape the jaws of a hungry shark.

The Yankee sloops diverged. One followed the *Fiske,* and the other headed straight for the *Margarita.*

"She's closing in on us fast!" Manuel shouted, and suddenly an ear-shattering *boom* broke the air.

A plume of water rose up several hundred yards behind their stern—this was a warning shot and signaled the *Margarita* to prepare to be boarded. Miguel knew that the Yankee sloop's gun would soon be in range, and he would never make it to the Manatee as planned. He threw the rudder hard to starboard and made a sharp turn into Terrasilla Bay.

His glance turned toward Egmont Key one last time before he slid inside the mouth of the bay and the mangroves hid them from view. Miranda's sloops were anchored off of the key's north end, but Miguel was elated by what he *didn't* see.

The Egmont light was out, but it was too soon to celebrate. Another *boom* sounded. This time the plume shot up only seventy-five yards short of the *Margarita*. The Yankee sloop luffed her foresail and came to a swift stop just outside the mouth of the bay. Her captain was unwilling to chance grounding in a shallow bay without the support of the other sloop that was chasing the *Eliza Fiske*. The gun crew on the vessel in pursuit of the *Margarita* feverishly reloaded for another shot, but Miguel slipped his boat behind a mangrove-covered shoal to get out of view of the hunter. He sailed the *Margarita* to the far end of the bay and dropped anchor at Peterson's Bayou. It was over, and they were safe.

It appeared that the mission had been a success! "We did it, boys!" "Ay, Dios mío!" Miguel said, as he wiped sweat from his face with his shirtsleeve. He laughed, "My friends, that was much, much too close!" Rofeno handed him a water jug and he took a long draught.

He could hear the Peterson children calling to them from the shoreline at his back. Mrs. Peterson waved from the porch and urged the men to come inside. A sullen expression crept over Miguel as he realized what he had done. Retreating to this place had been unavoidable, but it drew the enemy's attention to this peaceful haven.

What effect the removal of the light would have on the blockade, Miguel didn't know. But there was one thing he was sure of, it would only be a matter of time before the Yankee sailors expanded their invasion and traveled up the river and bays.

Yankee Boats on the Manatee, January 1862

The first hint of sunlight painted the eastern sky with rose-colored hues. It was a cold January morning, and the wind was nearly at dead calm, so the crew of the *Margarita* left her sails furled, set the oars in their locks, and pulled away from the Manatee wharf. The boat moved out into the morning fog that hung like a cloud above the flat, grey river.

Miguel, Asa Bishop, and Joseph Woodruff's boats brought up soldiers from Shaw's Point to Manatee Village. William Iredell Turner's horse company left the day before due to lack of fodder to feed their animals. The 20th Militia was being mustered out of service and being replaced by the newly-organized Florida Volunteer Coast Guard and two companies of the 4th Florida Infantry Regiment headquartered at Ft. Brooke. Miguel's services would no longer be required, and he could finally return to his family and fishing.

For six months, Miguel had been engaged in transporting men and supplies between the Manatee River, Fort Brooke, and coast watcher stations around Tampa Bay. He was lucky to spend two or three nights a week with his family. There was little opportunity to fish or tend to his nets and gear. He felt badly for Frederica, who was saddled with all of the responsibilities of raising their two young children. She was tending to the animals and the garden on her own and was exhausted.

Miguel and his neighbors were feeling the economic effects of the blockade. The shortage of supplies and loss of income was painful, but at least the Yankees seemed content to remain offshore. It was a blessing that they had not come up the rivers and bays as so many of the Floridians had feared.

Miguel sat at the helm, keeping *the Margarita* on course at a safe distance behind Asa and Joseph. Their yawls were halfway-hidden by the haze. The rhythmic sounds of the swishing oars and the lapping water soothed Miguel and he thought of home at Miguel's Bay.

Three nights earlier, he enjoyed sleeping in his own bed instead of on the deck of his boat or out in the open air. He fell asleep with Frederica lying in the crook of his arm—her head resting on his chest. During the night, a bright flash of lightning momentarily lit up the room, followed by a rumble of thunder that shook the walls. Miguel woke with a start, and for a moment he thought the gunboat had come into the bay and fired upon their cabin. He relaxed again when he realized it was just a storm.

As the lightning flickered in the woods, pale light lit the room. Miguel tilted his head toward Frederica and a calm feeling soothed him. He loved the way her wild, dark hair cascaded across the pillow. He kissed her forehead and a long, sleepy sigh escaped her lips. With her eyes still closed, she pushed back the strands of hair from her face. Her eyes opened, and she met his gaze, sad with the thought that he must leave again in the morning. Frederica cherished the moment, holding him tightly.

***

The fog was rising above the surface of the water, and Miguel could make out Joseph and Asa's boats up ahead. They were frantically turning back toward the *Margarita*. Someone on Joseph's boat was using a mirror to catch the morning sun, flashing a warning that something was amiss.

Boom. The sound of a cannon crashed through the misty air. Miguel looked toward the mouth of the Manatee River. The masts of three boats rounded the point, heading straight toward them. The lead boat was firing its howitzer and signaling for Joseph to *come to* and prepare to be boarded. Joseph and Asa tried to make a run for it.

"Come about port!" Miguel yelled, and the two oarsmen on the port side dug in their paddles in a breaking motion, allowing the starboard oars to bring the *Margarita* around and head back up river. A second howitzer sounded. A shot whistled past Joseph and a plume of water shot up between Asa's boat and the *Margarita*.

"Three Yankee cutters closing fast!" Manuel yelled, his voice cracking with panic. He had been watching the cutters operating in the bay for the past six months, so he knew that they were powered by sail plus up to ten oarsmen—there was no way to outrun them. He pointed his bow southeast in order to make a run for a large bayou on the south bank of the Manatee. Asa followed close behind, but Joseph had already run his boat aground just above Bishop's Point, and his crew was scrambling into the woods.

Boom, boom! Two more boat cannons sounded almost simultaneously. The shots landed dangerously close to the stern of Asa's yawl. Miguel realized the bayou was out of reach, so he leaned on the rudder and headed for the closest land where he could beach the *Margarita*.

"*Más rápido!*" he yelled desperately, and the crew pulled with all their might for shore. As soon as he felt the hull scrape across sand, Manuel threw the anchor overboard, and they abandoned the boat. Asa's boat slid up beside them and the men followed them into the woods. All of their gear, except the muskets, was left on the boats in the mad rush for cover.

The Yankees, who were only a couple hundred yards behind, opened up on them with a brisk volley from their muskets. A bullet made a whirring sound as it zipped past Miguel's head before it whacked into a tree trunk in front of him.

The firing stopped, but Miguel and Asa's crew kept running until they reached a high bluff. They stopped there to survey the situation on the river.

Three more cutters had entered the river and were offloading infantrymen at Shaw's Point cove. The three that pursued them were now moving toward the Atzeroth store across the river, with two boats in tow.

Miguel's eyes widened when he recognized that the two boats in tow were the *Margarita* and Asa's boat *Pokey*. He hung his head and slammed his fist into the dirt. His worst fear was coming to pass.

Miguel seethed with rage, "How am I supposed to support my family without a boat!" He turned and saw Asa running down the trail toward home. Asa grumbled to himself after seeing the second boat. Miguel got up, brushed the sand and sand spurs off his shirt and ran to catch up.

They paused at the edge of the woods bordering Asa's cabin just in time to see fellow militiaman Levi Heaton and another man being led away by Yankee soldiers. The sun reflected off of their bayonet-tipped muskets as they marched their prisoners down to one of the waiting cutters.

Asa and his men waited until the boat pushed off and rowed out into the river. They disappeared behind the mangroves on Bishop's Point and pulled the boat up on shore. Running at full-speed to his cabin, he yelled, "Martha!" He burst through the door and his heart sunk as he discovered evidence that his home had been searched. He immediately noticed that food had been taken and there was no sign of Martha and the children.

He took a deep breath, remembering what they had agreed to do in a circumstance such as this. "They've gone to the hammock!" he exclaimed. The men followed him as he ran down a trail that led south into the pine woods. As they rounded a large Oak Tree, they heard his father-in-law, John Andress, mimicking the call of a Loon, a bird with a distinct call. This was the signal that *all was well*. Asa fell to his knees and let out a sigh of relief.

"John! Where are Martha and the children?" Asa called out.

"Asa? *Asa*. Thank the Lord!" Andress said. "We heard the cannon and gunfire coming from the direction of the house and feared the worst. When I saw the Yankees coming, I sent Martha and the children out the back window and told them to come here to the hammock. But I can't find them, and they're not responding to the signal."

Asa didn't hesitate to put his tracking skills to good use and found fresh footprints heading in the direction of the village. The men set off through the woods like a pack of

239

hunting dogs locked onto a strong scent. They discovered bits of clothing hanging in the briars, broken branches, and trampled grass—all signs that his family had passed this way.

"I see them!" Asa called. Martha and the children were struggling to cross a little creek that meandered up from the river and into the hammock.

"Martha!" Asa's voice echoed through the woods.

Martha turned when she heard her husband's voice, took her children by the hand, and hurried back toward him.

Asa turned to the other men. "Thank you for helping me, my friends. You'd best go and see to your own families now." He remembered that Miguel would have no way of getting back to Terrasilla.

"Manuel, you and Miguel take my skiff. Its hidden about 100 yards up the creek due west of my place." Asa only cared about getting his family safely back home.

The Bishops disappeared into the palmettos with Asa trying to shush the excited children as they headed toward home. Miguel and Manuel ran down to the creek bed where they found the skiff pulled up on the bank in the underbrush.

They poled down the creek and waited at the edge of the Manatee for night to fall. A light breeze carried the little boat to Terrasilla. The men were exhausted, but adrenaline kept them headed toward home.

Miguel got a sick feeling in his stomach as he neared the long midden where his cabin stood. His heart was heavy with the fear that the sailors might have come up the bay and found Frederica and the children.

"Frederica, *¿Dónde estás?*" Miguel's voice thundered across the bay. "Frederica!"

Suddenly he heard the familiar lilt of her voice, "Miguel! Miguel! *Ich bin hier!*" Frederica called out his name as she ran down the side of the mound to the shoreline. She pulled her skirt up and waded out to meet the approaching boat.

She had been keeping a vigil for Miguel from the top of the mound, and she had seen the moonlight reflecting off of his sail. Miguel jumped out of the boat into the waist-deep water and waded the rest of the way to meet his wife.

"*Die Boote sind angekommen!*" Frederica exclaimed, and used her hand to signal that a boat had come through the pass toward their homesite. "*Aber nie gelandet*" she continued. The soldiers had come and gone, not coming ashore.

Miguel held her and thanked God his family was safe. Over Frederica's shoulder he saw Michael and Frederick running down to the beach—their white night shirts glowed in the moonlight.

Frederica watched Manuel pull the skiff to shore. "*Wo ist das Margarita?*" she gasped and gave Miguel a perplexed look.

When Miguel pointed in the direction of Egmont Key, she understood their boat had been captured. He anticipated her next question, "Whose boat is this?"

"Asa Bishop's," he told her.

Despite being safe in his own bed, sleep eluded Miguel that night. He was anxious about how the enemy had suddenly become aggressive. Up until now they had never left the safety of their ships or entered the rivers and bays.

He worried about his neighbors along the Manatee. It would only be a matter of time before the Union sailors came upriver again to destroy the mills and salt works. The Union would seize every resource that might be used to support the Confederate army. He had witnessed the ravages of war in Spain and he knew firsthand the savage toll it took on the people at home. He had never imagined that war would follow him to his island paradise.

Just before dawn, Miguel and Manuel set sail again with Frederica's skiff, *Maria* in tow. They sailed back to Bishop's Point to return Asa's skiff. Asa greeted them at the dock and invited them in for breakfast, but he avoided talking about the previous day's events with his wife and children present.

After breakfast the men went outside to smoke their pipes, and Asa told them what he had learned. The barracks on Shaw's Point were burned. Levi Heaton and another man were taken into custody and questioned. The Yankees wanted to know about the number of troops in the area and whether there were any big guns at Manatee. After hours of questioning, the two men were released.

Joseph Atzeroth had come to see Asa the day before. He reported that the Yankee boats hadn't reached the village or their store, but his wife's recent acquisition, the mail sloop *Mary Nevis*, had been captured on its way down from Tampa. Julia was livid and vowed to get it back.

"They're feeling us out, Miguel. I would bet that they are planning a trip upriver to the village and the sugar plantations. They'll take everything of value and probably destroy the mill," Asa told them.

Manuel and Miguel noticed the low-hanging haze on the river. If they left immediately, the haze would help conceal them from the ever-vigilant lookouts on the blockade vessels.

They climbed aboard the *Maria* and pushed away from the dock. With the boat's limited capacity to outrun the Yankee cutters, they would have to resort to using seine nets to fish the shallow bays close to home. He knew he could catch enough to provide for his family and barter with neighbors for other goods, but there would be no profit until the war ended and he could build a new boat.

243

Miguel turned and waved to Asa standing at the end of his dock with his little son, William, on his hip. As the *Maria* glided across the river, Miguel thought that all of Asa's predictions were coming true. He knew that all of the eligible men would have to go off to war if it didn't end soon.

Miguel's heart ached at the thought of having to leave Frederica and his sons.

Union Soldiers Arrive
at the Atzeroth Store

Frederica pulled off her shoes and put her tired feet into the cool water of the Manatee River. The sun was close to setting. She noticed that the air was getting cooler.

She and her little sons were living at the wharf with Aunt Julia, Eliza and Mary. She worked in the garden, helped in the store, managed the dock, and did her share of housework and cooking, just like she had done before she married Miguel.

There were big differences this time. She was no longer a young girl, free to have playful conversations and picnics at the beach. She was in her thirties, married with two young sons, four and six. She had a home of her own, and that came with some serious responsibilities.

When the Seminole War ended in 1858, the people of Manatee and the surrounding areas thought the worst was over. They began to feel safe and were anxious to move their lives forward. It was a wonderful time, and the community grew and prospered.

President Lincoln's election in 1860 broke the fragile peace between the North and South. Now the effects of the Civil War were felt in Manatee. Miguel and many other men and boys had gone to Fort Brooke to be mustered into the 7th Florida Infantry Regiment, soon to be sent to Tennessee.

Frederica had hoped and prayed for years that the animosity between the North and South would not result in an all-out war. The idea of Americans fighting fellow Americans and brothers fighting brothers horrified her. Surely this nightmare would not last long. Why couldn't Davis and Lincoln come to some kind of peaceful agreement before too many men were buried in distant battlefields? She knew that a peaceful result was not likely, since President Lincoln seemed hell-bent on preserving the Union.

A movement in her peripheral vision forced Frederica to glance toward the water. In the distance she could see the silhouette of a schooner—fear rose in her chest making her heart race. As the boat drew closer, she could see a group of men wearing blue uniforms scurrying about on the deck. Frederica didn't take the time to put her shoes back on—she gathered up her skirts and ran to the store.

She burst through the door to find Aunt Julia and Eliza in a panic, hiding supplies. Julia had already loaded the hunting rifle. What good that would do against a schooner full of Union navy! Mary, who had been outside urging the livestock into the woods, ran into the room and shrieked when she saw men walking up the dock.

Frederica screamed out, "Where are my boys?" She couldn't see Michael or Frederick anywhere. She bolted through the side door, scanned the surrounding area, and saw the boys in the grove. They were playing with their puppy. The panicked cry of their mother sent the boys running toward her. The tone of her voice told them in no uncertain terms that something was very wrong.

Both boys flew into Frederica's arms, and she instinctively lifted them up off of the ground. "We have to hurry to our hiding places," she said. "This is very real." The boys had practiced for this situation every day since Miguel had left, and she knew they would hurry.

As she turned to go back to the house, Frederica's heart skipped a beat when her eyes met those of a Union soldier. He was so young the hairs on his chin were barely noticeable. His eyes were cruel and cold, and Frederica's gaze was drawn to a long bayonet clasped in his right hand. His knuckles were white, and his jaw was set in a tight grimace.

Her heart pounded in her chest and her face grew hot. For a moment, she froze with panic, but she knew she had to think fast to keep herself and the children safe. She slowly placed the boys on the ground without letting her stare drop from the young man's eyes. Frederick ran behind her and buried his face in her skirt. Michael held Frederica's hand tightly and didn't say a word.

Judging from the soldier's posture, he seemed to be enjoying his newfound power over the unprotected woman. He strolled calmly up to Frederica and touched her face, then stroked her hair, letting the strands fall through his fingers. A chill ran up Frederica's spine, but she refused to show any outward sign of fear or weakness. "You are a beautiful woman, ma'am. The sea air must agree with you!" Little Frederick sobbed into his mother's skirt. Michael slowly let go of her hand.

The soldier pulled Frederica closer to him, and she could smell the sour breath wafting out of his open mouth. "I have a small favor I would like you to do for me. It's your duty to the Union, you see? It won't take long."

Suddenly the soldier cried out in pain. Michael had broken free, grabbed a shovel, and struck the soldier on the back of his head. Stunned, the man reached up and felt his head. His hand came away covered with blood, and he turned toward Michael, rage and loathing running across his face.

When he turned to face the boy, Frederica pushed him to the ground and jumped on top of him. She grabbed a heavy tabby brick with two hands and lifted it over the soldier's head. The door burst open, and before she could strike, she heard a booming voice call out, "Stop right there!"

A Yankee officer stood in the doorway with his Colt sidearm pointed at Frederica. As she stared, he pulled the hammer back with a click. Frederica rolled off of the young soldier, and her boys rushed to her side.

The officer lowered his revolver. A look of disgust passed over his face as he took in the scene. With a curse, he grabbed the soldier by the arm and pushed him back toward the house. The young soldier fell to the ground, but scrambled to his feet, holding the back of his head, as blood dripped through his fingers. The smirk had been wiped from his face, and his eyes were downcast with shame.

The officer nodded to Frederica. "We just needed a few supplies ma'am. I apologize for any worry that this boy may have caused you. We will be on our way directly."

Frederica let her shoulders relax. "Thank you, officer," she said softly.

Before he turned to leave, the officer looked at Michael. "You are a brave young man to protect your mother like that. You'll make a fine soldier someday."

Michael straightened up with pride. "Yes sir, just like my Papa." He kissed his mother's hand and smiled, and the officer left with the boyish soldier shuffling behind him.

On the Road to Knoxville, June 1862

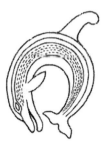

Tampa's citizens sent Company K off to war on June 27, 1862. Their departure was heralded with great fanfare and celebration. Women turned out in large numbers and cried as they waved handkerchiefs. The men of Company K marched through the streets of Tampa under a canopy of mossy oaks, and the old men gave them three cheers as the soldiers crossed the Hillsborough River and headed north.

The march to Brooksville took two days. The men averaged twenty-one miles per day as they trudged along on soft, sandy roads. During the third day out, it rained, and they found themselves marching in knee-deep mud. They were forced to take shelter from the storm in a flea-infested barn where they made a meal out of green corn.

Twenty of the men, including Miguel, hired two wagons at Brooksville to take them to Archer. There they caught the train for Tallahassee where they shouldered their knapsacks and marched to the Chattahoochee River. The steamer, *William Young*, waited to carry them to Columbus, Georgia.

After pitching their tents and stowing their gear, they had supper and spent that evening and the next day downtown. Columbus was the largest city Miguel had seen since he'd entered the country through the Port of New Orleans.

The next morning, they boarded a train and rode in an open boxcar. Many of the men hung over the side and vomited and cursed. Miguel assumed they were paying the devil for their drunken antics of the previous night. The train passed through Opelika, Alabama, headed to Atlanta, Georgia, and finally chugged into the depot at Chattanooga, Tennessee in the wee hours of July sixteenth. The men were too tired to set up camp, so they spent the night inside the car.

A shaft of sunlight found a place between a crack in the sideboards. It warmed Miguel's cheek and awakened him. It took him a moment to remember that he was still in the same corner of the boxcar where he had been cooped up for the duration of the fifteen-hour trip from Columbus to Chattanooga.

Miguel hadn't slept well and wanted to go back to sleep, but the smell of coffee brought him fully awake. He looked around and saw Alfred Lowe and several of the others were still sleeping off the peach brandy they had bought at the dinner stop at Opelika. Through the open door he spotted most of the others in his company huddled around a fire beside the track.

Miguel gathered his gear and paused for a moment in the doorway. The train was parked next to the train shed—a limestone and brick building with arched doorways. A train loaded with troops passed behind the building, and its smokestack belched thick, black smoke that shrouded the face of the rising sun like a widow's veil. Miguel looked back at the young, earnest faces of his sleeping companions. He wondered where they were headed and how many of them would not return home.

He was hungry and exhausted by the time they joined the rest of the 7th Florida Regiment at Camp Graham on the Tennessee River. They had gotten very little sleep over the past several days and had nothing to eat for over twenty hours.

The next morning, they headed to the quartermaster's tent to be issued their uniforms and other essential items. The quartermaster sergeant looked Miguel up and down and threw him a roundabout jacket. He tried it on and buttoned the six brass buttons. *A little bit large in the chest, which is good,* he thought. *I can wear a vest and a couple of shirts under it when the weather turns cold.* Miguel held up a sleeve and looked at the fabric. It was a very coarse wool—the color and texture reminded him of a corn sack.

The following day, Company K was sent to guard the railroad bridge at Loudon on the Tennessee River. Miguel took his turn on picket duty. His nerves were always on edge, for he knew that Yankees were all around them.

On occasion, pickets reported exchanging gunfire with Yankee snipers across the river, and his skin crawled as he walked the trestles, forever anticipating the whirring sound of a bullet streaking by his ear.

The next week, the regiment drilled together for the first time since they arrived in Tennessee. Pride swelled in Miguel as he looked down the line of sharply-dressed men in formation on the parade ground. They were beginning to look like an organized military unit.

On the first of August, they were sent to Knoxville and there they learned that they would soon be marching to Kentucky. On the twelfth, the men were issued three days rations and told to turn their tents over to the quartermaster. Miguel knew he would be sleeping under the stars for a while.

The following day, Miguel stood in the hot sun with the rest of the 7th Florida Regiment of Davis' 2nd Brigade. Their column stood four men abreast on the pike leading north out of Knoxville. They waited for the men of the 1st Brigade to move forward. The word was that the army was headed to the Cumberland Gap, where they were expecting to see their first action.

It was already late afternoon, and the ninety-degree heat was oppressive. Miguel removed his old brown slouch hat and poured water from his canteen over his head. The hat was stained with fish blood and misshapen by many Florida rains, but it was a symbol of his life in Florida, and he loved it dearly.

He was dressed in his new grey uniform, and around his waist he wore a cap box and bayonet scabbard on a black belt fitted with a brass-frame buckle. He carried a canvas haversack, canteen, and a leather cartridge box on a sling crammed with forty rounds of .577 ball cartridges for his brand-new Enfield rifle. His knapsack was loaded up with the clothing he had carried from home—three extra shirts, a black overcoat, and several pairs of socks. His old brown blanket was rolled up and tied around his body. He wore the old pair of brogan shoes that he had brought from home.

The order to move out was shouted at the head of the regimental column and relayed by the 1st sergeants of each company until it reached Company K. Sergeant Charles Berry barked, "Company. Forward!" Thus, fully accoutered, Miguel finally set off.

Miguel corrected his step to the cadence of the drum. Company K had marched with the rest of the 7th Regiment only a few times since they'd arrived in Knoxville two weeks ago, so there was a short period of adjustment before the company became a unified force. Far in the distance, he could see the head of Brigadier General Henry Heth's 2nd Division moving north along the Knoxville Pike. Their red battle flags streamed in the wind as they moved over the ridges like a great rattler hunting its prey.

The sullen utterances of the men of the great army hung in the air like the dust cloud kicked up by their boots. Miguel had a sinking feeling in the pit of his stomach—a queasy sensation that he blamed on excitement, but he knew it was fear. He tried to remind himself he was no longer a fisherman but a soldier. He felt the irony of this, for Menorcans tended to hate war, yet he had not been able to escape it since coming to America. He shook off the anxiety by recalling his days fighting the Seminoles. He was already a soldier. He had faced hardships before, and he could endure them again.

On the first day, the army passed through desolate farmland. Withered crops, brittle yellow grass, and dried up stream beds were the relics of a three-month drought. A flock of black crows, cawing wildly, appeared in the sky as they passed an apple orchard.

"Awww, hell no." Charlie Anderson said. "No sir, ain't a good sign at all. Them crows been sent to warn us what's waitin' up ahead."

"Shuddup, Charlie, It's jus' birds. Don' mean nuthin," his brother George scolded him. There was talk that there was bound to be a fight up ahead, and everyone felt they were headed for trouble. George knew everyone was as nervous as he was, and he didn't need to hear talk of bad omens.

When they halted at midnight, the men were completely used up. Miguel felt he had never been so tired in all his life.

He stripped off his gear, curled up in his blanket under a tree, and within moments fell fast asleep.

He dreamed that he was fishing on Tampa Bay with his oldest son Michael. *Dimples formed on the glass-smooth water, where little shiners fed near the surface. Suddenly a school of larger fish darted in among them, scales shimmering in the morning sun.*

"Michael, come look at the size of these mackerel!" Miguel shouted. Michael hurried to join his father by the starboard gunwale. He felt the warmth of his son's hand on his shoulder, and suddenly the hand tightened and shook him. Michael was pointing at the water.

A dorsal fin broke the surface and left a wide wake behind it. Miguel thought it was the largest shark he had ever seen, and it was headed directly for the boat. Its massive jaws broke the surface, and Miguel could see the whiteness of the shark's razor-sharp teeth contrasted against the raw reddish-pink flesh of its gaping mouth.

"Get up! Get up!"

He turned expecting to look into his son's eyes, but what he saw was the bearded face of Sergeant John Allison illuminated by the orange glow of the campfire. He was shaking Miguel's shoulder to wake him.

"Up! Rise 'n shine. Get some breakfast. We hit the road at daybreak," Allison said as he moved down the line and roused the slumbering men.

Miguel sat for a moment, head in his hands, and tried to compose himself. The dream had been so real. Seeing Michael's face and feeling his hand on his shoulder overwhelmed him and caused his throat to clench. What did the dream mean? Was it like Charlie Anderson's omen? Would he never see his family again? He cast the thought from his mind as if it was a scorpion in his bedroll, for he knew that fear is deadly to a soldier.

Miguel threw off his blanket and tried to get up, but his body wasn't cooperating. It felt like every bone had been broken. Shadowy figures of men with blankets draped over their shoulders moved about in the chilly predawn darkness. They shuffled off to relieve themselves while others hunted for firewood.

Miguel made his way over to join his friends and mess mates, Corporal Rofeno Fallis, Manuel Amon, and Francisco Diaz by the campfire. He poured water from his canteen into his tin cup and set it in the coals to boil. He fumbled in his haversack for his spoon and the little cloth bag of cane coffee Frederica had packed for him. He untied the string and poured the grounds into the cup.

"We march in an hour, Miguel. It's going to be a long day. Be sure to make yourself something to eat," Corporal Fallis said.

Miguel gave his coffee a stir with a spoon his wife had packed for him. The water spit and sizzled against the inside of the hot metal. After it boiled for several minutes, he pulled the cup out of the fire with a rag and waited for the grounds to settle. The spoon was one of Frederica's silver dinner spoons, marked "K" for Kramer. It was from her mother's silver set that she brought with her from Bavaria. Frederica only used it on special occasions. The last time he had seen it was when Frederica used it at Christmas dinner. His heart warmed as he realized his wife was reaching out to him across the miles.

Manuel Amon was busy rolling out dough on his tin plate and passing it out to the others. The frying pan and the rest of the cooking gear had been left with the baggage train, so the men improvised by twisting the wet dough around their ramrods and baking it in the fire.

Corporal Fallis' squad was made up of Spanish-speaking fishermen, so it was dubbed *Los Pescadores*, the Fishermen, by the men of Company K. Manuel Amon and Rofeno Fallis also spoke English fairly well, which was a great help to Miguel and Francisco, who spoke very little.

They were still drinking their coffee when they heard the call to form ranks.

"Fall in!" First Lieutenant Maloney called out.

Miguel pitched the rest of his coffee on the fire, tied his tin cup to the strap of his haversack, and fell into line next to Ben Asbury, a sailor from Manatee. Miguel wished him a good morning but got no response. Asbury's white hair and pale complexion made him appear corpse-like in the grey dawn. *Do I look that bad?* Miguel wondered, for his aversion to another long day of marching was surely sucking the life out of him. He could hear Frederica's voice in the back of his mind. *Gather yourself, soldier. A corpse won't raise your children.* Miguel let out a sigh before he took his first step into another day of war.

The Kentucky Campaign
August 1862

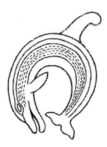

The army marched all day and crossed over a series of lofty ridges. Many of the Floridians had difficulty with the unfamiliar elevation, but Miguel's legs remembered hiking up Menorca's Monte Toro with his friends during his youth, so his steps were slightly less heavy than those of his companions.

The air was bone dry and hazy with the dust of the army's passing—it was as if they were trudging through a deep bed of ashes. Miguel looked at the men who marched beside him who were covered with dust from head to toe. Their grey uniforms had been relatively clean when they had left Knoxville, but this march turned them a dingy brown.

Ben Asbury's pale face was now black, and dirt ringed his eyes and caked around his mouth and nostrils. He was coughing uncontrollably. He asked Miguel to hold his musket while he dug in his haversack for his blue paisley handkerchief. He dampened it with water from his canteen, made a bandana out of it, and covered his mouth and nose to help him breathe. Miguel thought this was a good idea, so he did the same with the white handkerchief Frederica had made for him. Embroidered with his initials, it was much too fine for a soldier, but he silently thanked his wife for it all the same.

On the third day, they passed by a place called Jacksboro then turned northeast into the shadow of the Cumberland Mountains. That night they halted at Big Creek Gap. Company K rested in an orchard within the deep blue shadows of apple trees. When they were issued another three days rations and ordered to cook them, everyone realized they were soon going to cross the mountains into Kentucky.

Corporal Rofeno's squad was sent to forage for food and refill the company's canteens. Each of the six men headed down into the valley with six or eight empty canteens hanging on their shoulders. The tiny sounds of canteens clinking together reminded Miguel of cowbells, and this brought a smile to his face as he recalled summers spent driving cattle down the narrow stone-lined lanes of Menorca.

After a brief search, the men found a creek, but the bed was dry and cracked like most of the other creeks they had discovered over the last three days. Only one stagnant pool remained, and Miguel knelt by it and wiped green scum away from the surface. A school of water bugs scurried for cover.

"¡*No voy a beber eso!*" Miguel said.

"No, I'm not drinking that either," Corporal Fallis replied. "Let's keep going."

They continued down the valley, passed through a corn field, and emerged at the edge of a small farm. The men paused and surveyed the scene. The cabin had seen better days, but all the signs indicated it was indeed occupied. Chickens scurried across the front yard, and a cow grazed lazily in a field. A little girl was playing with a dirty rope doll on the front porch. A feather of smoke rose lazily from the chimney, and curtains billowed out from the open window. Miguel could smell the aroma of baking bread wafting through the air.

The men passed through a rusty gate and stopped next to a well. A large, black dog emerged from under the porch. Saliva dripped from his jaws, and his one jet-black eye glinted with menace. A low, threatening growl rolled out of his toothy mouth and was soon followed by angry barking.

The front door flew open and a thin, bedraggled woman emerged. Her clothes were worn and stained. She stood on the porch and stared at the men with fear in her eyes. A tiny girl peered out from behind her mother's skirts.

262

"We just want some water from your well is all ma'am. We'll be on our way after that," Corporal Fallis explained.

"Take what you want and leave us alone!" she cried and ran back inside the house, pulling the girl inside with her. The woman was about the same age as Frederica, and the sight of her touched Miguel in a way he hadn't expected. The war faded from his mind for a moment and his thoughts drifted homeward.

Manuel sent a bucket down the well with a splash, drew it back up, and filled the canteens with cool spring water. The clop of hooves made the men spin around and look toward the gate where two horsemen appeared seemingly from nowhere. Miguel and the others had been so preoccupied with thoughts of water they never heard the approaching horses.

A large man in a broad-brimmed slouch hat led a black man in chains behind him. A younger man, perhaps his son, followed behind the slave with a shotgun. The black man had a rope tied around his neck and was tethered to the older man's horse. Both men raised their shotguns and kept them trained on the intruders as they rode into the yard.

"What the hell you doin,' boys? You best git away from that well and git the hell off my prop-ty right now," the man bellowed.

Corporal Fallis held up his right hand. "We just needed some water, sir. We'll be on our way,"

"No sir, not for no Secesh scum, now git!" The sound of his shotgun's twin hammers snapping back to full cock told Miguel the man was serious.

"What's he done?" the corporal asked pointing at the black man.

"He's a runaway, not that it's any of your damn biss-ness," the younger man spat back.

Manuel and Francisco slowly brought their rifles up to the ready, but Corporal Fallis signaled for his men to put down their weapons.

"All right, all right. We're going!" he shouted back.

The older man kept his shotgun trained on the foragers as they backed out of the yard and turned down the road bordering the cornfield.

"He's a Tory, a Lincolnite if you will. He supports the Yankees," the corporal explained to the others. "Beats me why southerners support the Yankee cause. We're going to have to watch our backs. This state is full of those folks, and they are probably more dangerous to us right now than any Yankee soldier."

Manuel was grumbling about what should be done with southern men who supported the Yankees, but Miguel wasn't listening. He stared at the slave as the horsemen led him behind the house. Stripped to the waist, the man's black skin glistened with sweat, and his wrists were bloodied from the constant rubbing of his bonds. The look of sheer desperation in the man's eyes haunted Miguel.

"*Qué pasa?*" Manuel asked, noticing the somber expression on his friend's face.

"*Nada,*" Miguel lied. "It's nothing."

Once out of sight, the men stuffed their haversacks and coats with as much of the old Tory farmer's green corn as they could. They retraced their route back to the creek bed and found men from another company filling canteens at the stagnant pool. A queasy feeling crept into Miguel's stomach as he watched them. Company K was lucky indeed to have stumbled across the well of the Tory farmer.

The next morning the men were on the march again and headed for the Cumberland Mountains. Miguel thought that this must be the worst road he'd ever walked on in all his life. It was steep, deeply rutted, and littered with clothing and other items that soldiers had decided were non-essential. The road was strewn with the debris of a thousand weary men.

The brigade started across the mountains into Kentucky at a place called Big Creek Gap. The road was covered with a huge mass of soldiers that extended for miles and created a cloud of swirling dust that made breathing impossible. As the day wore on, the heat became almost unbearable, and men began dropping out of the ranks from sheer exhaustion.

Miguel's mouth was dry and his nose and throat burned with heavy dust. He supported his rifle in the crook of his left arm and reached for his canteen. He pulled the stopper out with his teeth and lifted it to his lips, but all he got was a warm mouthful of rusty sludge that he spat out in disgust. His back ached fiercely, and the straps of his knapsack rubbed his shoulders raw.

Miguel noticed Parson Edmund Lee marching several ranks ahead of him. The man was having a terrible coughing fit. He handed his musket to the file closer, 4th Sergeant William O'Neill, and fell to his knees by the side of the road as he hacked and gasped for breath.

The regiment continued to move down the road and left sick men behind to be picked up by a wagon train. Miguel was worried about Lee. The man had moved from Vermont to Florida in a last-ditch effort to survive consumption. He had recovered his health dramatically after moving to the warm Florida climate, but Miguel worried that the consumption had Lee in its filthy grip once again.

Miguel called out to the sergeant, "I'm going to check on Lee," then stepped out of the marching column and followed Lee down to the creek.

Sergeant William O'Neill, yelled out, "Make it quick!" Will, a friend of Miguel's, was married to Frederica's first cousin, Mary Nicholas. Will had been promoted to 4th Sergeant ten days ago, and it was now part of his duty to watch out for stragglers. Will knew that he could trust Miguel and was worried about Lee's health. He wondered why the parson had enlisted in the first place at his age.

Lee collapsed by the muddy bank of the stream bed. Miguel ran to him and rolled him over on his back. Covered in mud, Rev. Lee gasped, wide-eyed with fear, his lips turning blue. Miguel remembered the time when Frederica had saved their baby, Michael, once as he choked and stopped breathing. Lee looked much like Michael had on that awful day. Miguel sat Lee up and slapped him on the back hard several times. He cleared the thick mucus from his friend's nose and mouth using his now filthy handkerchief.

Miguel pulled the old man to the shade of a tree and leaned him against the trunk, then took the bandana from around his own neck and covered the parson's nose and mouth to keep out the dust. He reached for Edmund's canteen and shook it. There was still a little bit of precious water left.

"Drink." Miguel lifted the handkerchief and raised the canteen spout to Edmund's lips. Edmund opened his eyes and gave Miguel a slight smile. He sipped a tiny amount of water, hacked up some more thick mucus, and then drank a little more.

"Can't... breathe," Edmund gasped.

It's the damned dust, Miguel thought, and he feigned an encouraging smile for Lee's benefit. *I can hardly breathe myself.*

Miguel took their canteens and set off to see if there was any water left in the muddy stream bed. He found another little pool of stagnant water and managed to fill each of the canteens half-full. He returned to Lee, made a little fire, and boiled up some coffee.

As the 1st Florida Dismounted Cavalry was passing along the road behind them, Miguel knew that the supply train would be following close behind.

"Wagon's coming," Miguel told Edmund. "No more marching for you."

Miguel lifted the cup to Edmund's lips. "Here, drink this," he urged the parson. The hot coffee seemed to ease the coughing. When Miguel heard the rumble of wagons coming up the valley, he shouldered Edmund's pack and helped him up to the road.

One of the wagons was filled with sick men. Miguel jumped out in front of it, waved his arms, and urged the driver to stop. He helped Rev. Lee get on board and tried to make the parson comfortable by resting his back against his knapsack. Lee looked up at him with relief, "Thank you, Miguel, I won't forget this." Miguel patted Lee on the shoulder. "You good now, Parson. See you soon."

Miguel smiled, jumped off the back of the moving wagon, and stumbled over to the side of the road. The teamster slapped the reins against the rump of his horses, and the wagon lurched up the road.

Miguel knew he had to hurry to try to catch up with the 7th Florida He figured it must be several miles into Kentucky by now. He ran back to the trees to collect his gear.

He hoisted his pack, but when he felt his back muscles burning, he threw it down again. *I have to lighten this load*, he thought.

Anything that not absolutely necessary was accumulated in a pile at his feet—his extra pair of shoes, the suit of clothes he had worn from home, a pair of pants, four ears of corn, and the half dozen green apples that he had picked up back at the orchard.

He pulled out his black overcoat and paused—it was the one he had worn at his wedding. He couldn't part with it. Besides, it would feel so good in the winter. But, when he felt how heavy his pack still was, he yanked the coat out and regretfully threw it aside.

Miguel strapped on his pack, and this time, his back muscles didn't complain as loudly about the load. He slung his rifle over his shoulder and ran up the valley road into the swirl of grey dust.

Ambush at Big Creek Gap, September 1862

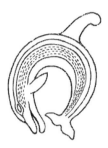

Miguel ran at the double-quick as he tried to catch up to his company. His side began to hurt, and his leg muscles cramped, but he pushed himself as hard as his aching body would allow. When he caught up with the 1st Florida Cavalry, he decided to fall in with them to catch his breath.

He shook his canteen—it was empty. A 5th Sergeant who marched behind the rear rank saw that Miguel was out of water and approached the exhausted soldier.

"What regiment are you with private?" the sergeant asked as he handed Miguel his canteen.

"The 7th," Miguel replied.

"They are way up ahead of the 6th, but you can fall in with us if you'd like."

"Gracias," Miguel answered, and he pulled the cork from the canteen's neck and took a long draught.

Davis' brigade was now in Kentucky and headed northeast along the narrow Wilderness Road, bordered on both sides by steep hills and thick woods. The infantry marched ahead of the supply wagons, so the soldiers had to live on the green apples and corn that they foraged along the way. The fields had mostly been picked clean by the time the 1st Cavalry reached them, so the men were out of luck until the wagons caught up with them at camp.

Miguel pulled a handful of parched corn from his pocket. Crunching on the hard kernels was beginning to hurt his teeth. A rustling sound in the woods to his right caught his attention and a flock of quail suddenly burst from the trees. He was imagining how a couple of them would taste roasted when he heard a whirring sound like a large bumble bee passing by his head. It was followed by a dull thud, a groan, and the crack of a rifle shot reverberating across the valley.

Someone behind him gasped, "Good God, I'm hit!" Miguel turned and saw a man lying on the ground. He desperately ripped at his coat to see where he was hit. As the victim's blue-checkered shirt turned red from the fountain of blood that spurted out of his abdomen, Miguel knew the wound was mortal.

There was a moment of complete silence and every man in the column paused as their fatigued minds struggled to process what had just happened. After what seemed like an eternity, one of the men cried, "Sniper!"

Tongues of flame shot out from the woods and filled the air with the hum of bullets. A man near Miguel was hit in the leg, and another man behind him was struck in the shoulder and spun around from the force of the shot. The column dissolved into confusion. Some men ran and sought cover while others stood their ground, raised their muskets, and returned fire. They aimed at the white puffs of smoke lingering in the trees and prayed that their blind shots would find a Yankee target.

Miguel felt helpless, so when a sergeant called for volunteers to flank the attackers he raised his hand. It seemed a better choice than remaining where he was. He ran with twenty-five other volunteers deep into the woods. They tore through scrub trees and vines—their rifles up at right shoulder-shift. They held canteens and haversacks tightly against their hips, so they wouldn't rattle. Another volley erupted from the bushwhackers hidden in the thick woods to their left.

The volunteers came upon a dried-up streambed a hundred yards or so behind the enemy position. "Take intervals," the sergeant whispered, and he signaled to his men to extend the line down the creek with a five-pace gap between each man.

The sergeant directed his men to take cover behind the bank and whatever brush they could find to conceal themselves.

The sergeant's next command was loud and clear despite the whisper, "Fix bayonets." Miguel's heart pounded even harder, it seemed all hell was about to break loose in this Kentucky forest.

The rest of the 1st Cavalry were pressing the bushwhackers directly toward them. He heard another volley of rifle fire echo through the woods, followed by the distinctive panther-like scream known as the rebel yell.

"Whoh-who-ey! Who-ey! Yai-yai-yi!" This was the first time that Miguel had heard the yell in action, giving a chill up and down his spine.

The bushwhackers returned fire on the advancing Confederate line, did an about-face, and retreated toward the secluded valley behind the creek bed where Miguel and his fellow soldiers lay in wait.

Miguel saw a group of twenty-five or thirty men wearing blue roundabout jackets and forage caps emerge from the woods. These weren't Tory militia men, they were a detachment of highly-trained Yankee infantry. Miguel's heart pounded even faster, and he had to remind himself to take a breath.

The 1st Cavalry sergeant called out, "Ready." Miguel and the others snapped their rifle hammers back to full cock.

"Aim." They raised their rifles to their shoulders, and Miguel sighted down his barrel at the shiny brass cartridge box plate of a Yankee soldier who ran directly toward him.

"Fire!" the sergeant shouted.

Rifles thundered from behind the creek bank, and a volley of hot lead crashed into the retreating Yankees. Several of the men were stopped dead in their tracks. Miguel swore, in later years, that the man he aimed at was thrown backwards by the force of the round that struck him.

Several dead and wounded lay on the ground, as the rest of the 1st Cavalry closed in from behind. Realizing they were trapped, the Yankees held their rifle butts high in the air to indicate they intended to surrender.

The Confederates emerged from their concealed positions and approached the Yankees with bayonet-tipped rifles. Miguel looked down at the youthful face of one of the dead soldiers lying at his feet. The Yankee's brown eyes stared blankly up at the clouds floating overhead. His brass cartridge box plate was splattered with blood from the mortal chest wound he had taken. *My God, he's just a boy*, thought Miguel, and a shudder of horror passed through him. He hoped it hadn't been his bullet that killed the boy.

The 1st Cavalry formed ranks again and headed back up the valley to the main road. Miguel's squad was put in charge of escorting twenty-two captured Yankees. Behind them lay the bodies of five dead Union soldiers along with several wounded men who were captured and would be paroled.

After dealing with the ambush, Davis' brigade continued on toward Barboursville. When they arrived outside the little town and made camp, Miguel found the 7th Regiment and walked into the campsite of Company K. He heard Lieutenant Maloney trying to calm down a group of red-faced men who were complaining that the 7th was being left here as a rear guard to escort the baggage train.

"Why should we sit here while the rest of Smith's Corps press on toward Lexington?" a stocky private yelled. The rest of the men muttered in agreement. The men were annoyed that they would probably miss out on their very first battle. Miguel wanted to tell them they shouldn't seek out the death and chaos that he had just experienced, but he knew they would never listen to him now that their blood was up. He trudged further into the camp, found Manuel, and threw his blanket down beside him.

The bothersome snoring of the sleeping men made it hard for him to fall asleep. Miguel kicked Manuel's foot hard. This stopped the snoring temporarily, but soon the irritating snorts began again.

He lay awake for hours, unable to get the young Yankee soldier and his soon to be grieving family out of his head. Thoughts of that family shifted to his own family back at Miguel's Bay. What would happen to Frederica and the boys if he didn't make it home? He looked up at the full moon as it rode high over the Kentucky hills. The thought occurred to him that the same pale moonlight was shimmering on the waters of Miguel's Bay at that very moment. He pictured his family safe in their beds, allowing Miguel to drift off to sleep.

***

In the week that followed, General Kirby Smith's Army of Kentucky, led by the 3rd and 4th Divisions, moved north toward Lexington. They sought supplies to feed his 19,000 troops. The general discovered, as his men knew well already, that food was in short supply. The 7th Florida followed behind with Heth's 2nd Division to escort the supply wagons.

As they neared Richmond on August thirtieth, the loud and continuous roar of cannon fire could be heard ahead. The lead divisions had engaged the enemy. The sounds of small arms and artillery mingled into one deafening roar and motivated the men of the 7th Florida. The night before, when they were issued only four ounces of beef and one biscuit as their daily ration, their morale had taken a turn for the worse.

"Whoo-ee! Churchill and Cleburne are kicking some tail up there, boys!" Captain Smith called out to the men of Company K. "Don't worry, you'll get your piece of this soon enough."

The long grey column continued to march through the endless miles of forest as they approached Kentucky's fertile bluegrass region. They were accompanied by the shrill sound of fifes and the rat-a-tat-tat of drums playing *Bonnie Blue Flag*, but the marching music could not quite drown out the thunder of the battle that lay ahead of them.

> *We are a band of brothers and natives to the soil*
> *Fighting for our liberty, with treasure, blood and toil*
> *And when our rights were threatened, the cry rose near and far*
> *Hurrah for the Bonnie Blue Flag that bears a single star!*
> *Hurrah! Hurrah!*
> *For Southern rights, hurrah!*
> *Hurrah for the Bonnie Blue Flag that bears a single star.*

The sound of singing abated, and the mood turned somber when they crossed over the last hill on the Richmond Road. The battlefield stretched out before them. In the distance, Miguel could see three churches. Their broken steeples jutted through a cloud of curling black smoke and flames, engulfing the neighboring buildings. Miguel remembered it was Sunday and it saddened him to think there were no pipe organs playing or singing to be heard.

The fields south of town were littered with the dead. Miguel saw that most of the corpses wore blue—the battle had been a brutal and costly one for the Yankees. The road leading into town was strewn with clothing and equipment cast off by the retreating Union army.

They marched past an exploded Confederate artillery caisson and Napoleon gun. The dead horses and contorted bodies of the gun crew lay scattered around a crater of burnt earth. In the surrounding fields, ambulance wagons attended to the wounded and details were already busy burying the dead.

As they marched down Main Street, the 7th passed one of the churches Miguel had seen from the edge of the battlefield. Through the open windows, he could hear the mournful wailing of men in agony. A man appeared in the doorway wearing a blood-soaked apron, carrying a bloody saw. Miguel knew he must be a surgeon.

The doctor touched the brim of his hat in salute as the regiment marched by. "Give 'em hell, boys!" he said. An attendant pushed by him with a wheelbarrow full of amputated arms and legs. He dumped them on the curb and scurried back into the church to collect more of his grisly cargo.

"Look at that," Manuel said to Miguel, and pointed to the pile. "Poor devils, I guess they won't be walking home." He smirked.

Miguel glared at Manuel disapprovingly, "That could well be us before this is over!" he said.
"Lighten up, amigo! If we can't laugh, we may go crazy," Manuel scoffed. "Look at what happened to these poor soldiers. They sacrificed their body parts, for what? Nothing.

Does that sound like a sane world to you? That's the good ol' C.S.A. for you—which stands for Corn, Salt and Apples, you know."

Miguel smiled wryly, for he knew his friend had a good heart. He certainly understood why Manuel hated the Confederacy. They were given half the rations the army regulations called for, and they relied on what they could forage for themselves in the fields. The lack of support from the Confederate government disgruntled the men.

Blood from the pile of amputated limbs trickled into the street. It stained their boots as they walked through it. Miguel looked at the faces of the green recruits around him, and he could see that they had all lost the urge to find the fight.

When they arrived in Lexington on the second of September, a huge crowd welcomed them. Hundreds of men, women, and children waved handkerchiefs, threw up hats, and applauded and shouted loud "hurrahs" as they celebrated the victory at Richmond. Confederate flags flew from every window, and patriotic banners hung across every storefront. Miguel had never witnessed such an ovation, and it lifted his spirits considerably.

The 7th Regiment and the rest of Heth's 6,000 troops were sent to threaten Cincinnati. The harsh terrain disappeared, so the long marches of nearly sixteen miles per day were much easier. When they arrived at the town of Crittendon, thirty-five miles south of Cincinnati, the men of Company K were again excited. They fully expected to cross the Ohio River and take part in the war's first invasion of the North. The city was incredibly well-fortified, causing General Smith to reconsider and withdraw Heth's Division.

The day they marched back to Lexington was particularly hot and humid. The order was given to fall out and take a fifteen-minute rest. Miguel found a shady spot under a large tree and sprawled out in the cool grass, using his knapsack as a pillow. He had learned early in the campaign that a soldier must sleep whenever he can.

Charlie Anderson was fumbling around in his haversack for something to eat. "I don't know about you fellows, but I'm getting plenty sick and tired of marching to God-knows-where and back again and seeing no action." he grumbled. Miguel reached into his haversack and tossed a green apple to Charlie. "Here you go, this will make you feel better," he said with a big smile.

Charlie threw the apple back. "Aw hell no, I don't ever want to see another apple for as long as I live once this war is over! Not another ear of corn neither." he said

On the march to Frankfort, they encountered a deadly and unexpected enemy. Some of the Company K boys, including Charlie and Manuel of the "Fishermen's Mess," became very sick one night with a disorder of the bowels. Charlie suffered from bloody diarrhea and burned with fever. Two days later, he collapsed and died by the side of the road.

Confederate generals Braxton Bragg and Edmund Kirby Smith had assembled a force of 12,000 Southern troops at Frankfort. When intelligence was received that the Yankees were marching out of Lexington and trying to outflank them with 60,000 men, orders were quickly given to evacuate the city.

"Word is, we're movin' south. They say there's bound to be a big fight comin'," Asa Bishop told his Manatee friends.

Manuel complained, "They'll kill us first with all this marching." He was finally able to keep food down but was suffering from chronic diarrhea. In his weakened condition he found it difficult to keep up with the others.

Miguel was concerned that his friend would be captured by the enemy if he dropped out by the side of the road, so he carried his friend's rifle and knapsack as far as Harrodsburg where they finally stopped and made camp. Manuel was placed on the sick list and was exempted from duty.

Miguel and the rest of the company spent the next several days on guard duty when they weren't looking for food. On the morning of October fourth, they were in the rifle pits on the outer perimeter of the camp when they heard heavy firing in their front. This meant that their skirmishers had made contact with Union forces. Battle was imminent, and it could come as soon as that evening or tomorrow.

The men were excited that the 7th Florida would finally earn its laurels in battle, but when they returned to camp later that afternoon, they saw that the regiment was moving out. They would be on the march again tonight. They were headed back to Knoxville, Tennessee.

A Fireside Chat

It was the fall of 1862. The War Between the States was dragging out much longer than anyone had imagined. Men would die, yes, but many would survive in a broken and hopeless state. They would all come home changed, never again would they be the men they once were. The women hoped desperately that the bodies and souls of their men would be spared. War does not respect gender, age, or social standing.

It was barely six in the evening, and Aunt Julia had barred the door. She closed the shutters on the windows in an attempt to block light from shining out into the darkness. The guns were loaded and placed by the front and back windows. The Atzeroth store would not be an easy target for raiders or ruffians.

Eliza put supper on the table then hurried back to the kitchen to hide the sugar, flour, salt, and other valuable ingredients that she used in her cooking. One never knew when a raid might occur, and hungry soldiers would take anything that wasn't nailed to the floor. Her set of fine dishes had been hidden in the barn for so long she could barely remember what they looked like. Supplies were buried in the garden for safe keeping.

Frederica brought in a pail of water. She washed the boys' faces and hands with part of it and kept the rest for cleaning the plates and forks. She longed for the day when they would have enough water for a hot bath. They spent as little time as possible outside these days—trips to the spring were even dangerous.

It was amazing to Frederica how Aunt Julia and Eliza could take simple ingredients and make such delicious dishes. Aunt Julia even made little cookies brushed with honey for the boys. She cut the children's initials into the tops of the cookies. The delighted boys gave her a hug and kiss.

It had grown very cold, and the wind whistled past the eaves. The darkness always brought an uneasiness to the women. Mary had wanted to stay in Manatee with some of the other ladies, but Julia insisted that the village houses and plantations would be targeted sooner by the Union troops than those north of the river or on Terrasilla Island.

Frederick put his little hands together and offered a blessing, "Please God, watch over Papa and Uncle Joe. Don't let them get dead or hurt. Help them remember how to get home." There was a silence around the table. He had forgotten to be thankful for the food, but, moved by the boy's genuine concern for his father and uncle, none of the women corrected him.

The four women gathered in front of the fireplace to relax after finishing the evening chores. The children were tucked into bed, and Frederica, Julia, Mary and Eliza were exhausted. The war was taking its toll on them, since they were forced to complete their normal chores in addition to the work usually handled by the men. They missed seeing their friends and neighbors. The weeks dragged on, and the war had become the new reality.

Frederica put her aching feet close to the hearth as the fire blazed. The mood was somber, no one spoke, and even the dog looked miserable. Finally, Frederica broke the silence. "Aunt Julia, would you like me to teach you how to weave a cast net tonight? I was planning on starting a small one." She attempted to sound cheerful as she spoke.

"No!" Her aunt snarled. I don't want anything to do with fish, or with any old fisherman!"

Frederica smiled, "Oh, c'mon Auntie, you know you love smoked mullet, and I know you love my Miguel, no matter what you say!"

"We have eaten so much fish lately that I fear I will wake up in the morning and find fins growing out of my back!" Julia snapped. "And Señor Guerrero looks like an old worn out egret with half of his white head-feathers gone."

Frederica laughed, "Oh, you are just jealous! Snow on the roof means fire in the fireplace."

Julia snapped, "Girl, you keep your marriage secrets to yourself." All four women giggled hysterically.

Frederica gained control of her laughter. "I am making nets for every woman I know," she said. "There are enough fish in the sea to provide food for all of us. Women just need to learn how to cast a net and there will always be food available. I am sure there are women up north starving to death because the winter cold keeps them from their gardens and cattle, but down here we have all we need to survive."

Eliza nodded in agreement, "Miguel will be surprised when he comes home and finds that every woman in this county owns a net of her own and knows how to throw a perfect circle. We may put his fishing buddies out of business!"

Julia stared into the fireplace. "*If Miguel makes it home...*" she said, her voice barely audible. "He and my Joe are older than any of the other men. They may not have enough food, and I am sure they are sleeping on the cold, hard ground. They will be easy targets for a young soldier's bullet, or they could be struck down by disease in their weakened state."

Frederica jumped to her feet. "You mark my words, Julia! Miguel Guerrero *will* return home in one piece, and he won't walk home like all of the others. He'll find every river between here and Tennessee, and he'll get a boat to make his way south. As soon as he gets to Gainesville, his feet will know the rest of the way."

Julia's voice warmed at Frederica's passionate speech. "Yes dear, he will certainly make it home. Nothing will keep him from his beautiful Frederica and his boys, and I hope my Joe will be by his side as they walk through that gate."

Return to Knoxville, October 1862

It was a hot, dusty march to Cumberland Gap. Miguel's lips were dry and cracked, and his mouth felt like he'd been eating cotton. He removed the canteen from his left hip, shook it—it was nearly empty. He decided that he'd better take a sip of the remaining water. The Drought of 1862 made it increasingly difficult to find water, so the men kept a sharp eye for any little creek or pond where they could refill their canteens.

As they marched along, they came upon a small swale between the ridges. Miguel, Parson Lee, and Joseph Atzeroth fell out to hunt for water. When Joseph reached the bottom of the swale, his boots sank in the mud.

"There's water here!" Joseph exclaimed with a broad smile. "Help me dig."

They reached into their haversacks, pulled out their tin plates, and dug down until they reached a tiny pool of murky, brown water. They filled their canteens with the liquid and were heading to the road when the Parson spotted movement to their right.

"Look! There's a cornfield." Lee said pointing up the ridge. Shadowy figures moved up and down the corn rows.

When they arrived, they found soldiers from another regiment filling their haversacks with ears of corn. It struck Miguel funny that they all seemed right at home in the cornfield, like scarecrows among the stalks of ripe corn and pumpkin vines. Many of the men were barefoot, and their clothes hung in tatters.

It was no wonder that their generals had decided to withdraw from Kentucky in spite of the success they'd achieved. The men were in a deplorable state—ill-fed and insufficiently clothed to survive the approaching winter. Miguel was glad that they were leaving Kentucky and going back to Knoxville, where they would have better rations and access to winter quarters.

After three days, men began falling out of the column. This included Parson Lee, who had to fall out and wait for the wagon after he developed a severe cough and began spitting up brown mucus.

Miguel's throat tightened and his eyes filled with tears when Edmund handed him a letter addressed to his wife Electa.

Miguel solemnly promised to mail it as soon as he reached Knoxville.

The regiment moved on toward the Gap and left the sick men by the side of the road. Joseph marched beside Miguel. The men were lost in their thoughts for a long time until Joseph put into words what was on their minds.

"I think Lee's goose is cooked," Joseph muttered.

Sergeant O'Neil overheard the conversation. "Well, don't count him out yet, he's a tough old bird. He's being discharged, which I knew would happen—didn't know if it would be signed by the Lord's hand or the Colonel's. I can tell you this, he's definitely not planning on quitting."

"Not quitting?" Joseph gave him a puzzled look. "What will he do then?"

"I overheard him talking to the Captain." McNeil said wryly. "He said he'll do whatever he can for the cause—maybe even work in a hospital as a chaplain. He was very insistent on *not* going home yet."

Miguel's thoughts turned to Manuel. He hated leaving him in Harrodsburg in such poor condition. He wondered if the same fate would befall him as it had Charlie Anderson and their friend Bill McLaughlin. Bill had been left sick at a hospital in Boston, Kentucky and died only days later.

Miguel sighed and wondered if he would ever see his fishing buddy again.

The following day a cold front blew in from the north. It was October tenth, but the wind, rain, and drastic temperature drop made it feel like winter had arrived. Miguel's only worry was how to stay warm and dry.

The men slept under the stars in fifty-two-degree weather with nothing but a blanket, laying in a half-inch of water made it even worse. Shivering uncontrollably, Miguel and his pards finally gave up and spent the night standing with their wet blankets wrapped around themselves. They huddled together like a herd of cows standing in a storm, waiting for the morning sun.

Under leaden skies, the column moved slowly through Cumberland Gap. Miguel shivered in his thin, wet jacket— unable to dry out and get warm. His empty stomach weakened him. He had, in fact, taken sick with fever, and a dreadful pain wracked his chest and sides. His Fishermen's Mess mates took turns carrying Miguel's knapsack and rifle as he struggled to put one foot in front of the other. After five days of steady marching, they arrived in Knoxville, and Miguel was sent directly to an old mansion outside of town that served as a hospital.

As Miguel stumbled up the front steps, he saw a group of men convalescing on the front porch. They were smoking pipes and playing cards. One of them shouted, "Miguel!

Miguel!" It was Joseph Woodruff, who had been sick and left behind when the regiment marched to Kentucky.

"Good Lawd, look at you, Miguel! I wouldn't have known you but for that old brown hat. Din't they feed you boys on that trip?" Miguel looked weak and thin—his face sweaty and flushed with fever. "Come in here and lay down, I'll git ya' some water."

Joseph helped Miguel inside and found an empty cot for him in the front parlor. "Ya' caught me jus' in time, ol' friend. I got my discharge papers!"

"*¿Te vas a casa?*" Miguel asked in a weak voice.

"Yes, I'm going home. I'll warn the mullet that you'll be coming right behind me!"

"Don't do that." Miguel laughed. "I want to surprise them!"

Joseph lifted Miguel's head with one hand, and with the other, he held a flask of whiskey to his friend's lips. Miguel's hair was soaked with sweat. "This might help break your fever, old friend. It will ease the pain."

The next morning Miguel's fever had broken, but he was still very weak. Joseph brought him a bowl of beef broth and slice of hard bread and sat with him as he ate. "Is there anythin' you want me to take to Frederica? Somethin' you want me to tell her?"

"A letter, I want to write her a letter," Miguel answered. "But she won't be able to read it."

Joseph thought for a moment. "There's a man I play cards with—a German who speaks English very well. I'll git him to help you with the letter."

"¡Magnífico! Now, I have to think about what I will say. Women never run out of words, but we are not so lucky." Miguel laughed.

Joseph returned later that morning with a young Confederate officer. Miguel dictated his words to Joseph in Spanish, and Joseph translated them to the officer in English. He carefully wrote the German words in beautiful, flowing script.

"She'll know that I didn't write that." Miguel chuckled. "My writing is like chicken scratch."

"Here, you sign it, she'll recognize your hand," Joseph reassured him.

Miguel took the pencil in hand and scrawled, MIGUEL at the bottom. Joseph took the letter from him, folded it, and placed it in his breast pocket. "The next eyes that read this will be Frederica's," Joseph said. He embraced his friend, picked up his pack, and disappeared through the mansion's front door.

***

Within a week the doctor proclaimed Miguel fit for duty again, even though his chest pain hadn't fully cleared. He was sent to rejoin the 7th Florida, which had been deployed along the railroad lines. Their crucial job was to guard the railway bridges that served as vital links in the supply chain.

It was bitterly cold—unusual for Tennessee this time of year. The men of Florida were unaccustomed and completely unprepared for these temperatures. The night wind numbed Miguel's face, and his eyes stung from the cold as he walked the trestles, keeping watch.

Tory militiamen were known to take potshots from across the river at the guards. Miguel was nearly frozen by the time his watch was over. He found a small campfire behind the log barricades and laid down to try to get some sleep, despite the bitter cold.

Miguel rolled up in the only blanket he had. He covered his head to trap his body heat, leaving a small opening just big enough to catch a breath. His hipbone grew numb and his backside cold, so he continually shifted positions like a hog on a spit. This resulted in night after night of restless sleep.

Come early November, Miguel and a dozen men in his company became ill with a respiratory ailment, and they were sent back to the hospital in Knoxville. Miguel was given laudanum to help with his pain and ease his violent coughing spells. The drug was given for several weeks as his terrible cough lingered.

A Welcome Visitor

Frederica dipped her pen into the ink well and carefully drew a large "X" through November 5, 1862. She closed the door to the cabin, walked around to the side porch, and sat on the wooden bench. She stared down the shell road as she did every evening about this time. *Am I looking for someone? Why don't I ever watch the sunsets from the front porch?*

Evening was the only part of the day she reserved for solitude and quiet reflection. She found that staying busy during the day kept her mind from drifting into bouts of worry and sadness. Sometimes she thought if she stared long and hard enough at the road, she might will Miguel's figure to appear. She could almost see his long strides as he approached the cabin.

During her reverie, the boys had scaled the fence and were walking the top rail like gymnasts on the balance beam in a Bavarian circus. In her mother voice, she yelled "Get down from there, boys, you might fall!" The boys turned to her, smiled and giggled in unison, each pretending he never heard her command.

The Guerrero boys had worn her slap out today, and she hoped they would use up every last bit of energy and fall asleep instantly when she put them to bed.

She turned her gaze back to the road. Her heart skipped a beat as she made out the figure of a man coming around the bend.

Frederica stood and leaned over the rail to get a better look. It wasn't Miguel, she could tell by his gait, but the figure looked familiar. As he drew closer, she recognized him.

"Joseph Woodruff!" she yelled at the top her lungs. Optimism and well-being shot through Frederica, as she ran down the steps and into the road to meet her visitor. Joseph smiled and raised his hand in greeting. The thought ran through her mind that he may be the bearer of bad news, but the exuberant grin on Joseph's face reassured her that the tidings would be good.

Joseph was one of Miguel's best friends. He lived south of the Guerrero's near Whitaker Bayou, and he once worked on the Snell Rancho with Miguel in his early fishing days.

Miguel and Joseph had not only fished together, but they also served in the Seminole War, and both men enlisted in Company K in support of the Confederacy.

Joseph was close to Miguel's age, and he could speak Spanish, English, and some German. He was a blessing to the Guerrero family because he readily volunteered his services as a translator when called on.

When Frederica reached him, she threw her arms around him and nearly knocked him down. She immediately noticed how weak and thin Joseph appeared. She pulled back, looked into his eyes, and could tell he had been sick. Frederica had expected the healthy, hearty man who had left for the war, but she was looking at an old man, dirty and worn.

She steadied him as they walked the rest of the way to the cabin, then she carefully pulled him inside and sat him down to rest. The boys were excited to see their Papa's friend, but they sensed they needed to be quiet and give him some much-needed peace.

Michael put Joseph's hat on the hook by the door and hurried to get him a cool drink of water. Frederick grabbed a wet rag and gently washed Joseph's face and neck to cool him down.

As Frederica fixed a meal for the weary soldier, he began to talk. "My dear, our men have already had a rough go of it. Eddie Curry and I took sick something terrible from the heat and dusty roads. Walking all day and sleeping on the hard ground every night was much tougher on us older men, not to mention that there was never enough food to go around.

We traveled by stage from Brooksville to Tampa last night."

"And Miguel?" Frederica anxiously interrupted. "Is he well?"

"He's hangin' in there" Joseph answered, "as far as I know. After we left Terrasilla we walked to Archer, then took a train to the Chattahoochee River. From there we boarded a steamboat up to Columbus, and then rode another train to Knoxville, where we met up with the rest of the 7th Regiment. That's the last time I saw your Miguel. We heard from some of the boys discharged from Kentucky that there was a big battle at Richmond, but I don't think the 7th Florida was in it. That's all I know Frederica."

She was disappointed that Joseph didn't have more current news, and he could see it on her face.

"I'm sorry I don't have better news for you," Joseph said. "But at least you know three months ago he was still breathin'!" He tried to sound encouraging. "Miguel made it to Knoxville, and that was not an easy journey, even for the younger men!"

Frederica was quiet as she envisioned the details of the trip. She wiped her hands on her apron while her imagination ran wild and conjured up horrific scenes of war and death.

Joseph got up from his chair, wrapped his arms around her, and whispered, "I know you miss him dearly and are worried sick. Maybe this will lift your spirits." He reached into his pocket and pulled out two tattered and dirty envelopes. "Papa Guerrero sends mail to his beautiful wife and handsome sons."

The boys squealed and grabbed for the envelopes. Joseph handed the precious delivery to Frederica over their heads. After a month of hard travel, he was relieved to finally deliver the letters.

Frederica carefully put the letters into the pocket of her apron. She was anxious for everyone to go to bed so she could read her husband's words in private.

A sudden rainstorm the day before had filled the rain barrel with enough water for Frederica to draw a warm bath for Joseph. She found clean clothes Miguel had left behind.

As her guest soaked in the warm, soapy water, the boys sat next to the tub like Seminole braves around a campfire. From the other room, Frederica could hear Joseph telling the boys stories of the war. He was careful to leave out the sad and gory details, and each story made Papa Miguel sound like a hero. He told the boys that the war would be over soon, and that their father would surely come home as quickly as he could.

***

After the long soak, Joseph dressed and came to the kitchen table. The bath had revived him, and he smiled as he looked at the wonderful supper that Frederica had prepared. He ate a plate full of fish and stewed garden vegetables with two hunks of cornbread. Being a simple man who didn't put on airs, he always enjoyed Frederica's hearty country cooking. Later Frederica served two pieces of blackberry pie and a piping hot cup of coffee. Joseph could feel his vitality return to him as the delicious food nourished his body, and the company of Frederica and the boys fed his soul.

***

The sun dipped into the warm gulf waters, and an evening shower pelted the cabin with raindrops. The boys insisted that Mr. Joseph sleep in their bed, since they loved having an excuse to join their mother in her big bed.

As Joseph lay down in the safety and comfort of the cabin, he pulled the covers up around his chin and didn't move again. His soft, rhythmic snoring could be heard from behind the drawn curtain.

Frederica hurried the boys to bed so that she could read Miguel's letter in peace and quiet. As she sat by the fire, she quietly laughed at the misspelled words and odd phrases but savored every word she could recognize. She knew that someone must have written this message for Miguel.

My Dearest Frederica,

How fortunate I am to have this opportunity to write you by the hand of a kind fellow who is fluent in both our tongues. Providence has put us together in this strange place.

I hope that you are not alarmed that this letter has been posted from a hospital. I have been here since early November. I assure you that I have not been wounded or disabled. I have contracted chronic rheumatism and was found to be unfit for duty.

How often I have wished that we could converse once again as husband and wife. Yet ours has been a love which has required no words to be spoken between us. Now that the opportunity has come to write, I hardly know what to say!

My time in this place of sickness and death has caused me to think about a great many things, but you have always been in the forefront of my thoughts.

It is true, as you have suspected, that I was married before in my home country. It was an impulsive marriage between two young people anxious to escape a war-torn country to seek opportunity in America.

Since her death, my heart's desire had always been to find true love.

The first time I saw you, my dear Frederica, the North Star was reflected in your brown eyes, and they immediately drew my soul into safe harbor. God surely favored me by sending you to save my drowning soul.

What strange magic it is when two souls meet and know instantly that they belong together! Their hearts become tightly bound and are able to weather the crashing waves of life. After finding you, I was once again able to navigate the troubles of this harsh world.

I feel complete and at peace when we are together, and I am so empty when we are apart. How cruel it is that throughout our short time together, the storms of life continually blow us apart.

Due to my poor health, I hope to be discharged from this place soon. I promise that I will summon all of the strength left within me to arrive safely at your door, and I will never leave you again. If fate conspires against us, and we are not destined to meet again in this world, then promise me, my love, that you will find me in heaven.

Your affectionate husband,

Miguel

P.S. - Michael and Frederick, your father loves you with all his heart. Continue to care for your mother as the men

of the house in my absence. Remember to keep the nets
washed and clean. I will fish with you again soon.
- Love, Papa

Knoxville Hospital, Tennessee
November 12, 1862

Frederica could sense her husband's love through the worn paper and faded ink. It gave her hope that she would see him in person one day soon. She traced his signature with her finger and imagined that she could feel his hand as he wrote each letter.

Frederica knew that "coming home soon" might mean Miguel had to be discharged because of an injury or a disability of some sort. She would need to prepare herself and the boys for the fact that their Papa might return to them with injuries of the body or mind. These thoughts filled her head as she climbed into bed with her sleeping boys.

The next morning Frederica cooked a huge breakfast of pancakes, mangoes, and fresh milk. Joseph savored every mouthful, and Frederica witnessed him transform into his old self again before her very eyes. She gave him a small jar of her honey and whiskey cough medicine along with a basket of food to get him through the day.

As she hugged him goodbye, she warned him that his homestead might not be in the same condition that he had left it.

As her friend walked down the path, Frederica silently prayed that his family would be found safe and sound with a roof over their heads and food in good supply.

Joseph turned back to the family when he reached the bend in the shell road and shouted, "Don't you worry, your old fisherman will return to you soon!"

The Christmas Care Package

It was an unusual November day on the island and the cold and dreariness of winter had given way to a warm, sunny day. Frederica had just put the boys down for their afternoon nap. Her aunt would check on the boys as she puttered around the house and store, so Frederica took the opportunity to climb into her little sailboat to visit the Lee's store in Manatee Village. The sun warmed her on the journey, and she was grateful for a little bit of time to be alone with her thoughts. These special days were like unexpected gifts that brought joy and hope.

As beautiful as the day was, Frederica felt a dark cloud looming over her. As the sun shone warm on her back, she could not help but imagine the brutally cold day Miguel might be enduring in Tennessee. He had been gone so long that his shoes must be worn through by now from the endless marching. She had heard that the Confederacy was struggling to outfit its soldiers, and his threadbare socks and clothes could not possibly keep wet snow and ice from chilling him to the bone.

Frederica's nights were spent in a soft, welcoming bed under a warm quilt. A fire crackled and popped in the fireplace each night. The wind howled outside, but she was protected from its cold sting. She imagined Miguel sleeping out in the open or under a raggedy tent.

Her husband would feel every icy blast of sleet that blew into his face. The frozen ground would cause his bones to ache and he would spend his mornings trying to loosen his stiff, sore muscles. Sleep would not come easily due to the coughs and moans of the sick and wounded during the night.

As she listened to the happy giggles of Michael and Frederick, Miguel heard the crying of men who longed for home and their loved ones. Nightmares plagued the men's sleep as they recalled the horrific scenes they may have witnessed during their days as soldiers.

***

The boat arrived at the Manatee wharf and she threw a rough hemp rope around a post. She hurried down the creaking dock to the Lee's Store—her small leather purse of coins clinking in one hand and her list, neatly folded in a pocket of her dress.

Notices were posted in community stores and churches that a shipment would be made to the Knoxville camps prior to Christmas. Anyone who had a family member at a camp or in one of the hospitals there was allowed to send one small box of supplies along with a letter.

Frederica rushed in the door to find Mrs. Lee working away at her sewing machine. Electa jumped up and greeted her with a hug. "Frederica my dear, you feel so thin. Are you getting enough to eat?"

Embarrassed by her gaunt appearance, Frederica replied, "Oh you know how it is with two growing boys around, they will eat the last crumb from the table and beg for more."

Frederica held a great deal of respect for Electa Lee. Her husband Edmund moved to Florida to convalesce after narrowly escaping consumption in the north. Once he'd recovered and thrived in the warm Florida sun, he settled on the Manatee River alongside his newfound friend Josiah Gates. He returned to Vermont briefly to collect his sweetheart, Electa. Shortly thereafter, they were married, and life opened up before them with promises of adventure and opportunity.

The trip to Florida alone was an adventure for the Lees, as they confronted the incredibly difficult task of clearing land and constructing a homestead. They persevered despite the heat, mosquitoes, tropical downpours, and stubborn vegetation. Soon they owned a store and a grove in addition to their home. The Lee homestead soon became a central part of the community. It served as a church for her husband's preaching as well as a school where Electa taught the children of the community. Additions were constantly made to the home to accommodate newcomers to the area, and new spaces were created for community meetings. Reverend Lee became the first judge of Hillsborough County, so their home was also used to settle many legal disputes, or to marry the young couples of the area.

Reverend Lee had performed the wedding of Frederica and Miguel, and Electa became a treasured friend and mentor to her. The two women now shared another bond—both husbands were caught up in this dreadful war, leaving them behind to raise the children, take care of business and protect their homes against the Union raiders.

The two women went into the kitchen, and Electa gently sat Frederica down into a chair at the large wooden table. She brought out a steaming bowl of stew and a glass of freshly-squeezed orange juice. "I know you can't stop thinking about Miguel, my friend. Edmund is in my thoughts every minute of every day, but we each have important roles to play here, and we can't fulfill those roles if we are constantly thinking about problems we can't control."

Electa cut a thick slice of bread, right out of the oven, and covered it with sea-grape jelly. "Let's slow down a minute and nourish our bodies, then we can talk properly about our troubles."

As Frederica savored the delicious food, Electa brought out a box and gently set it down on the table. Frederica hoped it was the grey woolen shirt that she had asked Electa to make for Miguel. The box did indeed contain the shirt. Electa handed it to Frederica to examine along with a thickly knitted scarf, some warm socks, and a crocheted hat. Next came paper and pencil, a bag of dried fruit, and a jar of jelly. There was an incredibly accurate portrait of Frederica with a space left below the image for a handwritten message. Electa pulled out a used coat that would be a bit too long for Miguel, but it would be warm and useful all the same. Beef jerky and a small can of coffee were the final items to fill the box.

Frederica stared at the pile of small treasures in amazement. "Where did all of this come from?" she asked. "Most people are struggling just to put bread on the table!"

Electa smiled and held out her hand to Frederica. "You, my dear, have saved many families with the castnets you provided. You've helped put food on your neighbors' tables and blessed us all with your generosity. When the hogs and cows were taken by Union raiders, you sent us fish you caught and dried yourself. The vegetables from your garden fed families when their unattended crops failed. Your knowledge of the sea, and even your fruit trees, have helped keep this community alive. Your neighbors have given you these gifts as a small token of their appreciation for you to send to Miguel."

Frederica put the treasures back in the box. She had so many wonderful women around her, and a bond had been forged between all of them during these days of turmoil. She simply couldn't find the words to express her gratitude for the outpouring of love she received from her friends and neighbors.

In a quiet voice filled with emotion, she asked Electa to write a note for her in her distinctively beautiful handwriting. Her friend put pen to paper in the space underneath the portrait one of her neighbors had so lovingly sketched.

The drawing was carefully folded and placed on top of the other items. The box was closed, and Electa wrapped twine around it several times to secure it. On top of the box, in large letters, she wrote *Miguel Guerrero*. Frederica drew a simple picture of a dolphin, a reminder of their first date, in the top-right hand corner. Electa took the box and stacked it with the others. They would be picked up the following morning and both women prayed that all the boxes would reach their destinations undamaged.

Frederica and Electa hugged, clinging to one another for a long moment. The women had powerful emotions that caught their words in a tight net and didn't allow them to escape. They wished each other well, hoping that both would survive these hard times, and that their husbands would return to them safely.

The Vision

As Miguel recovered from his drug-induced stupor in early December, he learned that Joseph Atzeroth had been discharged due to old age and disability. This troubled Miguel greatly, for he was deeply concerned about his friend, but his spirits were lifted when he saw a box had arrived for him.

When he saw the drawing of a dolphin in the corner of the lid, he knew it was from Frederica. The box was lovingly packed with dried fruit, jerky, a woolen scarf, new socks, a grey woolen shirt, and an overcoat. At the bottom of the box, he discovered a hand-written note under a beautiful portrait of his wife.

My Dearest Miguel,

I hope that this box finds you well. Stay warm, my love, and don't lose faith. Remember what waits for you at the end of your long journey home.

Forever Yours, Frederica

313

Miguel's eyes filled with tears and his heart felt as if it would burst from his chest when he read her note. He held the letter close to his chest and fell asleep dreaming of home.

***

By early February, the doctor declared Miguel once again fit for duty, even though he still suffered with chest pain and intermittent fever. He was sent to rejoin his company, stationed at Carter's Depot in East Tennessee. They were guarding the Watauga River Bridge, and they needed every available man.

After a few days there, he awoke one morning with a stiff back and swollen knees. The pain was so severe that he could hardly stand, so he was relieved of further duty. When the company was recalled to Knoxville at the end of the month, Miguel was again admitted to the hospital, which had once been a Catholic church.

When Miguel's stretcher was carried into the vestibule, the rancid smell of blood, decaying flesh, and human waste overcame him. The pews of the church had been removed, and the sanctuary was packed, wall-to-wall, with the sick and dying. Swarms of flies hovered around the filthy rags that lay in piles on the floor. Miguel's head pounded, and he burned with fever. *War has changed this house of God into a house of death*, he thought, and closed his eyes.

He was placed near the altar at the front of the church. Light streamed down through the stained-glass windows. Miguel tried to focus on the scenes portrayed in the windows in an effort to escape the stench, decay, and misery down below.

The light only made his head hurt more, so he closed his eyes to escape into darkness, but found that he could not escape the sounds of suffering that echoed all around him. Miguel's spirit drifted into a desperate place. He thought of Manuel. He'd been left behind in Harrodsburg and never made it back to Knoxville. Miguel was sure his friend was dead like McLaughlin and Anderson. He resigned himself to the fact that he would never see his family again. He wanted to give up and join his fallen friends.

A young man named Sawyer occupied the cot next to Miguel, and his long stories distracted Miguel from his morbid thoughts. Sawyer had been shot by a Tory, and his wound had grown infected. This resulted in the removal of the young man's right leg from the knee down. He spoke to Miguel for a long time and told him more than he wanted to know. Miguel couldn't understand Sawyer with the soldier's heavy southern accent. When the nurse finally gave Miguel his dose of laudanum, Sawyer's voice and the pain faded, as Miguel drifted into unconsciousness.

When he awoke from the effects of the drug, the cot next to him was empty. He called out to an aide who was passing by, "Where is he? Where's Sawyer?"

"Died in the night," the aide answered, very matter-of-factly.

Sawyer's death sucked the wind out of Miguel's sails. He had been shuffled in and out of hospitals over the last three months, the pain in his chest and sides seemed to be growing worse. The fevers were more frequent, and now the back and joint pain was unbearable.

Miguel's head pounded like a drum, and he felt as though he was floating high up near the rafters of the church. Someone placed a cloth on his forehead and distant voices swirled in the background.

Miguel was lost somewhere in a hallucinatory dream. *It was a stormy night on the raging Gulf of Mexico, as dark a night as he had ever experienced in life. He was sailing just short of Passage Key Inlet when the wind snapped the mast and dropped the sails into an angry sea. The boat tipped to starboard as the canvas quickly filled with seawater, but he managed to cut the rigging free, cast the anchor, and furiously bail the water out of his boat.*

The waves raged against the hull so violently that, sometime during the course of the night, he lost the anchor and was set adrift. Deeper and deeper he drifted into the Gulf, as if he was being pulled out to sea by a giant octopus. He tried to keep his bearings and strained to see a fixed beam that radiated from the Egmont lighthouse. He watched the light with an increasing sense of panic and hopelessness until finally the darkness swallowed it, and all was black.

As suddenly as it had started, the wind and rain ceased. Miguel felt himself floating, timeless and alone. He was utterly lost.

So, this is death, he thought, and he resigned himself as if he were letting go of a lifeline and sinking into the infinite depths of the sea.

Suddenly, a piercing white light enveloped him. Colors radiated from it, and it reminded Miguel of the Great Northern Lights that the old sailors described as they sat around telling tall-tales over a pint. As he watched, the waves of color merged into ghostly images, and he recognized the faces of the Virgin Mary, the disciples, and Jesus.

Miguel awoke and sat up straight in his cot. Light streamed through the multi-colored pieces of glass in the windows and painted everything in brilliant hues. He studied the scene in each window—they were the images that he had seen in his dream.

The window scene of the Virgin Mary reminded him of his mother and the faith she had tried to instill in him as a child. The Palm Sunday window reminded him of the palms back home on Terrasilla. The window depicting Jesus and the children reminded him of Michael and Frederick, and he remembered how much they needed him. Finally, the scene of the disciples fishing made him miss the salty smell of the sea and the feel of a rough net in his hands.

When his eyes finally rested on the scene portraying Jesus and his disciples on the stormy Sea of Galilee, the light fully penetrated his soul. All the dark places inside of him were lit up. Jesus beckoned to him just as he had called to Peter. "Have faith in me. Trust me and step out of the boat."

Miguel felt a new strength rise up in him. He realized he was not alone and would fight to live. Now more than ever, he wanted to go home.

Miguel is Home

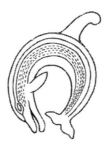

Miguel sat in the back of the boat and tried to get comfortable. It was a chilly spring morning, and he couldn't wait to see the sun rise over the water.

As the boat launched into the familiar waters of Tampa Bay, he wanted to feel relieved and safe, but he knew the war wasn't over, and danger could still be lurking along the mangrove coast.

He leaned on his backpack and put his trunk between his legs. His back ached, and his joints felt stiff. His feet were raw, and they bled through his worn-out socks. He was hungry and exhausted from the grueling trip.

Weeks of walking on the stony mountain roads of Tennessee and Georgia, then riding on bumpy paths in the backs of wagons had taken their toll. He had been so relieved when he finally found a fisherman headed south along Florida's west coast. The sailor was too old to fight in the war, but he was doing his part by shuttling veterans back home. Gliding through the smooth water felt so good to Miguel and he finally relaxed enough to allow his mind to wander.

Bright oranges and golds crept over the horizon, and the air grew slightly warmer. Miguel vowed he would never again travel through snow and ice or sleep on the cold, hard ground.

He thought of the endless days of marching with Company K. The men were like a small herd of cattle with painful yokes around their necks. The yoke was lifted for many of them when they were discharged for medical reasons, but most found themselves slaves to their new disabilities. The men of Manatee had begun to trickle home like water through a dry creek bed. Miguel would continue to support the war effort in his heart, but he would do it from home.

As the boat neared his little island, the familiar smells he loved filled the air. He put his hand over the side of the boat and felt the spray of saltwater. He saw quicksilver swirls of fish, and birds congregated near the sandbar. Miguel was afraid he might be dreaming, and he would wake up around a dead campfire on the side of a frozen hill.

The hull of the boat scraped against sand and shells, and it was Miguel's turn to disembark. He turned to the other men in the boat and waved farewell. What a weary group of men they were, some of them bringing home wounds that would never heal. Crutches, eye patches, empty shirt sleeves that strong arms used to fill, and head injuries that caused slurred speech and permanent mental problems were the souvenirs they carried home.

The boat pulled away, and Miguel let his feet sink into the warm, sandy shore. He was just an hour's walk from the cabin. Fatigue lay heavy on him, but he would not stop to rest. He wondered if Frederica had gotten the news that he would be arriving today. *She and the boys may not even be at the cabin*, he thought, and worry lines creased his forehead.

Many families had moved in with their neighbors for protection. It was possible that his cabin had been raided by Union soldiers. Miguel prepared himself for the possibility that his home had been destroyed.

It was still early morning, and there were no signs of people on the dirt roads or paths. The land looked neglected, but he saw no signs that fields had been deserted. He passed a few cows sleeping in a pasture and saw that a few fields had been planted for spring.

A large rabbit appeared in the bushes just feet away from Miguel. The animal froze when it saw him, and Miguel's first instinct was to grab his rifle and shoot it. He was used to foraging, and a good soldier never passes up a chance for meat. He took aim, breathed slowly, and then lowered his gun. The rabbit bolted into the underbrush and disappeared. *I've heard enough gunfire to last forever*, he thought, and the peace of the morning remained unbroken.

He walked on, and after a time oyster shells crunched under his boots. He was finally on the shell path that he and Frederica had blazed years before. His cabin was just around the next bend.

A queasy feeling grew in Miguel's stomach as he drew closer to the cabin. He didn't feel the rush of excitement he had expected to feel upon arrival. He stood under a tree and took some time to gaze on the homestead he dreamed about for so long.

It was eerily quiet and still. His dogs didn't bark at the crunching noise of someone walking up the path. The animal pens were empty. The shutters on the side of the house were closed. No one was there. His heart sank in his chest.

The mid-morning sun was high in the sky, and the water of Miguel's Bay glistened. Two small figures appeared against the backdrop of the shining waves. It was Michael and Frederick! *How could they have grown so much in just one year?* He smiled as he saw them struggling with a huge basket—he supposed it was full of fish that they had caught from the dock.

Miguel's steps quickened as his excitement grew. Now he was much closer to the cabin and he could see it was undamaged. There were some minor repairs to be done, a shingle out of place here and there, but his home was almost as he had left it. The yard had been cleared and a fresh row of wild petunias lined the side of the house. *Even in the midst of war she found time to plant flowers.*

The tree he had planted by the back porch was already tall enough to offer some much-needed shade. The wagon must be hidden in the pinewoods, and his boat was surely tied up in the creek to hide it from the prying eyes of brigands. His wife was very wise, and he marveled at how well she had prepared the homestead in his absence.

He wished he had been able to bathe, shave, and change into clean clothes before seeing his family. It was possible that they might not even recognize him. He had left them as a tanned, strong, and clean-cut fisherman, and he was returning a thin, sickly, and exhausted man with tattered clothes that hung off his malnourished frame.

Miguel ran his hand through his thinning hair and touched the wrinkled skin of his cheek. He wondered if Frederica would be shocked and disgusted at the sight of him. How could she ever be attracted to such a worn out old man?

He reached for his handkerchief to wipe his face. He wondered if the emotional toll of war had damaged his soul. If he could not fulfill his duties as father and husband, his life would not be worth living.

He rounded the mango tree and dropped his bags on the ground. The front door of the cabin flew open with a bang, and Frederica hurried down the steps to the path. She ran to her husband, and strength rose in Miguel as his eyes met hers.

Frederica also looked worn, and in that moment, Miguel understood he was not the only one affected by the war, but Frederica's beauty was undiminished to him, just as captivating as she had been on their wedding day. Miguel embraced her tightly and all of his apprehensions faded in the precious moment of reunion.

The two boys heard the commotion and ran toward their mother, concerned something was wrong with her. When they turned the corner and saw their father, they froze, screaming, "Papa!" Miguel rushed to meet his sons. The boys jumped in their father's arms, laughing and crying at the same time.

They were a full crew again. Life could begin once more. Miguel was alive, and he was finally HOME to stay.

Frederica's Cabin Christmas, 1863

Frederica woke with a jolt. The floor boards creaked as two sets of small feet walked toward her. She lay very still and tried to appear as if she was still asleep. Then the giggling began. Why did Frederick always have to get up at the crack of dawn, and why did he always have to wake up his brother?

She let out a sigh and accepted the inevitable fact that her day was about to start. No one could resist those tiny, smiling faces, and Frederica knew they were hungry and ready to start their day.

She let out a long sigh as she sat up. It was difficult for her to get out of bed these days. This new pregnancy brought the usual sickness every morning, but it happily reminded her that another little Guerrero was on the way.

It was an unusually warm day for December, and Frederica was glad she could get the boys outside to play. The water would be too chilly for swimming, but the morning air was warm and refreshing, not like the unbearably hot summer days. This weather was the very opposite of the Christmas seasons that she remembered from her childhood.

Instead of trudging through a soft blanket of freezing snow, her bare feet pushed through soft, white sand. Instead of leafless, barren trees of the Bavarian countryside there were mangroves and flowering shrubs filled with buzzing bees. The island was such a beautiful place full of life, but Frederica nevertheless felt a twinge of homesickness. It saddened her to know that her sons would never know the Christmas traditions of their ancestors. She could pass on some of them here, but there was nothing like Christmas in Bavaria.

She looked around the small cabin and realized she needed to decorate, despite the fact that she was miserable, tired, and not in the mood for more activity. She wanted to teach the boys the Christmas story, and wanted them to learn Christmas carols.

Frederica and her little shadows walked into the brush after breakfast and cut down a four-foot pine tree. She knew that the little tree was all she could handle at the moment, and the boys tried to drag it back to the cabin to show their mother how strong they were. She oohed and aahed at their overdramatic grunts and groans.

There were no expensive, sparkling ornaments of glass to decorate the cabin, but she had beautiful shells that Miguel brought her from his fishing trips, and she hung them from

326

green twine. There were no red cranberries or holly, but she had bright crimson blooms from the tiny hibiscus bush that she had grown from a cutting—they would supply the dash of red that Christmas demanded. There was no star of gold for the top of their tree, but a dried and bleached starfish seemed more exquisite anyway.

Cuttings of pine and cedar went into a large piece of pottery one of the Indian girls had given her in return for a small bag of sugar. They perfumed and masked the seaweed smell that permeated the air. Frederica taught the boys how to buy small gifts for people they loved—sometimes a homemade gift was even better than a purchased one.

The baby would come by summer, so they would soon be a family of five. She and Miguel would need to think about adding a room or two to the cabin. The space was already feeling cramped.

Her thoughts turned to the boys, and she gave them pen and paper so that they could start their lessons. She was determined to educate them in spite of the isolation of the island. She would teach them as much Bavarian and English as she knew. They would hear many languages in this melting pot of a state, and they picked up new words every day from all sorts of people. The old saying about children being like sponges was true. Miguel often spoke to the boys in Spanish, and sometimes they would laugh at their mother's confused stares.

The boys were developing many of the skills that would make them successful Floridians, and this made Frederica hopeful about their futures. They could already tend to the garden and help their mother as she cooked. They were learning to work with wood and build practical items—this knowledge came from their Kramer blood, for sure. Michael and Frederick showed a great deal of creativity. Children who grew up in the wilderness had to be fearless and industrious just to survive, and her boys had a good start.

Miguel taught them how to fish and shoot, and they felt comfortable being on water and land. They knew the names of the stars and how to sail and navigate without a map. The Indians had shared the knowledge of how to live on this land, including which plants were good to use as medicine, and which ones should be avoided. Knowledge was such a precious gift, and she and Miguel were intent upon making their children rich with the gifts of understanding.

Despite her physical discomfort, and the effects of the Civil War blockade, Frederica knew this would be a wonderful Christmas. She felt so much love for her little house on the estuary and friends and neighbors were a blessing. *Feliz Navidad*, she thought as she sat next to her bright, happy boys.

Another Son

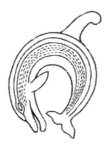

Miguel was always incredibly excited when Frederica went into labor, although she didn't appreciate his giddy spirit while she was doubled over in pain. She knew his giggling and pacing was just a product of his nerves, but it was annoying. She sent Michael and Frederick away from the cabin—she needed peace and quiet to get through this birth. She hoped help was on the way, because she sensed that the baby would arrive by nightfall.

Papa Miguel had insisted on being at his wife's side during the births of his first two sons. He completely ignored the commands of the women who were assisting Frederica. He was trying to be helpful, she supposed, rubbing her head and singing to her to take her mind off the pain.

His singing had irritated Frederica so much during Frederick's birth that at the height of pushing she yelled, "*Halt maul!*" and slapped him. The doctor and midwife in the room tried to hide their amusement, but Miguel could still hear their snickering.

The weather was stifling hot that June, so they had opened all of the windows and doors to pull a breeze into the house. Michael and Frederick periodically poked their heads through the front door to see if the baby had arrived, and Miguel did his fatherly duty by chasing them back into the yard.

The boys desperately wanted more brothers to round out a full crew for Papa Miguel's boat. They dreamed of an all-Guerrero fishing dynasty, and when Frederica mentioned that a sister might like to fish as well, they laughed hysterically. Michael and Frederick begged their Papa to take them on a voyage to Menorca when they got older, and Miguel promised them he would.

After five hours of labor, three massive pushes, and a final scream that sounded like a Seminole war whoop, baby Christopher Guerrero entered the world. The child was immediately cleaned and wrapped by Grandma Tinsley, the local midwife. She put the sweet newborn into Miguel's arms. He carefully carried his son to the front porch. He held him up for the small crowd of friends and relatives that had gathered. Everyone cheered as he said, "*Otro hijo!*"

Miguel had chosen the name Christopher because he loved the story of Saint Christopher, the martyr. He vividly remembered the nuns at the Iglesia de Santa Mariá in Mahon as they told of a man named Christopher who had helped a child cross a river. Halfway across, the child had grown very heavy, and the river was swollen and swift. The man's own life was in danger. Christopher used every last bit of his strength, managing to get the child safely to shore.

Safely on the other side, the child revealed himself as the Christ. Christopher then understood what it was like to carry the weight of the world. The child disappeared, and Saint Christopher was blessed with a new understanding of the burdens that Christ is willing to bear for mortal men. St. Christopher became the patron saint of travelers, and small images of him were often worn around the neck.

This story came to mean more and more to Miguel as the years passed. He also knew what it was like to carry a heavy burden. He had fought in wars, buried a wife, and lost friends and family to death and disease. Despite these grievous wounds, God had blessed him with his own family and opportunity in the New World.

Miguel looked down into the face of baby Christopher. Here was another great responsibility, but the joy of having another son far outstripped the worry of another mouth to feed. Beaming with pride, Miguel stepped back into the cabin and delivered his youngest son into the waiting arms of his beautiful wife.

He marveled at the sight of Frederica bonding with her third, perfect little son. He felt for the gold chain that hung around his neck. He pulled it from beneath his shirt, kissing the image of St. Christopher on the small, round medallion suspended from the chain. The memory surfaced of his precious grandmother's smile as she presented the gift to him on the morning he boarded the ship at Port Mahon for protection on his journey to America.

Smooth Sailing Ahead

Two years after the birth of Christopher and four months since the Civil War had ended, Frederica and Miguel were finally experiencing life together as it should have been all along.

It was a hot, humid day during the summer of 1865 and Miguel and Joe had gone hunting. Frederica desperately hoped they would return with some fresh meat for dinner. She had grown so very tired of fish. She decided to gather the boys and visit Aunt Julia's store for some supplies. Michael and Frederick thought it was funny to call their Great Aunt Julia "Madam Joe" behind her back like some of her patrons did. They knew, of course, not to let their mother hear them, or they would get a sharp pinch on the ear and extra chores to do when they got home.

Frederica undid a few buttons on her skirt to relieve the pressure on her bulging waistline. With each pregnancy she seemed to grow bigger and faster than the one before. Thankfully she had not felt as sick with this boy—after having three sons she felt destined to have a fourth. When the skirt loosened, the baby stretched out and moved into the new available space.

Michael had the boat prepared by the time she had the two younger boys ready to board. He was quite the navigator for only being eight years old. Miguel had brought a seaman's hat home from the war for him and he wore it every day, even though it was much too big for him. Frederica had sewn a canvas strap onto the hat that could be tied under his chin, so it wouldn't blow away. Michael had taken her ink pen and scribbled a big "M" on the strap.

With great creativity, Frederica improvised a safety belt for little Christopher. First, she took a piece of an old cork float and covered it with fabric. Then she took one of Miguel's belts and ran it through the middle of the float, so she could tie the contraption around Christopher's waist.

Miguel laughed at her invention. The very next day she tied it around the waist of her little water bug after breakfast. Sure enough, Christopher found an open door, wandered outside alone, and fell off the dock into the water. Frederica, always alert to the whereabouts of her children, was in hot pursuit of the toddler and saw him topple off the dock.

Christopher popped right back up to the surface with a smile on his face. After that, Miguel didn't make fun of the cork contraption anymore. Drowning was entirely too common for folks living on the coast of Florida, and nothing was more heartbreaking than finding a child's body floating along the shore. She was not sure she could ever survive the loss of one of her children—what could be worse than that?

When the last three passengers arrived on the dock, Michael blew the wooden whistle that Uncle Philippi had given him and yelled, "All aboard!" He held out his hand to collect their imaginary tickets as they boarded. This had become a tradition for Michael, and it made Frederica and Frederick laugh every time he did it.

Little Christopher squirmed to get out of his mother's arms. He wanted to get in the water so badly after taking his maiden voyage just the day before. Frederica was certain that he would be swimming before his second birthday.

She settled the children into their places and untied the rope from the dock. "Ready to set sail, Captain Michael!" He loved being in charge of the boat when his Papa was not there.

Frederica had also become an excellent sailor and was now a big part of Michael's training. She would give him the helm for this journey but would be ready to step in and take charge at the first sign of trouble.

Christopher immediately crawled into her lap. Frederick was already scanning the water looking for dolphin fins. Sure enough, once they cleared the mouth of Miguel's Bay, four dolphins appeared alongside the boat. They swam at the same speed as the small craft and seemed to be challenging their human counterparts to a race. Frederick pointed to them and yelled, "Look Mother!" so that the others would not miss out on the show. Two smaller dolphins swam behind the boat and enjoyed the foamy wake.

As they rounded the bend into the Manatee River, Frederica thought about Miguel and how the war had affected him. He did not speak much about his experiences, but she could tell that he dreamed about them. His health had slowly returned and his stamina for fishing was coming back, but it was a long process.

To make up for many sleepless nights while on patrol, he seemed to need so much sleep at first. Some nights he would cry out and wake up in a cold sweat. He was sensitive to loud noises and was overprotective of Frederica and the boys. Sometimes he would sit on the dock and stare at the water for hours while Frederica held his hand. She hoped time would heal him and fishing would bring back his peace of mind. The homesteaders now looked forward to times of peace and prosperity. Surely the Guerreros were destined for smooth sailing from here on out.

Frederica shook her head to clear it of daydreams. She looked up and realized that Michael had guided them safely to the Atzeroth dock. She could see Eliza running toward them recognizing their familiar sail. Frederica carefully passed Christopher into Eliza's arms then took Frederick's hand to help him out of the boat and onto the dock. She glanced over and saw Michael writing the date and time in his little leather book—it was a "captain's log" his Papa had given him. She hoped that someday he might control his own fleet of boats and continue to build the tradition of the proud Guerrero men.

Eliza greeted the boys with hugs and then set out for the store. As they walked, Frederica breathed deep of the clean air and took in the sights and sounds of the bustling wharf. These were people who had survived the horrors of war and were beginning to enjoy their lives again. She thanked God once more that her family had not been shattered like so many others. They were whole and healthy with a bright future in front of them. For the first time in a great while, Frederica felt that all was well.

The Reunion

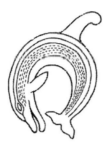

Miguel wasn't sure if he trusted the promises that came with the fragile peace, especially with occupying Union soldiers, carpetbaggers, and other strange folk prowling the area. He was amazed at the stories he heard of the strength and endurance the women had shown when left alone to defend their property and children. He was sure they didn't share too much of the trials they went through knowing their husbands would be tormented by guilt.

The best medicine for Miguel was time with his boys. He spent hours with them making nets, carving wood, looking for Indian treasures, and teaching them to hunt. He was trying to make up for lost time. Despite these good times, the light in Miguel's soul seemed a bit dimmer than it had been before he left for the war.

Mrs. Peterson called out and waved as she arrived in her wagon. Today Frederica would go with her friend to pick oranges with Uncle Joe. Miguel was home with the boys, and she could get a lot done without the distraction of her children. The two women tried to time their visit just right so that Aunt Julia would fix them lunch.

They enjoyed chatting on the way to the grove. Sometimes weeks would go by without seeing a neighbor, so visits with friends were cherished. As they pulled into the small grove, Joe and Julia were picking the sweet-smelling fruits. Aunt Julia had her slingshot loaded for any squirrel that had the nerve to steal an orange. Frederica often thought a scarecrow fashioned after *Madam Joe* would keep Indians, soldiers, wild animals, and any other form of danger from entering their homestead.

Frederica hugged Uncle Joe. "I missed you dear uncle, especially your big hug!" When she pulled away from him she noticed that the twinkle in his eye had not yet returned. Almost emaciated, he looked like he had aged ten years during his time served in the war. Frederica pulled Aunt Julia aside and whispered to her, "Do you think Joe and Miguel will ever fully come back to us? They have witnessed so much destruction and death. I wish we could do something for them."

"Men will not talk about their memories like women do." Julia said. They guard their secrets from their women because they fear that we are not strong enough to help bear their grief." Julia's eyes widened as an idea came to her. "We need to have a party. We need music and dancing and good food," she exclaimed. "We will have lots of mullet and cheese grits. I'll bake a cake, and we'll break out the good coffee and beer!"

Frederica loved seeing Aunt Julia get so excited.

"A week from Saturday, Frederica! Be at my river dock at high noon and bring your special biscuits and guava jelly! Get ready to dance!"

With deft hands, the women quickly picked six crates of oranges and headed back home with enough to share with neighbors along the way. The mothers loved this season. It seemed that the children didn't get sick nearly as much when they had fresh fruit to eat. When they arrived at the cabin, Miguel jumped up from the porch to help unload the crates. The boys had spilled some milk inside, and she could hear their panicked whispers as they scurried to clean up the mess. She waited a few moments before she went in so they would have a chance to finish.

"Aunt Julia is hosting a small party a week from Saturday at high noon." Frederica watched Miguel's face turn sour as he recognized the word *party*.

He didn't say anything, but he let out a disappointed sigh. A party was not his favorite way to spend a Saturday. Miguel knew that Joe would not be looking forward to a party either, but at least misery would have company.

For two days, the men were enlisted by their women to prepare for the big party. All they could do was pray for rain and hope that it might be cancelled.

Much to Miguel's disappointment, when the day of the party arrived, the weather was beautiful without a rain cloud in sight. Frederica made Miguel and the boys dress in their Sunday clothes, comb their hair, and clean their teeth. A passerby might have thought that the children were being tortured inside the cabin hearing the loud moans and groans. The objections intensified in volume and pitch when Frederica told the boys that, YES, they would be wearing shoes this afternoon.

The family took one of the fishing boats in order to shorten their traveling time. Frederica hoped that a change of scenery and some good food would brighten Miguel's mood.

Once Miguel and the three boys were seated in the boat and ready to launch, Frederica stood up and said she had something to tell them. Miguel had noticed she hadn't been herself the last few days and hoped she wanted to cancel the trip and stay home to rest.

The boys listened anxiously to hear what she had to say.

"I want to let you know of a little Christmas gift that has been ordered for you this year."

"A new rifle for me?" Michael exclaimed.

"I hope it's a guitar for me!" said Frederick.

"How about some more help around here for me," Miguel joked.

Frederica smiled, "Papa, guessed right! Right now he has three sons to follow him around and soon there will be a fourth child to make him the happiest man on Terrasilla Island."

Miguel winked as he said, "You have already made me the happiest man on Terrasilla Island!"

***

The water birds were out in the shallows by the hundreds. Frederica loved the large, pink flamingos that lined the mangrove coast to feast on baby fish. While she gazed at the beautiful birds, the boys snuck a couple biscuits out of the baskets of food. They ate them quickly but were found out when Frederica noticed the crumbs sticking to their sweaty cheeks. She tried to act mad at them for not asking permission, but her anger faded as she looked at their adorable faces.

The boys searched for the dock as they entered the river. In the distance, Miguel could see fifteen or more boats surrounding Julia's dock—too many for a small party. Frederica pretended to be concerned that something terrible must have happened to bring so many boats to the wharf.

"Look at all the boats! Has someone gone missing or drowned? Maybe there was a fire or a boat accident?"

Miguel was visibly anxious as well. The worried look on his face bothered the boys, and they began to fidget in their seats. As they drew closer to the gathering, a wonderful scene unfolded. Julia was waving a giant American flag, and it looked like it might catch the wind and catapult her into the river at any moment. There were other familiar faces standing on the dock, and they all waved small flags in the air calling out greetings to Miguel.

These men were his band of brothers—fellow fishermen and farmers, settlers and businessman, all of whom had fought beside him in the Civil War. They had all come home, but they had not been together in months because there was so much to tend to with their own families and property.

Miguel's eyes welled up with tears when he saw the face of Manuel Amon, whom he feared had been left dead in Kentucky. Standing alongside Manuel were Asa Bishop, Joe Atzeroth, George Anderson, Reverend Lee, and John Wilhemson. Other men started down the dock as Miguel's boat tied up. They had different occupations and worshipped in different churches, and their skin colors and languages varied. In spite of these differences, they had become a community, and they were ready to celebrate new beginnings.

The families of the men stood on the shore waving homemade streamers and cheering. Miguel realized this reunion was a celebration of the men who returned, and a time to reminisce about friends who had not come home. That day the deep sadness in Miguel was broken, and joy returned to his spirit. His excitement for life rekindled, and his love for this wild and wonderful land was reborn.

He looked back at his beautiful family, the water sparkling behind them as they laughed with friends. Miguel whispered under his breath, "I have finally come back to you, Terrasilla."

Meeting Captain John

Miguel gathered the three older boys to go to Lee's Landing and left Frederica and baby Robbie to have a quiet day together. Frederick kissed his mother and promised to bring her a treat. Michael brought in an extra bucket of water, so she would not have to go out. Christopher cried to stay home, but Miguel scooped him up and put him on his shoulders. "It's your Papa's turn to play with you boys now that I'm home from being a soldier. I have been away too much of your lives, but now I'm here!" Within seconds Christopher was giggling, and Miguel ran down to the dock with the boy bouncing on his shoulders.

The fourth Guerrero son had arrived, as was foretold by his mother, the week before Christmas. Arriving at a healthy nine pounds, Frederica predicted he would be the fearless, adventurous one.

At first, Miguel felt guilty about leaving Frederica alone with the baby, but she said she would relish the opportunity to spend some alone time with her newest son. Miguel was thrilled to have another boy to spoil.

The river was crystal clear on this bright Tuesday morning, and many of the neighbors were out in their boats taking advantage of the perfect weather. Miguel waved at the boats as they passed, and the boys took off their hats and waved them in the air as friendly neighbors greeted them.

As they neared the Lee dock, Miguel spotted a new sloop he didn't recognize. He lifted each boy up and out of the boat, and they took off to find Miss Electa and Sarah. The boys knew there would certainly be something good to eat in the kitchen, and there were always other children to play with. Miss Electa had started a school, and she made no secret of the fact that she hoped the boys would enroll someday.

The bells on the tall wooden door alerted Edmund Lee someone had entered the front of the store. He bolted out from the back, "*Hola, amigo!*" He frantically motioned for Miguel to come to the back with him.

After a firm handshake, the men walked into the supply room to find a man loading some boxes onto the shelves. "Miguel, meet Captain John Fogarty. He is going to be our new neighbor. He plans to settle westward down the river on the south side." Miguel reached out his hand with a smile, and John gripped it tightly.

"*Saludos, Miguel. ¡Estoy emocionado de ser tu vecino!*" Surprised that the Irishman greeted him in nearly perfect Spanish, Miguel's jaw dropped.

Lee and Fogarty chuckled at Miguel's reaction.

Thrilled that he could communicate with someone without having to stumble through English, Miguel was immediately at ease with John. The two men exchanged information about themselves, and Miguel was excited to find that boats, fishing, and the ocean were passions they both shared.

Miguel promised his new friend he would help him navigate the waters of the area and introduce him to Terrasilla. He also vowed to show him where to find the best wood for building his home.

John promised he would help Miguel build the boat he had been dreaming about since he had settled on the island. In just a few minutes, the two men became friends.

The three boys scurried in from the kitchen, each with a large cookie clutched tightly in his hand. Reverend Lee's eighteen-year-old daughter, Sarah, followed the boys, and Miguel was not surprised to see her carrying Christopher—Sarah tended to dote on him more than the others since he was the youngest.

Electa entered the room and told Miguel to sit down before turning to her daughter. "Sarah, fetch me the box for the

Guerreros, it's just beside the door." When her daughter returned with it, Electa held it on her lap. "This is for Frederica," she said. "As I recall, you two lovebirds have a wedding anniversary coming up soon, and I wanted to send her something special." Electa smiled. "I remember your wedding as one of the best my husband ever officiated.

Madam Joe had the place decorated so beautifully, and the food was outstanding. "And look at your beautiful family!" She took the lid off the box, "I made her a beautiful white nightgown trimmed with lace. With all the men in her house, she needs something pretty and feminine."

Miguel smiled as he gazed at the beautiful gift. "*Muchas gracias, Electa. Ha bendecido nuestra boda desde el principio.*"

As Electa struggled to understand Miguel's words, Captain Fogarty stepped up to translate. "He says, 'You blessed our marriage from the beginning." Miguel nodded at Electa, sincerity shining in his eyes. "*Usted nos apoyó cuando otros no lo hicieron. Le agradecemos.*"

Electa looked to Fogarty again. "He says that you supported the marriage when many others would not. He and Frederica thank you."

"You're both welcome." Electa's broad smile lit up the room. Reverend Lee took advantage of the chance to easily communicate with Miguel. "We would love for your family to come and worship with us on Sunday. Electa would be willing to help your boys with language and writing, and you need to get that application in to the State of Florida. It's time to own that prime piece of property you've invested so many years in."

Miguel nodded in agreement and spoke in Spanish. When he finished, Fogarty translated, "Yes, it is time to concentrate on my family and friends. That's all that I want to do now that I am home."

The Lees walked Miguel and his boys out to the boat and helped load the supplies Miguel purchased. Captain John shook Miguel's hand vigorously, and Miguel hugged Electa and thanked her again for the gift.

As the boat nosed its way into the current, Miguel looked back at his friends. They were still waving from the dock, and at that moment, he realized that they might be the finest people that he had ever met.

Off the Beaten Path

Frederica pulled back the curtains and looked outside at the beautiful morning. It was warm and breezy, and there was not a cloud in the sky. Once again, she reflected on how wonderful it was to live in Terrasilla during the winter. The biting insects and humid air had departed along with summer. How fortunate she was to have made this place her home.

Miguel had been gone for a few days, and she and the boys had developed a case of cabin fever. It was torture to stay inside the house for too long. She had grown to love the outdoors and the water.

Michael was the same way. When he got bored he would often say, "I need to go stare at the water, Mama." He always came home wet. "I just fell in... sorry," was his excuse. The big grin on his face usually made up for the water he dripped on her floor.

Frederica pondered what to do with the day. She and the boys loved to eat their meals outside under the gumbo limbo tree, and the birds didn't object to cleaning up any food that fell on the ground or table. She thought her mother would be shocked that they dined outside with no tablecloth, fine dishes, or fancy candles, but what better lighting for a meal could there be? A long walk in the sunshine always helped the little ones sleep more soundly, and Frederica loved the fresh air.

Her decision was made. It was time for a picnic. "Let's go, little Guerreros!" she called, "We are going to the spring for a picnic! If we are lucky, Eliza and Mary might be there with some of Aunt Julia's delicious cookies!"

The children knew the drill. So that the shell path wouldn't cut their tender feet, they put on their Indian-made moccasins that Miguel had traded for. The brothers took turns combing each other's hair, and Michael tied the leather laces of little Robbie's moccasins. "On my back little brother!" said Michael, lifting him up on his shoulders. Robbie had to be carried because his little legs couldn't keep up with the others.

Frederick helped Christopher load the picnic basket, and the two boys carried it between them. Christopher grabbed the blue hat he wore everywhere he went. He said it protected him from "mean birds and big bugs." Frederica loaded Miguel's old double-barreled shotgun and looped the thick, leather strap over her shoulder. It had served him well in the last Seminole War, and he let her use it when she left the cabin. She had become a good shot, and she could easily take out a rattlesnake at close range. An unwelcome intruder would suffer a bitter end if he threatened Frederica or her family. She reached for her sturdy walking stick that could be used as a weapon if the need arose. *No dainty parasols for the women of Florida*, she thought. She tied her hair back with net twine since it would take too long to brush, and she didn't want the children to get restless.

Normally, their dog, Gator, would walk alongside them like a bodyguard, but he was nowhere to be found today. *He must be out chasing squirrels*, thought Frederica. *He will be home when we get back.*

***

The boys and Miguel had grown to love the old dog since Miguel had found him. One day while hugging the shoreline on the north part of the island, Miguel saw the dog sleeping on the sand. From a distance, he watched a ten-foot alligator making its way through the mud toward the unsuspecting animal.

Miguel laid the monster to rest with one shot, and it took three men to haul the huge carcass into the boat. The dog looked scared, sick, and hungry, so he gave the hound the bacon and biscuit that he had packed for his lunch. He slowly wagged his tail and looked up at Miguel optimistically. Before he knew it, he was taking his first boat ride. The dog stayed on the opposite end of the boat from the dead gator—the look in his brown eyes showed he feared a sudden resurrection of the beast.

When Miguel came home that day, the boys were so excited to have a new pet. Frederica had to remind them to lower their voices so that they didn't scare the skittish animal.

That night they enjoyed a fried alligator feast. The irony of the dog eating the gator that had hunted him did not escape Miguel, and he grinned with a mouthful of tender meat. At first Frederica wasn't thrilled to have another mouth to feed, and she knew there would be messes to clean up. But Miguel and the boys loved the dog, and she quickly grew to love him too. He became a dependable guardian of the family and patrolled Miguel's Bay like a soldier standing watch. From that day on he was named *Gator*, and he was a big part of the Guerrero family.

***

They marched out of the front door in a single file line with Frederica leading the way. The family looked like little ducks following a mama duck down the path. Frederica walked about ten feet ahead of her children, and her head panned from side to side as she looked for anything dangerous that might do harm to her brood. Halfway to the spring, Christopher had to relieve himself. Michael sighed, "Christopher, you always have to stop. Hurry up! We're almost there."

Frederica smiled as Christopher looked for the right spot. He was very modest, so he went a little farther off the path than the other children would typically go. She thought that he looked like a little dog that marked his territory everywhere he went.

A noise in the brush caused Frederica to turn around. She scanned the area and tried to determine the source of the sound. Once again, she heard a soft crack, and she tightened her grip on her walking stick. "It's probably an armadillo or opossum," Frederica whispered to the children.

Suddenly, a huge female panther leapt out of the palmetto thicket. The angry beast landed on all fours directly in front of Frederica. The cat's ears were laid back flat against its skull, its ivory white teeth were bared, and a deep growl emerged from its throat. The panther's emerald, green gaze met Frederica's eyes, and she knew that she could not look away.

The shock of the panther's sudden appearance made Frederica freeze in panic. She gripped her walking stick tightly, wishing that her white knuckles were holding the shotgun instead. She slowly extended her free hand out to her side to let her children know to be still and quiet. She had spoken to them many times about dangerous wild cats, and she hoped the boys remembered her words.

To Frederica's horror, she heard Christopher coming out of the thicket behind her. She turned her head slowly around to look at him, and her heart skipped a beat when she saw a panther cub in his chubby little arms. He continued to walk toward his mother, proud of his extraordinary find—completely unaware of the deadly situation he had created. When the panther saw her cub, she began to shriek. Through the demonic howl, Frederica heard Frederick whisper to his brother to put the cub down on the ground.

Frederica tried to gather her composure, knowing that she had to decide on a quick course of action. Should she go after the panther with her stick, or should she try to unsling the shotgun and fire a shot? If she missed, she knew the panther could tear them to pieces. One powerful lunge and the predator could be atop little Christopher. One swipe with her long claws would take off half of his face. One bite to the neck and he would bleed to death.

Frederica took a deep breath and stared into the jade eyes of the seething animal. It was just a few feet in front of her now and was inching closer. Frederica and the cat feared the same thing—both their babies were in grave danger. Both mothers would gladly give her life to save her little one, and both didn't know how best to solve this stalemate.

Frederica slowly lowered her stick and dropped her eyes to the ground. She heard soft padding steps behind her as the baby panther walked toward its mother. It caught the mother's scent and began to run, but when the cub reached Frederica's feet it stopped and laid down. The pounding of Frederica's heart grew even more frantic.

The mother panther rose up out of her attack position and cautiously approached her cub. She stopped at Frederica's feet, close enough to touch, and licked her little one as she looked for an injury. After what seemed like an eternity, the panther picked up her baby by the scruff of the neck and gently carried it off into the thicket.

Frederica's legs went weak and she dropped to one knee. She was physically exhausted from the sheer terror she had experienced. She cried tears of relief and gratitude for the protection that God had given her. Christopher came up to her, stroked her hair, and put his arms around her neck. "He was lost Mama," he said. "He was looking for his mudder."

"I know sweetheart. You were so kind to help him find her, but next time you must let him find his mother on his own." Frederica held him tight. "That mother panther and your mother are the two happiest creatures on this island right now."

Michael and the other two boys joined the hug. The older children knew they had narrowly escaped a tragedy. They stood and wiped the dust from their clothes, gathered what they had been carrying, and continued down to the spring.

They would have quite a story to tell their Papa when he returned.

By the Light of the Moon

It was May of 1867, and Frederica Guerrero had long been in bed. She was drowsy, and with that drowsiness came an open and reflective mind. Carefully examining her thoughts, she was the last one awake in the house. During the evening hours of the summer, time seemed to slow down. *Perhaps it's because today was so busy*, she thought. Nonetheless, the clock would not stop, and tomorrow would be the beginning of another day.

Frederica hoped the summer and fall would be healthy for the Guerrero clan. It would surely be a season of peace and prosperity now that wars were in the past. Many families were moving into the area to start new lives, and the optimism in Manatee was like the fresh scent of honeysuckle on the breeze.

The bright, full moon could be seen through the triangular window of the bedroom. It was warm, and the wind moaned through the pine trees. Miguel's rhythmic breathing comforted her. She had slept without him for too many nights during their eleven years of marriage. His fishing kept him out on the water for extended periods of time. She had known that from the start, but she had not been prepared for the impact of war on her family. Frederica stared at her husband's profile in the moonlight. She loved him.

How she wished her mother could come to see her home and meet her family. She would absolutely adore her little grandsons, and they would love her dearly. She imagined her father coming to Terrasilla and meeting her husband. He would be so impressed with Miguel's strong character, business sense, and determination. The fact that he made a life out of this rugged wilderness would amaze him. He would see Miguel's devotion to his children and would share in Miguel's love for them.

She quietly eased out of the bed to get a drink of water and check on the boys. For a precious moment, she watched them while they slept. It was the only time during the day they were still. Their little boy instincts sent them off in different directions each day. How perfect they were. Each child was so different, and each one held a piece of her heart.

Frederica walked across the floor to stare out the windows at the moonlit water. She supposed that dodging mosquitoes was a fair price to pay for living in a place so much like Eden. She watched as Miguel's boat rocked gently on the water. Her husband loved his work, and his sons were developing a passion for the sea. Frederica could see the pride in her husband's eyes when he heard them talking about how to mend a net or how to set a sail.

Frederica made her way back to the bedroom. Each floorboard creaked in protest as she walked, and she wondered why they never sounded this way during the daytime. As she slipped back into bed, Miguel stirred. He opened his eyes and looked at her curiously. "Nothing to worry about dear, go back to sleep," she said. Suddenly Frederica's eyes widened as she felt a flutter deep in her stomach.

Miguel sat up and looked at her with concern, "What is it?" he said.

"I think we are going to meet another little Guerrero this winter," Frederica said, and Miguel's ivory smile shone in the moonlight beaming through the window.

The Broken Wall

Frederica's fifth pregnancy was turning out to be more difficult than her previous ones. Maybe it was because she was older, maybe it was because she had four boys to care for and was exhausted all the time, or maybe it was a sign that this would be her girl. But the weeks were not passing by quickly enough for her, and she was anxious to have this child join the family.

She sat on the front porch with her sore, swollen feet resting on a bucket and wondered what she would cook for dinner that night. Cooking was such a chore for her now that she had reached the latter stages of pregnancy, and she never had enjoyed it as much as some women did. *Cooking takes up so much of the day,* she whispered to herself. *It's so much nicer to be outside enjoying the sea breeze and the sun!*

Feeding Miguel and the boys was like feeding a small army—they laid waste to every dish she placed in front of them. She tried to eat her meal while she cooked, otherwise she and the baby wouldn't have stood a chance against the male appetites in her care.

The gate squeaked open and Uncle Joe walked up the path to the cabin. "Don't get up my dear!" he called. "You must rest whenever you can."

Joe Atzeroth seemed to always show up when she was at her wit's end. He was like an angel in that regard. Joe was incredibly kind to her, and he loved Frederica as much as his own daughters.

He took off his hat and kissed her on top of the head. "Julia told me to come fetch the boys for the day. You and Miguel can come up later for supper, and you don't have to bring anything but each other. Would that be all right with you?" He gave her his signature wink that melted her heart every time, and Frederica felt a huge grin spread across her face as the possibilities of an afternoon free from children blossomed in her mind.

An afternoon of peace and quiet was something she and Miguel rarely shared. Frederica's thoughts turned to a cool afternoon bath, a nap, and then Aunt Julia's cooking. It had suddenly become the perfect day, and it was all due to the kindness of her aunt and uncle. Uncle Joe gathered up the boys, and Frederica waved as they hopped into the wagon and disappeared down the shell road.

Uncle Joe's old wagon rattled down the oyster shell road, as the boys bounced around in the back. He narrated the trip as if they were northerners visiting the area for the first time. He taught them the names of trees, pointed out a dead snake on the side of the road, sang Bavarian songs, and described how Terrasilla had looked when he and Julia and Eliza first arrived. The place had been a wild jungle, he said, and the boys loved his stories of danger and adventure. Not all of them were exactly true, but most of them were. Still, he couldn't be blamed for engaging in a little exaggeration when his wife wasn't around to correct him.

Frederica and Miguel enjoyed their afternoon of freedom and peace at the cabin. It wasn't often that they were alone together at home, and this afternoon was so quiet they could hear the waves as they lapped gently on the shore. The seagulls called to each other in the distance, and the bees buzzed around the orange blossoms.

Miguel hummed quietly while he mended one of his nets. He looked over at his wife, put down the net, and disappeared into the cabin. Frederica wondered what new task had captured his attention. He returned with a bucket of cold water from the rain barrel. Still humming, he threw a handful of salt into the bucket and stirred it around with a stick. "What are you doing?" she wondered aloud.

Miguel brought the bucket to Frederica and placed her tired, swollen feet into the refreshing water. He then pulled out her hairbrush and brushed her hair. He began to sing a

Menorcan song. For all Frederica knew, it could have been a Christmas carol, a love song, or a child's lullaby, but regardless of the lyrics, his deep voice soothed her soul. She had never felt so loved by Miguel, and she drifted off into a blissful sleep.

A brief afternoon rain shower woke Frederica from her nap. She knew that it was time to get ready to go to Julia's house, and she began to imagine what her aunt might serve for dinner. Aunt Julia was, without question, the best cook for miles around. She had cooked for officers at Ft. Brooke, and they loved her food so much that she was able to make some extra money by feeding them from time to time. Frederica's thoughts were filled with images of fresh-baked bread, golden-fried chicken, steaming plates of fresh vegetables, and flaky, delicious pies. Her mouth watered in anticipation of the upcoming feast.

Miguel and Frederica could smell Aunt Julia's cooking long before the wagon reached the Atzeroth house. When they walked through the front door, the boys ran to greet them as if they had been separated for weeks. Frederica loved being away from the boys for short amounts of time simply because she loved to feel their little arms wrap around her waist in greeting. After they greeted their mother, the four boys attacked their Papa until he fell to the ground as if he had been ambushed by a Seminole warrior. Miguel begged for mercy, but his sons tickled him relentlessly. Peals of boyish laughter rang through the house, and not all of it came from the children.

The table was beautifully set with china and silver flatware, the boys were clean, and their hair combed, and the food looked divine. Julia had made a special spicy grilled snapper for Miguel with thinly-sliced mango on top and a mound of saffron rice on the side. When Julia served it to him, he grabbed her hand and kissed it. She jerked away from him and made a disgusted face, but Frederica knew that her aunt was starting to love Miguel, and his love for her cooking helped the process.

Frederica wondered how Julia could cook so much food in such a short amount of time. If *she* had tried to prepare this feast, there was a good chance the cabin would have gone up in flames.

They all joined hands to bless the food, and Uncle Joe said grace. Aunt Julia allowed Miguel to bless the food once, but his prayer had taken so long that she never asked him to pray again. Frederica suspected that this was exactly the result that Miguel had wanted.

Frederica opened her eyes during the prayer and studied the beautiful family seated around the table. She couldn't imagine what she had done in her life to deserve all of them. Her sons were intelligent, unique, and so very much like their father. Aunt Julia was stern and opinionated, but she had a heart of gold. She was the strong, old oak tree of Terrasilla. She'd weathered storms, Indians, soldiers, sickness, and disappointments, yet her roots remained planted firmly in the ground.

Julia adored Frederica's sons and spoiled them. The boys mended a hole in her heart that had remained open since the death of her own sons back in Bavaria. She had special nicknames for each one of them, and she knew all of their favorite foods. Frederica considered Julia's two daughters, Eliza and Mary, to be her sisters. It was truly a blessing, she reflected, that God had put the Atzeroths in her path.

Everyone said a loud "amen," and the feast began. Aunt Julia loved the sounds of satisfaction the boys made as they ate. Her reward was seeing them fill their plates a second time, and Miguel sneaked a third plate before she brought her famous strawberry cake out from the kitchen. It had been so long since they had eaten something sweet that the sight of the cake set them to salivating once more.

***

After the last bite of strawberry cake was eaten, everyone leaned back in their chairs and groaned. The men and the boys felt so full that the slightest movement might kill them, so Julia allowed them to sit for a few moments while their dinner settled. The contentment on each of their faces made her afternoon of hard work worth it.

Julia sighed at the sight of the post-meal table, rose to her feet, and started clearing away the dishes. Miguel intercepted her, pulled her into the parlor, and sat her down in her rocking chair. He motioned for Uncle Joe to get up, and together they cleared the table. The two men carried the dishes out to the porch, filled the large, metal wash tub with water and soap, and began the washing, while the boys helped rinse and dry.

Julia, Frederica, Eliza, and Mary were so entertained by watching two men and four little boys wash dishes and clean the table that they were soon paralyzed with laughter.

The boys bumped into one another and the men lacked any grace whatsoever. Miguel dropped a slippery, wet bowl, but little Frederick dove and caught it in mid-air before it crashed to the ground. Uncle Joe slipped on a patch of lard while putting dishes back in the cabinet, and he skated wildly across the floor, his arms flailing in an effort to regain his balance. Michael gagged repeatedly and dramatically as he cleaned up the leftover chicken parts and fish heads. Christopher stayed in the outhouse and only returned when he heard the commotion subside, but he was met at the door by his father, who was holding a bucket of food scraps to give to the pigs. Christopher hated those smelly pigs, and his grumbling set off a fresh gale of laughter from the women, who fought not to lose their breath.

An hour and a half later, the boys stumbled into the parlor, totally exhausted from their work. Frederica knew they had learned a valuable lesson that would be passed down to their own sons—when your womenfolk are happy, your home is a peaceful place.

Mary played a game of marbles on the floor with the older boys, and the younger boys snuggled with Aunt Julia in her big wooden chair. The men had retreated to the front porch for a smoke, and Frederica could hear the pleasant tone in their conversation as they discussed fishing, family, and other common interests.

As the sun began to set, the young family gathered their things for the journey home. Julia gave Miguel an awkward side hug, which made Frederica smile, knowing how she truly felt about her husband.

Mary is Born

Frederica hoped that her baby would be born in December, but the Christmas season of 1867 passed, and she carried her child into 1868. And, as all mothers know, babies aren't born until *they're* ready.

As Frederica struggled to pull herself up out of her chair, she decided she had eaten too many of Eliza's special Christmas cookies. *I'm eating for two,* she thought, and mentally pardoned herself for eating so many of the delicious treats. With a sigh, she carefully wrapped the last wooden figurine from the nativity set Uncle Joe had carved for her family's Christmas gift.

Frederica had planned to name the Christmas baby Mary if it was a little girl. This would be a name with deep meaning because of its ties to the Christmas story, and it would also be an honor to her younger cousin, Mary. She definitely needed another female to help her wrangle the Guerrero boys, and she was running out of male names after giving birth to four sons.

Miguel tiptoed into the room to check on his wife. He was always very considerate of the fact that she needed peace and quiet during the late stages of pregnancy, so he kept the boys busy outside whenever possible. He pulled Frederica into a hug and then patted her stomach. "*Nombre?*" he inquired.

Frederica recognized the Spanish word for "*name*" but she acted like he had no answer for Miguel. She shrugged her shoulders. "I just can't decide!"

Miguel slipped her a small piece of paper. Frederica carefully opened it and read the contents slowly. The note said, "*María, mi hermana menor a quien amo.*" Frederica spoke each word in English as she translated the note, "Mary, my younger sister who I loved." She had her answer. If the child was a girl, they would name her Mary.

Frederica looked up at her husband and spoke the name aloud once more, "Mary!"

Miguel smiled and nodded, "*Maria!*"

Frederica's eyes suddenly grew wide, and the color drained from her face. She put a hand beneath the blanket that covered her. "*Agua,*" she murmured. "*AGUA!*" The murmur turned into a shout, and Miguel realized that Mary had heard her name spoken aloud and deemed this an invitation to join her parents in the outside world. She was on her way.

After six hours of labor for Frederica, and pacing for Miguel, the Guerreros welcomed their fifth child. She was a beautiful baby girl, and her name was, of course, Mary. Frederica couldn't wait to make her a little pink dress and a lace bonnet. Finally, another girl in the house.

All four brothers begged for the right to hold their baby sister, and each boy cradled her gently in his arms as if she was as fragile as a porcelain doll. Miguel stood back and beamed with pride as he watched his children. He wished his mother and his sister Maria could see all of them together, for they truly were a beautiful family.

***

April 3, 1868

It was early in the Spring of 1868, and at the end of the Guerrero dock, Miguel was busily mending nets and cleaning traps in the cool morning air. It had been a busy season of fishing, and he was weary from the drudgery of his six-day work week. He looked forward to some quieter days of rest with his family at the cabin.

He stood up, slowly leaned back, and tried to stretch out the tightness and pain in his lower back. He had always appeared much younger and stronger than his age suggested. Miguel never exposed his weaknesses to the people around him. He rarely asked for help with anything and he powered through everything he did.

He squinted into the bright sun and looked out into the bay. A small sailboat was approaching through the pass, and he immediately recognized the captain. *My eyes are still like an Osprey's,* thought Miguel. A smirk of satisfaction crossed his face.

It was Captain John Fogarty, who was a trusted and loyal friend. He was waving his cap in the air, and his long Irish mustache was blowing in the wind. He had not seen Fogarty in a while, and a friendly visit would be a welcome diversion from the nets. Fogarty had spent time in St. Augustine and spoke Spanish well, so Miguel always enjoyed their conversations.

The stout Irishman waved to Frederica, then his gaze shifted to the four little Guerrero boys who ran down the shell mound to greet him. "Come see your Uncle John!" he bellowed in his deep Irish brogue. The children jumped on him and stuck like barnacles, and they giggled and pulled on his hands and legs.

Michael grabbed Fogarty's cap and put it on his little head, then held a wad of Spanish moss over his upper lip to mimic Fogarty's mustache. He sucked on a mangrove shoot to imitate the man smoking his clay pipe. John doubled over with laughter at Michael's clever imitation, and he rewarded them with hard candy from his deep pockets. They popped the candy into their mouths, quieting the giggles.

With the boys satisfied, Fogarty produced a box for Frederica from his wife Mary. Wives do not always bond with their husband's friends' wives, but Frederica and Mary had quickly become like sisters.

"Lads," Fogarty said, "I'll be taking your Papa away for a quick trip. We will be back in an hour. If you go help your mother with your chores and the baby, I'll take you for a ride when I return. They scurried back to the cabin to finish their work, and Miguel and John boarded the boat.

They rigged the sails instinctively, every movement a subconscious expression of each man's mastery of the sea. The wind gave them a swift start, and they glided across the bay. There was no fishing gear on the boat, which made Miguel wonder what his friend had up his sleeve. John could not keep a grin from spreading across his face, and Miguel suspected a surprise of some sort.

John pulled the tiller to head toward a sandy landing, and the sloop coasted into the shallows. Miguel looked around for a clue as to why they had stopped in this place, but nothing stood out to him, and his confusion deepened. As the boat scraped on the sandy beach, John reached under the bench for the package that he brought. He carefully untied the string from around a stack of papers. He pulled out a bottle of ink and a pen.

"Miguel," Fogarty said, "*This* is an application for us to fill out so that you can own the land that you have lived and worked on for so many years. The State of Florida's Homestead Act has given you, a fisherman from Menorca, the chance to be a landowner in America. Tomorrow, I will send these documents off to Tallahassee, and perhaps by mid-summer you will have a deed to your beautiful Terrasilla. Miguel's Bay will be on the map of Florida for all of your descendants to see!"

Miguel looked up at his friend, his eyes shining with gratitude. His throat was too choked with emotion to speak. He had always struggled with the English language, particularly with reading and writing—he could barely sign his own name, and this was an embarrassment to him. Frederica had to do his business paperwork, and sometimes even she would require assistance with the words and numbers. Captain John had known this about his friend, so he had taken it upon himself not only to organize the application for Miguel, but to take him to a private place so that his family would not see him struggle over the papers. *John is a true friend,* thought Miguel, *and I will never be able to thank him properly for this act of thoughtfulness.*

Together the two men began to work through the tedious, endless pile of papers. The last step was to date and sign the final page, and Miguel hesitantly took the pen from John's steady hand. Slowly and carefully, the fisherman signed his name, M-IG-E-L G-E-R-R-E-R-O, April 3, 1868, Manatee County, Florida.

Miguel and John sat for a few minutes and waited for the ink to dry in the breeze. Each man contemplated the importance of these papers and what they would bring to the Guerrero family. What an opportunity Miguel had been given! The dream of passing rich land on to his sons would not have been attainable in Menorca.

Once they were dry, John carefully placed the documents in the heavy envelope. Miguel secured it with a string tied with a fisherman's knot. "Miguel," John chuckled, "Don't make it too hard for those soft politicians to open!" They both laughed at the thought of a skinny, pale-skinned man in a suit peering through thick glasses at the impossible knot.

Captain John wrapped the precious package of papers in a piece of an old sail to protect it. The two friends paused and looked at one another, each cherishing the experience that they shared.

Miguel reached out and firmly grasped the hand of Captain John Fogarty, "Gracias, mi amigo."

John answered him, "Let's head on back to *Miguel's Island* and tell your beautiful wife the good news!"

Hurry Home

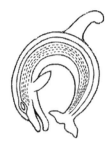

Miguel had always loved to sail alone when he was close to home. By himself, he was better able to appreciate the sights and the sounds of the sea. Pleasant memories of his past were free to surface, and the solitude enabled him to think without interruption.

Times had changed. His fishing trips with Michael and Frederick were his favorites now, and he missed them terribly when he was away from home. The boys teased Frederica that some trips were for the men only, and how they had secret adventures about which she could never know. Michael claimed to be the first mate, and Frederick always made sure he packed snacks for each trip.

Today, they were headed to Hunter's Point. It took a while to get there, but the shallow waters were safe, and the boys loved to collect shells on the beach of Palm Island. They could sell the dried starfish they found to travelers at Aunt Julia's store, and they used the money to buy candy or little presents for their mother.

It was a perfect day for sailing. Gentle breezes easily moved the boat along, and fluffy clouds blocked the sun so that Miguel and the boys didn't get sunburned. Frederica always insisted the boys wear hats and shirts until they swam to protect their skin from the hot Florida sun.

Miguel was in a great mood, and he sang old Menorcan fishing songs at the top of his lungs as the boat cut through the waves. He marveled that the boys had learned the songs and could sing along, despite the fact that they didn't know the meaning of the words.

They fished, swam, explored the old Indian mounds, collected shells, and played in the sugar-like sand until almost sunset.

As he prepared the boat for the return to Terrasilla, Miguel saw something disturbing in his peripheral vision. He turned and saw Frederick collapse on the beach. He ran to his son to see what was happening.

Miguel had Michael fetch water from the boat, and he made Frederick drink. Perhaps Frederick was just dehydrated? Yes, that must be it. The water and some rest would make him right.

The hope his son was simply dehydrated began to fade as Miguel moved him back to the boat. He burned with fever and went completely limp in Miguel's arms. Frederick's eyes closed, and he was unable to respond to his father's voice.

Frederick laid his head in Michael's lap as Miguel sailed home. His father took every shortcut that he could find. Miguel prayed through bitter tears that his son had merely become overheated, and this was not the demon fever that had so recently crept into the area.

The Heart Breaks Twice

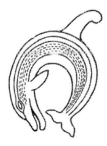

No parent should ever have to bury a child, thought Miguel as he wiped sweat from his eyes. Fiddler crabs scampered into their holes as he lowered the crude pine box into the grave. This box contained the body of his son, Michael, who would now rest along the creek bank next to his brother.

Why wouldn't the tears come? Miguel wondered if his heart had turned to stone when Frederica looked at him with accusing eyes after Frederick had taken his last breath. Now they were both heartbroken after watching Michael follow his brother into the afterlife.

He turned as Frederica came out of the house. She held little Mary tightly to her breast, and Christopher and Robert trailed behind. She joined Miguel at the graves and dropped to her knees beside the box that contained Frederick. She cried softly at first, then began to emit a long, sorrowful wail that came from the very depths of her soul. It was as if the maternal spirits from all of the preceding ages joined in her grieving. The wails of every mother who had ever lost a child could be heard in that scream. Mary began to cry.

Frederica quickly composed herself. She stood and looked at Miguel as he lowered Michael into the hole. She wore a dull, blue-grey dress—it was the closest to black of any of her garments. A tattered black veil concealed her tears from the younger children. Robert, the youngest child, was throwing oyster shells at a dragonfly perched on the branch of an overhanging mangrove. Christopher stood with his face buried in the folds of his mother's skirt. No doubt he was sensing that something wasn't right.

Miguel stood on the opposite side of the open grave from Frederica. He strained to hear her utter a soliloquy that was almost inaudible. "*Mein Gott, warum hast du mich getotet?*" Whatever she had said, he was sure it was meant for God's ears, not his. There was a long, awkward silence as they stood in the shade of the mangroves and stared down at the yellow pine box in the bottom of the dark pit.

Miguel tried to say some words, but the lump in his throat strangled every attempt. *What could he say to lessen the grief of his family? Nothing.* He thrust the point of his shovel violently into the earth and tossed the black mud mixed with oyster shells on the lid of Michael's coffin.

"*Warte mal!*" Frederica cried. She removed her veil and stepped to the edge of the grave, lifting her face upward.

With closed eyes she began to speak into the blue morning sky. It was a final litany that only she could understand.

Her display of courage and inner strength shamed Miguel who found himself lacking those qualities. "Boys, say goodbye to your brothers," Frederica whispered as she pointed down toward the grave so the children would understand. Christopher, who had been concealing himself in the fabric of his mother's skirt, walked up to the grave and tossed a little wooden boat onto the top of Michael's coffin. He waved goodbye and turned away.

Frederica put her hand over her mouth and looked at Miguel. He had made the little boat for Michael when he was about Christopher's age. Their favorite pastime had been sailing the boat along the little creek, their imaginations aglow with thoughts of sea voyages, jungle adventures, and pirates.

Miguel's eyes were swollen with tears. He looked upward to keep them from rolling down his flushed cheeks. Thoughts of Michael and Frederick filled his mind. He pictured them sailing along with the white clouds. The rising morning sun tinted the sky yellow-orange, and the boys were happy and free from the cares of this world. Miguel wished he could rise up and join them on their lofty voyage.

When he looked down again, Frederica and the children were gone. They had made their way quietly back to the cabin and left Miguel to the solemn task of filling in the little graves. Every shovel of dirt was a reminder that he would never see his sons' smiles or hear their laughter again on this earth. He tamped down the damp mud and covered the little mound with oyster shells. He whispered, "*Hasta nuestro próximo viaje*," as he placed the two little crosses that he had made from branches of an ancient live oak. The tree stood sentinel on the Indian mound where the boys had liked to play.

Miguel felt like he was suffocating, and he needed to get back out on the water to busy himself and try to forget his grief. As he gathered his gear from the work shed, his heart told him he should go to Frederica and comfort her, but his pride restrained him. His wife's body language, and how she avoided eye contact, convinced him that she blamed him for exposing her sons to the fever. He had taken the boys sailing with him last week to Tampa for supplies, and they had fallen ill soon after their return.

Miguel walked down the mound and out onto the dock. He threw his gear into the boat. When he turned back to the house, Frederica was watching from the door. He thundered out coldly, "I'm going fishing". The words surged up from a deep well of pain, and he was sorry for them as soon as they escaped his lips. He pushed off and jumped into the boat. He looked back, intending to shout to Frederica that he was sorry, but she was gone.

A Trip to the Spring

Frederica walked through the back door of the cabin and steadied herself against a rough post. She closed her eyes for a moment and felt the sun on her face. She had to draw strength from somewhere for the sake of her children.

She was so tired and weak, and her body had not yet forgotten the pain of childbirth and sleepless nights that had followed, but how could she complain? Mary was the most beautiful baby girl she had ever seen. She was a little angel, pure and innocent. Frederica had been given the gift of another child before disease and death snatched her first two sons out of her arms. Their bodies now rested in mounds of sand and shell not far from the cabin.

The death of Michael and Frederick continued to burn like a white-hot knife in her heart. She had to force herself not to dwell on their memories, because they would drag her into a bottomless pit from which she could not escape. Despite being so young, Christopher and Robert were sensitive to her heartbreak. They were obedient and loving

382

to their mother. They would hold her face in their hands, smile, and wipe her tears with their little fingers.

Frederica knew she had to pull herself together. She needed to be healthy for her family. She would only see her older boys again when she took her last breath on this earth, and for the sake of her children, that could not be soon.

Snap out of it, Frederica. You have three living children who need food and water. She wrapped her shawl tightly around her shoulders and noticed that the air was unusually cool for a summer day. The wind picked up as a storm brewed in the Gulf. Her thoughts focused on Miguel.

He had left on a short trip to obtain fish and buy supplies. Their stores had become low since the birth of the baby— neither parent had time to keep up with their normal routine. Miguel promised that he would be back as soon as possible, since he knew how much Frederica and the boys needed him right now.

She stared at the dark clouds as they rolled toward the land. A cold, misty rain started, and it would only get worse. This could be one of those dangerous gales that takes you by surprise and becomes serious very quickly.

Frederica had to get to the spring for water before the children woke up. The horse and wagon had been borrowed by a neighbor, so she would have to walk in a hurry.

The door was secured so the boys would not be able to come outside until she returned, and Frederica prayed they would not wake up for at least another hour. Mary should sleep for at least two hours before needing to be fed again.

Two big wooden buckets hung from nails on the side of the cabin. Frederica thought about how heavy they would be when full of water. As she walked into the wind, it blew her back toward the cabin. The rain hit her in the face and she squinted. She wished she had grabbed her hat, but she didn't want to take the time to go back for it. Her stomach started to cramp, but she pushed through the pain as she hurried down the shell path. *Walk faster, Frederica!*

When she arrived at the spring, she was soaked and shivering. The cool water churned around her feet as she filled the buckets. She shivered uncontrollably as the sheets of rain washed over her face. The buckets of water were so heavy that she had to walk bent over, and the pelting rain made it difficult to see the path. The wind caused her to stumble frequently, and she nearly fell several times.

Her feet stuck in the mud, so she decided to cut through the woods. She tried not to panic as she thought about the children waking up and finding her gone. *Hurry up, Frederica! They need you!* The wind howled as her hair blew around her face. She couldn't see the path and she stared at her feet as she walked in order to stay on course.

A scream of frustration escaped her throat as the water sloshed out of the buckets. *Almost there! Keep going!* She was dizzy, and she had to focus on putting just one foot in front of the other. *It can't be too much farther.*

When she finally reached the porch, she dropped the buckets in relief. As she straightened up, a sharp pain in her back brought her to her knees. Something was terribly wrong. *Let me just get inside,* she thought.

Because of the wind, the door stubbornly refused to open—once it did, it slammed shut behind her as she dragged the buckets inside. She spilled much of the precious water onto the floor. Frederica fell into a chair to catch her breath. Somehow the children had slept through the noise of the wind and rain. She was relieved they had not awakened without her there.

She pulled off her shoes and wet clothes and considered building a fire even though it was almost July. The shivering would not stop, so she wrapped herself in a blanket and sipped a cup of hot coffee.

As much as Frederica didn't want to admit it to herself, she suspected the worst about her symptoms and was terrified. *Could this be the same fever that had killed her boys?* She prayed to God that he would miraculously bring Miguel home to her. She had never needed him more than at this very moment. She felt alone and helpless. *This could not be happening. Why was this happening?* The wind abated for a time and the cabin grew quiet. With the windows closed the cabin was dark, and Frederica realized this was probably why the boys continued to sleep.

Her body stopped trembling for a little while and she dozed off. The rain outside continued to fall, and the wind rattled the shutters again.

When she opened her eyes, Mary was stirring in her cradle. Christopher was sitting up in his bed playing with a toy, and Robert was making his way toward her with his little blanket—he wanted her to pick him up for a snuggle.

Frederica tried to appreciate this moment. She cherished every detail of her life—the children, the cabin, and the sounds and sights that she had come to love on this wild island. She glanced through the window and looked for the familiar sails that always brought Miguel home to her.

As the heat of fever rose in her body, she realized she was about to face the biggest storm of her life, and she would have to ride it out alone. Two cups of spring water made her feel slightly better, and she put Mary in a sling, so her hands would be free while they started the morning ritual.

The first stop for the family was to get eggs from the chicken house. They would then walk in the woods to check the rabbit traps, and finally they would pick oranges. Frederica used to love the morning walk, but since the fever took the older boys, she used it as her time to cry. She walked behind

Christopher and Robert, so they would not see the tears that flooded her face. Two pieces of her heart were buried by the creek side. The pain of losing the boys was unbearable, but her other children still needed her. They were the reason she got out of bed in the morning.

After gathering eggs, they looked for special treasures to put on the graves. Robert found a bird feather. Christopher found a small turtle shell and what he described as, "the most beautiful stick he had ever seen." It was somehow comforting to visit the graves. Maybe if her boys could see her from heaven, they would know that she constantly thought of them and ached to be near them. It also helped Christopher and Robert understand that their older brothers could not come home to them ever again. It was a painful lesson to have to learn at such a young age.

Upon reaching the creek, the boys placed the new treasures on the fresh graves beside the other offerings that had been brought just days before. Frederica envisioned herself removing the layer of oyster shell and reaching into the loamy soil to pull up their bodies and hold them one more time. Now she could only dream about having them with her. How cruel for them to be taken after such a short time on Earth! They had fallen ill, suffered, and then died together. They were best friends as well as brothers, and they had always been inseparable.

Back at the cabin, Frederica struggled to finish all of the necessary chores. She grieved for Miguel's losses. His children were his greatest source of pride and joy. She imagined him making his way home through the storm.

A wave of nausea washed over her as she peeled vegetables and she had to sit down. She drank more water and tried to eat, but her appetite was gone. The boys listened gravely as she explained what was happening to her. She urged them to stay on the porch and wait for their Papa so that they would not catch her illness. Christopher cried. Just days earlier he watched his brothers die, and now his mother was sick.

Robbie held up his hands and a bewildered look appeared on his face when she did not respond. She was simply too weak. Heartbroken, she pointed to the door and urged the boys to leave her.

She tried to be so careful to protect her family from this terrible fever. Some folks suspected that the disease came from mosquitoes, so she and the children wore long sleeves and covered their legs, even in the tremendous heat. They always came inside at dusk to avoid the twilight swarms of insects. While Michael and Frederick were sick, she kept them away from the rest of the family and washed everything they touched. She kept the windows open so that the fresh sea breeze would keep the house from becoming hot and still.

Dizziness overcame Frederica again, and she stumbled out to the back porch. The vomiting began as she leaned over the porch rail. She was burning up.

388

When she came back into the cabin, she changed into a clean, white nightgown and braided her long, brown hair as if she was preparing for bed. She knew her sons would carry this vision of her for a lifetime, so she wanted to look peaceful, as if asleep. She tried to feed Mary one more time, but the fever had caused her milk to dry up. Her sons had been prepared for this scenario weeks ago. She and Miguel had taught them what to do if something happened to her while their father was gone. They even knew how to put drops of milk and water into Mary's mouth to feed her until help came.

Frederica put Mary in the bed beside her and prayed that she would be safe until help arrived. She pulled back the sheets, so she wouldn't become entangled in them.

As she waited for death to come, she wondered, *Will it be terrifying? Will I experience excruciating pain? Will I look disgusting to Miguel when he finds me?* She hated the thought of leaving him with a gruesome image of her that would haunt him for the rest of his days. How sad that such a kind and loving man must experience so much heartbreak in such a short time.

In her delirium, memories of her life filled her mind. *Michael and Fredrick had been two perfect young boys just on the brink of becoming men. Miguel had taught them to catch fish, and he had even made them their own small nets for Christmas one year. They could hunt small animals with their bows and arrows.*

They climbed trees like little monkeys, and they swam like fish. They lived every day of their lives to the fullest.

Her boys had treated Frederica like the queen of her castle. Miguel taught them to stand at their chairs and to not sit at dinner until she was seated. They helped her with the daily chores of the house with no complaints. Frederick loved to brush his mother's hair at night, and Michael told funny stories that made her laugh.

Miguel put the children to bed when he was home to give Frederica a break. He told them wild stories of pirates and Indians, of terrible storms in the ocean, and giant sea creatures that lurked in the deeps. Then he would calm them by describing soothing images of the boys floating on water that looked like glass or laying in the soft, warm beach sand under a golden sunset.

A breeze blew through the bedroom window and made the thin curtain flutter. The cool air was refreshing, and Frederica felt something release in her body. A sudden sense of calm overtook her, and the shaking and fever was gone. For a moment she thought she might be getting better.

She sat up in the bed and looked out of the window toward Miguel's Bay.

A small sailboat had docked, and two figures walked toward the cabin. They carried bouquets of flowers in their arms.

Her heart pounded as they drew close enough for her to recognize them. Michael and Frederick walked through the door of her bedroom with the sweetest smiles on their faces. Their skin was healthy and gleamed in the light, their white clothes were brilliant and clean, and the flowers emitted the most intense, wonderful smell.

Michael spoke first in perfect Bavarian, and it sounded as if he had grown up with her in her native land. "Mother, we have come for you. You don't have to suffer anymore, and we can be together in a place more beautiful than Terrasilla. The boat is waiting. Our little brothers and the baby will be cared for and loved. Papa will be home soon. We passed him on the way here."

Frederica sat up. She hugged Mary one more time and gently kissed her on her forehead. They passed by Christopher and Robbie as they left. They were asleep on the front porch bench. She stroked their hair and kissed each of them on the top of their heads. She noticed a huge, yellow butterfly hovering over them, and she wished they were awake to see it.

 The older boys took her by the hand and led her out to the boat. Together they sailed away.

True Love Lost

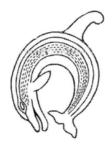

Miguel was awakened by the squawking of seagulls. As he opened his eyes, he saw that the birds were on his boat. Their black-tipped wings were fluttering as beaks pecked frantically at his catch of fish. He attempted to get up to chase them off, but he was too weak. He watched helplessly as they destroyed his catch.

It took him a few moments to figure out where he was. He had been becalmed, and because he was too weak to row the rest of the way home, he had anchored just off the coast of Terrasilla Island.

A storm was brewing out in the gulf. A sharp breeze made him shiver uncontrollably as it passed over his sweat-soaked skin. Mustering all the strength that remained in his weak, aching muscles, he pulled up anchor, hoisted the mainsail, and pointed the bow toward home. How good it would be to sleep in his own bed.

A sense of relief enveloped him as his boat passed through the mouth of Terrasilla Bay. He drifted in and out of consciousness, but the sound of the hull scraping over oyster shells awakened him fully as the boat glided through the shallow, mangrove-lined cut into his bay. The orange sun rose above the eastern shoreline where his cabin stood. It burned through the grey mist rising from the surface of the water. His head throbbed, and he raged with fever. Miguel felt he was drifting in a dream.

His eyes brightened when he came within sight of his cabin, and he hoped to see Frederica standing on top of the midden with her beautiful dark hair blowing freely in the morning breeze. She often watched for him to return from his fishing trips, but he wasn't overly concerned when he didn't see her. *It's still early*, he thought. *She's probably inside feeding the baby.*

As the boat pulled near shore, a terrible premonition overcame Miguel. His experience as a guide during the Seminole Wars told him that something wasn't right. No smoke rose from the chimney, nor did he hear the sounds of Christopher and Robert playing. Most alarming was the sight of the black buzzards circling high above the cabin. The scene reminded him of the Seminole villages that had been abandoned in the Everglades during the war.

A feeling of panic overcame him as he made his approach to the dock. He bumped it hard with the boat, tied the bowline swiftly, and jumped onto shore leaving the sails up and the stern swinging out into the bay. He ran toward the mound and called out desperately, "Frederica! Christopher!"

Miguel struggled up the slope using both hands and feet. There was still no answer from the cabin. When he reached the summit of the mound, the door of the cabin had been left wide open, and the curtains were blowing out through the open window. There was definitely something wrong.

Then he saw Christopher and Robbie running toward him from across the yard, and he breathed a sigh of relief. Bella followed a few yards behind the boys. They were filthy, and they were crying uncontrollably.

"*¿Dónde están Mamá y Mary?*" he asked. He swept the children into his arms and hugged them close. Christopher looked toward the house. Then Miguel smelled it—the unmistakable odor of death coming from the cabin.

Miguel told the boys to stay where they were and ran to the cabin. As he reached the porch, the rancid stench nearly overwhelmed him. He covered his mouth and nose with his shirt and walked inside. He was petrified by what he saw— Frederica lay on their bed with her face turned slightly toward the open window. Her eyes were open as if she was looking at something across the bay. She had a slight hint of a smile on her face. Little Mary was cradled in the crook of her arm.

"Frederica! Dear God!" he whispered and crossed the room to the bedside to collapse across her. "What have I done?" he cried, as his lips touched her cold forehead. From the condition she was in she had been dead for some time. "You must have fallen sick right after I left home. How you must have suffered! I should've been here with you!" he cried. Miguel's heart was crushed under the weight of his guilt.

He sensed a slight movement on the bed to his right, and then he heard a faint whimper. *Mary is still alive!* He pulled her carefully from her mother's stiff arms. They were frozen around the child as if Frederica would not let her go. Miguel took his daughter out into the fresh air.

The baby was limp, glassy-eyed, and burning up with fever. As he carried her down the mound and away from the putrid air in the cabin, he felt faint and it was becoming difficult to breath.

"Christopher, *agua!*" he shouted. Christopher ran for the water jug and followed his father to a shady spot beneath the trees. Miguel took the jug and dripped small amounts of water into the baby's mouth. He took a drink himself and stretched out in the grass.

He stared with tear-filled eyes at the twin crosses by the creek. Now it was Frederica who must be laid to rest. Mary would probably come next, and then it would be his turn. He wondered if Christopher and Robbie would show symptoms soon. Why did this have to happen? He was losing everything—his whole family was being destroyed. Why would God allow this to happen to them? How could he have left Frederica and the children alone?

Miguel stopped himself. There was no time for grief or blame. What would happen to the children if he died? Somehow, he must get them to safety. He thought of the Atzeroths—they were the closest homestead by land, but he knew he was too weak to make the trip.

He coughed hard and noticed that his white shirt was splattered with blood. Michael and Frederick had begun coughing up blood just before they died, and he'd seen it in the Knoxville hospital during the war. He looked up— buzzards circled overhead. He thought of Frederica. He knew he was running out of time and must give her a proper Christian burial—he owed her that much.

Miguel told the boys to wait for him outside as he entered the cabin. Mary was tucked in the crook of his left arm, and under his right arm was a roll of sailcloth. Their home now felt like a tomb. He laid the baby on the bed, so she would be safe from the buzzards outside that were slowly becoming more brazen. He closed Frederica's eyelids and washed her body clean of all the marks of her suffering. He marveled at how beautiful she was, even in death. He felt a wave of emotion cresting within him but shook it off for the sake of the boys.

Miguel rolled his wife's body into the old sail and lowered it carefully to the floor. As he dragged the canvas shroud over the threshold and out into the backyard, he remembered the first time he carried Frederica across the same threshold after their wedding. They had been so happy, but that day seemed like a distant memory.

Miguel knelt beside the canvas and sewed it close with a sail needle and linen thread. The memories of the times spent with Frederica flooded his mind. The emotions overwhelmed him, and he could hold them in no longer. He sobbed uncontrollably and collapsed beside Frederica on the oyster shells—he was unable to continue. He felt too weak to move his wife, and he knew he might die right there beside her. He cried out again, "Why is this happening?" He thought of Mary, who was still lying on the bed inside the cabin. He looked to his right and saw Christopher and Robbie run into the mangrove jungle screaming in terror. "My children! My God, what will become of my children?"

The blistering summer sun was high in the sky, beating down mercilessly on Miguel. He laid himself down on the eastern slope of the midden next to Frederica's body. Oyster shells cut into his chest and forearms. He was delirious, and he was on the verge of losing consciousness altogether. Darkness hung over Miguel's Bay. The smell of death overwhelmed him.

An Anchor in the Storm

Asa Bishop had been home on the river for over a week. He needed to work, but the outbreak of sickness had kept many people close to their families and away from town. The pestilence lurked around every corner, and no one knew when it might enter their home and steal away a loved one.

He looked toward the dock and saw a steamer arriving from Fort Brooke. There would not be many passengers, but supplies would be on board, and hopefully the mail would be delivered. He knew this would be a quick stop, and he very much wanted to hear any news. He grabbed his wife's burlap grocery sack and hurried off toward the dock.

The captain jumped on the dock and walked toward Asa, who instinctively put out his hand to greet the man, but the captain did not offer his in return. Instead he said, "Mr. Bishop, the fever has spread like wildfire. It's not only in Tampa, it's spreading out to the farms and coastal families as well. The doctors are baffled as to how to treat it."

The captain continued, "The last three times I have been by Terrasilla I have looked toward Miguel's cabin and there have been no signs of life—no flag, no sign of Miss Frederica or the boys, nothing. Can you go check on them?"

Asa took off toward his boat at a full run. He prayed that the tide was high enough to allow him into Miguel's landing, and that the wind would be strong enough to get him there quickly. He had made this trip often, but the voyage seemed to take forever, this time. The whole way there, he prayed he would glide up to the dock and hear the children playing as the pleasant smells of Frederica's cooking hung in the air. He knew that Miguel was away on a quick trip, but surely, he was back by now. Miguel knew he couldn't stay away for long since Frederica needed his help with the baby.

Asa rounded the corner and his heart sank. He took in the eerie silence and the utter stillness of the place. There was no smoke from a cook-fire, no animals in the yard, and no voices coming through the windows. There were no signs of life anywhere. The door stood wide open as it swung back and forth, creaking in the wind.

He felt a momentary sense of relief when he noticed that Miguel's boat was anchored. Then he observed that the boat was poorly secured and was still fully-loaded. Birds were eating the fish as they rotted in the sun, and the sails had not been let down. Something was terribly wrong.

He called out the children's names as he ran toward the cabin. He stormed through the door and the smell of death immediately made Asa feel as though he might be violently sick.

Little baby Mary was faintly crying in Miguel's bed, but no one else was there. Asa's first impulse was to pick up the baby and soothe her, but he knew he had to find the others. As he pushed open the back door of the cabin, his friend Miguel hovered over his sweet Frederica's lifeless body. He was sobbing as he wrapped his wife's corpse in an old canvas sail.

"Miguel! I'm here!" Asa called.

Miguel was too distraught to speak. His face was ashen as he tried to sew the canvas around his wife's body. When Asa looked into the fisherman's eyes, he could see that Miguel was utterly shattered by shock and grief. Miguel rose to greet Asa and collapsed in his arms, hot with fever and very weak.

Together they were able to bury Frederica by the creek where Michael and Frederick had been laid to rest. Miguel was becoming delirious from the fever, and Asa knew he had to get his friend and the baby to a doctor as soon as possible. He looked around, but he didn't see Christopher and Robert. He would have to get Miguel and Mary to his boat and then search for the boys. Asa called out their names one more time, but no answer came.

Asa struggled to get Miguel onto the boat. The baby went quiet and still as she lay in the fish basket that Asa had lined with a blanket. He wondered if he could get them back to his house alive. He begged God to help him—he felt so helpless.

Out of the corner of his eye, Asa saw movement in the shallow water near the mangroves. Two little boys stood motionless and paralyzed with fear. Asa went to them and gathered them up. Once they were in his arms, they clung to him and cried. Their clothes were wet and filthy. He lowered them into the boat, but he made sure to keep them away from Miguel. The last thing that they needed was to be exposed to the fever again.

He tried to get Miguel to drink some water as they made their way toward the river. The fisherman spoke nonsense and occasionally called out Frederica's name. Asa dipped a cloth into the water and squeezed it into Mary's tiny mouth. He was relieved to see her swallow the small drops.

When Miguel shivered uncontrollably in the wind, Asa took off his shirt and coat to cover him. He wrapped Mary up tighter in the blanket and held her close to his chest to keep her warm. He kissed her forehead, and Asa's heart skipped a beat when he realized the baby felt feverish too. The sun was beginning to set, and darkness was descending.

Before Asa had left for Terrasilla, his wife had hurriedly gathered up sandwiches, bananas, and milk and packed them in the boat. When Christopher and Robert were offered the food, they ate as if they were starving. Asa could not imagine how exhausted they must be after the horror of the last few days. He showed the boys where the soft nets lay in the bottom of the boat, encouraged them to lie down, and the gentle lapping of the water rocked them to sleep.

Asa was overcome with emotion as he looked at Miguel and his sons. It didn't seem right to leave Frederica on the island, but he was sure that he and Miguel would go back later to bury her properly. He thought about his time spent serving with Miguel in the militia and then in the Confederate army. They had survived so much—surely this fever would not take him.

The boat made the wide turn that headed up the river, where a group of concerned neighbors waited for them to arrive at the dock on Bishop's Point. Two men met the boat and carried Miguel to the house. Granny Tinsley grabbed the baby. Mary Bishop and her sister-in-law each carried one of the boys. The children never stirred and were put directly to bed.

The women whispered amongst themselves. "What a horrible tragedy these children had endured at such a tender age." They wept over their friend Frederica and wished that they had sensed her need. The image of the dying mother holding her baby would torment all of them. Granny Tinsley was able to mix up a baby formula. Mary took it, but she was very weak.

While Asa waited for Dr. Pelot to arrive, he prayed that he would suddenly wake from this horrific nightmare and look around to see that all was well with the family. Then he would walk out to his amigo Miguel. The fisherman would be smiling and laughing, his two boys would be sitting on his lap. Asa shook his head and let out a long, terrible sigh. His heart told him that this was no dream.

Asa Bishop's House

A thin beam of light found its way between the bedroom curtains and settled on Christopher's face. He was still so tired that all he wanted to do was sleep. He reached out his arm and felt Robbie next to him, snoring softly like he did every morning.

As he lay with his hand touching his little brother's shoulder, images and memories of the last few days invaded his waking thoughts. He remembered seeing his mother lying in her bed, very still and quiet. The contrast of her long, brown hair against her nightgown made her look like an angel. She told him that she might not wake up, and it scared him. Frederick and Michael hadn't woken up either, and he missed them terribly. If Mama didn't wake up, that would mean she was with his brothers in heaven. That was good, because Heaven was a happy place, but it was bad because he didn't want his mother to leave him. She told him he would have to take care of Robbie and Mary until Papa returned.

Christopher knew where to find the bread and water that was left, and he knew how to get milk from the cow. He could pick fruits and vegetables all by himself.

A long day dragged on and Papa did not come home. Christopher was terrified when the light faded, but he was hopeful he would see his Papa's boat at the dock in the morning. Another day went by, and then another sleepless night. The food was all gone, so the boys ate raw potatoes and tomatoes out of the garden. Christopher was able to get a little milk from the cow, but she was spooked by a rat and chased him out of her pen.

Mary cried a lot. He tried to put milk into her mouth with a spoon, but she started to choke so he stopped. He didn't want his sister to die, too.

Christopher and Robbie sat on the dock and stared at the horizon until the sky was dark. Papa did not come. They were hungry and scared, so they barred the door. Christopher got a splinter under his thumbnail that made him cry even more. He rubbed Robbie's hair until his brother went to sleep. Mama had done this every night until she went to sleep forever, never to wake up.

Papa's voice woke them up on the third day. The boys were so happy to see him, and they knew that everything would be all right, but Papa didn't act right. He tried to help Mama by carrying her outside. He told them to stay inside the cabin with Mary until he returned.

Christopher found Papa asleep in the grass by the creek. He hoped he would feel better when he woke up. There was sweat on his Papa's face, but he shivered a lot. He put a blanket over him and tried to make him drink water.

When they heard noises from the shallows, they ran to the shore and saw a big sailboat coming toward them over the breakers. It was almost sunset, and they couldn't see the man's face very well. He didn't look like one of Papa's fishing friends. The man yelled out in a deep voice, but Christopher couldn't understand him. A scary thought gnawed at him. What if this was a bad man coming to take them from their family since Mama died? He knew that Papa was too sick to fight a bad man.

Christopher took Robbie's hand and ran. They hid among the mangroves and tried to be very quiet and still. The brothers hid for a long time and watched as the big man carried Papa to the boat in a blanket. *Had he taken Mary too?* The man went back into the cabin and brought out a fish basket with a blanket falling over the sides. He must have Mary.

The boys continued to watch as the man stood on the dock and carefully studied the land around the cabin. They clung together in fear when he caught sight of them. As he slowly walked through the water toward them, his face came into view. He softly called their names and held out his arms. Christopher recognized Mr. Bishop and ran to him. He knew that Mr. Bishop would save the rest of his family.

Collapsing into his arms was the last memory he had before waking up in this house.

Christopher was wide awake now, and he wondered who had brought him to this bed. He smelled bacon frying and heard lots of unfamiliar soft voices in another room. He sat up, and through a doorway he could see a woman with yellow hair. She wore a blue dress and stirred something in a bowl. The woman was too busy to notice that he was awake. Suddenly his thoughts turned to Papa. *What had happened to him? Did he wake up?* Christopher realized that he had to get up and find him.

Across the room, was an open door. Christopher tiptoed quietly over to see where it led. It opened into another bedroom and lying on a large bed underneath a brown blanket was his Papa. Relief poured over him and he ran to the bed and cried, "Papa! Papa! You *are* alive!" Miguel could barely open his eyes, but he held out his hand and Christopher grabbed it. He rested his head on his Papa's chest and cried. He thought that all would be well now that they were together.

Mary Bishop came into the bedroom, gently took Christopher's hand, and led him out to the kitchen. "Sweetheart, I bet you're hungry for some breakfast," she said, leading him to a big round table.

Someone had gotten his brother out of bed and he sat in a young woman's lap eating a biscuit smothered with red jelly.

Every now and then he would reach up and touch her curly red hair, and she would smile back at him.

*****

Asa burst through the front door with Rev. Edmund Lee right behind him. Without a word they went straight to the room where Miguel was fighting for his life. Lee rushed to Miguel and leaned over him, but Miguel raised his hand to stop his friend. The message was clear, he didn't want the men to catch the fever. Edmund muttered, "God, protect me," and moved right in to talk to Miguel, against his wishes.

Miguel's fever raged, but he felt comforted by the presence of his friends. The sight of Edmund brought back memories of his wedding day, their patrols together during the Seminole War, and marching side by side from Fort Brooke to Kentucky during the Civil War. What a kind man he was.

Miguel clutched the Reverend's arm and whispered the words, "Mis hijos."

Edmund spoke in his low, reassuring voice, "Your children will forever be loved and taken care of by your friends and neighbors. Electa and I will take Christopher and baby Mary, and John and Mary Fogarty will welcome Robbie into their home. We will cherish them and prepare them for a great life. They will inherit your property on Terrasilla when

408

they are old enough to receive the deed." Edmund choked back tears. "We will never let them forget you and Frederica. We will speak of you often and tell great stories of their brave and courageous father. Be assured, they will become excellent sailors. They will make fine nets, and they will be feared by all the fish in these waters!"

Miguel tried to smile when his friend spoke of fishing.

Edmund continued, "They will speak perfect Spanish, and Julia and Eliza will continue to pass on Frederica's Bavarian heritage—I promise."

Miguel sighed, "I can't..."

Reverend Lee, who had been with many dying men over the years, knew that his time had come. "You rest easy, my friend. You have fought the good fight and finished your race. You can let go. Your Lord and Savior is waiting for you along with those precious loved ones who have gone on before you."

Miguel's grip loosened and his hand slid off his friend's arm. His body felt light, and a euphoric feeling washed over him. A door swung open in his mind, and a familiar voice said, "*Buenos días, mi hijo*. The wind is right, the sails are full, and the sea is calling. You have many friends waiting for you at the next port." Miguel quickly rose to embrace Josep Miguel Guerrero-Rossello, his own Papa. How wonderful it was to feel his father's strong arms around him again after so many years. Miguel and Papa Josep passed by the boys as they ate their breakfast. He stopped and kissed their heads, whispering "Papa loves you" in their ears. Mary turned and smiled at them as they passed.

***

Christopher could hear the men as they moved Miguel out of the back room, and he wanted to be there to help. He knew that the men were going to bury his father just like his mother and brothers had been buried. Overwhelmed with fear and sadness, he looked out the window and started to cry. He was suddenly scooped up into Electa Lee's arms, and he rested his head on her shoulder. She held him tight and swayed back and forth until he calmed down. He sat in her lap for a long time and she spoke soothing words in his ear.

Another woman brought in a large tub and filled it with warm water and soap. When they finished eating, the boys were scrubbed with a big sponge, dried off, and dressed in clean clothes. The woman brought some sweet-smelling oil to rub in their hair and on all the bug bites they had gotten while hiding in the mangroves. She combed out their hair and cleaned their teeth with a little brush that tasted good.

She had a big canvas bag. Inside were little boats and animals made out of wood. She pulled a tiny, brown puppy out of a perforated box.

Robbie sat on the floor, mesmerized by the puppy. It licked his face and neck and made him giggle. They played for a long time, and the women smiled as she watched the two of them. "I'm Mary Fogarty," she said, as she sat on the floor beside Robbie. Her eyes brimmed with tears. Without warning, Robbie crawled up into Mary's lap and she held his little hand. The puppy curled up and went to sleep and was put back into his box.

Christopher walked out of the kitchen and into the large room with the fireplace. He had suddenly remembered his sister and was frantically looking for her. He found an old woman rocking Mary in a chair. The baby had been cleaned up and wrapped in a pink blanket. She wasn't crying, so he figured someone had found a way to feed her. Her little eyes were open, and she was looking around, curiously. Christopher bent down and kissed her on the hand, and she reached up and touched his face. He knew his mother would be proud that he had taken care of her and Robbie.

An hour passed, and some close neighbors arrived at Bishop's Point. Sarah Lee stayed inside with Robbie and Mary as they napped. Everyone else walked outside to the place where Miguel's body was laid to rest in a simple grave marked with a plank of cedar. Reverend Lee read scriptures about Heaven and spoke of Miguel being reunited with Frederica and his older boys. These images provided some comfort to the mourners, who were devastated by the passing of this family they knew and loved. The women gathered and made plans to assure that Christopher and

Robbie would have an easy transition into their new families. They vowed to give these two special boys an added measure of love and attention as they grew.

The boys were fortunate to have the Atzeroth family to treasure and nurture them. How grief-stricken they would be when the terrible news of the deaths finally reached them. The Atzeroth's would be sad beyond measure, but they would surely approve of the two families that had so graciously invited Christopher and Robert into their homes.

***

Despite his young age, Christopher would remember the day of his father's death his entire life. At four years old, he had endured much pain and loss, but felt peaceful knowing his mother and father were reunited with his older brothers. This would give him much needed comfort as he moved through his childhood years.

A Trip Back to Miguel's Bay

Christopher whispered his new name to himself as he walked through the village of Manatee. *Edmund Miguel Lee*, he said with pride. He was proud to have Papa's name as his middle name, always writing out his full name on his school papers. His new father, Reverend Lee, reminded him often that his papa had been a good and courageous man. Miguel was never far from his son's thoughts.

It was very different waking up in a large house with so many rooms. In his Terrasilla cabin he never felt alone—there was always someone nearby. In this house, it was often quiet at night, and he had to go down many stairs to find someone to talk to.

His new mother, Electa, was very sweet and kind, but strict. She spent a lot of time with *Edmund* and was very impressed at how quickly he began to speak and understand English. When she was teaching the other children upstairs, his new sister, Sarah, would help him practice his reading, writing, and arithmetic. She loved to play school and store with him during the hot afternoons beneath the oak trees.

Every day before supper, Edmund would go outside to play with the children in the village. In Terrasilla, his brothers were often the only playmates to be found, but Reverend Lee's large store and dock brought so many different people to buy supplies or to rent rooms for lodging. Many of the visitors had children, so he could always make new friends.

He and the Indian children would climb giant trees and look out over the river toward the sea. In Terrasilla, he and Robbie stayed along the protected bay and mostly played among the mangroves. One of the trees in Manatee was so tall, a small house was built up high among the branches. People passing through were welcome to rent it for a night, and its perch in the treetop protected renters from animals and insects.

The Lees dug a long canal that connected the river to the store. It had been built to move goods to and from the boats that docked at the river's edge, but in the evenings, Edmund was allowed to take his little canoe through the canal and out into the river as long as he was home before dark.

He loved the river. The water was clean and clear and didn't taste bad when he got it in his mouth like the water he was used to on the island. The bottom was sandy, and it didn't cut his feet like the oyster shells of Miguel's Bay had. Some of the older boys taught him to bend a sewing pin to make a small hook, and he had mastered tying it to a string and piercing it through a small piece of bacon. He and his friends caught small fish for hours on end as they sat at the end of the dock.

When the Spanish fishermen came to the store, they flattered Edmund and told him that he was a great fisherman like his Papa. They gave special attention to Edmund and Robbie, and they made sure the boys kept their Spanish fluent and sharp.

Captain Fogarty often brought Robbie to the store, so the boys could play together. If Electa allowed it, and if Edmund had his schoolwork completed, Captain John would take the boys out on the sailboat for an adventure and a sailing lesson.

One fine day, the Captain and Parson Lee gathered the boys for one of these sailing trips. Edmund thought it was strange that they would pack so much food and water for a short trip on the river. He also thought it was odd that both fathers had taken time away from their work during the middle of the day.

"The day is bright, and the wind is right." The Captain would say. He let Edmund navigate, and the boy barked his orders to Robbie and his father. They all laughed when the boat hit a sandbar with a jolt and Robbie was catapulted overboard. The water looked so inviting that they all decided to join him for a refreshing swim. The two fathers pushed the boat back out into deeper waters, and they continued on their way.

They skirted around small islands and cut through passes, and Edmund felt as though they had really gone far from home. As they turned and steered straight for land, Edmund developed a strange feeling. He could see the cabin, the thatched huts, and the overgrown garden and fence. They were heading into Miguel's Bay, and he recognized his old home even though two years had passed. The color and smell of the water, the feeling of the thick, warm air on his skin, the scent of fruit trees blooming, and the tall white birds wading along the shore were all so familiar. The men grew quiet, and they watched the boys closely to see how they would react to seeing their old home.

Edmund stepped onto the dock that his Papa had built. He longed to see his mother hanging clothes on the line or cutting her flowers in the garden. He remembered Miguel hanging his nets out to dry and cleaning fish on the shore. The memories swirled around him. The vivid images, sounds, and scents flooded his mind. He was overcome with emotion.

The Lees had always been honest with Edmund about what had happened to his family, and they answered every question he had. He was four when the fever took his two older brothers, his mother, his father, and eventually, his baby sister. Mary had fought hard against the fever, but eventually died and was buried in the Lee Family Cemetery.

He would always harbor memories of those awful days. Maybe time would eventually take some of the sting away, but here at his old home, he felt it as if the pain was new.

The Fogartys also told Robbie bits and pieces of the Guerrero's story. They would tell him more as he grew older. Adopted at the age of two, John hoped he would not struggle too much with unpleasant memories.

As they stepped onto the dock, Reverend Lee took Edmund's hand, and the Captain picked up Robbie and carried him. Robbie could walk fine on his own, but he loved being carried by his father. They all stood quietly for a few long moments and stared thoughtfully at the cabin.

The memories continued to flood into Edmund's mind, but they felt more like pieces of dreams than full memories. Small and seemingly insignificant scenes played out in his mind–his mother's hand as she stirred a pot, his father's scratchy stubble scraping his cheek during a hug, these indelible memories and a multitude of others surfaced in young Edmund's mind.

The cabin door was barred, and the windows were boarded shut. A tattered net hung from a tree branch and swayed in the wind. Edmund remembered taking baths in the old metal tub on the front porch. White roses had overtaken the fence on the side porch, and weeds surrounded the fruit trees. As he looked down the shell road, Edmund vaguely remembered Aunt Julia's old wagon and how it made so much noise coming up the bumpy road.

Edmund closed his eyes and leaned into Rev Lee, finding himself holding back tears. His father lovingly put his arm around his little son. "Eddie, you were a tiny lad the last time you were here. I wanted you to come see the wonderful gift your Papa and mother have left for you and Robbie. This will all be yours when you get older."

Robbie piped up, "Edmund, can I live here with you when I'm grown up?"

Captain Fogarty, in his strong Irish accent said, "Robbie I would like you to live with *me* forever, but if you insist on growing up, I will let you live here. The only condition is that you build me my own bedroom to visit often!" The Captain's comment made them all laugh, but Robbie answered, "Oh, I will!"

Little Edmund remembered all of the happiness and love he had experienced living on Miguel's Bay and dreamed that he would have his own family live here someday.

They walked around to the back of the cabin to see the cow pen, the chicken coop, and the vegetable garden. Edmund instinctively bent down and pulled some weeds from the loose soil. He remembered enjoying helping his mother in her garden. Robbie carefully picked a yellow rose, mindful to avoid the thorns. "I want to take this flower home to

Mother, you know, the one I have now." The tough old Irish sailor had to turn his face away from the boys, so they would not see him push back tears at this sweet gesture.

One at a time, they peered into the one window that had not been boarded up. Nothing had been moved since the day Asa Bishop rescued the family. Frederica's beautifully carved wooden table was fully visible. On it sat a stack of the German plates that she loved to use.

Miguel's old boat was pulled up into the creek and tied to a tree to protect it from storms. Captain John could see in the distance the two graves of Michael and Frederick on the creek bank, but he chose not to point them out to the boys. *That will be another time*, he thought, and steered them toward the Indian mound.

The old homestead felt peaceful and calm. It was so different than the night the two little boys had been whisked away. Edmund felt his nightmares would subside after coming back to see it in the light of day, for he was able to remember the happy times when he had grown up wild and free on this little island.

They took out the picnic basket and ate lunch on Miguel's dock. John told funny stories about Miguel, and Reverend Lee told them the story of how their parents met, and how they fell in love despite all odds—how he had married them on a perfect spring day.

With a full tummy and the breeze in his hair, Robbie fell asleep with his head in John's lap. The captain looked down at the precious little boy—he was such a blessing, especially since he and Mary had not been able to have children of their own. He couldn't possibly love a biological son more than he loved this child.

Edmund asked if he could take the old tattered net in the tree back home with them. Reverend Lee told him, "You may bring home anything that you see here. It is yours, and all forty-six acres will belong to you Guerrero boys when you are older. Your parents left you a wonderful gift of the land and this cabin, to give you a great start in life."

"Will you help me mend the net since you're my father now?" Edmund asked. "Then, I'll have something to keep from both of my fathers." Rev. Lee pulled him into a strong hug to answer the boy's question.

When Robbie awoke from his short nap, the preacher asked the four of them to hold hands and make a circle on the shore of the bay.

Captain John chuckled, "Do you Presbyterians have to pray every time the clock chimes?"

In his serious preacher voice, the Reverend prayed for God to bless Miguel and Frederica's property and to keep it safe from storms and destruction until the sons could come back to claim and restore Miguel's dream. He asked God to give

Edmund and Robbie good health, sweet wives, and many children to bless them in their old age, and to let the tragedies that had befallen the Guerreros be remembered and appreciated by their descendants.

A huge, yellow butterfly landed on Robbie and Edmund's intertwined hands, and the slight tickle made Edmund open his eyes to look at it. Like a cool breeze blowing over his face, a memory surfaced of him and his mother catching a similar butterfly so very long ago. He turned and found that Robbie was looking up at him. He whispered, "I remember her." Edmund said, "Me too." For a fleeting moment, he envisioned her— beautiful, healthy and smiling at her sons.

The vivid memory left as quickly as it had come. Both boys felt calm, peaceful, and safe. They boarded the boat and set sail for the Manatee River. The brothers were thrilled when a group of dolphins playfully swam alongside the boat and then went after a school of mullet. The day ended well and the bonds between the orphaned boys and the special men who took them in as sons were strengthened.

**

Losing their parents at a young age gave Edmund and Robert a sense that you can't really control life.

The Lee and Fogarty families raised them to turn adversity into opportunity. Surrounded by a community of friends and people that loved them as their own, they thrived and went on to have large, wonderful families of their own.

The Guerrero bond kept the two brothers close, forever best friends.

Epilogue

The Boys and Their Paths

Growing up with the Lees, Manatee Village

The Lees of Manatee were well-educated people. Edmund Lee moved to Florida from Vermont because of his poor health. He greatly improved in the warm climate and decided to settle on the Manatee River. He returned to Vermont to collect his sweetheart, Electa Arcott. The newlyweds moved back to become one of the first families to settle in the village of Manatee.

Electa began the first school in Manatee, and Edmund preached to the people who settled there. Reverend Lee was very active in local politics, serving as a Hillsborough County judge from 1844 to 1845, and was appointed the first Clerk of Circuit Court when Manatee County was formed in 1855. Edmund performed the wedding of a young couple who had chosen to settle on Terrasilla island. Their names were Miguel Guerrero and Frederica Kramer.

Edmund and Electa, along with their daughter Sarah, ran a general store, trading post, and boarding house. The all-purpose rambling home was used for court hearings, church services, a school, community gatherings, weddings, and funerals until other buildings were constructed in the village. Fishing, farming, and citrus groves supported the Lees and surrounding neighbors.

Parson Lee, as he was known, fought in the Seminole Wars and the Civil War alongside Miguel Guerrero and the other enlisted men from the area. He was discharged for health reasons and advanced age but stayed in Savannah for three more years in order to serve as a chaplain to the soldiers. Like the others, he had to walk home when his duties were finished.

Electa fell ill and died two years after taking in Edmund Miguel. This left the raising of six-year-old Edmund to Sarah and Reverend Lee. In 1872, Reverend Lee married widow Adeline Frierson, and she brought her three children into the home. Little Edmund, who was eight-years-old, welcomed the new siblings and was particularly close to Adeline's son, John. Sadly, Addie died the very next year. This was also the year Sarah married a widower named James Vanderipe. His children moved into the Lee homestead, so the big house was always bustling with activity. Sarah became mother to all of them.

Edmund Lee's third wife Elizabeth O'Dell outlived the beloved Parson.

Edmund Miguel lost three stepmothers and acquired many stepbrothers and stepsisters along the way. A stepbrother, John Frierson, became a close friend.

Edmund Miguel helped run his father's store and the orange grove, and he served the patrons of the boarding house. It has been said that he spoke several languages. These probably included Seminole, Spanish, English, and some German. He learned to build houses, fish, sail, farm, run a business, and he was an avid reader. He was a member of the Manatee Methodist Church. Edmund Miguel was known to be meticulously clean and well-dressed, even when working in the fields. This tendency probably had its roots in the training he received while running his parents' boarding house under the supervision of three strict mothers.

When they reached their early twenties, the day finally arrived for the Guerrero sons to claim their father's land on Terra Ceia Island. Edmund Miguel was eager to leave Manatee and start his own life, so he and John Frierson renovated Miguel and Frederica's old log cabin and began to farm the surrounding land. Miguel's little Christopher was finally home and ready for a fresh start as an independent adult.

John Frierson eventually married and moved out of the cabin, which left Edmund to run the farm alone. When he wasn't farming, he worked the postal route up the Manatee River to Ellenton and Parrish. On one of the routes, he met

Susan Berryhill, who soon became the love of his life. They married in the Palmetto Baptist Church in 1892. This was the same year that Edmund and Robert received the deed to the forty-seven-acre Guerrero Terra Ceia homestead.

Edmund and Susan's first home was Miguel and Frederica's renovated log cabin on Miguel's Bay. By 1896 they had welcomed three babies and outgrown the cabin. To accommodate their family, they built a roomy frame house on the slope of the Indian mound. The Lees went on to have ten children, but sadly only six survived to adulthood. Their names were Mattie, Robert Edmund, Miguel, Susie Annie, Dewey, William Clyde, Esther Amelia, Louis Justin, Margaret Inez, and Miller Herman.

As the family grew, Edmund sold his portion of the Terra Ceia property and moved to Rubonia. He built a large home nearby on the mainland. They continued to farm and take in guests for boarding. Tragedy struck the Lee home when Susan became ill and died at the age of forty. Edmund was left with four younger children to raise, under sixteen years old. He never remarried. His sixteen-year-old daughter, Susie Annie, helped him with the younger children. The Rubonia house later burned down, and Edmund moved his family to the Palm View area. He continued to farm, fish, and raise his children.

When his children were older and had families of their own, Edmund Lee had the opportunity to move back home to Terra Ceia. He rented a tiny two-room cottage from a family that lived on the original property that Miguel and Frederica had first settled.

He spent his final days on Miguel's Bay teaching his grandchildren how to fish and weave cast nets by hand. He played with them on the Indian mounds and by the little creek where he and his own brothers had played so many years before.

Edmund was remembered as being kind, sweet-natured, quiet, reserved, and always clean and well-kept. He did his own cooking and cleaning, and he dressed in a suit every day to walk up to the Terra Ceia Post Office to retrieve his mail. He went to church every Sunday, and he often had lunch with friends afterward. Edmund had green eyes and a mustache that curled up on the ends. He had an old Victrola phonograph and loved music. He peacefully lived out his golden years on Terra Ceia Island.

At the age of seventy-five, Edmund passed away after a short illness, leaving behind six adult children. His funeral was well attended at the Terra Ceia Methodist Church on April 29, 1940. He is buried in the Gillette Cemetery with his wife Susan and his daughter Inez. Edmund began and ended his life on Terra Ceia Island.

Growing up with the Fogartys, Fogartyville

Robert Guerrero Fogarty immediately became "Robbie" to new parents, Captain John and Mary Fogarty. The young couple did not have children of their own, so he received all the love and attention that a little boy deserves.

Fogartyville had been settled by three brothers, John, Bartholomew, and William Fogarty. The settlement was on the south side of the Manatee River. The fourth brother, Jerry, stayed in Key West and had a career as a merchant. The three Fogarty brothers were masters of shipbuilding, fishing, and sailing. Their schooner trade with Gulf of Mexico and Caribbean seaports was very successful, and they connected many traders from distant places to the Manatee area.

Like the story of so many other American families, the story of the Fogarty family began with the Irish Potato Famine. In 1836, Patrick and Eliza Fogarty left Ireland on a schooner bound for America. They were determined to start a new life that would provide happiness and opportunity for their daughter Julia. The family arrived safely in New York City, and they were lucky in this respect, for many immigrants became ill and perished on the voyage.

The crowded city and poor living conditions were hard to endure, so after a dismal winter, Patrick and Eliza made their way down to St. Augustine, a port with a flourishing sea trade and a milder climate.

428

While in St. Augustine, Eliza gave birth to three sons, named John, Bartholomew, and William. Jeremiah was born into the family in 1845, so he was the first family member to be born a citizen of the new State of Florida.

Patrick was an adventurous risk-taker, and he became restless after the Seminole War. He moved his family to Key West to take advantage of a booming sea trade economy. The family adjusted well to the new island settlement and thrived. Patrick was content for a while, but like so many other men, he was lured by the gold bonanza that was taking place in the west. He left his wife and five children and promised to return a rich man.

Patrick safely navigated the dangerous journey to San Francisco, but in 1851 he met his death and was buried in California soil like so many other hunters of the seductive glint of gold.

In 1865, young Captain John Fogarty sailed up the west coast of Florida from Key West. A monstrous storm loomed in the distance, and he spotted a vessel in distress. Fogarty rescued the men aboard but could not save their boat from sinking.

He loaded the extra crew in his dinghy and entered the mouth of the Manatee River for the first time. He had heard about the village of Manatee and was pleased by what he saw. Locals directed him to Reverend Lee's General Store to buy provisions for his trip back to Key West.

John was enchanted by the beauty of the area. The waters were shallow, calm, and full of fish. The soil was fertile, and the climate was mild compared to Key West. He saw trees perfect for ship-building and lots of open land ready for the taking. A plot of land between two creeks on the south side of the river really sparked his interest, and he knew that he must return to settle there.

On the day of John's first visit, Reverend Edmund Lee sold Captain John the entire inventory of his store for forty dollars. He also sold him on the potential of the beautiful land along the Manatee River. Captain John returned to Key West and talked two of his brothers into coming with him. His sweet Mary didn't need much convincing.

Captain John Fogarty married Mary Bethel of Indian Key. Their sailing honeymoon brought her from Key West to the new homestead, which was built on the Manatee River. The first year of Mary's great adventure included a new husband, a new homestead, and the adoption of her precious little Robbie. The Fogarty aunts, uncles, and cousins accepted Robbie with great excitement. Frederica's own Aunt Julia and cousin Eliza moved closer to the Fogartys and provided Robbie with a link to his birth family.

The year 1866 marked the start of the boat-building industry in Manatee County. Boats were the main form of transportation in the area, so the industry flourished. The three Fogarty brothers, John, Bartholomew, and Tole developed a thriving business that built smacks, schooners, sloops, and yawls as well as smaller boats.

Together they claimed 135 acres known as *Fogartyville*. The settlement included homes, a general store, a bakery, a small dairy, two churches, a cemetery, warehouses, wharves, and buildings for the construction of boats.

From this little community on the south side of the Manatee River would sail seven Fogarty ship captains. These captains, including Robbie, would sail the Tampa Bay area, both coasts of Florida, and throughout the seas of the world.

Robbie was a bright boy. He attended school and church and spoke several languages. As a teenager, he ran Captain John's General Store with Manuel Amon, a Spanish fisherman who fished and fought in wars with his father, Miguel. They made a great team and kept a good trade going with the Cuban fishermen as well as the settlers in the area.

Robbie became an expert sailor, builder of boats, fisherman, and farmer. He could harpoon jewfish better than anyone around. He seemed to excel at everything he did, and he played an important role in Fogartyville in spite of his youth.

Reverend Lee and Captain John made sure Miguel and Frederica's sons saw one another often. They were the best of friends. Both families attended the Methodist Church in Manatee, and the boys were baptized by Reverend Gates.

Captain John helped Miguel apply for and secure his Terra Ceia land immediately before his death. In 1885, John Fogarty paid the remaining $6.16 balance to the state which secured the deeds for Robert and Edmund. In 1892, the deeds were filed separately for the two sons, and the dream of a Menorcan fisherman to own land in America was finally realized.

As a young boy, Robbie met a little girl at school who had just moved to the area from Cedar Key. Her name was Mattie Tillis, and as soon as he saw her curly hair he told a friend, "That's the girl for me." To everyone's surprise, she *was* the woman he ended up marrying many years later.

In 1888, Robbie's life almost came to a end when a second outbreak of yellow fever blazed a path through Florida. Captain John and Mary were very afraid that he would fall to the fever just as his mother and father had years before.

Dr. Leffingwell came to see if he could save Robbie. Mary stood vigil around the clock. She prayed for him and withheld water from him—such was the treatment at that time. She kept a wet cloth pressed to his forehead, but he did not improve. Mary prayed aloud constantly and read scripture to the ailing young man.

Family legend says that Robbie waited for his mother to finally leave the room, and then he drank the entire pitcher of water that sat on the nightstand. The healing spring water gave life to his frail body and he fully recovered. The yellow fever had come, but it had failed to take another Guerrero.

Robert Fogarty was married to the little girl with the curly hair. Reverend Edward F. Gates performed the ceremony in the John Fogarty home.

Robbie and Mattie built a two-story frame house just north of the Tillis house. The location made it easy for Mattie to visit her mother and brothers anytime she took a notion to do so.

The women of Fogartyville were a force of nature. They gardened, fished, sailed, and planned great social events for all of the Manatee River settlers. They also learned to sell their vegetables, fruit, and guava jelly, which was shipped by steamers to Mobile and New Orleans. They raised their children and protected their property during the Seminole and Civil Wars when the men were called to fight.

The new Fogarty home was made complete upon the arrival of Robert John on September 23, 1890. Robbie and Mattie went on to fill their home with eleven children, and all of them survived to adulthood. Their names were Robert John, Henry, Martha Irene, Mary Myrtle, Samuel Edward, Jeremiah Emerald, Hubbard Gerrero, Walter, Annie Jewel, Susie Elizabeth, and William Patrick.

Edmund and Robbie had twenty-one children between them, and seventeen survived to become adults. Miguel and

Frederica's dream was to fill Terra Ceia Island with Guerreros, and when the two families got together, they pretty much did.

Uncle Robbie would load up the schooner with his own children, the neighbor's children, and anyone else they could fit on the boat and sail over to Terra Ceia to visit Edmund and his crew.

Madam Joe was interviewed by Rose Abel of Terra Ceia in the late 1800s. In the interview, Julia told Rose that one of the sons of Frederica and Miguel had located the bodies of his parents and eventually moved them to the Palmetto cemetery.

Robbie took baskets of supplies from Captain John's store to share with them, and in the summer, he would supply each family member with an oversized straw hat.

When the Lee children saw the sails in the distance, they would run to Bill Fogarty's dock to greet the schooner. The children would play in the fields and woods, and sometimes they would venture to the Indian mound area—where they were probably not supposed to play. There was swimming, fishing, and lots of food to be enjoyed.

When Edmund's family lived in Terra Ceia, they traveled to Fogartyville by boating across the river, docking, and then walking to see their friends and family. When the Lees moved to Rubonia, Edmund would drive his horse and buggy to the Manatee River, take a ferry to Bradentown, and walk to Fogartyville.

In 1916 old Captain John took his last voyage after making a two-week trip to Tarpon Springs. He fell sick and died while there, and his beloved store was closed to the public.

Mary, known later as "Grandma Togey," lived until 1929. She was taken by a stroke at the age of eighty-six. She and John lived to see a thriving community form because of their vision and hard work.

In 1923, Robbie and Mattie built a house of cypress wood near the river. It was east of the original Warner home site. The large, six-bedroom home comfortably housed the remaining five children. The spruce-studded land yielded countless loads of white sand, which was sold and hauled to builders. The sand was used in concrete, cement, and plastering, and it was highly sought after for its pure, sugary consistency and color.

Robbie continued to supply contractors with sand until his failing health ended his active working years. He was sick for a long time, and it was necessary for him to receive full-time care at a sanatorium.

After a long illness, Captain Robbie was called home to the Lord on February 14, 1933. He was sixty-eight-years-old. Funeral services were held at Wakeman's Funeral Home, and Reverend E.H. Gates, pastor of the Allentown

Methodist Church and friend of many years conducted the ceremony. Robbie was buried in the Fogartyville Cemetery.

Mattie Fogarty lived in the large house adjacent to the sand pit for a number of years after Robbie's death. She finally closed the home and moved to Tampa with the two youngest children so that she could be nearer to her daughters.

When her nest was empty, Mattie returned to what had once been Fogartyville. She lived in the cottage which had been the home of Captain John and Mary. She eventually moved back to Tampa to live with her daughter, Annie Jewel, and she lived with her other daughter Martha for a time. Her life ended on June 21, 1956 after a long battle against illness.

Mattie was buried by her husband's side in the Fogartyville Cemetery.

Source: Taken from the unpublished notes of Mrs. Hubbard Fogarty (Ollie), used for her book *They Called It Fogartyville*, Manatee Village Historical Park collection.

Fishermen's huts of the type Miguel and Frederica would have
lived in on Terrasilla when they first married in 1856

An old pioneer road on Terrasilla

Manatee County Historical Records Library

Miguel & Frederica's marriage license, March 15, 1856,
officiated by Rev. Edmund Lee, Clerk of Court

Land Entry Files, NA, RG 49

Miguel Guerrero's signature on his application for homestead,
certificate #645, April 3, 1868

438

ARMY OF THE CONFEDERATE STATES.

CERTIFICATE OF DISABILITY FOR DISCHARGE.

(To be used, in duplicate, in all cases of discharge on account of disability.)

Pvt. McGill Guerrero _____, of Captain _R. B. Smith_ Company, (_H_,) of the (_7th_) _Fla._ Regiment of Confederate States _Volunteers_, was enlisted by _Capt. R. B. Smith_, of the _7th_ Regiment of _Fla. Vols._ at _Tampa, Fla._ on the _5th_ day of _March_, 1862, to serve _3_ years; he was born in _Spain_ in the _City_ of _Navarra_, is _53_ years of age, _5_ feet, _6_ inches high, _dark_ complexion, _grey_ eyes, _light_ hair, and by occupation when enlisted a _farmer_. During the last ____ months said soldier has been unfit for duty _____ days. (Here consult directions on Form Med. Dept. Gen. Dir.)

STATION: _Watauga Bridge_

DATE: _March 1st 1863_   _R. B. Smith Capt._
                                    Commanding Company.

I CERTIFY, that I have carefully examined the said _Pvt. McGill Guerrero_ of Captain _Smith's_ Company, and find him incapable of performing the duties of a soldier because of (Here consult par. 1134, p. 213, and directions on Form 12, p. 203, Med. Dept. Gen. Dir.) _Chronic Rheuma-tism, & General Debility the result of old age —_

L. S. Lewis of 7th Surgeon.
7th Regt Fla. Vols

DISCHARGED this _9th_ day of _March_, 1863, at _____

R. Bullock Lt. Col   Commanding the Post.

NOTE 1.—When a probable case for pension, special care must be taken to state the degree of disability.
NOTE 2.—The place where the soldier desires to be addressed may be here added.

Town—   County—   State—

(DUPLICATES.)

Compiled Military Service Records, NA, RG 92

Miguel Guerrero's Civil War Certificate of Disability for Discharge, Watauga Bridge, Tennessee, March 1, 1863

Old Hillsborough County Courthouse

Manatee County Public Library Historical Digital Collections

Edmund Lee and daughter, Sarah Lee Vanderipe

Manatee County Public Library Historical Digital Collections
Frederica's Aunt Julia Atzeroth, known as *Madam Joe*

Third Seminole War foes, Capt. Leroy G. Lesley
and Chief Billy Bowlegs

Manatee County Public Library Historical Digital Collections

Photo courtesy of Jonathan Davis

Asa Bishop, who rescued Miguel and his three children
and took them to his cabin on Bishop's Pt. (above)

443

Confederate camps around Tampa Bay looked much like this
camp at the Warrington Navy Yard, Pensacola, FL

Lt. John A. Bethell, Company K, 7th Florida Infantry

Manatee County Public Library Historical Digital Collections
Edmund & Susan Berryhill Lee, children, and visiting cousin

Marian Bailey Anderson Collection
Susie Annie Lee Bailey (daughter of Edmund Miguel Lee)
& family, late 1930's

445

Robert Fogarty Family with visiting cousin, Mollie Kramer

Robert Fogarty Home, Fogartyville

Manatee County Public Library Historical Digital Collections

Capt. John Fogarty's river sloop on the Manatee River

Manatee County Public Library Historical Digital Collections

Robert and Mattie Tillis Fogarty Family

Manatee County Public Library Historical Digital Collections
Capt. John Fogarty and the steamer *Manatee*

Collection of Mickey Lee, Granddaughter of Robert Fogarty
A harpoon point allegedly passed down to Robert
from his father, Miguel Guerrero

448

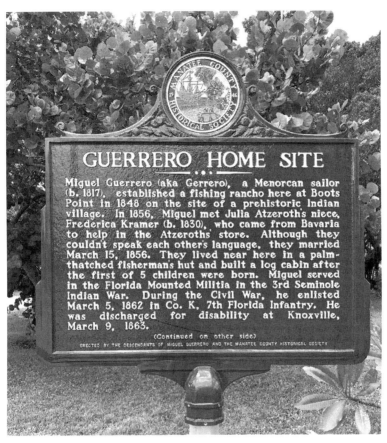

GUERRERO HOME SITE

Miguel Guerrero (aka Gerrero), a Menorcan sailor (b. 1817), established a fishing rancho here at Boots Point in 1848 on the site of a prehistoric Indian village. In 1856, Miguel met Julia Atzeroth's niece, Frederica Kramer (b. 1830), who came from Bavaria to help in the Atzeroths' store. Although they couldn't speak each other's language, they married March 15, 1856. They lived near here in a palm-thatched fisherman's hut and built a log cabin after the first of 5 children were born. Miguel served in the Florida Mounted Militia in the 3rd Seminole Indian War. During the Civil War, he enlisted March 5, 1862 in Co. K, 7th Florida Infantry. He was discharged for disability at Knoxville, March 9, 1863.

(Continued on other side)

ERECTED BY THE DESCENDANTS OF MIGUEL GUERRERO AND THE MANATEE COUNTY HISTORICAL SOCIETY

Photo: Peggy Donoho

Historical marker side one erected on the Guerrero homestead at Boots Point, Terra Ceia Island

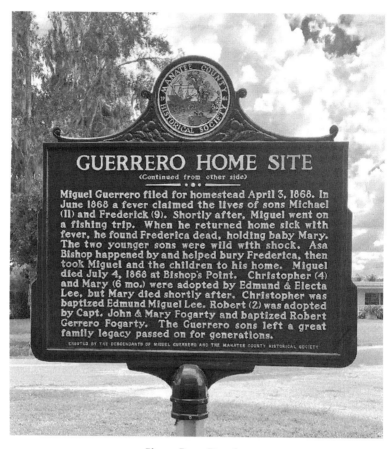

GUERRERO HOME SITE
(Continued from other side)

Miguel Guerrero filed for homestead April 3, 1868. In June 1868 a fever claimed the lives of sons Michael (11) and Frederick (9). Shortly after, Miguel went on a fishing trip. When he returned home sick with fever, he found Frederica dead, holding baby Mary. The two younger sons were wild with shock. Asa Bishop happened by and helped bury Frederica, then took Miguel and the children to his home. Miguel died July 4, 1868 at Bishop's Point. Christopher (4) and Mary (6 mo.) were adopted by Edmund & Electa Lee, but Mary died shortly after. Christopher was baptized Edmund Miguel Lee. Robert (2) was adopted by Capt. John & Mary Fogarty and baptized Robert Gerrero Fogarty. The Guerrero sons left a great family legacy passed on for generations.

ERECTED BY THE DESCENDANTS OF MIGUEL GUERRERO AND THE MANATEE COUNTY HISTORICAL SOCIETY

Photo: Peggy Donoho

Historical marker side two erected on the Guerrero homestead at Boots Point, Terra Ceia Island

Hubbard Fogarty Family Collection
A Fogartyville Gathering

Manatee County Public Library Historical Digital Collections
Adult Children of Robert and Mattie Fogarty (far left)

Photo: Peggy Donoho
Edmund Miguel Lee & Susan Berryhill Lee,
Gillette Cemetery, Palmetto, Florida

Photo: Peggy Donoho
Robert Gerrero Fogarty and Martha Tillis Fogarty,
Fogartyville Cemetery, Bradenton, FL

Ron Prouty searching the Mahon Public Records with
historical document translator, Gordon Byron in
the Biblioteca Publica de Mao, Menorca

Landon and Peggy Donoho researching the Guerrero family
genealogical records at the Arxiu Diocesa Menorca with
historian/author Marc Pallicer Benejam

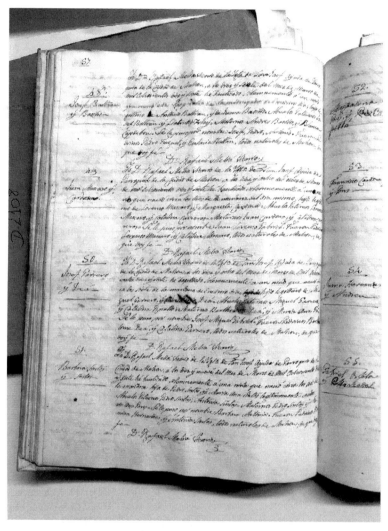

Baptismal record of Josep Miguel Gabriel Guerrero-Deya,
March 18, 1817, Mahon, Menorca

Marc Pallicer Benejam and Josep Gornes, historians at the
Arxiu Diocesà de Menorca, Ciutadella

Nieta Cardona & Gordon Byron, Biblioteca Pública de Maó

Peggy Donoho, great-great-granddaughter of Miguel Guerrero
visits Església de Sant Josep de Maó, Menorca
where Miguel was baptized

Genealogy of Miguel Guerrero-Deyà

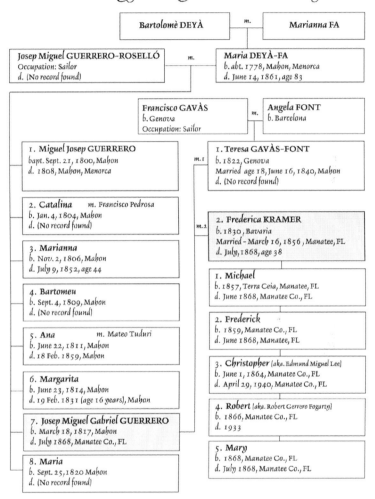

| Bartolomè DEYÀ | m. | Marianna FA |

| Josep Miguel GUERRERO-ROSELLÓ
Occupation: Sailor
d. (No record found) | m. | Maria DEYÀ-FA
b. abt. 1778, Mahon, Menorca
d. June 14, 1861, age 83 |

| Francisco GAVÀS
b. Genova
Occupation: Sailor | m. | Angela FONT
b. Barcelona |

1. **Miguel Josep GUERRERO**
bapt. Sept. 21, 1800, Mahon
d. 1808, Mahon, Menorca

m.1

1. **Teresa GAVÀS-FONT**
b. 1822, Genova
Married age 18, June 16, 1840, Mahon
d. (No record found)

2. **Catalina** m. Francisco Pedrosa
b. Jan. 4, 1804, Mahon
d. (No record found)

m.2

2. **Frederica KRAMER**
b. 1830, Bavaria
Married - March 16, 1856, Manatee, FL
d. July, 1868, age 38

3. **Marianna**
b. Nov. 2, 1806, Mahon
d. July 9, 1852, age 44

4. **Bartomeu**
b. Sept. 4, 1809, Mahon
d. (No record found)

1. **Michael**
b. 1857, Terra Ceia, Manatee, FL
d. June 1868, Manatee Co., FL

5. **Ana** m. Mateo Tuduri
b. June 22, 1811, Mahon
d. 18 Feb. 1859, Mahon

2. **Frederick**
b. 1859, Manatee Co., FL
d. June 1868, Manatee, FL

6. **Margarita**
b. June 23, 1814, Mahon
d. 19 Feb. 1831 (age 16 years), Mahon

3. **Christopher** (aka. Edmund Miguel Lee)
b. June 1, 1864, Manatee Co., FL
d. April 29, 1940, Manatee Co., FL

7. **Josep Miguel Gabriel GUERRERO**
b. March 18, 1817, Mahon
d. July 1868, Manatee Co., FL

4. **Robert** (aka. Robert Gerrero Fogarty)
b. 1866, Manatee Co., FL
d. 1933

8. **Maria**
b. Sept. 25, 1820 Mahon
d. (No record found)

5. **Mary**
b. 1868, Manatee Co., FL
d. July 1868, Manatee Co., FL

Source: Arxiu Diocesà de Menorca;
Manatee County Historical Records Library

457

Edmund Miguel Lee
& Susan Berryhill Lee Family

EDMUND MIGUEL LEE	June 1, 1864 - Apr. 29, 1940
SUSAN BERRYHILL LEE	Mar. 16, 1874 - Nov. 11, 1914
Mattie	d. Mar. 18, 1893
Robert Edmund	Mar. 16, 1895 - Oct. 22, 1962
Miguel	1896 - 1897
Susie Annie Lee	Jan. 20, 1898 - Jan. 18, 1969
Dewey	b. 1900
William Clyde (Butch) Lee	Feb. 12, 1902 - Apr. 14, 1958
Esther Amelia	Aug. 3, 1903 - Jun. 28, 1950
Louis Justin (L.J.)	Mar. 5, 1905 - Sept. 24, 1953
Margaret Inez	May 18, 1909 - July 1, 1922
Miller Herman Lee	Nov. 23, 1911 - Jan. 20, 1980

Robert Gerrero Fogarty
& Mattie Tillis Fogarty Family

ROBERT G. FOGARTY	Dec. 18, 1865 - Dec. 14, 1933
MATTIE TILLIS FOGARTY	Dec. 16, 1875 - Jun. 21, 1956
Robert John	Sept. 23, 1890 - July 4, 1964
Henry	May 2, 1893 - Oct. 22, 1974
Martha Irene	Sept. 21, 1895 - Feb. 13, 1970
Mary Myrtle	Aug. 21, 1898 - Dec. 22, 1955
Samuel Edward	Aug. 22, 1900 - Apr. 20, 1928
Jeremiah Emerald	May 23, 1903 - Nov. 16, 1969
Hubbard Gererro	Sept. 11, 1906 - Dec. 18, 1995
Walter	Jan. 11, 1909 - Nov. 9, 1959
Annie Jewel	Oct. 28, 1911 - May 11, 2004
Susie Elizabeth	Aug. 13, 1914 - Jan. 10, 1962
William Patrick	Aug. 12, 1917 - Apr. 21, 1970

Bibliography

A number of resources were helpful in developing the historical background for the novel, these in particular:

Catherine Bayless, *Terra Ceia Island History and Historical Sites*, 1979.

John Beale, *Manatee History Matters: Cuban Fishermen Set Up Ranchos in Manatee*, Bradenton Herald, 2-19-2016.

Ripley P. Bullen, *The Terra Ceia Site, Manatee County, Florida*, 1951.

Bill Burger, *What's In a Name, Terra Ceia Island*, Terra Ceia VIA Newsletter.

Andrew P. Canova, *Life & Adventures in South Florida*, 1906.

James W. Covington, *The Billy Bowlegs War*, 1855-1858, 1982.

Ollie Fogarty, *They called it Fogartyville*, 1972.

Robert E. King, M.D. , *A History of the Practice of Medicine in Manatee County, Florida*, 1985.

Marion B. Lawrence, *On The Banks of Manatee*,1978.

Janet Snyder Matthews, *Edge of Wilderness*, 1983.

Lillie B. McDuffee, *The Lures of Manatee*, 1961.

D.B. McKay, *Pioneer Florida*, 1959.

Ronald N. Prouty, *War Comes to Tampa Bay, The Civil War Diary of Robert Watson*, Tampa Bay History Magazine, Vol. 10, 1988; transcript at Chickamauga-Chattanooga National Park.

Jonathan C. Sheppard, *By the Noble Daring of Her Sons*, 2012.

Cathy Slusser, *From a Heavenly Land, Eliza's Story*, 2013.

Cathy Slusser, *From an Heavenly Land, Julia's Story*, 2014.

Cathy Slusser, *From a Heavenly Land, Caroline's Story*, 2016.

Marvis R. Snell and Jacob Randolph Snell, *The Gillette Cemetery, A Pioneer Cemetery in the Gillette Community, Manatee County, Florida*, 2002.

Margaret F. Stack, *An Archaeological Appraisal of Spanish Indians on the West Coast of Florida in the Eighteenth and Nineteenth Centuries*, 2011.

Samuel C. Upham, *Notes from Sunland on the Manatee River, Gulf Coast of South Florida*, 1881.

Unknown Author, *Palma Sola, The Youngest and Largest Town in Florida*, 1884.

Joe Warner, *The Singing River*, 1986.

Zack Waters, *Tampa's Forgotten Defenders: The Confederate Commanders of Ft. Brooke, Sunland Tribune*, Tampa Historical Society, Vol. 17, 2018.

Printed Interviews:

Phaedra Carter, *Pioneer Fogarty Family*, Manatee Historical Park, 1-11-2011.

Ollie and Hubbard Fogarty, *Fogartyville*, Manatee County Historical Society, 9-17-1991.

Col. G.W. Johnson, *Dedication and History of Manatee County's First Courthouse*, Manatee County Historical Society, 1977.

Carl King, *The History of Manatee County*, Manatee County Historical Society, WTRL: "Manatee Speaks", 4-26-1974.

Joseph Herman Simpson, *History of Manatee County, Florida, Chapter 16*, Sarasota County History Center, 1915.

Author Unknown, *130 Years of Service*, Manatee United Methodist Church, 1979.

David Kirkland Walker, *Recollections of Old Manatee*, Manatee Historical Society, 1983.

Archival Records:

Board of State Institutions, *Soldiers of Florida in the Seminole Indian-Civil & Spanish American Wars*, Florida, 1903.

Records of the 7th Florida Regiment, Record Group 109, National Archives, Washington DC.

Church records, Arxiu Diocesà Menorca, Ciutadella, Menorca, Spain.

Civil Records, Biblioteca Pública de Maó, Mahon, Menorca, Spain.

Newspaper articles:

Phaedra Carter, *It was a long way from Tipperary to Manatee County for the Fogarty clan*, Bradenton Herald, 11-17-2015.

Authentic Story of Pioneering, as told by Josiah Gates, the first white man to be born in Manatee County, taken from *Tampa Daily Times*, date unknown.

Lectures:

Jeff Moates, *Cuban Ranchos*, lecture by at Florida Maritime Museum, 10-18-2017.

Peggy Anderson Donoho

I had a wonderful childhood growing up in Bradenton, Florida. I didn't realize then that I was fortunate to have such a large extended family who were very close-knit and available to me. Some family members lived within walking distance of my house; others lived in faraway states, but they visited regularly on holidays and special occasions.

Any occasion for a visit was special. There was always great food, lots of conversation, laughter, and stories. Those stories took on new meaning for me as I became an adult and started to experience life on my own.

Every two years we went to the Lee family reunion on the 5th of July. It was held in a different location each time we met. We had aunts and uncles and cousins from Ohio, North Carolina, Louisiana, Alabama, North Dakota, and

California. When I say that I have family all over the country, I really mean it.

At every reunion, the history of the family was told, we prayed before the shared meal, and the kids just wanted to get outside and play. Then we would try to get what seemed like hundreds of people together for a picture.

The out-of-town cousins always loved it when the reunion was held on Anna Maria Island, which was our favorite playground. This is where we all felt at home. It is the island of my youth, and the fact that our family began on another island just across the bay gives it a special kind of symmetry.

One year my mother, who is affectionately known as *Tookie*, researched the facts and dates and then wrote down the story of Miguel Guerrero for us. I remember scanning it at times when I ran across it in my papers, but honestly, I didn't feel an urge to know more about these characters until I moved back to Bradenton in 2016.

Miguel Guerrero's life could be made into an action-drama movie like those about Indiana Jones. He sailed the oceans of the world, fought in wars, homesteaded on an unclaimed island and raised a family whose descendants still talk about him five generations later.

Frederica Kramer Guerrero's life was never easy. She left a comfortable life in her homeland of Bavaria and crossed the ocean to live in the wild, untamed tropical jungle of Florida.

In researching this book, I have found a new respect for this young woman's strength, courage and determination as she faced unimaginable trials.

I believe that I will meet Frederica one day, and I suspect that she will tell me that she is proud to have been chosen for such an important role in life. She truly left her mark on the world. Her story is told in this book, and I hope that it pleases her. My wish is that family members, friends, and strangers will be as inspired by her life as I am.

Ronnie Prouty and I spent the last two years searching local historical archives for new information about the Guerrero family. We discovered important genealogical information on a trip to the beautiful island of Menorca with my son, Landon, in 2018. We visited old church archives and uncovered two more generations of family members. We walked the same streets that Miguel walked in Port Mahon, and we caught a glimpse of what his life was like before he crossed the ocean.

It has been said that a family tree can wither if no one tends to its roots. It is a gift for me to know that I came from Frederica and Miguel Guerrero, and I hope that future generations of my family will be inspired to protect our Family Tree. I also hope that those who read this book will draw strength and inspiration from the story of Miguel and Frederica.

This book would never have happened without the friendship and talents of Ronnie Prouty. He has been a blessing to my family and the time and work he put into this book is a beautiful gift to us.

My biggest joy in life comes from my three sons, Landon, Andrew and Evan. I hope reading this book will make you proud of your mama and connect you to your roots.

Peggy Donoho
2018

Ron Prouty

Marian Anderson, great-grand-daughter
of Miguel Guerrero with Ronnie Prouty

My fascination with Manatee County's pioneer history began at age five, standing under the majestic oaks on the playground of Manatee Elementary School, staring with fascination across the fence at the lichened headstones of the Old Manatee Burial Grounds. I remember wondering who these people were.

My interest in history grew over the years, encouraged by my parents on family trips to historic sites and listening to my grandmother's stories of my fourth great Grandfather Moses Lufkin, a drummer in the Massachusetts Line during the Revolutionary War.

During the 1980s, I was immersed into the study of Manatee County's Civil War history as a member of the Confederals,

467

a Civil War Living History organization. The local Confederate unit we portrayed was Co. K, 7th Florida Regiment, and that's how I first became acquainted with Pvt. Miguel Guerrero.

Several years ago, I sought out descendants of Company K soldiers while writing a story for the *Manatee-Sarasota Herald-Tribune's* "Look Back" column. To my amazement, I discovered that Marian Anderson, a fourth-generation Floridian who was a close friend of my mother, is Miguel's great-granddaughter.

After reading Cathy Slusser's first historical novel, *Eliza's Story*, the idea entered my mind to try my hand at writing a historical novel about one of Manatee County's pioneers. In a conversation with Cathy, she suggested I write a novel about a Company K soldier. The first soldier who came to mind was Miguel Guerrero.

In 2016, I became re-united with Marian's daughters Karen, Peggy, and Cindy, who I grew up with in church as a child. Over time, I discovered that Peggy and Cindy shared my love for Manatee County's pioneer past. At dinner one night, I mentioned to Marian how much she reminded me of my mother, who I lost in 1995. The family graciously "adopted" me as the son and brother they always had wanted. The Andersons, as well as Miguel and Frederica, were now my "family".

One fall day, after attending an author's talk, Peggy suggested that I write the story of her great-great-Grandfather Miguel. I told her it was funny she should mention that, and I agreed, under one condition: That she would help me research it. And with great enthusiasm, she did!

But Peggy became much more than a research assistant; after she surprised me one day with the draft of her first chapter, it was evident that she would be my co-author, writing Frederica's story, and I would write Miguel's. The work she has done on this book has equaled, if not surpassed my own, and she has continually amazed me at the energy she put forth, spending hours of research in libraries and historical records looking for clues to Miguel and Frederica's past.

Two years later, the result is this book. We realize any work of historical fiction falls short of what probably really happened; however, we have taken great care, based upon the historical clues we could find, to remain faithful to Miguel, Frederica, and their pioneer neighbors in telling their tale.

Ron Prouty
2018

Ron Prouty (left), portrays Pvt. Miguel Guerrero, Co. K, 7th
Florida Infantry at the 125th Anniversary reenactment of the
Battle of Chickamauga, 1987

Ron and Peggy in the 1960's, growing up in
Bradenton, Florida and loving it!

Frederica's chapters
written by
Peggy Donoho

Miguel's chapters
written by
Ron Prouty

Made in the USA
Columbia, SC
07 October 2023

1b13cf63-68b9-410e-aba4-bada452909d2R01